THE ENEMY WAS READY AND WAITING...

The fight has been much more intense, more difficult than predicted in initial assessments. I attempt to establish contact with Space Strike Command. I pick up some disjointed communications from several vessels, but cannot raise either the flagship or the 4th Regimental Command Craft. The communication fragments, those I can decode and reconstruct, are disturbing.

"Ranger three! Ranger three! Bogies coming in on your tail!"

"Veloceras reporting. Star drives are out. We're not going anywhere. . . ."

"Emynian has been hit! I say again, Emynian is hit!"

"God in heaven, look at her burn! . . ."

"We need to stop those gunboats! The KKMs are killing us! . . ."

The fighting in near-planetary space is not going well. I must face the possibility that I and my fellow Bolo combat units may soon be on our own, with no hope of orbital support or reinforcement.

My radar detects large amounts of wreckage in space, much of it falling toward the surface. I locate the command craft, which appears to be damaged and falling toward Caern. I estimate it will enter the planet's atmosphere within the next two minutes. Since its communications are out, I have no means of determining whether or not those on board are still alive.

A bright meteor streaks through the predawn sky overhead, followed by another, two more . . . and then a shower of them. Debris from the battle is beginning to enter the atmosphere and burn up from the friction of entry.

My Commander, my Battalion CO, the regimental commander, and other senior staff personnel will face the same threat very soon, if any are alive now in that tumbling hulk.

And there is nothing I can bring to bear that will help them. . . .

ALSO IN THIS SERIES:

The Compleat Bolo by Keith Laumer

Created by Keith Laumer:
The Honor of the Regiment
The Unconquerable
The Triumphant by David Weber & Linda Evans
Last Stand
Old Guard
Cold Steel
Bolo Brigade by William H. Keith, Jr.
Bolo Rising by William H. Keith, Jr.

ALSO by WILLIAM H. KEITH, JR.

Diplomatic Act (with Peter Jurasik)

BOLO STRIKE

CREATED BY
KEITH LAUMER

WILLIAM H. KEITH, JR.

BOLO STRIKE

This is a work of fiction. All the characters and events portrayed in this book are fictional, and any resemblance to real people or incidents is purely coincidental.

Copyright © 2001 by Bill Fawcett & Associates

A Baen Books Original

Baen Publishing Enterprises
P.O. Box 1403
Riverdale, NY 10471
www.baen.com

ISBN: 0-7434-3566-4

Cover art by Dru Blair

First paperback printing, October 2002

Library of Congress Catalog Number 2001035395

Distributed by Simon & Schuster
1230 Avenue of the Americas
New York, NY 10020

Production by Windhaven Press, Auburn, NH
Printed in the United States of America

Prologue

IGC S-83,938,253. Perseus Arm, Columbian Sector.

Sallos A,B. Stellar class: both F9, radius: 1.07 Sol, radius: 1.14 Sol, luminosity: 1.9 Sol. Estimated time remaining on the main sequence: 3.5×10^9 years.

Planetary System: Seven major planetary bodies . . .

V, *Dis*. Mean orbital radius = 4.85 a.u., period = 10.004 years.

Orbital eccentricity = .0312.

Apastron = 5.00132 a.u.; periastron = 4.69868 a.u.

Equatorial diameter = 198,673 km.

Density = 1.034 g/cm^3.

Surface gravity = 2.92 G.

Axial tilt = $2.03°$.

Rotational period = $9_h\ 12_m\ 27.112_s$.

Magnetic field = 6.4 gauss.

Atmosphere: H_2, 84% ± 3%; He, 16% ± 3%; CH_4, 0.15%; NH_3, 250 ppm; C_2H_6, 15 ppm; H_2O, 2 ppm; HCN, .08 ppm; C_2H_2, .034 ppm; CO, .003 ppm; GeH_4, .0004 ppm.

1

Satellites: 25 with diameters > 100 km, 3 with diameters > 5,000 km. . . .
One major satellite, *Caern*, is of special note. . . .

Satellites: Sallos Vf, *Caern*.
Orbital semimajor axis = 1,002,354 km, rotational period = $4_d\, 8_h\, 46_m\, 6.87_s$, orbital eccentricity = .0004. . . .
Equatorial diameter = 8368 km.
Density = 6.228 gm/cm^3.
Surface gravity = .74 G.
Planetary mass = 1.91232×10^{27} g.
Axial tilt = 0.04°.
Rotational period = tidally locked at $4_d\, 8_h\, 46_m\, 6.87_s$.
Magnetic field = 1.21 gauss.
Surface area = 219,985,074.4 km^2.
Surface temperature: 12% of incidental thermal radiation is derived from the primary.
Temperature = locationally variable, –30° C. (anti-Dis side) to 50° (sub-Dis point).
A habitable band exists between the hemispheric regions of permanent ice and desert.
Atmosphere: Mean surface pressure 0.8 bar.
N_2, 77.08%; O_2, 21.04%; Ar, 1.02%, H_2O, 0.05–1.5% (mean 1%); CO_2, 350 ppm; Ne, 12.2/ppm; He, 6.34 ppm; CH_4, 1.9 ppm; Kr, 1.98 ppm; CO, 1.3 ppm; SO_2, 3.4 ppm; H_2, 0.4 ppm; N_2O, 0.33 ppm;
O_3 .05–1.9 ppm; Xe, 0.09 ppm; NO_2, 0.03 ppm.

Notes: A habitable satellite of the gas giant Dis with its own native biosphere, Caern was colonized by Terran-human stock late in the Concordiat age. Military depots and communications centers at Paimos and Grendylfen gave the planet some minor strategic import in that struggle, but the system was located far from major areas of conflict and not directly involved in the fighting. Cut off from all contact with human space during the final phase of the Melcon Armageddon and the subsequent Dark Era, Caern was eventually absorbed as an outpost of the then-unknown Aetryxha Reach. Recontact with Caern in cy 375 has led to a period of steadily escalating tension between the Confederation and the Reach. . . .

Space Navigator's Ephemeris
Confederation Technical Press
37th Edition, cy 378

Six Confederation naval vessels, huge, irregularly patterned in swaths and stripes of black, gray, and blue, decelerated into Disian space, weapons charged, spiked snouts clawing at the clotted stars. Ahead, the ringed, back-lit globe of the gas giant loomed vast within its necklace of crescent moons. Sallos A and B, the local suns, glowed hot, white, and arc-light dazzling, made tiny by distance.

On board the battlecarriers *Esan* and *Helias*, the command cruiser *Galahedron*, and the three destroyers that made up the battle group, nearly ten thousand Confederation naval personnel waited at their stations, waited to see what shape the Aetryx response to their arrival in-system would take. At this point, little was known of the aliens. All that could be said with certainty was that their reaction would likely be . . . *alien*. In truth, little of the xenosophontological reports garnered thus far from the planetside merchant factors and X-Corps scouts made sense. Making sense out of the situation—and ascertaining the fate of some hundreds of millions of humans resident on Caern— was the Battlecarrier Task Force's primary mission.

Officially, the BTF was engaged in what was euphemistically termed "diplomatic service." The military forces of another age and place might have called it a show of force, or even "gunboat diplomacy." The Aetryx Circle had defied the Confederation Senate. Millions of humans living on Caern languished in alien slavery. Admiral Cellini, commanding BTF-74, was determined that there would be a full accounting.

At the very least, they would get the Aetryx to talk. . . .

And then everything started going wrong.

Dazzling flares of silent light erupted in the darkness. Space fighters, sleekly streamlined and knife-blade deadly, streaked through the Confederation squadron, loosing missiles, Hellbore bolts, and high-velocity kinetic-kill projectiles. Thermonuclear horror engulfed the *Helias*, vaporizing her aft works and sending the rest, accompanied by glittering fragments, pinwheeling into the night. Hellbore fire sliced through the bridge and primary turret decks of the destroyer *Calavas*, until her crew modules erupted in a spray of liquid metal and hard X-rays.

Orders snapped from the *Galahedron*. Firing at their attackers in barrage upon barrage of disciplined chaos, the surviving members of the squadron accelerated. The laws of physics being what they were, to continue deceleration until they could return the way they'd come was suicide, plain and simple. Their only hope lay in maintaining their course, whipping past Caern and giant Dis and outrunning their ambushers until they could again slip into the relative safety of hyper.

Another volley of incoming kinetic-kill missiles loosed shattering radiance within the infalling coterie of warships, peeling back armor in half-molten strips, shattering the hull of the destroyer *Tubek*. The battlecarrier *Esan* shuddered as multiple warheads vented their hellish fury scant kilometers from her hull; battlescreens failed, and a second volley sent a storm of hard gamma radiation sleeting through her crew modules. Every man and woman aboard was dead when the leviathan vessel detonated as a tiny sun minutes later.

The surviving vessels were clear of the first onslaught now and racing for the minimum distance beyond the local gravity well where they could kick over into hyper and vanish. Dis wielded an immense influence over local space, however, and at maximum acceleration, *Galahedron* and the destroyer *Kurbal* would need another hour at least to work their way clear.

The second flight of needle interceptors raced in from a quartet of Aetryx battlecarriers in close orbit over Caern . . . blunt-nosed penetrators flashing in at accelerations so high they could only be robotic or manned by suicide crews. *Galahedron* survived until she was sweeping in periplanetos past Dis, skimming the hydrogen fringe of the gas giant's upper atmosphere . . . and then a barrage of missiles hunted her down in a blaze of thermonuclear fury. The radiation storm touched the hurtling *Kurbal*, burning out secondary drives and knocking her weapons off-line, but her captain kicked in auxiliaries to stabilize her fall and let the massive gravitational drag of Dis slingshot his hell-scorched vessel clear of the planet. The interceptors followed but were too far astern now to have a chance of closing to complete their kill. Ninety-eight minutes after the engagement began, *Kurbal* slipped into hyper, the sole survivor of BTF-74.

Admiral Cellini had been sister-in-law to the Senate president. The firestorm that erupted within the Confederation Senate upon *Kurbal's* return to her base at Endymion far surpassed the pyrotechnics that attended the destruction of the *Galahedron*.

Chapter One

Input . . .

Somewhere beyond the sphere of my awareness a switch is thrown, power flows through control umbilicals, and I return to full consciousness at Status Ready-Three. It is 2712.78 hours, Confederation Standard Time, on Day 410 of cy 381, some 515.92724 hours since I was powered down for loading aboard the transport.

I initiate a status check. All primary and secondary power plants are online at one hundred percent output, all offensive and defensive weapons systems read fully operational at standby mode, and communications are nominal, with clear channels and data feed lines both to the other members of my unit and to the human component of the Invasion Strike Force.

My visual feeds are off—I scarcely have need of sight while sealed inside a Type 7 Assault Landing Pod within a transport cargo bay—but I can sense the life of the ship around me, and of my comrades, as the Battalion is brought to full consciousness.

I exchange data with Bolo Mark XXXIII serial 837987, "Ferox," the other Bolo in my battalion, then with the other members of my unit, the 4th Regiment, Second Brigade, First Confederation Mobile Army Corps.

7

I sense deceleration and the steady ticking of the transport's drive and feel the shudders in the vessel's hull that indicate she is maneuvering toward a primary approach vector. I estimate that action is imminent and that deployment will begin within the next three hours. I require only my tacsit briefing and operational orders before launch.

Colonel Jon Jarred Streicher entered the enclosed walkway above the main cargo bay and paused, looking down through the slanted windows opening above the canyon vastness of the bay's seemingly bottomless depths. Major Carla Ramirez, his Executive Officer, paused with him.

"What do you think, Major?" he asked. "Are they ready?"

"As ready as they can be, Colonel," Ramirez replied. "I'd feel better if we had a clear intel report. I don't care *what* Moby Dickhead says, we're going in at a disadvantage."

"Watch that," he warned, glancing down the walkway at a group of technicians just beyond earshot. Euph sang in his blood. He'd just taken a tab minutes before and was well into the manic phase of the drug, powerful and completely focused.

She shrugged. "The man's an idiot."

"He's ConSAGCom, and Skymarshal in charge of this whole damned show. And he knows what he's doing. I won't have his authority undercut, Major."

"As you say, sir." She didn't sound convinced. "We're still at a disadvantage, even if we had the God of Battles running the show."

"We have the technological advantage," he reminded her. "We know the Trixies don't have anything like the Mark XXXIII."

"They have a *planet*, Jon," she reminded him in turn.

"A planet is a big place, an enormous place, even for a full corps of planetary siege units. We're up against a planet's entire population, both the Aetryxha and the indigenous human population. *And* they have Bolo technology of their own, even if we don't have a good idea of how up to date it might be. *And* they have a culture shaped and molded by a long, long tradition of endless warfare. They could so easily surprise us."

"Of course, of course." He hesitated, trying to put into words what he was feeling. "But . . . I mean . . . just *look* at them!"

He gestured at the black, swollen shapes beyond the transplas barrier. Most of the cargo bay beneath the enclosed catwalk was in darkness, so vast was that immense maw, deeper and broader and more voluminous than most planetside buildings short of orbital towers or city arcologies. Floodlights nestled among shadowy webworks of struts and support beams cast pools of light across curved hulls and fairings; worker bees drifted among the leviathan pods, each bearing dazzling lights beneath outstretched mechanical arms and grippers and bringing life and motion to the mountainous tableau below. The bay was kept in vacuum; when the time came, it would take too long and be too wasteful to depressurize such a huge volume, and it wasn't as though the cargo needed atmosphere.

The Assault Landing Pods were stacked in staggered arrays, two racks of four files stacked three deep with space around each vessel to allow all-round access by work pods and the intricate, drifting spaghetti of power conduits and cable feeds.

A single Mark XXXIII Bolo massed 32,000 tons—as much as a fair-sized warship—120 meters long, 38 meters broad, and reaching 25 meters from ground to main deck, not counting the three squat and massive turret housings for the machine's incredible main armament. A Type 7 ALP was just large enough to house one such monster, 200 meters long overall, with a blunt, egg-shaped main pod and a trefoil drive and maneuver assembly aft. The whole was clad in night-black ceramplast, folded, studded, and embellished with sensor pods, drive sponsons, and field projector arrays.

The Mark XXXIII was, in fact, the first Bolo mark possessing enough internal contra-gravity generators to allow it to serve as its own landing boat for planetary assault. The Confederation Navy was conservative, however, heirs to the long-faded glories of the old Concordiat and of near-mythic Earth, who tended to rely on hand-me-downs from earlier ages rather than investing heavily in R&D. There were tried-and-true advantages to using ALP variable-geometry landers, and the Navy wasn't going to give them up.

Twenty-four ALPs filled the belly of the Confederation assault transport *Heritas*, an entire brigade of Bolo planetary siege units. Beyond the transport's outer hull, in the darkness of space about them, five more brigades of Mark XXXIII Bolos rode toward Destiny aboard other *Shehuva*-class star transports.

"They're impressive," Major Ramirez said after a moment. "And the plan is good. Just so long as we don't forget just what it is we're up against." She turned and peered closer at him. "Jon? Are you okay?"

He wiped his forehead, trying to steady the bounce he felt in his shoulders, his gut. Okay? He felt fracting *great*!

But Carla didn't know about the euph and wouldn't understand if she did.

"Fine," he said. "I'm fine." He checked the time on his implant. "Let's go, Major. It's time for the final briefing."

They turned and strode off down the catwalk side

by side, leaving the enormous black pods and their shrouded charges in the floodlight-starred darkness.

Major General Weslen Ricard Moberly was not a foolish man. He knew exactly how complex was the task set before him, and he knew the power of delegation and military staff command. As Confederation Supreme Army Group Commander, he'd been given the special executive title of Skymarshal and assigned the monumental task of organizing, deploying, and directing a planetary invasion from space. To that end, he'd marshaled a small army of tacticians, military theoreticians, and technicians—the "T-cubes," as he referred to them in his frequent Fleet e-memos.

Only through such an army, coordinated and accessed through the flagship's VR net, could he hope to stay on top of the situation once it began unfolding . . . in just another few hours.

From his command chair high up within the cavernous recesses of the Combat Command Center on board the task force flagship *Denever*, he could gaze down on the trivid tanks and plot boards of the invasion planning team; with a touch of the controls in the arms of his seat, he could *be* there, immersed in the lights and symbols of each simulation through the consciousness data relay links in his VR helmet. So far, only the fleet tacsit tanks were active, displaying the cone-shaped formation of the task force as it approached the objective, now less than five astronomical units ahead. Local resistance, he was pleased to note, was almost nil, far less than the best simulations had predicted. Perhaps they'd caught the damned Trixies and their human Janissaries with their shorts around their ankles after all. K-fighters and photon interceptors, most of them robots and teleops, snapped and flashed at the task force's flanks, but so far none had been able to penetrate the outer picket screen of destroyers and light escorts. The dreaded Aetryx carriers, so much on the planning staff's collective mind for the past months, were nowhere in evidence. The diversion at Draelano must have worked.

Yes! . . .

If General Moberly was not a foolish man, neither was he a patient one. Opening Channel 12 in his helmet CDR link, he summoned forth the image of Colonel Garrity, his Fleet Liaison Officer, her hard features projected by the helmet interface directly onto his retinas. "More speed," he told her. "Tell Admiral Hathaway that we need more speed. I want to brush past these pickets and enter approach orbit within three hours."

Her pale green eyes met his through the VR interface. A wisp of dark red hair fell across her eyes and she impatiently brushed it aside. "I'll tell him, General, but you may get an argument. We're pushing the e-mass-c barrier now, and he's bitching about how we should have started deceleration as soon as we dropped out of hyper."

"Remind the good Admiral who's in charge, Colonel. Or shall I talk to him personally?"

"I'll pass the word, General."

"Do it. I have to fire off the final briefing. Let me know if there's any problem."

"Yes, sir."

Garrity's face faded from his view as he electronically dismissed her. He'd expected opposition from Hathaway, a conservative and somewhat stodgy old-Navy type with limited imagination and drive. The e-mass-c barrier was always trouble. The closer a ship in normal space crowded c, the speed of light, the more relativistic mass it possessed, and the more energy per kilogram of rest mass it took to accelerate it . . . or to slow it down.

Hathaway was husbanding the task force's limited energy reserves in case they needed to do some hard maneuvering later on.

But if the Aetryx carriers and other fleet heavies were gone, combat maneuvers wouldn't be necessary, and the fleet could refuel from Dis, the system's inner gas giant, once absolute space superiority had been achieved.

Which wouldn't be long at all, now.

A tone chimed in his ear. "Final briefing," an AI voice said in dulcet tones.

"Okay," he told it. "Set me up. Let's get this parade on the march!"

LKN 8737938 was his primary designation, but he was Elken to his friends and the other members of his crèche social. He awoke, stretching . . . and then the fear hit him in deep, shuddering waves, like the icy surf at Gods' Beach. The last thing he remembered . . . no . . . what *was* the last thing he remembered? Memory eluded him, like fragments of a dream.

He opened his eyes, then wondered why he couldn't see. He reached out with a trembling, sweat-slicked hand, then realized he couldn't feel anything, that the tremors, the sweat, the cold were all imagined, anchors for the mind adrift within a vast and lightless void.

Concentrating, he summoned memories from deep, deep within. Surgery? He'd been going in for somatic surgery. Yes, he remembered that much. His god had promised him a new body, a new and unending life free of pain, of sickness, of fear. The god had promised him transcendence. Immortality, and eternal youth.

What had gone wrong? . . .

Nothing is wrong, a voice, deep and quiet, spoke

within the terror-haunted depths of his thoughts. *All is as it should be.* <calm reassurance>

"I can't see," he said, shouting into darkness. "I'm blind!"

You are not blind. Your optical processors are not yet online. <calm reassurance>

The voice of his god! He was not alone after all.

Do not thrash about in your mind so, the voice continued. <growing concern> *We do not wish you to injure your new body.*

New body! "Then . . . the operation worked? I'm immortal?"

The god did not reply immediately. Elken tried to conjure the being's image in his thoughts, clinging to memory as a defense against the fear. All he could manage was the memory of his god's eyes, deep and golden and piercingly beautiful, the last time he'd seen them. How long had it been?

What was wrong?

Nothing is wrong, the voice said, reassuring in tone and unhurried pacing. *You have been . . . chosen, LKN 8737938, chosen for greatness in your service to Caern.*

Elken forced himself to relax. If a god said that all was well, then well it was, without question, without the possibility of doubt or question.

And yet it was so dark here.

And . . . just where in the Twelve Black Hells of Shrivash was *here*? . . .

"What do you mean . . . 'chosen'?" Elken asked after a moment's uncommunicative silence.

Caern is in great danger, the voice of his god replied. <concern masked by self-assurance> *Invaders, fallen demons of the Evil Beyond, threaten now our world and all within it. You have been chosen to help repel the demon-horde invasion.*

"You . . . you promised me a new body, one that worked. . . ."

This you now have. It will take a few moments for the neural pathways to be attuned and their signal strength balanced.

"You said I would be immortal. No more sickness. No death."

This you will have soon. <calm reassurance> You have but to join Caern's defenders in repulsing the demons, and we know you are eager to reach for immortality this way. If you vanquish the Enemy, your new and immortal body awaits you.

"And . . . if we don't win?"

Then Caern and the Assembly of the Gods will be no more. <sadness, mourning for what might have been> Immortality must fail, for the gods will be dead and forever Worldpromise shall be broken. And you, LKN 8737938, will cease to exist.

Fresh horror stirred within the churning recesses of Elken's thoughts. "The gods cannot die! That's impossible!"

The gods will not die, for our servants, you among them, shall defend us. <confidence> Behold your new form, LKN 8737938.

Light shimmered into Elken's awareness, and the light took form. He was in an armored cavern, duralloy-walled and crisscrossed with walkways and work cranes. To either side, Elken was aware of vast, squat forms, slab-sided, multi-tracked, blister-turreted, massive military vehicles of some sort painted in rippling patterns of black and gray that shifted at the touch of light.

He'd seen such machines before, though without particular interest. A storehouse of the things had been buried on Caern, relics of the long-vanished Concordiat. The gods had taken charge of them ages ago, or so he'd heard through a history feed documentary once.

But he was looking for himself. There were humans before him, but they seemed impossibly small, tiny and scurrying. There were even a few gods in the chamber. Where? . . .

Turning his head, he was startled by the shrill whine of a high-energy mass-converter engine. His sense of perspective shifted, and he became aware . . .

By the living gods of Caern . . .

"What has happened to me? . . ."

He was trapped within a cliffside, no, a mountain of metal, a consciousness pinned immobile in the heart of a machine too vast to be easily comprehensible. In another horror-cold moment, he realized the truth. He was a tracked vehicle of some sort, exactly like the other metal monsters now in his field of vision. When he'd tried to move his head, a turret on his upper deck had slued sharply to the right.

The vehicle in which you now find yourself was called by its creators a Bolo, Mark XXXII, his god explained. *<patience> We have taken your brain and certain parts of your central nervous system and wired them directly into the Bolo's Combat Command Center. In effect, you are the brain, the Bolo is your body.*

"I'm . . . a . . . monster. . . ."

You are an extremely powerful, adaptable, and efficient combat unit, and a vital asset in the defense of our world. You show considerable leadership potential. You will adjust. You will adjust. Your strength as a human is your adaptability.

"I'm not human anymore! . . ."

<bafflement> Of course you are human. What does exterior form have to do with your true nature? <patience and reassurance> Do not despair. This transformation was necessary to preserve our world and vrefylsh'ye *. . . what you would call worldview or, perhaps, your way of life.*

Elken's horror was receding somewhat, as the initial shock wore away. The gods themselves took many forms. They were brilliant in their ability to generate new bodies as cradles for their *r'ye*, their essential life force and being. The godforms that took as their responsibility individual humans like Elken were quite different in outward appearance from the godforms that ran the cities or grew the sea crops or flew between the stars.

The god was following his thoughts. *Yes.* <approval> *You see the way of it, LKN 8737938. This transformation is but a first step toward the total freedom of form that you shall inherit as one of the immortal gods.*

"I . . . I'm not worthy of this honor, Lord."

You are worthy if a god says you are worthy. And you will prove that worthiness soon, by defending the World of the Gods from the invading demons.

"Y-yes."

It was payment, of a sort. He helped defend the world, he received godhood as his pay. He just wished someone had seen fit to warn him about this ahead of time. He'd found out he could tap into camera feeds from various locations and actually see his own huge, gray-black form, a hulking, brooding mass of duralloy and lethal-looking weaponry, squatting on the ferrocrete pavement of the cavern. There were scars along his flank, like plow furrows, and there were incrustations of rust and dried vent discharge at odd angles and corners of his suspension housing. The machine that was now his body was old, and it had seen combat in the distant past.

"Just one thing," he said. "I'm a monk. A *student* monk, in the *Dyi'jikr*, the Way of the Gods. I don't know about war. I've never fought anyone, or anything. I've never fought a demon. I . . . I . . . wasn't even sure the sky demons were real!"

<amused surprise> *Did you believe, then, that the*

Histories were mere fantasy? Mythology without form or substance?

"The idea had crossed my mind. I mean, we of the Brotherhood serve the living gods . . . but stories of vast empires spanning the night sky, of other worlds circling the lights in the sky we call stars . . . it's all a bit fantastic. Many of us believe the Histories to be . . . allegory. Metaphor."

The histories are accurate, or as accurate as such records can be, given the passage of millennia and the erosion of social order by time.

"I've never even seen a weapon." Mentally, he indicated the hulking presence of his own body. "I certainly don't know how to operate this . . . thing."

We will be feeding you a great deal of information within the next few periods, his god said. *This information will help you learn how to operate your new body efficiently and what to do when the time comes to fight. All you need do is perform the tasks I or others of the gods set before you.*

"I . . . I'll try my best."

And you shall succeed. <complete confidence> *It is foreordained, and the gods have declared it to be so.*

Elken wished he could savor some of the confidence he felt radiating from the god's presence and mental bearing.

He had the feeling that earning immortality was not going to be easy.

Tami Morrigen stood on the rocky beach, feeling the cold wind from Starside ruffling her hair a final time. Gods, she was going to miss this.

It would be full-light in another six hours; already the sun was staining the eastern sky in golds and silverblues with the slow-paced advance of dawn. Northward, auroras flamed, billowing, silent curtains of red and green and ultramarine shivering and flaring in the sky.

In the east, of course, Dis hung in golden-ringed glory, spectacular as always. The banded giant, spanning close to twelve degrees of the sky, was nearly full, the shadow of her arcing rings sharp and curved across her pale green and pink cloud bands. By Dislight, the city dome of Ghendai rose above its own reflection in the still waters of the bay. Clouds gathered in the south, illuminated by Dislight, piling high to blot out the few stars bright enough to shine through the bright Caernan night.

Storm coming, she thought, then chuckled at the irony.

"Mother! It's time to go!"

She turned at her daughter's call. Marta, willowy slender, her long brown hair in pleasant disarray from the sea wind, waved from the dunes behind the beach.

"Coming!" she called back. She didn't want to go.

Morrigen had been among the first free humans to arrive on Caern, five years ago. Pityr, her husband, had been an assistant manager to the principal factor for Daimon Interstellar then, bright, eager, and looking for the fast ladder up. Since then, he'd become a factor in his own right, still ambitious, but less . . . frantic. That was the word. Less frantic about commissions and percentages. There were more important things in life. Caern was a beautiful world, a good place to live.

She hated what was about to happen, even though she'd helped set the onrushing events in motion.

With a final lingering gaze at the low, deep-emerald swell of the Storm Sea, she turned and scrambled up the rocks to the hard-beaten path she'd descended from the dunes. On the plain beyond, at the edge of a gold and scarlet forest of bloodtrees and leaf fungus, the tiny corporate interstellar runabout was waiting, silver in the Dislight, coolant spilling from its pressure vents in billowing white clouds of steam. Flat, sleek, and hulled over with a mirrored surface that caught the light from the sky like a faceted jewel, the runabout was their ticket to safety from the approaching storm.

Men and their toys, she thought, bitter . . . then reproved herself. There were as many women as men working within DI Corporation. And the sleek little starship was their only way off this world, their only escape from horror.

Damn, but she wished that escape wasn't necessary.

Most of the others were already on board. Her husband and daughter waited by the open hatch, along with Senior Factor Redmond, and Redmond's servant. A last few stragglers from the home office were arriving as well, clambering off grounded flitters and making their way to the starship, children and baggage in tow.

"Step lively, Ms. Morrigen," Redmond called to her with that oily, patronizing laugh she despised. "We don't want to be caught at ground zero now, do we?"

Morrigen wondered about Redmond. Did the man really want to free the locals as passionately as his speeches over the last few months implied? Or was he thinking about the profits, once the indigenes were freed from the Trixies and turned into dutiful and grateful consumer-customers of DI? With Sym Redmond it was always hard to tell. She glanced at Veejay, Redmond's stolid servant. *He* was a local, his freedom purchased from one of the minor gods in Ghendai two years ago. What did he think about all of this?

There was no reading the man's placidly emotionless features.

Another flitter arrived from the city, touching down in the field a hundred meters away. The exodus had been going on for hours, now. The corporate starship had been flown out here during the night; it was unlikely that the Trixies would give permission for her to boost off-world, and Redmond had decided not to chance their probable refusal.

But there were Bolos on the way, a lot of them. It would be healthier for DI's Caernan branch office if the senior trading partners and their families were safely off-planet when the hammer fell.

Movement caught her eye, a flash of Dislight on metal or glass.

"Pityr?" she asked, pointing toward the distant city. "What's that?"

"Uh-oh," Pityr Morrigen said. "Trouble, is what."

It was a godflier, huge, stoop-winged, insectine, its oddly faired and blistered hull garish in black and yellow. It raced low across the plain toward them, overtaking the families still hurrying toward the ship and coming to a dead-stop hover overhead.

"You will please step out of the ship," an amplified voice called from the metallic threat hanging overhead.

"Let me handle this," Redmond said, reaching inside his jacket. "The rest of you get on board."

"No, sir." Veejay's voice was as calm, as implacably unhurried as ever.

"Pityr!" Tami cried. "That man has a *gun!*"

Redmond's servant had stepped back, and he held a wicked-looking needler in his hand. "The gods do not want you to leave," he said. "Please step away from the hatch."

"Veejay!" Redmond snapped. "What kind of nonsense is this? Put that thing away!"

"No, sir. Please take your hand away from your jacket slowly. That's good. Now keep your hands where I can see them, all of you. Ms. Morrigen?" He gestured at Tami's daughter and she felt a stab of ice-sharp fear. "Would you tell those on board to begin coming outside?"

"Daddy?"

"Do what he says, honey," Pityr Morrigen told his daughter.

"Damn it, Veejay!" Redmond snapped. "You can't do this! We're trying to help you, you and all your people!"

"We were not aware that we needed help, Mr. Redmond. The gods, after all, are on our side. All of them!"

A second godflier had arrived from the direction of the city . . . and a third. As two mounted guard overhead, one touched down a short distance away. The somas on board were enforcer types, lean, heavily scaled, and menacing with their leather garments and stunsticks. Their eerily human faces, weaving atop slender, snake-supple necks, made Tami queasy. There were human warrior somas as well, hulking, brutish-looking men with leathery skin, upsweeping, curved horns growing from their foreheads, and oversized, night-seeing eyes.

"You can't do this!" Redmond screamed. "You need us! You need our help if you're ever to be free of these monsters!"

"On the contrary," Veejay replied, "it is you who need our help now, just to stay alive. Please do exactly what the gods tell you, or you may be injured."

"I'll see you all in hell first!" Redmond screamed, groping for the weapon holstered beneath his jacket.

The enforcers started toward them, stunsticks upraised. . . .

Chapter Two

On board the transport *Heritas*, inbound for Caern, Colonel Streicher and Major Ramirez settled back on the reclining seats within the transport's briefing theater and allowed the technicians to adjust their input helmets and mikes. Only a handful of other shipboard officers shared the room with them, but when the VR tech touched a screen on the main console, the theater vanished and they found themselves within a stadium packed with thousands of uniformed Confederation officers.

Their bodies were still in the theater aboard *Heritas*, but in their minds, beneath virtual reality helmets and the needle-slender beams of light flicking across their retinas, and with low-frequency electromagnetic beams stimulating the tiny net of cranial implants touching their brains, they were elsewhere, beneath a green transplas dome on a world thousands of light years distant from the star system of Sallos. At the stadium's center, towering above them all, was the richly beribboned and impressively martial form of Major General Weslen Ricard Moberly.

"We are fighting," he said, his amplified voice booming through the virtual theater like thunder, "against gods. . . ."

23

A ripple of amusement danced through the bleachers, seating alcoves, and tables encircling the General's titanic form.

"At least," the apparition thundered on, "Intelligence informs us that that is how the Aetryx see themselves.

"In fact, our xenopsychological people suggest that they evolved socially with an innate worldview that essentially hardwired them to think of themselves as the masters of the cosmos. It might be a religious compulsion—think of all the human religions that told their followers that they were lords of creation. More likely, there's a biological root. Maybe their ancestors learned to breed domestic animals to fit specific needs, and they developed from that a philosophy that saw all other life as *tools*, as things to be used for their gain, comfort, and safety. We just don't know.

"We do know they have an advanced biological science that lets them manufacture bodies, or *somas*, to order, both within their own species, and in others. Here's the form we're most familiar with. . . ."

Moberly's form faded away, and in its place, suspended in midair above the stadium center, was an alien being at once shockingly strange, yet almost hauntingly beautiful. Centauroid—four-legged and two-armed—it had a body as sleek and as graceful as that of a jungle cat, with glistening ebony fur marked by streaks of silver. The head was oddly shaped and angled, but the face was eerily human, with large, expressive eyes that looked like orbs of shattered, golden crystal with jet black, slightly elongated pupils.

The being looked at once muscular, sleek, and benevolent; when those magnificent eyes blinked, Streicher had the feeling that a powerful mind resided behind them.

"Intelligence calls this form the Diplomat," Moberly's voice explained as the image slowly rotated in space.

"It was apparently gene-tailored specifically for the purpose of communicating with humans."

The black and silver being vanished, and was replaced by another, also centauroid, this time massively armored with bony plates embedded in a leathery hide, a walking tank in mottled patterns of olive green, brown, and black. The head on this one was a horror out of some ancient mythology, dragonish and snake-necked, with a saw-toothed crest of black spines, and red slits for eyes within bony protective turrets.

Interesting. The diplomat form had inspired an almost instinctively positive response in Streicher. This one inspired an instinctive dread. Streicher wondered how the image alone was able to affect him emotionally and with such power.

"This is one of several warrior forms," Moberly said. "Warrior, Type One. And this . . ."

The warrior was replaced by yet another centaur form. It possessed the same basic body shape, but the upper torso jutted forward instead of up and was capped by a nightmare tangle of multiple red-gold eyes, palps, and wetly gleaming mouth parts. "Our intelligence sources call this an Aetryx protosome. We think, we *think* that all of the subspecies derived from this one.

"General," one of the officers in the virtual room asked, "what are you saying . . . that *all* of these different forms are Trixies?

"We're not privy to the Trixies' biological labs," Moberly replied, "but our xenobiology labs think that the Aetryx genome must be highly plastic. Think of dogs, with all the different sizes and shapes and breeds they come in, and yet they're all *Canis familiaris*, from a palmpup squeaker to a Nordanian riding hound.

"Our sources tell us that the Aetryx don't attach the same importance to body image that we do. They may gene-tailor themselves to fit specific roles in their society. They may also have the capacity to so perfectly pattern the thoughts and memories of their own brains that they can download them into computers or possibly specially grown organic brains. This is all guesswork, at this point, but our intelligence sources claim this is the basis for the Aetryx claims of godhood. They don't die. They're effectively immortal. When their body ages, they download their minds to another one. At least, that's the claim.

"We have evidence that the Aetryx also use intelligent beings in their bioengineering schemes. And that, of course, is one reason the Confederation has declared war on these monsters."

The Aetryx protosome faded away, replaced by the image of a human.

Or was it? It was humanoid, certainly, with human features emerging from the broad, flat, muscular face. It was nude and male, though the genitals were missing, along with every bit of hair, right down to the eyelashes. Like the Warrior, Type One, the being's skin was leathery and protected in places by bony plates that followed the shape of the sharp-etched muscles underneath. The horns curling up from the being's temples added a peculiarly sinister aspect, as did the fangs protruding from an elongated jaw.

"A Warrior, Type Two," Moberly continued. "Also called a troll. It appears to have been gene-tailored from human stock."

Streicher heard groans and gasps from others in the virtual audience.

"Apparently, wherever the Aetryx go as they expand into the galaxy, they tinker with the genetics of any species they come across. We don't know the details of how they do this, but it's easy enough to see why. By altering the gene pool of any given world, they can tailor its population to their specs, make them tractable, docile, loyal, whatever is necessary. This makes them extraordinarily dangerous as military opponents.

"Caern was once one of the outlying frontier worlds of the old Concordiat, far up the Perseus Arm and pretty well off the beaten track of trade routes and military defense districts," Moberly went on. The troll's image was replaced by the swollen orb of a planet, a ringed gas giant, circled by a drifting coterie of moons. One of those moons, large and cloud-streaked as the camera angle zoomed in for a closer look, showed the colors of life—greens and olives and russet golds, with the telltale gleam of ocean blue beneath dappling clouds.

"Caern," Moberly continued. "A major moon of Dis, Sallos V. It's located just outside the traditional habitable zone boundaries, but the gas giant exacts tidal stresses enough to keep the surface warmed in the liquid water range. At last census, Caern was home to nearly three hundred million humans.

"That, however, was five centuries ago. When the Concordiat collapsed, all contact with Caern was lost. The Aetryx must have arrived shortly after that, conquered the planet, and enslaved whatever was left of the human population.

"We know very little about the Aetryxha. We know they have star travel, but we don't know how large the Aetryx empire is, or even if they *have* an empire along the lines of the Confederation. We've had minimal contact with them so far . . . at Jolhem, at Draelano, and here at Sallos, and our diplomatic exchanges with them in the first two have been limited to radio. Intelligence believes they may be slowly expanding through the Perseus Arm, settling only on worlds that offer them good . . . building materials. Congenial hosts they can work with, mold to their specifications. This appears to be the first time humans have run into them face to face, as it were."

Streicher felt a growing anger . . . or was it fear? An alien species with a technology evolved along biological lines, rather than the traditional methodologies of physics, chemistry, and math . . . their arsenal might be expected to include impressive biological weapons. And their conquests of other worlds would involve literally reshaping the inhabitants of those worlds to meet the new masters' specifications.

Jon Jarred Streicher was a military man from a military family, but his roots were on Aristotle and within the quasi-religious doctrine of Ethical Eudaimonics . . . which stressed that each individual had the right to develop his or her full potential through creativity, artistic endeavor, and individuality. *The greatest good for the greatest number.*

The idea of an outside intelligence reshaping an entire world population to its own ends . . . the very idea was disgusting.

And yet, he thought, no wonder the Caernan human population reportedly thought of the Aetryx as "gods." The impulse to worship higher powers might well be genetically enhanced or even grafted in whole.

But Moberly was still lecturing. "Confederation traders rediscovered Caern five standard years ago," he went on. "The condition of the human population on Caern was only gradually uncovered after several trading settlements were established on the fringes of the Storm Sea."

As Moberly spoke, words and names overlaid the slow-turning holographic globe, showing continents, cities, seas and other geographical features. As would be expected for the moon of so large a gas giant, Caern was tidally locked with its primary, one side forever facing Dis, the other looking outward, toward the stars. Because Dis was large enough to generate a fair amount of thermal radiation through gravitational collapse, the Disward side of Caern was desert, while the antipodes were ice-locked tundra, glacier, and solid-frozen ocean. Between the two extremes was a chain of landlocked seas girdling the planet from pole to pole. Rugged mountains had crinkled and gnarled the planetary crust with fractal geometries too complex for the eye to follow. Ice melt from mountains and outside glaciers had carved crazy-quilt jumbles of canyons, rivers, and badlands, and active volcanoes glowed and grumbled everywhere. Most of the cities—the old Concordiat population centers— were scattered along the seas and fertile plains pinned between desert and ice.

Planetographic data scrolled through Streicher's inner awareness, cold facts and figures inadequate to describe so vast and complex a thing as a living world. Smaller than Earth, with a surface gravity only three quarters of a G, and a low atmospheric pressure as well, .8 bar., Caern circled Dis in four days and eight hours, rotating once in that time as it faced its primary.

Two suns crawled slowly across the Caernan sky through the long, long day. With so much thermal energy falling on Caern both from the stars and from Dis, storms were large, violent, and frequent, though the slow rotation and small seas together meant that large Coriolis-induced storms were nonexistent.

Local storms, though, could be fierce, sudden, and fast-moving, with torrential downpours, tornadoes, and brick-sized hail. Thick ozone layers and a planetary magnetic field measuring about 1.2 gauss protected the surface from the vast bands of radiation flung off by giant Dis; the night skies were ablaze with auroras.

Caern, Streicher thought, must be a world of wild and spectacular beauty.

It was also a world that would be filled with unexpected dangers, even deadliness, all quite apart from any surprises the Trixies might have arranged for unwanted visitors.

Moberly was still talking behind the image of the slowly turning moon, describing the history of contact with Caern since the first traders had arrived five years earlier.

"Requests that Confederation officials be allowed to inspect the living conditions for Caern's human population were ignored or rebuffed," he said. "Those Caernan humans we were able to interview showed signs of having been brainwashed or otherwise conditioned emotionally into believing the Aetryx are actually gods of some sort. Demands that full civil rights be extended to Caern's humans were ignored. So were demands that our merchants have direct access to the human population.

"Tensions escalated when the Aetryxha Circle, as their government styles itself, rejected the Persean Doctrine. You've all received downloads on the legalese. Essentially, the Doctrine guarantees the rights of humans throughout the Confederation's sphere of influence, and establishes the Navy as the guarantor of those rights."

Images shifted and drifted across Streicher's vision, replacing the holographic globe of Caern. Confederation naval vessels, huge, irregularly patterned in swaths and stripes of black, gray, and light blue, moved into Disian space, the ringed, back-lit globe of the gas giant looming vast within its necklace of crescent moons.

"Since Caern is well within the treaty boundaries of Confederation influence, the Confederation Senate authorized military intervention. Two months ago, the battlecarriers *Esan* and *Helias*, the command cruiser *Galahedron*, and three destroyers arrived at Caern as part of a show of force to win Aetryxha acknowledgment of the Doctrine's provisions. You've all been briefed. You all know what happened. . . ."

Silent pulses of light illuminated the squadron of warships drifting across Streicher's inner vision. Through computer simulation, the virtual watchers observed again the ambush of BTF-74, the eye-searing disintegration of the *Helias* and the *Esan*, the two destroyers and the *Galahedron*.

"*Kurbal* recorded four battlecarriers moving out of Caern orbit as she swung past Dis," Moberly said, as the enemy vessels were highlighted in the scene by flashing red reticule boxes. "We don't know whether those ships are stationed permanently in the Caern System, or at some other Aetryxha base at another star. Third Fleet has engaged enemy forces at a known Trixie base at Draelano, ten parsecs from here, in an operation designed to draw local forces off . . . and it appears to have been completely successful. Our lead fleet elements have now reached Caern and begun the preliminary bombardment. They report that the carriers aren't here now, which means we will be able to achieve and maintain complete control of local space.

"With total air-space superiority, we will be able to land the special assault units without delay and without concern for counterattack or unpleasant surprises from enemy spacecraft. We will follow Landing Plan Brilliant Lightning. Targeting and LZ data is being downloaded to the Bolo Strike Force as we speak.

"And so, ladies and gentlemen, we are on a mission of mercy . . . and of rescue. Hundreds of millions of our human brothers and sisters are enslaved on Caern, and we are going in to save them! And we'll prove to the damned Trixies that they *aren't* gods, if we have to kick them all the way back to heaven!"

The virtual audience around Streicher erupted in

cheers and shouts. Streicher exchanged a glance with Ramirez as she arched one perfect eyebrow, then shrugged.

"Not all of them have seen combat before," he told her. "They don't know . . ."

"They're going to find out," Ramirez replied. "We all are."

We certainly are. For Streicher, in fact, shared the major's doubts about this mission. Things had come together so swiftly, with such *enthusiasm* during the two months since the destruction of BTF-74. But he wondered if anyone had thought about the real risks involved. . . .

"All personnel, report to your combat stations," the general told them, shouting above the ongoing cheers. "We hit atmosphere in ninety-three minutes!"

For the past eighty-one minutes, I have been receiving data feeds through the ship network AI nexus, with constant updates as more information becomes available. The invasion force has entered Disian space. The cruisers, destroyers, and gunships have begun the planetary bombardment, and the transports are now maneuvering for an approach path that will place us on the necessary vectors for release and insertion. So far, there is still no sign of the Enemy battlecarriers reported to be in this system, and no serious opposition to our approach. I remain confident that the initial phases of the battle plan have succeeded to a greater degree than is often the case with operations as large and as complex as this one. I calculate a probability in excess of 82 percent that we will be able to establish a beachhead on the target planet with casualties of less than five percent.

My regimental commander is not so sanguine about our chances for immediate success, however. On our private comm channel, he warns me to "stay on my toes," though the anatomical allusion baffles me for a full 0.0031 second, until I locate the appropriate phrase definition in my slang dictionary files. Colonel Streicher, it seems, is concerned that the Enemy may not be so unprepared as he seems and may have hidden reserves that could seriously upset the projected timetable for deployment or battle prosecution.

"The Enemy's best opportunity for blocking the invasion," I tell him, "is during our approach to the objective. Once our heavy units have been deployed and reached the surface, he will be unable to bring sufficient firepower to bear to hinder our movements."

I do not add the obvious, that the Bolo Mark XXXIII has won the appellation of "planetary siege unit," with each single Bolo possessing, as it does, sufficient firepower to overcome most typical planetary defense garrisons. Our first wave consists of the entirety of First, Second, and Third Brigades, a total of seventy-two Mark XXXIII units, with three more brigades in orbital reserve. It is what ancient strategists referred to as a powerhouse punch, designed to eliminate all Enemy resistance in a minimum of time and with a minimum of friendly casualties or collateral damage. It is the hope of the Confederation High Command that principal Aetryx resistance on Caern can be broken by L-plusthirty hours with minor damage to the local infrastructure, allowing the humans held in Aetryx slavery to take over the governing of their own world with a minimum of cost and delay.

"There was an important military base here five centuries ago," Colonel Streicher informs me after several long seconds. Human speech is appallingly slow, but I collect the words as they are spoken, storing them for processing and response when appropriate. In the meantime, I continue seven separate diagnostic routines

on various integrated software and satellite systems.

"Much of the hardware must be obsolete by today's standards," he continues, "but. . . well, you know there's a good chance that there are Bolos on Caern, right?"

That fact, of course, is in my briefing files. The Concordiat's Perseus Arm, Twelfth Military District Headquarters, was located on Caern, including an aerospace base, army command post, and a Bolo reserve depot.

"According to my records," I tell him, "ninety-three Bolos were left here at various reserve bases. Forty-one were advanced Mark XXXIIs, while the rest were older models, Mark XXVII through XXIX. It is unknown how many may still be in operation."

"Exactly," the Commander says. "It's unknown. You guys could find yourself in quite a fight down there."

"The Bolo Mark XXXIII Combat unit is vastly superior to all previous marks," I tell him. I am aware that human AI psytechnicians still argue whether my kind knows emotions such as pride or self-satisfaction, but that is only because they have not questioned me directly. I am fiercely proud of what I am and of my potential. "Obsolescent combat units on the objective world will not pose a serious threat."

"You sound smug." He sounds surprised.

"I merely state fact," I tell him. "I have been fully programmed with the tactics, communications protocols, and access codes of earlier Bolo marks. Unless the Aetryx have made major reprogramming changes, the Bolos on Caern will not even be able to attack. We will simply co-opt their major control systems and shut them down."

"I hope it's as easy as you think it will be," my regimental commander tells me.

I comprehend. He is warning me against overconfidence.

But I am a Bolo, Mark XXXIII, and in my case, at least, overconfidence is not a part of my psychotronic profile.

Streicher rose from the padded chair in the Bolo Combat Control Center. As always, there were ghosts here.

Peace, it seemed, always came with a price. You had to buy it, first in blood, privation, and suffering. Later, though, when peace was a way of life, you paid through unpreparedness and the inevitability that someone bigger and stronger than you was going to come along and try to force *his* version of peace down your throat. The Confederation had been at peace for a long time now and was not, in Streicher's professional estimation, ready for war . . . even so small and easily won a war as the Caern Incursion promised to be. Unlike his fellow Confederation officers, Streicher had had far too much experience with war. He'd seen the elephant, as an ancient and somewhat incomprehensible military adage put it, and he'd not liked what he'd seen.

His earlier charge of euph had worn off, the joy and self-confidence failing. Instinctively, he reached for a breast pocket on his uniform, clawing at it before he remembered he'd left the packet of small, intensely blue tablets in his quarters. He was trying to ration himself, but it seemed as though the need was coming more frequently these days.

"Colonel, Lieutenant Tyler has just come on board," the Bolo's voice announced, a calm, almost thoughtful male baritone filling the tiny compartment from above. "She is on her way to the battle center via personnel conduit one."

"Very well. Thanks, Vic."

Ducking to keep from banging his head against the lower rim of the 360-degree holoscreen dome hovering above the command chair, he made his way aft toward the hatch. A monitor in the bulkhead showed Lieutenant Tyler's lanky frame coming up the moving way aft of the battle center.

Bolos had been fully autonomous, not requiring a human commander on-board, since the Mark XV . . . and those dated back as far as the late 24th century, at least. Still, sheer conservatism, and the centuries-old fear that Bolos might start thinking for themselves and slip out from under the figurative thumbs of their human builders and masters, had kept this tiny compartment with its battle command center, reclining seat, and holoscreen buried deep within the duralloy mountain of most Bolo combat units.

He laid one hand on the curved, metal wall of the control center, feeling the faint pulse transmitted through layered duralloy and ceramplast. The heart of the Bolo, beating along in its centuries-old rhythm. The heart of a living mountain.

Or of a god of war.

Streicher often came to the BCC, sometimes to talk with his enormous charge, sometimes simply to be alone and to think. He'd started out nearly twenty-five years ago as a very young, very junior lieutenant on a Bolo maintenance crew on his home world of Aristotle, out on the remote marches of the Confederation, and that was where he'd discovered this safe haven from barked orders, hassles, and overly anal authority. Later, after the horror of the Kerellian Incursion, he'd been the human liaison with a Bolo in the old 4th Star Guards and then been transferred to Asetru, where he'd commanded a company of two ancient Mark XXVIIs.

Now he was a colonel, in command of a regiment of six Mark XXXIIIs. On each world, in each command, he'd found it necessary for sanity's sake to seek this metal-walled haven out, a place of escape when he needed one.

For Streicher had seen far too much of the folly men called war. He'd been wounded—not with visible scars or missing limbs or the cancerous burn of radiation, but with deep and ragged tears etching his soul.

The agony of losing his family and people, his entire world . . .

God, he needed another euph.

He'd been taking the little blue chew-tabs for twenty years, now, ever since Aristotle. A sympathetic doctor had prescribed them, at first, back when it wasn't even clear if the grief-stricken band of exiles from the scorched world would survive.

Euph tablets had been popular on Aristotle long before the Kerellian Incursion. Streicher, like nearly everyone throughout the Confederation's Thousand Worlds, carried a cerebral implant in his brain, part of the microsymbiotic hardware grown molecule by molecule throughout his body that helped him link in to AI simulations or data feeds or connect mind-to-mind with other people.

Euphorinase was an artificial molecule, an enzyme that catalyzed a reaction between sugar molecules in the blood and the cupric-hafnide neuron receptor sites within the implant. When chewed in tablet form, the molecule entered the bloodstream through the capillaries beneath the tongue and almost immediately began bonding to the implant receptors in the brain. Over the course of the next hour or so, sugar was broken down, yielding a thin flow of free electrons as it did so.

The result was a kind of trickle charge directly into the implant where it bonded with the brain's key memory and sensory areas. It felt *good*. More than that, it tended to inhibit painful memories, dull them and push them into the background, without interfering with the normal functioning of the brain. Not physically addictive at all, it was widely used by medtechs to relieve stress and aid patients dealing with serious loss or mental trauma.

And if there was some emotional addiction for some, well, it was easy enough to reprogram the implant to reject euphorinase and break the craving once and for all. He could stop any time he wanted to at all.

Euph was forbidden to Confederation military officers, but everyone knew that plenty of people at all ranks took the stuff. It was harmless, after all, and could even help a man focus, to think harder and straighter, without the distractions of whatever memories had driven him to the drug in the first place.

Once, twelve years ago, a spot physical check had caught traces of euph in Streicher's implant and bloodstream, but the discovery hadn't hurt his career in the least. His implant had simply been reprogrammed. Within two weeks, he'd found a civilian medtech willing to program him back.

And life went on, made bearable by the occasional chewing of those bright, beautiful blue pills.

A tone sounded, and the battle center hatch irised open. Lieutenant Kelly Tyler stepped through, ducking to avoid banging her head. "Oh!" she said, rising to meet Streicher's gaze. "Excuse me, Colonel. I . . . I didn't know anyone else was in here."

"You can always query the machine, Lieutenant," he told her.

"Yes, sir, but, but I didn't think of that. People don't usually come up here."

"I do. So do you, apparently."

"Uh . . . yes, sir." She seemed nonplussed. She had long red hair, which at the moment she was wearing at a most nonregulation length down her back. She started to run her fingers through her bangs, then realized what she was doing and stopped. "I, uh, just wanted to run a prelaunch on Victor, here, from his command center."

"I've already done that," he told her. "For the whole regiment. But please feel free to check me if you want."

He could see her hesitate, see her weighing the best possible reply. He was pretty sure that Kelly, like him, came here to be alone.

She was a strange one, he'd decided almost as soon as he'd joined the regiment. Shy, unwilling to put forth her own ideas in conference, she was nonetheless an excellent Bolo unit commander, with a decided rapport with her huge charge. She could talk to the Bolo, he knew, far more comfortably than she could communicate with most of her human comrades.

And, just maybe, he thought, she was a little in love with her titanic charge, and wanted to say goodbye.

He knew exactly how she felt. "I'll be in the launch center," he told her. He checked the time on his implant. "Make it fast. You have ten minutes."

"Yes, sir. Thank you, sir."

"And . . . your hair."

"Sir?" She flushed.

"It's attractive hanging down that way, but regulations say you wear it up, high and tight, at least on-duty. Don't want you catching it on the instrumentation."

"S-sorry sir." She reached up and began tucking it into a bun.

"Besides . . ." Streicher raised his eyes toward the ceiling, indicating the Bolo. "I don't think *he* notices your hair style."

She stammered something unintelligible, her blush growing darker. Grinning, he ducked through the hatchway and into the narrow, green-painted passage-way beyond. Streicher knew what she was going through and would give her what time with the Bolo he could.

But in another handful of minutes, the regiment would be on its own.

Chapter Three

I employ the final seconds before pod release completing a final diagnostic on all combat, power, navigation, and sensory systems, and report to Central Combat Command that all systems are working within the expected parameters. Through external shipboard monitors, I can see the objective planet now, a ruddy crescent touched with white and ocher, now less than five hundred kilometers distant. Heritas has established an approach vector which will bring me down on the night side, but close to the dawn terminator. Ringed Dis, swollen, pole-flattened, storm-banded, rises above the curved horizon of its largest moon.

"Fourth Regiment, First Battalion!" sounds over our communications relay from C^3. "Sound off!"

"Invictus, ready," First Battalion's Unit One replies.

"Horrendus, ready," adds Unit Two.

Then it is Second Battalion's turn.

"Second Battalion. Sound off!"

"Victor, ready," I reply.

"Ferox, ready!"

"Third Battalion. Sound off!"

"Terribilis, ready!"

"Fortis, ready!"

41

Elsewhere in the sky, the stars, formerly banished by the brilliant sun, emerge. . . .

Colonel Streicher ushered Major Ramirez through the hatch before him, then followed, stooping to ease his tall frame past the hatch combing and into the sunken, circular compartment beyond. Soft and indirect lighting glowed from the walls; in the center of the room, a comfortable sofa couch surrounded the sunken conversation pit.

No instrumentation was in evidence. It didn't look much like a spaceship at all.

VR techs began helping the two officers with helmets and commlink mikes. Major Dylan King, the Regimental Tactical Officer, was already on the couch, his eyes lost in the flickering patterns of laser light that tied him into the Combat Command Network. With him were the three battalion commanders and members of their staffs.

Streicher took a seat and allowed a tech to complete the physical links with C^2N. As his feeds went hot, he sensed presences about him—Ramirez and King, the vehicle's pilot, members of Moberly's command staff aboard the flagship *Denever*, the quick awarenesses and nervous thoughts of the regiment's six unit commanders and the three battalion commanders, and all the others. The process was called Extended Command Distribution, or ECD, and it was a tried and tested strategy for military operations, especially mil ops as large and as complex as this one.

Also present within the ghostly kinesthetically sensed host were six large and brooding thought-forms, the virtual presence constructs of the six Bolos of the 4th Regiment.

As the link switched on, Streicher could see the view being transmitted by an external camera on *Heritas's* outer hull, with the curved blue and black-painted duralloy above, the dark orb of Caern below and ahead. *Heritas* was now in the world's shadow; both Sallos A and B, the local suns, and Dis, the world-moon's primary, were below that slowly flattening horizon. The side of Caern that forever faced away from giant Dis was a cold and lonely place with few settlements and no targets of any military significance. It lay in night, now, the surface illuminated only by starlight and the ghostly glow of the planet's highly charged auroras, visible as pale green, red, and yellow patches circling the poles.

Streicher could see the pinpoint orange and red gleams of several large, active volcanoes stretched in chains across the night side, where lava seas illuminated smeared plumes of ash, and a glacier the size of an ocean shone in pale starlight, like a ghostly cloud obscuring much of Caern's anti-Dis hemisphere. The data feed on Caern had indicated that the side facing away from Dis was cold, never getting much above minus ten degrees, even during the long, fifty-two-hour period of daylight. At this distance from brilliant Sallos A and B—almost five astronomical units—the temperature of any free planet would remain far below zero. Dis, however, through thermal radiation and the heating effects of tides alternately stretching and compressing the world, kept Caern's sub-Dis side unpleasantly hot for humans.

The major settlements and military strongholds all lay along the shores of the chain of seas that stretched from pole to pole to pole again, girdling the world between the realms of fire and ice. That would simplify somewhat the basic strategy for assaulting Caern. It wasn't as though the Confederation fleet had to conquer an entire world of some 220 million square kilometers. Only about ten percent of that area lay within Caern's habitable band, and of that less than half—say, ten million square kilometers all told—was land.

Still, that much sheer open ground comprised a vast area. The Caern strike force of necessity would focus on key targets—cities, military stores depots, communications centers, spaceport facilities. Secret allies among the Confederation trade delegation to Caern had provided most of the necessary information.

The bombardment would help.

"Give me tactical," Streicher said, and the view of the planet became cluttered with targeting and tracking reticules, icons, and symbols. Ahead, orbiting toward the horizon, an echelon formation of destroyers—their ID blocks picked them out as *Cateran*, *Delphis*, and *Tritheladee*—were commencing a bombardment run. Their Hellbore blasts were optically invisible at this range, of course, but the data feeds showed fire cones and firing angles, primary and secondary targets, and the flash and shockwave spread of each shot. Grendylfen was getting a real working-over, Streicher thought. Those destroyers mounted 200cm main weapons with an output of five megatons per second apiece, the same as the Mark XXXIIIs in his regiment. Whatever they knocked down would *not* get up again soon.

He tried not to think about the devastation taking place at that moment across the world's surface. He'd seen that sort of thing firsthand, on Aristotle. . . .

Damn. I should have gone ahead and taken a euph before coming here, he thought. This was going to be rougher than he'd expected.

"Command craft, stand by for release," a voice whispered in his ear.

"Here we go," King said. "I hope the scouts knew what they were doing when they reported the area clear!"

"Why's that?" Major Beswin, the First Battalion CO, asked.

"Because I feel exposed in a lifeboat, damn it!"

Streicher chuckled. "Don't worry, Dylan. If the bad guys start shooting back, the transport is a *much* bigger and easier target! You'll be damned glad you've already taken to the boats!"

In fact, the command craft was considerably larger and more comfortable than any lifeboat. But Streicher knew what Major King was feeling. *Heritas* was so big; it was hard to imagine being safer in a squat, domed saucer barely fifty meters across.

"Command craft release in five," the voice continued, "... four ... three ... two ... one ... *release!*"

Inertial fields kept Streicher and the others from feeling anything, but the clang of hull grapples releasing provided the illusion of a sharp jolt. The vast curve of the *Heritas*'s hull fell away, and as the saucer-shaped command craft rotated and stabilized, the larger vessel seemed to swing off to the side, receding quickly.

Other saucers, as tiny, comparatively, as minnows swarming out from the sides of a thousand-kilo bladeshark, spilled into space, along with a glittering cloud of myriad decoy satellites.

With nuclear interceptors and anti-ship hunter-killers, even a vessel as large as the *Heritas* was vulnerable. No matter if she had battlescreens up at full, one nuke close alongside could render her helpless, and a single salvo was guaranteed to reduce her to a cloud of hot, metallic vapor. ECD had been evolved to assure the survival of as many members of the command staff as possible, even in the face of an all-out nuclear assault.

But Streicher had to admit that he did feel a little more helpless now, adrift in the black void above Caern's starlit hemisphere.

Heritas was maneuvering now, dropping rapidly toward the planet and slowing sharply as well. From the vantage point of the command craft, and with the visual enhancements possible through the fleet-wide netlink, they could follow the transport's descent as she stooped toward Caern's night-shrouded surface.

Other transports maneuvered elsewhere along the night edge of Caern's daybreak terminator—the *Vangled*, with the 3rd Regiment, further north, and the *Kalahad* with the 1st, to the south. Streicher found himself holding his breath, and he forced himself to release it, to draw a new one. If the enemy had any hidden reserves, weapons or forces concealed from the trading consortium spies, this, logically, would be the time for them to strike, when the drop pods were vulnerable to ground fire, when the Bolos they carried were still unable to deploy their fearsome armaments.

The watchers switched to a view relayed from a camera satellite paralleling *Heritas's* course, as the horizon ahead flattened to a gentle, silver-and-gold-edged curve bowed back from a rising sun of pinpoint, eye-searing brilliance. She had her main bay doors open now and was decelerating hard to match the planet's rotational velocity, to reduce her ground-speed to effectively zero. A moment later, the first of the Bolo ALPs dropped from her swollen belly.

Each was considerably larger than a command craft, but tiny compared to the transport nonetheless. They dropped two by two, maneuvering clear of *Heritas* and of each other, pivoting in space, aligning themselves with their drives aimed against the sky, their blunt noses toward the ground. Their drive flares were invisible, but the data tags on Streicher's virtual readout showed that the pods were accelerating, dropping from space and beginning their long plunge toward Caern.

❖   ❖   ❖

Two by two, we are released from our docking grapples. Brief bursts from contra-grav projectors nudge us free of Heritas and into the void.

First Battalion—Invictus and Horrendus—are first to clear the ship's bay. I follow, along with Ferox, and the Third Battalion drops after us. Our pods handle the separation and drop-vector insertion maneuvers. Though not possessed of true AI, the processing power of their computer brains are more than ample to handle these tasks. My inertial sensors record our passage through Heritas's idling drive fields and pick up the jolt as my pod's drive switches on and the acceleration swiftly builds.

A quick scan by long-wave radar verifies my position and vector. Heritas has successfully released us at a point that very nearly matches the slow rotational vector of Caern—a ground velocity of approximately 69.7 meters per second. The value is extremely low for a planet— some three to five times faster is more common—but I note that this is due to Caern's low rotational velocity— one rotation about its 26288.8 kilometer circumference in 4 days, 8 hours, 46 minutes, 6.86 seconds.

With a lateral descent vector component matching the planet's rotation, however, I effectively have been released directly above my drop point at an altitude of 127.3 kilometers. My pod's drives are accelerating me to a velocity of 1500 kph, straight toward the surface. At this speed, impact will occur in 5 minutes, 4.8 seconds.

I have other things to worry about, however, for the next several minutes. The Enemy, while severely handled by the Fleet's orbital bombardment, is beginning to respond with heavy anti-space and -aircraft fire.

The sky around me blazes with light, heat, and hard radiation. . . .

✧   ✧   ✧

"Kind of hard, all this waiting," Captain Meyers, of the regimental logistical staff, observed.

Lieutenant Kelly Tyler had to agree, though she never would have done so aloud. For now, from orbit, all she and the rest of the 4th Regiment's command staff could do was sit about the circular well and watch the landing approach, painted directly on their retinas by flickering pulses of light. Cameras mounted on the pod hulls gave unsettling views of the Bolos' descent, nose-down toward a darkened, cracked and broken plain. Myriad flares like brilliant stars—plasma projectiles, white-hot kinetic rounds, and the exhausts of anti-air missiles—floated up from the shadows below to meet them.

It was hard to keep in mind that they were over six hundred kilometers above Caern's surface and not in that fire-ringed plunge into night, so persuasive were the virtual scenes unfolding in their thoughts. At one point, Kelly felt a biting pain in her palms. It took a moment to realize that the pain was caused by her own fingernails digging into the heels of her hands.

She focused on the commlink she shared with Victor. She could sense his thoughts as though he were there in the Sky Strike command craft with her, or she with him in his battle command compartment. "How are you, Vic?" she asked.

"All systems functioning nominally, my Commander," was Vic's typically flat reply. Was there a hint of rebuke there, a subtle suggestion that she should shut up and let him do his job?

Now I'm getting way too sensitive, she thought. *Vic understands.*

Dear Vic . . .

Kelly knew she had a lot of trouble relating to other humans, especially to men, and she knew that others thought of her as quiet, shy, even withdrawn. She'd imagined that they'd accepted her on the command staff because she was undeniably good with Bolos, especially with Victor, with whom she'd been teamed now for over a standard year.

The only entities, the only *people* she'd ever really been comfortable with were Bolos. Like Victor. He didn't come into her room at night the way her father had, hadn't beaten her or "played games" with her, never got drunk on joybrew. Victor didn't scream at her the way Wayne had, or hit her and humiliate her like Fred. He was cool, self-sufficient and self-possessed, always rational, always presenting a thrilling, deep masculinity that had nothing to do with sex. He accepted her and extended to her *respect*, in that calm "Yes, my Commander" he always used.

For Kelly, he represented perfect power—complete, perfectly controlled, and balanced.

She pretended sometimes that she was in love with Victor, though she knew that it was nothing more than a private game, a fantasy, perhaps.

Usually.

At ninety kilometers, they were well into the thin, upper reaches of Caern's ionosphere. Hull temperature rising . . . atmospheric pressure increasing. A dazzling flare of star-bright radiance expanded at the edge of her vision, swelling, brightening . . . and then flashing past as the landing pod dropped. Data readouts recorded the EMP surge, the intense heat and searing radiation, and Kelly imagined she could almost feel the shudder as the pod rode out the shock wave.

So, the Trixies weren't afraid to use nukes. That was not a real surprise; the records from the *Kurbal* showed the Trixie interceptors using nukes against BTF-74, after all. Still, some in the command staff had suggested that the Trixies wouldn't resort to nuclear weapons on or near their own world.

She remembered that Streicher had not been persuaded by the arguments and had pushed the planning team to adopt tactics that acknowledged the possibility of NBC warfare on the planet, with maximum dispersal of assault force assets. He'd been prescient on that one. Had he been prescient enough?

The ground below appeared to spark and twinkle. The assault force was redirecting its bombardment now to suppress enemy batteries and strong points within the LZs, and the Hellbore strikes were punching out craters filled with molten rock, each shot liberating a megaton per second or better of sheer, raw heat. The fleet's two battlers, *Ajecerras* and *Validente*, had turned their kilometer-long railguns toward the planet below and were hurling relativistic projectiles down the gravity well, targeting enemy defense bastions and command-control centers.

It seemed impossible that anything could face such a rain of devastation and survive. . . .

LKN 8737938 could feel the thud and reverberation of the bombardment as he rumbled slowly through the tunnel. The underground tubes, a labyrinthine maze his people called the Caern Deeps, crisscrossed their way through the planet's crust, connecting the human cities with the deeply buried Aetryx communal centers and nests. He'd been in the tunnels countless times since his emergence from the vats two and a half Disyears before, but his memories of them were of vast tubes beneath the ground, with high-arching ceilings all but lost in the darkness overhead. To his new senses, and from this new vantage point within the duralloy hull of a Mark XXXII Bolo, the tunnels were brightly lit—at least at infrared wavelengths—and almost claustrophobically low and narrow. The gods had assured him that the tunnels were deep enough and strongly enough reinforced that no weapon could touch them. Even so, he felt a quickening of fear. Had he still possessed a heart, it would have been beating rapidly now.

The detonations above increased in intensity and frequency, a shuddering, rolling thunder as the enemy warships passed over, slamming the surface of Caern with high-energy plasma bolts, each liberating the heat and shock of a fair-sized nuclear warhead.

He wondered if his family had survived. The city of Paimos had almost certainly been among the first on the enemy's list of targets.

Your family lives. <assurance> *Most of the civilian population was evacuated into the sub-city tunnels as the enemy approached.*

"Thank you. Can I see them? Talk to them, maybe?"

Not now. <regret> *You must focus on your mission and upon our cause.*

It was just as well. What would either of his mates think if they saw him in this form now? Jaennai, especially, with her neurotic dislike for the plasticity of the Gods' Way, the mutability of their appearance.

His parents too, might be distressed, though there were few emotional bonds remaining with them. Removed from his mother while still the size of a pea, nurtured within the spawning vats, and born and raised in the warmth and joy of Paimos Crèche 4937, he'd not even met them until he was half a Disyear old and now knew that he had very little in common with them.

But they'd visited him in the hospital before his surgery. He knew they were concerned. And he didn't want to cause them worry.

A branching appeared in the tunnel ahead, the left

leading up, the right down. *Go right,* the god's voice said. *You will wait out the bombardment at Trolvas.*

"What is Trolvas? A city? I don't know the name."

It is one of our . . . special places within the Caern Deep. A city of the gods.

Elken felt a shiver of anticipation and just a little fear. He'd heard of such places, of course. Caernan myth was filled with stories of the fabulous caverns of the great Deep, of the treasure troves laid up by the gods, of the places of joy and judgement.

But he'd never expected to actually see one before his physical death.

The tunnel floor dropped away, leading him deeper into the planetary crust. How deep was he, now? He realized that both the ambient temperature and the air pressure here were controlled, so he would find no clues there. He could only guess that he was kilometers beneath the surface already, if only because the multi-megaton blasts were muted now to a distant, ominous thunder.

How far down did the labyrinth reach? The gods alone knew. Myth from the Dark Age before the coming of the gods whispered that humans had begun these tunnels as they'd probed Caern's crust, searching for precious metals and rare elements. But Man's scratchings at the rock were insignificant compared to the power of the gods.

The thunder overhead redoubled, booming and rumbling through the tunnel maze. What, Elken wondered, was it like on the surface now? Was there even anything left of the cities, the towers, the farms, the droma ponds, the habspreads, the soaring, golden temples of the world he'd known?

LKN 8737938 pressed onward, and down. He might not yet have come to terms with his own change of appearance, but one thing he knew.

The Enemy would pay for the desecration of the Holy Places of the gods, and pay dearly. . . .

Hellfire explodes around me, nuclear detonations ranging from half-kiloton tactical anti-air bursts to five-megaton thermonuclear blasts designed to scramble the electronics of incoming spacecraft. Both my internal electronics and those of my drop pod are hardened and well-shielded, however, with fiber-optic data feeds and EMP-grounded processor mounts, and while the pod's outer hull heats alarmingly, I pass through the blaze unscathed.

The friction of my passage through thickening atmosphere is heating the hull as well. I monitor the rate of temperature increase, as well as sensors reporting hull stress and flexure. All systems are still well within normal parameters.

I fall through a cloud of anti-radar, anti-lidar chaff blasted from ejectors on the pod's outer hull. From the ground, the sky must be a nearly opaque shield of chaff clouds, for my own view of the target area is now increasingly obscure. A trio of nuclear explosions detonate some ten kilometers below me, and I surmise that the Enemy may be trying to clear the chaff cloud with shock waves and thermal radiation.

Then I am through the chaff layer, technically in free fall, but feeling deceleration now due to atmospheric re-entry friction. The pod's outer layers are ablative, shedding excess heat as they break away, the half-molten fragments in turn providing additional radar and laser shielding. The fireball of my descent ionizes the air around me, which both increases my radar cross-section to sensors on the planet and interrupts my HF and VHF communications bands with the transport and the command craft overhead. No matter. I continue falling, and in another 158.4 seconds, I have slowed enough that the ionization trail begins to dissipate and full operational communications is restored.

I sense the brush and tickle of the Enemy's search and targeting radars and laser-ranging detectors. I am in the center of a vast and very rapidly played game, of sorts. Each time the Enemy attempts to paint the incoming pods by radar, sensors in orbit pinpoint the source of the transmitter, and shipboard Hellbore batteries pound the target until the signal goes dead. The Enemy, for his part, uses a large number of radar emitters at widely scattered, remote stations, switching among the different transmitters quickly so as to avoid providing the ship sensors with a signal of great enough duration to allow a target lock.

Nonetheless, with each passing second, fewer and fewer of the Enemy's radar and laser emitters remain active, and those that do are having a harder and harder time penetrating both the electronic jamming from ECM satellites and spacecraft and the clouds of metallic debris filling Caern's predawn sky.

The Enemy is not helpless, however. Below me, another nuke detonates, and a light layer of clouds at the ten-thousand-meter level suddenly glows with a pulse of intense reflected light. The shock wave brushes my pod, sending me into a momentary tumble, but its idiot brain recovers and restores itself to the proper vector.

But one of my regimental data feeds has just gone dead. Bolo serial 837989, Horrendus of First Battalion, whom our handlers fondly referred to as "Horry," is no longer transmitting on any frequency. I must surmise that that last nuke detonated close enough to his drop pod to score a kill.

Resistance, I note, is far more active, more fanatic than anticipated by either the Bolos of the regiment *or our human counterparts. I am concerned about what this may mean when I finally am able to grapple with the Enemy.*

"Damn!" Major Beswin shouted, breaking the silence within the command craft's observation center. "Horry's gone!"

Streicher had felt the snap of the communications link with the First Batt Bolo and known immediately what it meant. There was a chance, of course, that the pod's communications suite had been destroyed but the craft itself was still intact . . . but Streicher had seen the flash of that last nuke and knew from his telemetry that the missile had detonated less than a hundred meters from the pod bearing Horrendus.

It was hard imagining something as large, as powerful, as heavily armored as a Mark XXXIII Bolo being destroyed by *anything* . . . but a near-direct hit by a nuke at an altitude of twenty-five kilometers would certainly do it.

"Steady," Streicher said gently. "We knew there was a chance things would be rough going in. You've still got Invie to get down."

"Y-yes, sir."

"Lieutenant Bucklin?" Jaime Bucklin had been Horry's unit commander, and he knew the two were close.

"Sir." His voice broke.

"Hang on. I'll need you as regimental reserve. Don't go to pieces on me, now."

"No . . . sir. I'm okay."

Like hell you are, son. Unit commanders and Batt COs alike tended to form pretty close bonds with their titanic metal charges. The shock of losing one was always tough.

The loss hurt Streicher as well. He'd liked Horry,

the short time he'd been able to work with the machine. But he still had five other Bolos in the regiment, all of them dropping through hellfire.

The orbit of the constellation of command craft was sweeping them across the Bolo LZs, bringing them closer to Caern's dawn terminator. Within the scene painted by flickering, low-energy laser light across Streicher's retinas, sunlight burst above the curved horizon of Caern, as silver and gold arcs rimming the planet's edge raced away from the dazzling point of sunrise, slowly thickening into the slenderest of crescents.

Below, the land was still in night, but lit enough by the coming dawn that Streicher and the others could see the crinkle of mountains, some ice-capped, some wreathed in ash-cloud and the sullen glow of lava. The seas were dark and still, the shorelines intricate fractals of dune and black rock, of pale shallows and twisting rivers knotted within the molted hues of spreading, alluvial fans.

Most of the cities were burning, with dense clusters of yellow and orange pinpoints of flickering light shotgunned into the larger tangles of artificially geometric shapes that were the Caernan population centers. Smoke palls hung downwind of each target area, lit by ruddy glows from within and beneath. Here and there, fires burned in the cratered ruin of other targets apart from the cities, the aerospace bases and communications centers and command complexes and other defense installations that comprised the Aetryx military infrastructure.

They'd tried their best to spare Caern's population centers, though most cities had at least one major Trixie base or command complex. The bombardment had savaged all of the major targets and most of the lesser ones, though the low-orbiting destroyers were still seeking out the smaller bases nestled in among mountain crags and desert canyons. Fast-pulsing sparkles of blue-white light to the north marked the bombardment of a radar-lidar tracking station in the mountains above Yotun.

Enemy resistance was unexpectedly fierce, and he could tell from the data feed that they had a lot more in the way of ground defenses than had been expected. New radar, laser, and planetary defense positions were revealing themselves every moment, none of them were on the original list of pre-invasion bombardment targets and objectives.

Well, it wouldn't be the first time in military history that intelligence had failed to provide accurate and timely data.

He just hoped that the intelligence shortfall wasn't going to be the deciding factor in this contest, because if it was, those Bolos down there might well find themselves in a trap from which there was no possible escape.

Chapter Four

I have fallen to the fifteen-thousand-meter level. Much of the ground below me is covered now by clouds of smoke rising from several destroyed targets, making direct observation difficult.

I note that there are numerous Enemy ground positions that do not correlate with known positions in my target files. Some positions, in particular, are evidently deeply buried, well fortified and shielded, and mount heavy weapons—planetary defense bastions of unexpected strength. They will need to be dealt with on an individual basis once I land.

Assuming I am able to land successfully, that is, and do not share the fate of Bolo serial 837989. Laser and particle beam fire is searching the sky, scattering from the droplets of ablated hull material in quick, rainbow flashes of color and puffs of expanding vapor.

And I have now reached an altitude of twelve thousand meters and must begin decelerating, a maneuver that is certain to attract unwanted Enemy attention. . . .

"Here we go, everybody," Streicher said. "Be alert."

They watched as VR graphics traced out the courses of the five surviving Bolo drop pods. Each had begun braking savagely, pushing fifteen Gs to kill their downward plummet. Enemy fire was tracking more accurately, as their fire control computers picked out the targets from the clutter that were maneuvering independently.

One by one, though, each pod's finned tail assembly broke free, then split, continuing to maneuver to further confuse enemy fire. At the same time, telemetry showed the pods opening, their blunt hulls unfolding to create broad delta wings with wide-open air brakes. They began pulling out of their dive as well, nosing up second by second, battling against the inertia of their Mach-two dives.

They were fighting hellish G forces, and if any flesh-and-blood pilots had been facing them without inertial dampers, they would have been immediately unconscious and possibly dead.

Bolos were not flesh and blood, however, nor were the artificial intelligences piloting those pods. Data continued to stream into the command craft, with only occasional data dropouts or static fuzz from bursting thermonukes. The heaviest anti-air fire was slackening now, as the pods dropped close enough to the surface that they were below the horizon for the more distant weapons launch sites. At the same time, tactical fire was picking up, lasers and particle beams from vehicles on the ground, from ships, or from low-flying aircraft.

Streicher accessed the time readout, which painted itself in the corner of his vision. Two more minutes to go. . . .

Vibrational . . . levels . . . increasing . . . as my pod . . . pulls . . . out of its . . . dive . . .

Contra-gravity thrusters . . . at maximum. . . .

The pod . . . pulls . . . fifty Gs. . . .

My dive is flattening out as I continue to decelerate, the G-load dropping. Twenty gravities now . . . fifteen . . .

The maneuver is a tight one, designed to avoid my slamming into the ground at twice the speed of sound. Inertial dampers might ease the stress but are too large and require too much power for a disposable landing pod. I am unaffected by high-G maneuvering, though I am concerned that the pod's variable-geometry wings are approaching G-load stress tolerances.

In any case, the worst is over. I am flying level now across a dark sea at an altitude of 1200 meters, with a velocity of 436 meters per second, roughly mach 1.5 for this altitude and air pressure. Several remote shards from the pod's tail assembly accompany me, maneuvering independently. My pod in this configuration has external stealth characteristics which give it an apparent radar cross section of less than five centimeters, while the shards reflect the image of a much larger target. Some of the decoys begin to maneuver now, drawing attention away from my position.

Ahead, the sky is aglow, partly with the approach of dawn, but judging from spectral analysis of the light, much of that glow is from cities set ablaze by orbital Hellbore fire.

I begin dropping toward the water. . . .

LKN 8737938 entered the cavern the gods called Trolvas. The place was deep, so deep that he entered the compound across a bridge spanning a deep chasm, at the bottom of which bubbled and seethed a black-crusted river of molten rock. The walls themselves were aglow with ruddy light, and sulfurous fumes steamed and roiled in the air, collecting beneath the rocky, sulfur-encrusted ceiling high overhead.

The thunder of the bombardment continued, but it was so distant now, so muffled, that Elken was scarcely aware of it. The throb of power shackled to the gods' service, booming and rumbling from the generator stations and factory complexes ahead, was much more evident.

Awaiting his arrival, drawn up in three ranks on a broad parade ground before the squat, black and brown Aetryx buildings, were forty machines identical to Elken's new form . . . huge, broad, tracked, with slab-armored sides and low single-turret weapon mounts, each bearing the ugly snout of a 200cm General Polydynamics Hellbore.

And . . . he realized that he recognized the minds, the thoughts behind many of those blunt, metallic facades, though he wasn't entirely sure *how* he knew. There was VBR 9383733, an old friend from his crèche. And that was NGK 2225344, from Paimos, a friend, he thought, of his parents. He'd thought both of them had moved on to the Gardens of the Gods long ago.

And the mental voice of that one in the front rank had to be SND 9008988. She, like him, he knew, had volunteered for elective surgery some cycles ago, her bid for immortality.

He was distracted enough that, just for a moment, he searched about himself for a cockpit release and a hatch . . . until he realized that he was not riding one of the crawlers popular for ground transport in Caern's more formidable outback terrains. He *was* the crawler, a huge, tracked warfighting monstrosity with a human brain, and the thought brought a fresh rush of fear. What was going to happen to them . . . to him?

Everything is going to be all right. <confidence> *All is as it should be.*

"Hey, Elken!" A Bolo that Elken somehow knew was PLT 94635469, a teenaged kid from the city who'd just graduated from the crèche a few twelves of daycycles ago. "Look what I can do!"

The Bolo shifted back on its tracks, shuddered,

then popped its forward contra-gravity projectors, lifting its ungainly prow high into the air. For an ominous moment, Elken was treated to the sight of a 21,000-ton Mark XXXII Bolo standing upright on the back curve of its rear tracks at an angle from the ground of about sixty degrees, holding that precarious balance with short, sharp, quick back-and-forth nudges from its hind drive wheels.

"Huh?" Elken heard Palet's voice answering an unheard command. The Bolo dropped back to a solid connection with the ground with a thud that rattled Elken's suspension. "Uh, sorry. . . ."

Many of your comrades are still adjusting to their new forms, the voice in Elken's thoughts explained. *Adaptation will not take long. Move there . . . take your place in the front rank.*

He ground forward, swinging into line alongside SND 9008988. He felt Sendee's warm thought of welcome. "Elken! I'm so glad you joined us!"

"I . . . wasn't expecting this," he replied. "A new body. I thought it would be human . . . or at least have some human left in it, like the Specials."

"We *are* Specials now," she told him. "The most Special there are! . . ."

"It's taking some getting used to."

Attend, children. <earnestness> *We know many of you are surprised at your new bodies, surprised at this form the gods have chosen for you as your first step into golden immortality. Trust us when we say that our first and greatest desire would have been to welcome you all to the ranks of immortality directly, without the need for this intermediate form. Events, however, have forced drastic measures upon all who live upon this world, gods and humans alike. Behold. . . .*

An image formed in Elken's mind, unfolding with

a depth and a clarity startling in its realism, and startling, too, because he had never been in space.

He seemed to be hanging in space high above Caern's dawn terminator—he recognized his world, of course, from maps and news feeds. Great Dis was visible in the background, swollen and huge and golden-ringed. A vast armada of alien spaceships drifted above Caern, and he could see the flash and twinkle of titanic explosions sparkling here and there within the night-shrouded portion of Caern just in front of the transition from night to day.

The view, he thought, must be computer generated, a fiction mirroring actual events. How, otherwise, could the gods be getting this image from the midst of the invading fleet?

But then, the gods could do anything. He refused to question that.

The image expanded, as though he were swooping in toward his world's surface, the horizon opening up from tightly curved to scarcely curved at all. At this much lower altitude, he could see whole cities wrecked and ruined, vast, mountain-high piles of smoke as thick and as ash-laden as the pall from any volcanic eruption.

The city of Ledelefen. <deep sorrow>

Ledelefen? That was in the south, not too far from Paimos. He'd been there many times, visiting the Hall of Histories in the course of his studies as a student monk of the Brotherhood, and he knew it well. What he was looking at now . . . rubble and the broken-off stumps of towers, obelisks, and hab centers, peppered by numerous craters each with a seething, still molten bottom . . . no. This could *not* be Ledelefen.

No, that was the Tower of Learning, still standing next to a circular emptiness that once had been the Park of Divine Prospect, scorched and blackened, canted now at an angle.

By all the gods and the world they made. . . .

The Sky Demons ravage our garden world. <righteous anger> *Their bombardment blindly smashes our cities, our crèches, our places of learning and study. This wanton destruction is intended to bring us all, humans and gods alike, to cowering submission. This strategy will turn and strike back against its fomenters. The Sky Demons will learn that savagery, barbarism, and treachery cannot break the spirit of civilized peoples living in harmony with their gods.*

For this reason, you have been recruited to serve the gods and your people. You are here now, within the warm and molten depths of Trolvas. The Sky Demons' landing vessels approach, and soon the bombardment of our world will cease.

And when it does, you shall strike . . . to wipe this scourge from our world.

I drop to within ten meters of the surface of the Storm Sea, flying east at a velocity of 1230 kilometers per hour. This is well above the speed of sound for the ambient air pressure. The shock wave of my passing raises a towering wall of water and white spray in my wake as I outpace the thunder of my passage.

I am paralleling the shoreline, here. The Kretier Peninsula lies 32.7 kilometers north, on my left, but 58.1 kilometers ahead of me the shoreline curves to the south, and at my current velocity I will pass from sea to land in another 19.8 seconds.

My targeted landing zone is the rocky beach just north of the city of Ghendai, one of the larger and more populated of Caern's cities. My intelligence download identifies Ghendai as an important logistical, communications, and command-control center, as well as the location of at least two underground Bolo storage depots. Since the storage depots are deeply buried and well defended against orbital attack, my primary mission is to engage local forces, neutralize the depot defenses, and hold the position for the arrival of Confederation military specialists who will secure any Bolos still operational at the site.

I spend almost a tenth of a second speculating about Bolos stored here on Caern. They will be Mark XXXIIs, machines nearly as capable as myself on many levels, though massing only 21,000 tons and possessing only a single 200cm Hellbore in a dorsal turret mount. Although our records of this sector are fragmentary, these Bolos would have been transported here for storage as a strategic reserve during the chaos of the near galaxy-wide Melconian War of nearly five centuries ago. They will have been powered down and placed on the lowest operational standby alert, and will require considerable preparation and maintenance work to bring them back to awareness. Still, if this can be accomplished by Confederation Bolo technicians, we will have a large local force to draw upon for scouting, patrol, and garrison duty as the strike force completes its investment and reduction of the planet's defenses.

It would be interesting to speak with Bolos awakened from that past age. I and most of my comrades date from nearly two centuries later, when the conflict known to humans as the Melcon Holocaust had largely burned itself out. So many records from the beginning of that war were lost, especially with the scorching of Old Earth. Much could be learned from these old veterans of that devastating galactic conflagration.

Unlike my human commanders, I have no fears at all that the Bolos on Caern might be reactivated and used against us by the Enemy. Mark XXXII Bolos possessed a sophisticated psychotronic AI nearly as powerful as my own. A revolutionary neural-psychotronic interface allowed direct human-Bolo communications through optical net or laser communications links. The Mark XXXII's basic loyalty and doctrinal operating systems programming would prevent its use by any non-human agency, even if that agency could access the layers of codes, program traps, firewalls, logic cut-outs, and destruct-sequence barriers protecting the basic AI function.

Rumors do persist of a machine intelligence in toward the Galactic Core which suborned a Bolo on a world called Cloud nearly a century ago . . . reportedly a Mark XXXIII, though that seems incredible. If true—and I cannot accept much of what I have heard as fact without more proof than evidently exists—that suborning of a Bolo AI can only have been possible because the Enemy in that case was itself a highly sophisticated artificial intelligence of a technological capability considerably in advance of the human culture under attack.

In this case, the technology of the Enemy, the alien Aetryx, is self-evidently on a par with our own. They cannot have the programming skills, or the knowledge of our technology, necessary to bend the Mark XXXIIs stored on Caern to their will.

Even if such a thing could be managed, it remains true that I am vastly superior in technology, firepower, and tactical management skills to the Mark XXXII, to say nothing of earlier, more primitive machines in the local arsenal depots. The local forces have managed to mount a surprisingly savage and well-fought defense against our landings but will be no match at all for the Confederation deployment, once the invasion force has come to grips with the planetary defenses.

With eighteen seconds to go before I reach the coast, I use the pod's external sensors to probe in all directions, searching for possible centers of Enemy resistance. My intelligence briefings indicate a large planetary defense bastion at Dolendi, on the Kretier Peninsula to the north, but I am receiving no electronic signs of life from that direction at all. Dolendi had been the focus of a far-flung web of radar sites and fire-control bases, but the bombardment appears to have successfully neutralized them all.

Encrypted signals employing frequencies and keys not employed by the Confederation forces are coming from several points up ahead, at 078, 091, and 095 degrees, respectively. Clearly, these are leakage from Enemy tight-beam communications equipment, but they are low-powered and weak, possibly undetected from orbit.

No matter. I assign the location and destruction of the radiating sites to my combat priorities list.

Fifteen seconds to go. It is time to slow to landing speed. Airbrakes unfold from the trailing edges of the pod's delta wings, taking hold of the air in a shrieking, shuddering deceleration. Its ventral contra-gravity generators angle forward, applying a hard four Gs of thrust. I feel the shudder as I go subsonic. The pod also initiates a slight bank to the left, moving from a heading of 089 degrees to 082 degrees, in order to put me down near the storage depot complex just north of Ghendai.

And then everything starts to happen at once.

"Vic is under attack!" Lieutenant Kelly Tyler yelled. The regimental Space Strike Command team looked down on open ocean dotted with scattered islands and a hurtling, delta-wing landing craft. "I've got a reading on a launch, coordinates Sierra one nine by Oscar five three!"

"Impossible!" Major Lawrence Filby, Second Battalion's CO, snapped. "That's open water!"

"No, I check her," Major King said. "There's a ship

or submersible there, something rising up out of the sea."

Streicher saw it, a long, black shark-shape running with upper decks awash. It must have been lurking behind those islands, possibly under water.

"I read three small nuke warheads, half-kiloton range," Ramirez said. "They're locked onto Victor's pod. Range five kilometers . . . three . . ."

"Target them," Streicher ordered. "Take them out!"

"Too late!" King said. An instant later, three dazzling brilliant white suns blossomed above the water, and all communications telemetry with Victor was lost.

The Enemy missiles arc over an island to the south, racing at low altitude across the water at hypersonic speeds. The pod has defensive weaponry—antimissile gatling lasers and kinetic-kill gauss guns—but they are currently aimed forward, and the pod AI is distracted for a critical instant by the need to apply its full attention to the low-altitude bank.

I attempt to take control of the pod's weapons system myself, but lose a full 0.08 second negotiating with the pod AI through an outdated interface. The first missile warhead detonates less than five hundred meters to the south.

The pod's battlescreens dissipate and absorb much of the thermal energy, but the shockwave sends me tumbling, the pod wildly out of control. A second airburst, this one at a range less than two hundred meters a scant 0.45 second after the first, shreds the pod's right wing, overloads the battlescreen generators, and melts critical control circuits in the pod AI suite.

I initiate override protocols and take control of the landing craft myself. The wings are no longer generating lift, but I can use the ventral contra-gravity generators to raise thrust enough to regain control and bring me down for a soft water landing.

But a third nuclear blast follows the second by 0.34 second. I feel the pod's skin melting . . . and then I lose all external sensation as the pod's sensory data feeds are catastrophically closed down.

In utter blackness, I feel the pod's wreckage tumbling.

I have few options. I must get clear of the pod, or risk serious damage upon impact. With luck, the jettison charges are still intact. . . .

The god Ulyr'ijik saw the sky light to the north, saw the target vanish from his screens aboard the submersible *Dannek*. The vessel was already sliding beneath the surface as the shock wave reached them, a disk of pure white sea-froth and a wall of shrieking, hurricane winds. The vessel shuddered and lurched, then steadied as its launch tower submerged completely, leaving the raging storm to roil and slash the sea's surface, while the *Dannek* rode in comparative calm and silence.

An excellent job, Ulyr'ijik told the submarine's human crew, wired to their control panels and couches. *You have brought down one of the Sky Demon Bolos! You will be remembered forever in the Gardens of the Gods!* . . .

The god knew just how lucky that shot had been. Had he been any farther away, the Confederation landing pod's defenses would have had time to react to his sneak launch; had he been closer, his own weapons would not have had time to acquire the target after launch and home on it.

To say nothing of the fact that they would not have survived the triple firestorm of the warhead detonations.

A very good job indeed.

Now, though, they needed to make their escape. The launch, the destruction of one of the Sky Demons' landing craft would not have gone unnoticed, and their retaliatory fire would be swift and deadly. . . .

And the god Ulyr'ijik intended to survive a bit longer, to claw a few more Sky Demons down in nuclear flames.

The charges fire and the landing pod's hull shatters. White-hot flame scours my outer hull . . . some from the jettison charges, true, but most from the seething nuclear fireball of the last detonation.

Sensors fail. I am tumbling a scant few meters above a flame-lashed sea of steam and spindrift. My hull temperature soars, approaching 900 degrees Celsius. The radiation flux is terrific, well above 1500 rads, and it is possible that my external hull has become hopelessly contaminated.

These are minor problems, however, since they pose no immediate threat within the next two to three seconds. Of more immediate concern is my landing.

I engage my contra-gravity generators. Mark XXXIII Bolos, unlike earlier marks, have internal contra-gravity generators. This increases their battlefield mobility, of course, and also allows a direct assault landing capability, something the Mark XXXII could manage only with special auxiliary modules. Landing pods were employed for this assault, however, because it was expected that the landing would be contested, and the pod provided stealth and decoy characteristics that helped insure a safe landing.

At least, that was the idea, before I found myself tumbling in a cloud of wreckage through a superheated nuclear fireball.

Thunder shrills all about me. I trigger the contra-gravity generators . . . and nothing happens. A critical circuit has overloaded and burned out. Approximately 3.1 seconds later, I strike the water in my left side, still traveling in excess of 200 kilometers per hour. A cloud of wreckage—the shredded and half molten remnants of the landing pod—follow me into the depths.

"Victor is . . . gone," Kelly Tyler said, her voice ragged. Then she seemed to collect herself, to realize where she was. "Sir."

It was hard not to project yourself into these virtual reality simulations, even knowing that you were safe, sitting back on a command deck thousands of kilometers out in space.

It was especially hard when you cared about the machines you were watching in the sim, when you thought of them as people.

"Stay linked," Streicher told her. "Vic may have pulled out." It was a fragile hope, staring down into the holocaust of steam and incandescence rising above the ocean, illuminating sea and clouds in a baleful green-yellow deathlight, but it *was* a hope. The Bolo might have survived the blast . . . though there was a terrifyingly good chance that it would be smashed when it hit the water, crushed by the pressure of the depths, or trapped if it landed upside down and, turtlelike, was unable to right itself.

"Oh, God," he heard Kelly say.

"Besides," he continued, "I need you in reserve. Pull it together. We have a long way to go yet."

He wanted to reach out to both Kelly and Jaime, to clap them on their shoulders and tell them it was okay, that he understood . . . but that was less than perfectly professional behavior, and he held back. They all needed to stay focused right now, and not be distracted. The inevitable fruit of combat was casualties and missing friends, and it was tough to deal with, even when those friends were machines.

"He'll pull through," he heard Kelly mutter over the command sim's comm channel. The depth, the sheer ferocity of her emotion surprised him. She was usually so withdrawn. "He'll pull through! He's *got* to! . . ."

Chapter Five

I can still hear the roar of the explosion, and the light, even twenty meters down, is still searingly brilliant, a hot, shimmering white glow above me. The particulate and gamma radiation flux is gone, however, as is the direct thermal radiation. My hull temperature drops rapidly in the cold, thick embrace of the sea. My immediate concern now is not vaporization or the stress of impact, but simply landing upright when I hit the bottom. If my tumble takes me to the seabed upside down, I may not be able to right myself.

Righting myself would have been simple with working contra-gravity projectors, but their failure forces me to investigate other means of attitude control. I am currently sinking toward the bottom on my left side some 110 degrees out of the upright position, nose down at a 56-degree angle. The bottom, I sense, using sonar, since laser ranging is largely useless in this medium, is fifteen meters below the front of my left track, and I am sinking at a rate humans would refer to as rocklike . . . at twenty-five meters per second.

There is no time for experimentation. If I can reduce my yaw to the left by something in excess of 20 degrees, I should be able to land ventral-side down on both tracks.

My secondary weaponry consists of fourteen 20cm ball-turret-mounted Hellbore infinite repeaters arrayed in two lateral banks of seven apiece. I pivot my seven starboard secondaries to maximum elevation, pointing above my hull in relation to my body, but, in this upside-down configuration, they aim at the fast-approaching bottom.

I fire all seven weapons simultaneously. The shock of seven one-gram pellets of fusing hydrogen plasma accelerated by magnetic induction to a fair percentage of the speed of light jolts me like the near brush of a nuclear warhead. The water around me turns to steam, and my upper deck heats dangerously.

But the momentum of those seven relativistic rounds jolts me hard, like the firing of heavy missiles. The recoil as I drop is enough to push my starboard side over to the right by a good thirty degrees. I'm going to hit hard . . . but I'm going to hit more or less upright.

My left-front track slams into the bottom at an estimated twenty meters per second . . . and sinks into mud. My surviving external sensors note that almost my entire length plunges nose-first into the blanketing ooze before I finally come to rest.

Above me, the dazzling light of the nuclear fireball fades, plunging the depths once again into their normal lightless murk. I have survived the near-miss of three half-kiloton nuclear warheads. But the situation I find myself in now seems scarcely better.

I seem to be entombed in mud.

The problem, Streicher thought, was this feeling of helplessness, this being trapped in a tiny command craft high above the planet's atmosphere utterly unable to do a thing to influence the battle . . . or help in the location and rescue of a downed warrior AI. The Confederation tended to be ludicrously top-heavy in its military hierarchies, and Bolo regiments pushed that imbalance to the limit. A single Bolo had a unit commander, a battalion commander, and a regimental commander, and none of them could do much of anything short of make suggestions, at least so long as they were so far to the rear.

Ancient combat, millennia ago, had required commanders who led from the front, who inspired their men, who made a difference simply through their presence. Modern combat, though, was peculiarly lethal to flesh and blood. The life expectancy of a human on a modern NB^2C battlefield—with Nuclear, Bolo, Biological, and Chemical weapons—was measured not in minutes, but in seconds. Only units as heavily armored as Bolos had a chance of survival.

And when things started to go wrong—and they invariably did in combat—there wasn't a damned thing all of those brass-heavy commanders could do but watch and maybe do a little heavy-duty cursing.

Or praying.

God I need a euph. He had a store of them here on the command craft, tucked away in his personal locker below decks. A foil packet with twenty-four tabs . . . though he'd already gone through five of those. Nineteen doses left. Nineteen gloriously blue, blue chewtabs that could take away the stress, take away the anguish that lingered still, every time he thought of lost Aristotle.

He shook himself, dragging his thoughts back from the tantalizing blue of euphoria. He had to think, had to concentrate, to *focus*.

Two Bolos down out of his original regimental strength of six. He shifted his command sim to an overview of the entire regimental op area again, noting positions and times to landing. Invictus was only seconds from touching down on the Kretier Peninsula, just south of the planetary defense bastion at Dolendi. Ferox was one minute out of its LZ at Kanth. Third Batt was still over the Storm Sea, minutes from landing.

"*Go*, you goddamned brutes," he muttered, not realizing he'd spoken aloud. . . .

I require 2.035 seconds to completely catalog my assets. All systems, save for the onboard contra-gravity generators, are fully functional. Twelve psychotronic circuit boards, despite being fully hardened and shielded, have burned out in various other systems, but all have multiple redundant backups and do not at all limit my options. In particular, my power plants are at full combat operational output, and my drive train is operational at 100 percent capacity.

The problem is that by using my tracks alone I cannot escape this nose-down attitude, with more than three-quarters of my length buried in mud. There's nothing to grip, nothing to work against, and my total mass—while amounting to only 23,680 metric tons in Caern's .74G gravitational field—is far too great to lift from the mud, no matter how furiously I spin my tracks. I sense that my weight is slowly dragging my rear portion down deeper into the mud. My nose appears to be pressed against solid bedrock beneath the mud, but the raised portion of my structure is sinking through the viscous stuff at a rate of approximately three meters per minute.

At this rate, I will again have all four sets of tracks resting on more or less solid ground in another five minutes. However, the viscosity of the mud is such that my movement will be seriously hindered.

I have downloaded reports of lower-mark Bolos that literally tunneled through hundreds of meters of ferrocrete, duralloy, and concrete to escape subsurface tombs prepared for them. I will be able to move, but it

*may take hours, even days, to win my way through mud.
I would actually make better process if I were entombed
in ferrocrete; at least then my tracks would have something against which to push, a means for applying the
not inconsiderable power stored in my accumulators.*

*I do not have hours, or days, in which to get free
of this trap. My presence on the battlefield is required
now, in accordance with the battle plan currently being
employed. While my commanders must have assumed
me destroyed in the explosion that brought me down
and by now be changing their plans to reflect my loss,
it is my clear duty and responsibility to reach the
battlefield as quickly as I can and bring my armaments
to bear on the Enemy.*

*If I can reduce the effects of my mass, I might still
be able to swim my way out of this predicament. If I can
at least partially repair my contra-gravity generators,
there is a chance, albeit a slim one.*

*The diagnostic has shown me where key power feeds
picked up the magnetic pulse of the nuclear detonations
via induction and melted, despite shielding, battlescreens,
and other safeguards. In addition, the vaporizing power
leads have damaged five of the twelve projector assemblies on my ventral surface. The power feeds can be
replaced, and I deploy ten damage control robots—
"techspiders," as humans call them—to replace the cables
and bus bars. The damaged projectors can only be
replaced, and that is an operation requiring refit within
a major maintenance depot. If seven CG projector
assemblies are not sufficient—something which I believe
is borderline under these less than ideal conditions—I
will not be able to repair the units at all.*

*I have no option but to try. I deploy the spiders to
the damaged sections of my hull.*

*I wonder, though, how the battle is proceeding on
shore without me.*

✧   ✧   ✧

"I'm going to stretch my legs. Beep me if there's a change."

Colonel Streicher broke contact, sat forward, removed his headset, and rubbed the spots from his eyes. The landings were going as well as could be expected, and there was little now for him to do. The tough work now was up to the unit commanders . . . and their mobile warrior mountains below. He needed a break. He needed . . .

No.

The others of the 4th Regimental Command Staff remained in the circled couch, faces blank, the rapid green flicker of light across their eyes and brows blocking the real world from their consciousness as each played voyeur within the less substantial electronic world of data feeds and AI simulation.

The lighting within the command craft was low and indirect, and the view screens encircling the room were on, allowing shipboard personnel to gaze out into space. He went first to the hatchway leading down to their personal lockers. Space was at a decided premium aboard ECD command craft, so there wasn't much in the way of amenities—narrow bunks, no private rooms for senior officers, a single small locker for a change of uniform . . . and any other personal effects.

He palmed open his locker, its recognition pad accepting his touch. Inside, tucked into a breast pocket of his number two uniform, was the packet of euph.

He broke one free and held it in his palm a moment. Such a pretty blue color, so deep, so pure. He popped the tab into his mouth and chewed it slowly, savoring the warmth that spread from tongue and jaw up through his face and back through his head.

It felt so *good.* . . .

He knew he was going to need the charge to get through this next part.

No . . . it wasn't that he needed it, not really. It was just that the blue chew-tablet helped him be more himself, more focused, more observant. Clear-headed.

And no thoughts of . . . what he didn't want to remember. *That* was what was important. . . .

He used the lavatory, then returned to the main deck where he accepted a cup of kaff from an aide. Padding silently across the thick, white carpeting, he leaned against a sill and stared for a long time down at the world of Caern.

Below and ahead—the saucer was tipped with one rim pointed directly at Caern's heart—glowed a panorama of spectacular beauty, swirled cloud whites and wrinkled browns and ochers, verdant greens and deep sea-blues. The command craft had decelerated and matched the planet's slow rotation, which meant they were no longer in orbit. Poised six hundred kilometers above Caern's dawn terminator, they were held aloft now solely by the thrust of the spacecraft's contra-gravity generators. It was the only way they could maintain line-of-sight communications with the regimental ground elements, without enduring a long comm blackout as they circled around to the far side of the planet.

To Streicher's left, the slash-ringed disk of Dis hung heavy against the sky, its night side faintly glowing in deep red and orange-brown swirls and bands of color and internal heat, while beyond the arc-brilliant flare of Sallos painted a slender crescent across the Disian limb. Other moons were scattered across the gas giant's ecliptic, tiny crescents bowed away from the glare of the distant, closely paired white suns.

Without the electronic visual acuity of the virtual reality feeds, the other ships of the Confederation invasion fleet were lost in distance, motes in a vast gulf of emptiness. The planet's surface itself gave few clues to the savagery of the assault from space. He could just make out some smudges here and there, catching the dawn's first light, that might be vast plumes of ash and smoke rising from ruined cities, and across the terminator into the night there was a scattered handful of ruddy pinpoints which might be active volcanoes . . . or the funeral pyres of Caern's centers of population.

He felt a sharp pang at that. While major defense installations located within population centers had been targeted, the kinetic energy released by each projectile directed planetward from orbit had been calculated to destroy as little of civilian structures as possible. No one had expected that the enemy would use nukes against incoming landing pods, however, and large sections of the human cities on Caern had been set ablaze or knocked flat by nuclear air bursts ranging from a few kilotons into the megaton range.

It demonstrated how desperately the enemy intended to defend himself on Caern. The enslaved human population, though, was caught in the middle and was suffering accordingly.

It always happened like that, with war. . . .

Caern's surface was pocked and scarred by ancient craters and the eroded shadows of craters, ghosted crescent-shaped mountain chains and ring lakes. A chain of circular seas stretched from equator nearly to the north pole, and one, the Storm Sea, was the focus of a hellstorm loosed upon the world. They were hovering directly above that thousand-kilometer circle of water now, and Streicher thought of the Bolos fighting their way into the burning enemy cities around its northeastern rim.

"In order to save the village we had to destroy it." The words were from an ancient war, a blood-letting so far

in the past no records of it remained, but the aphorism had survived within some military traditions. How many of the human slaves held on Caern had been killed in the preliminary orbital bombardment, or by the nukes deployed by their Aetryx masters to stop the first wave of the assault? And how many more would die before the Aetryx bases and planetary defense bastions and fortresses and depots were neutralized or under Confederation control? The Aetryx's free use of nukes against incoming drop pods suggested a fanaticism bordering on the suicidal.

"Are you on Aristotle again?" a soft voice said at his back.

He jumped, startled. Carla Ramirez had emerged from the VR simulation as well and stood behind him now, a cup of steaming kaff in her hand.

"I suppose maybe I am," he admitted. "It puts a different perspective on it, seeing it from *this* angle."

"For war," she said, "there *is* no good angle."

"We're doing the right thing," he insisted, as much to convince himself as his Executive Officer. He felt the power, the *rightness* of what they were doing. "Hundreds of millions of humans down there . . . in slavery. . . ."

"How many millions will we kill to free the rest?"

"I don't need to hear this now, Carla."

"Sorry. It's . . . been on my mind for a while."

"And mine . . ."

He still remembered the bloody fighting on Aristotle. He'd been a young junior staff officer in the planetary militia, serving aboard the battlecruiser *Alexander*. Aristotle had been anything but a warlike world. One of the wealthiest and most prosperous of the Confederation's Thousand Worlds, it rarely involved itself in galactic politics. The majority of its citizens were Eudaimonians, with a fanatic regard for the greatest pleasure for the greatest number that was as much religion as philosophy.

Twenty years ago, the Confederation had found itself in a brief, savage little bastard of a war, the Kerellian Incursion. A Kerellian raiding fleet had entered the Aristotelian system and hit the world, hard.

To say that the attack had been unexpected was almost criminal understatement. Aristotle lay well off the major space lanes and trade routes, a hundred parsecs from the Danforth Cluster, where most of the fighting was taking place. They used meteor bombers to shatter the cities, spaceports, and military facilities first, then followed the first strikes up with nuclear warheads. Then the landing boats had swooped down from smoke-clotted skies, disgorging Kerellian raiders and human mercenaries intent only on killing, plundering, and rape.

The *Alexander* had been on patrol with the Confederation 453rd Fleet when the attack came. Streicher didn't see his homeworld, didn't see what it had become, until nearly two months after the raid. His parents, his wife, his daughter, all had died in the raid; at least, he *hoped* they'd died. None of their bodies had been found, and it was possible the Kerellians had carried them off.

Carla Ramirez had been on Aristotle when the raiders came, a child of eight. She'd hidden in a blast shelter as the high-velocity projectiles shrieked from the sky, shattering cities . . . then taken refuge in the ruins of a library in the forests outside of New Athens, eluding the patrols and slaver gangs and hunterbots and drunken marauders.

She'd lost her family in the holocaust as well.

Aristotle had had a global population of nearly half a billion. One hundred million—twenty percent—had died in the flaming city-pyres. Another two hundred million—possibly more, though the numbers would never be known with precision—had died in the months following of starvation, disease, radiation sickness, and exposure during the brutal onset of the southern hemisphere's winter. The pall of dust hanging in the sky, swept around the world by the jet streams, promised a winter that would last for decades and might well signal the onset of an ice age.

Tens of thousands of Aristotelians had escaped to other worlds . . . the lucky ones. The *rich* ones. Several million more had taken the only other route off of a shattered and poisoned homeworld, joining the Confederation military, while their surviving friends and families began the generations-long task of rebuilding.

The Bombardment of Aristotle had proved to be *the* challenge to the philosophy of Eudaimonics. How did one find joy in life and productivity when his homeland had been reduced to ice-locked rubble, dying forests, and starving bands of survivors?

Twenty years later, there were a number of Aristotelians in the Confederation Navy who remembered that day. They tended to find one another, to form small and tightly knit cliques, to serve together where possible. They were an elite, of sorts, for they'd experienced first-hand war at its most violent, senseless, and horrific. Relatively few other Confederation military personnel had ever seen war. The Kerellian Incursion had been the only real fighting faced by Confederation forces in the past fifty years, and few veterans of that conflict still served. The Aristotelians had stayed in, however, most of them; the military was now the only home they knew. Other Confederation military personnel tended to look at them a bit strangely, to keep their distance, as though fearful of contracting their fanaticism . . . or their ill fortune. It didn't matter. They thought of themselves as an elite who knew the true meaning of war and its true horror. They retained their Eudaimonic philosophy, but it was a philosophy tempered now by horror, blood, and nightmare.

The greatest pleasure for the greatest number now lay in the death of enemies and in a battle plan well developed, well deployed, well fought.

Their password, the phrase spoken *sotto voce* that allowed them to recognize one another, had been used before in the remote past, and with similar feeling. *Never again.*

"How can we do this?" Carla asked, her voice soft.

He knew that what she meant was how could survivors of Aristotle employ the same tactics that had destroyed their world. "We didn't start this war," he said. "No more than we started it with the Kerellians. We didn't nuke their cities. It wasn't our fault. *It wasn't our fault! . . .*"

With a small, nightmare snap of horror, he realized that his thoughts had wandered into forbidden territory. *Damn it, this isn't supposed to happen!* He'd just taken a euph. He should be feeling the blue singing in his blood right now. He should feel powerful right now with the drug's first upward surge, strong, right, on top of things . . . not wallowing in a black and blasted past.

He'd been dreading this moment, knowing it was coming. Perhaps it would have been better had he offered his resignation, left the service, as several friends back on Primus had suggested.

No. He would beat this thing. His fist clenched at his side.

I'm going to beat it! . . .

Together, he and Carla watched the cities burn at the edge of the Caernan night. He put an arm around her waist, drawing her close. They'd been lovers, off and on, for nearly a year, now, ever since she'd transferred to the 4th.

And after a long time, he heard her whisper, "Never again."

It has been 14 minutes, 27.503 seconds since I deployed the techspiders to begin repairs to my contra-gravity assemblies, an eternity in combat or to an advanced AI battle intelligence capable of awareness at microsecond levels. Throughout that time, I have been monitoring the repairs directly through the electronic eyes and senses of the spiders as they clamber through access ducts and repair conduits to reach and replace the damaged circuitry.

The contra-gravity projectors are General Psychotronics Model 78s, each with a listed lift rating, at full power, of 4000 tons. Six of the twelve damaged systems have been brought to optimal capability by replacing power feeds, bus bars, and melted circuit modules. The remaining six, I have now determined, cannot be repaired in situ, and I require the services of a Bolo maintenance/repair facility to have them replaced.

Six CG projectors with a total lift capacity of 24,000 tons. I have a mass of 32,000 tons, with another thousand tons, approximately, of on-board cargo, remotes, and expendables. Even in Caern's .74 G, I weigh nearly 24,500 tons. I am not going to be able to fly—or even float—my way out of this trap.

Still, there may be other aspects of basic physics I can bring to bear on the problem. I have braided diamonofilament tow cable on board, of course, with a robotic deployment system, but with only 500 meters of cable overall, I would be unable to reach the shore and the nearest suitable anchor point necessary to drag myself free.

I consider the design of my tracks.

I have a total of twelve sets of tracks, twin-mounted in six suspension assemblies, three along each side.

Each set is four meters wide, and set with half-meter flanges to increase ground traction and to grip slippery slopes. They are not enough to provide adequate traction in twenty meters of mud, but they may assist my escape in another way.

I set my drive trains in motion, the tracks turning. At the same time, I engage all operational CG projectors. Immediately, the water above my canted upper deck turns opaque as vast, swirling clouds of silt rise, obscuring all of my external vision pickups. I increase power. On land, on an open plain, my driver wheel rate would translate to a velocity of sixty kilometers per hour. Here, underwater and in the mud, I feel my mass shifting forward a bit, feel my nose coming up, but the only direct measure of the tremendous energy going into my spinning tracks is a sharp rise in suspension temperature. I will need to monitor that carefully to avoid further damaging my drive systems.

I increase turn rate by ten percent. My contra-gravity projectors have succeeded in reducing my apparent mass to approximately 500 tons. I am very nearly there.

If my unsupported weight in Caern's gravity is only a bit more than 24,000 tons, however, my inertial mass is still well over 32,000 tons. Contra-gravity can support most of my weight, but I retain my full mass. Getting that mass moving is going to be a major problem.

I increase my driver speed again, this time by five percent. The temperature is rising quickly throughout my suspension and drive elements. The water surrounding them is an effective coolant, but the silt is so thick the drive efficiency is being seriously impeded.

I change tactics, putting my drive train in reverse. After a moment, I shift forward again, repeating the maneuver a number of times, attempting to rock myself free of the mud's grip. The attempt fails.

There is one possible trick left which I can try, but it is a dangerous one. I run several sets of calculations first, seeking some reassurance that I will not be seriously damaged or even disabled by this maneuver, but find none. With no other viable option that I can see, however, I elect to implement it.

Swinging my forward turret until it is aligned dead ahead, I elevate my forward primary weapon to 45 degrees and fire.

The effect is immediate, and remarkable. Hellbores use magnetic induction to accelerate gram-slivers of cryo-hydrogen to relativistic speeds, along vacuum paths tunneled by a high-energy laser pulse. The acceleration is sufficient to induce fusion within the cryo-H, and the kinetic energy released is in the 2-megaton-per-second range.

The range of the tunneling laser is sharply limited within water, however, and much of the energy is absorbed by the surrounding medium before the pulse reaches the surface. The cryo-H sliver reaches fusion temperatures and pressures just beyond the muzzle of my primary weapon, then begins to heat—violently— the water above and ahead of me.

The result is a titanic blast which creates a region of hard vacuum surrounded by a fast-expanding bubble of superheated steam and water plasma. The shock wave envelops me, as violently devastating as the nuclear fireball I flew through earlier.

A number of other effects occur in rapid sequence. As the vacuum ahead and above me collapses, it draws an enormous volume of water and silt into itself. At the far end of the collapsing bubble, the fierce energies of the disintegrating fusion-plasma sphere break through to the open air, creating a fireball that swiftly boils into the sky. Tremendous energy—heat, mostly—rises with the fast-forming mushroom cloud. The updraft of the cloud adds to the powerful current of steam and super-heated water sweeping across my hull from back to front.

In addition, the shock wave strikes the sea floor beneath my tracks, rebounding violently. The net effect is powerful enough to drag me forward and up, setting me in rapid motion.

My upper deck and primary turrets break the surface and are engulfed at once in the firestorm. For a brief instant, my outer hull temperature registers 970 degrees, a temperature which would break down even duralloy if sustained for more than a few minutes.

I increase the rate of turn on my tracks, literally swimming now as my hull skims through water well above the worst of the silt. My less than perfect streamlining cannot sustain this drift for long, of course, but I can generate lift enough to carry me clear of the worst of the sediment which, in any case, has been scoured from the sea floor and hurled aloft with the Hellbore shot's fireball. It may have taken a great deal of energy to get my inertial mass moving; once moving, I am very hard to stop.

Inevitably, though, friction takes its toll and I begin to sink once more.

Interlude I

Across the ravaged landscape of Caern's habitable belt, the Bolos were coming down. While the 4th Regiment was landing in the district Intelligence called Kanthuras, 3rd Regiment was hitting Vortan, northeast of the Kretier Peninsula. Both 1st Battalion/3rd Bolos grounded safely outside of the enemy command control center and naval base at Othelid. Both 2nd Batt machines landed safely as well, one at Gron, the other at Yedethelfen. One of 3rd Battalion's Bolos had been hit by a ground-to-space nuclear interceptor however, while still forty kilometers up, a near-direct hit in the five-megaton range.

The other 3rd Battalion Bolo managed to jettison itself from its damaged drop pod and make an emergency landing on its contra-grav units in the Ethyreat Sea. Since 3rd Batt's planned target had been a planetary garrison at Vled, the surviving Bolo was going to have its figurative hands full.

In skies lit by light-suffused palls of smoke and the pyres of cities, by auroral glow and the strobe and thunder of high-altitude nuclear detonations, the ponderous, delta-forms of the ALPs drifted down over forests and rugged, broken stretches of black basalt and erosion-scoured badlands, free, for the most part, from enemy attack for the final seconds of their approaches since they were low enough now that the horizon itself offered some shelter.

Slowed by wide-open airbrakes and contra-gravity thrusters, the deltas drifted in one by one, searching for relatively open ground. Landing skids deployed, and the aerial monsters, several with steaming, half-molten scars in wing and nose surfaces, slammed into the ground, rumbling forward for dozens of meters before finally grinding to a creaking, shuddering halt.

Side panels blew off, inner armor unfolded like opening petals of a flower, exposing the blocky, slab-sided black-and-gray combat units locked within. Restraints parted with the high-pitched bangs of release charges and the whistle of highly stressed cables whiplashing through air. Bolo engines engaged, and the titanic machines lumbered off their opened pods, their tracks biting into the soil of the flame-wracked world.

Caern was a rugged planet with a surface pocked by near-circular seas and lakes, the evidence of past meteoric bombardments in the world-moon's stormy youth. Much of the land between the scattered cities was forest, mountain, or badlands, with few habitations outside of the heavily built-up, farm-encircled population centers. The mines and the major industrial centers appeared to be deep underground, where the planet's geothermal energy was easily tapped. A few roads and magtubes connected the cities, but most transport on Caern was by air or sea. The wilderness stretches had provided the invasion's planners with one of their two biggest challenges—the other being the rumored underground factories, depots, and power plants. Only the size, speed, and supreme mobility of the Bolos would make the conquest possible at all.

And it *was* conquest, after all, that the

Confederation wanted to achieve on Caern, and not obliteration. The ostensible purpose of the invasion was the rescue of the human population from slavery, though most critics of the war back on the major worlds of the Confederation pointed out that Caern's rich mineral resources and the high density of its heavy-metal-rich crust were more attractive to the Confederation economic planners than the freedom of a few hundred million humans.

In either case, the planet had to be secured and the Aetryx presence neutralized. The Aetryx were still something of an unknown quantity, especially since it was assumed that most of their numbers and military strength were hidden underground, safe from orbital bombardment. The first step in the conquest of Caern, however, would be to seize the cities and other surface facilities. That would give the Confederation forces freedom of movement on the surface and the luxury of bottling up their opponents underground to be dealt with later.

Each Bolo LZ, then, had been chosen with considerable thought, a choice seeking an ideal balance between open, uninhabited wilderness and a primary objective that, usually, was in or near a city. That ideal was not always possible.

Invictus of the 1st Battalion/4th Regiment, for instance, overshot its LZ and came down almost on top of the southern wall of the planetary defense bastion at Dolendi. Though the bastion had been savaged by half a dozen big-gauge Hellbore blasts from space, knocking out the main radar and lidar facilities and smashing the big particle beam turrets, there was plenty of small-caliber fire coming from the wreckage, as troops poured out of underground bunkers to take up defensive positions in the rubble. Invictus was taking heavy ground fire even before the landing pod touched down. By the time the craft had skidded and gouged its way to a halt, it was the center of an all-out barrage of everything from small arms fire to 100cm plasma guns mounted on light, teleoperated armored vehicles. As the craft doors opened, freeing the Bolo on the load pallet inside, the fire intensified, raking the armored sides and exposed tracks of the combat machine within.

And everywhere else on the inhabited portions of Caern, the defenses were coming fully to life.

Disaster at Caern:
A Study of the Unexpected in Warfare
Galactic Press Productions, Primus, cy 426

Chapter Six

I sink swiftly but am able to slow my descent rate somewhat by manipulating the current set up by my fast-spinning tracks and by careful play of my CG projectors. When I touch bottom once again, I note with relief that the silt here is less than three meters deep, inconsequential. Consulting my terrain maps of the AO, I conclude that the sediment I landed in first was a portion of the subsea alluvial fan formed by the egress of the Duret River into the Storm Sea, the result of geological ages of sediment carried down from the Kanthurian Mountains and the High Desert Plateau beyond.

I pause for 5.24 seconds while I run a thorough complete series of diagnostics and damage control checks and wait for the seething, churning seawater to cool my hull to temperatures less threatening to its molecular integrity.

I note that my primary ground-to-orbit communications suite has suffered major damage. External antennae have been swept away and several circuit modules overloaded and melted. I deploy techspiders to initiate repairs. There is other damage to secondary systems, all minor.

Then, with all primary operational systems showing

93

*green, I resume my approach-vector heading toward
the coast and begin to advance, crawling across the
bottom of the sea at fifty kilometers per hour. Within
moments, the bottom shoals, and soon my upper works
are above the water. Artillery fire and missiles seek
me out from five directions, but it is all low-caliber,
no threat to a hull that has twice withstood the fury
of close-proximity nuclear detonation. My point-defense
lasers, operating on automatic, knock out the larger
shells and warheads while they are still kilometers distant. The others strike my battlescreens and explode
without effect, further churning the roiling waters
about me.*

*Behind and above me, the top of the mushroom
cloud from the Hellbore blast that freed me rises high
enough—an estimated 6,000 meters—to catch in gold
and purple glory the predawn light of a sun still below
the horizon as seen from the surface.*

*Ahead, my optical and infrared sensors detect the
flames of a burning city.*

Streicher and Ramirez were lost deep in the kiss
when the alarm sounded in his ear. He pulled back
from the embrace, touched the clip attached to his
right ear, and muttered a heartfelt curse.

She read his expression and the gesture, shrugged,
and smiled. "We knew it couldn't last," she said. "To
be continued?"

"Absolutely," he growled. "With the Greatest Pleasure."

"The Greatest Pleasure," she replied formally, but
still smiling. "I'm looking forward to it."

They'd found a bit of privacy for themselves in a
lounge area off the main simview chamber, on a couch
looking out on the stars and *not* down into the hell-
blasted burning of an inhabited world. He pressed

down on the ear clip, activating its microtransceiver. "What?"

"You'd better come back in, sir," Major Lawrence Filby's voice said. "Something's happening. I think we've reacquired Victor."

"On my way."

Something in Filby's tone galvanized Streicher, and he hurried back into the simview chamber still adjusting various parts of his uniform. The techs waiting for him there studiously ignored his open tunic and disarrayed spray of hair. He settled back into his place on the ring couch. Major Ramirez entered and took her seat as the techs adjusted his virtual-feed headgear.

"We picked up a two-megaton Hellbore burst ten klicks off Ghendai," Filby's voice said, "just about at the spot where Victor went down." Second Batt's CO tended to be a control addict, precise, fussy, and a bit dogmatic. He'd never seen combat and was pretty much a career desk pilot from what Streicher could tell about the man, and he compensated with an anal attention to detail that might pass on a dark night for career dedication. Streicher normally found it easy to ignore the man as a gnome-shadow of the Confederation's mil-bureaucracy, but the crisp urgency in Filby's voice suggested that there was something here beyond properly filed maintenance reports and end-of-quarter fitness evaluations.

"Got it," Streicher said as the light flared in his eyes, the command craft's sim compartment vanished, and he floated once again over the 4th's AO, his visual input relayed from flying robotic eyes high above the battlefield. Zooming in, he could see the IR hotspot on the sea west of Ghendai, superimposed on the visual of a tangle of mushroom clouds. Three small, kiloton-range nukes had been disrupted and subsumed into the larger umbrella-capped steam-pillar of a Hellbore blast.

Zooming in closer still, Streicher could see the rectangular black slab of a Bolo, its upper deck barely awash, moving into the harbor at Ghendai. The churning wake streaming out behind it in a broad V suggested that it was moving at a considerable speed.

"Looks like Victor's back in the game," he said.

"I *knew* we couldn't count him out!" Kelly Tyler said, back online, her voice jubilant. "He survived the attack and just kept on going!"

"Do you have a data feed from him yet?" Streicher asked. "Has he suffered any damage?"

"No data yet, Colonel," Tyler replied. "We're trying to reestablish contact. There may be a comm fault."

"With all those nukes popping off, I'm not surprised. Keep on it."

"Yes, *sir!*"

"Give me a projection. Where is he coming ashore?"

Lines of light drew themselves across Streicher's virtual view of the terrain below. "On his current heading," Kelly said, "just north of Ghendai. But he'll be taking a lot of fire."

"Mark XXXIIIs can take it," Streicher said quietly. "And they can dish it out, too."

Gunfire crashes as I rise from the sea, water streaming from my flanks. I use point-defense laser fire to burn down three 200mm artillery rounds inbound, disintegrating them harmlessly at a range of 7.2 kilometers. Lighter rounds snap and sparkle against my battlescreens. A particle beam flares from the north, scattering from my screens in coruscating flashes of light and heat. I backtrack the beam, target an armored vehicle of unfamiliar design hull down behind a rocky cliff face, and return fire with a 20cm Hellbore infinite repeater. The cliff shatters and the vehicle, reduced to flaming wreckage, tumbles down the slope in a crumpled heap. As I pass, the wreck explodes, and I hear the sharp zing and hiss of shrapnel impacting my battlescreen.

The beach is narrow and rocky, backed by a sharply eroded cliff five meters high. Advancing, I grind across the beach, rocks popping and shattering beneath my tracks, and I claw down the cliff in a crashing avalanche of mud and stone.

Ahead, I see the ruins of Ghendai, a sprawling city edging the shore of a broad, open harbor. The orbital bombardment has flattened most of the taller buildings and habitation domes, reducing the place to rubble, the twisted skeletons of shattered towers, and steaming craters. The background radiation count stands at 157 rads.

Shifting my primary vision to infrared, I scan my surroundings for signs of life, but there are too many hot spots to allow me to easily or reliably pick out the body heat of enemy troops or the heat from vehicle engines. I switch back to optical/low-light mode and continue my advance, grinding over the glittering but shock wave–twisted span of an antenna farm and snapping the gently curved, elevated arc of a monorail line stretched across my path.

I pick up an incoming salvo on radar, ten targets coming over the horizon at a bearing of 085, range 132 kilometers. Mass and thrust characteristics allow me to tentatively identify them as intermediate-range ballistic missiles under remote teleoperation. Whether the warheads are nuclear, high explosive, or something more exotic I cannot determine; high background radiation counts prevent me from accurately determining whether the warheads carry radiation sources.

It is a simple matter, however, to lock on, track, and fire with my 20cm Hellbores, slamming fusing slivers of hydrogen into each incoming missile. The night-shrouded horizon to the east lights up in a popping chain of strobing, arc-brilliant flashes. One warhead detonates, illuminating the landscape with a false dawn that fades to blood and silver as the fireball rises. One of the IRBMs, at least, was carrying a nuke. I estimate the yield at 5 kilotons.

The enemy salvo eliminated, I return counterbattery fire with a salvo of my own—40cm mortar rounds shrieking off into the night. It is difficult to pinpoint the launch site, which was screened from me by a range of mountains, and since the missiles were under teleoperational control, determining their point of origin is not simply a matter of backtracking their trajectories. I blanket the valley beyond the mountains, however, with nuclear mortar rounds of 10-kiloton yield. It will make them keep their heads down, as the human slang phrase has it, and may eliminate any surface antennae or tracking/control sites serving as part of their fire control network.

Twelve seconds have passed since I emerged from the sea, and I have entered the outskirts of the ruined city. At close range, now, I become aware of a number of humans sheltering within the rubble and fallen structures. None appear to present direct threats to me. I detect no weapons, no explosives, no indication of tactical maneuver.

Indeed, it occurs to me that these humans represent the proximate reason for our insertion here. According to my briefing downloads, the humans on Caern are held as slaves by the alien Aetryx, and our mission is to liberate them.

Unfortunately, their cities have been liberated in a manner inconsistent with their continued structural integrity.

A form stumbles from the shadows beneath a partially fallen wall, and I track it with an antipersonnel battery—Number 32—locking on at a range of forty meters. Normally, my AP batteries are left on automatic, but the nature of our mission here has caused all of my automatic AP close-defense systems to be overridden by moral inhibition subroutines designed to prevent a general massacre of civilian personnel in the confusion of the invasion—a good idea in light of the fact that these are the people we are here to save.

The form shambles closer, and I can see that it is a male human, his left arm mangled, his face hideously burned. The background radiation count stands close to 300 rads now; the man has already accumulated a more-than-lethal dose. He must have been caught within the line-of-sight of a nuclear airburst, at a range short enough to cause those burns. Or possibly the burns are from a near Hellbore strike, and he simply had the bad luck of wandering into a portion of the ruins irradiated by a nuke.

"Ghe'el ni!" he cries out. He doubles over, vomits, then cries again, "Ghe'el ni, poless!" My Caern translation routines transform the words, heavily accented by the Kanthurian dialect, to their Galactic equivalent.

"Kill me! Please!"

I consider the request for a full .02 second. With the radiation he has absorbed, the man has but hours to live. I am under no obligation to accede to his request. Besides, he is a civilian. I have control over the moral inhibitor subroutines controlling my AP batteries, but other inhibitors govern aspects of my programming to avoid collateral damage to the civilian population, where possible and when consistent with overall mission directives.

And yet the man is in great pain, and no medical facility accessible within a reasonable amount of time could save his life. I override my primary moral inhibitions and switch off the governor subroutine responsible for suppressing the automatic triggers for Antipersonnel Battery 32. The radar-guided mount pivots sharply and releases a high-kinetic burst of AP needles, and the human is shredded in a vivid splash of scarlet. I switch on the governor subroutine once more and continue my passage through the ruined city.

It appears that the shattered population center has not been defended, and my only targets are helpless, dying civilians.

I yearn to find the Enemy and come to grips with him.

Elken was feeling better about his new body. For a number of minutes now—strange how minutes now passed for him like hours—he'd been receiving downloads, programs and data files and a kind of behavioral matrix that helped him adapt to this new, alien form. Control, he found, was a matter of practice . . . but he could practice in his mind, picturing a maneuver or a movement, then experiencing what it felt like and how much force to apply without actually carrying it out, and possibly bringing down a wall or smashing into the armored flank of one of his fellows in the process.

The other Bolo-equipped warriors were becoming practiced as well. They exchanged rapid-fire barrages of data, establishing secure communications links.

Then the voice of the god was speaking in Elken's thoughts, addressing them all.

The Sky Demons are destroying everything on the surface, leveling our cities in fire, cutting down our people in the streets. <great sadness> *You, our children, must stop them before there is nothing left with which to rebuild.*

An image formed in Elken's mind—a vast, lumbering shape emerging from the sea near Ghendai. Though he would not have recognized the machine before, something within him now identified it as a Bolo Mark XXXIII, part of the Confederation Strike Force assault upon Caern. He watched, his thoughts running cold, as it destroyed a Krakess mounted gun, then rumbled slowly into the outskirts of the ruined city of Ghendai. There was no sound on the data feed . . . but he saw the human stumble from the wreckage, saw the man cut down an instant later by a cloud of high-velocity AP flechettes.

They murder civilians, your friends, families, neighbors, without provocation or reason. <sadness> *There can be no negotiation with such monsters.*

"Let us at them!" NGK 2225344 yelled, and the others took up the battle cry. "Kill them! Kill them all!"

It is time, my children. Forward, to face the enemy! Salvation for Caern and your gods!

Yelling with the rest, Elken rumbled forward, thundering onto a ramp leading up.

I swing clear of the city, moving north. A massively armored facility five kilometers beyond the city's edge is listed by Intelligence reports as the Ghendai Command-Control Center. A fortress, it is part of the extensive Caern planetary defense system, with logistics and maintenance depots. The facility has a high target priority rating because of the probable existence of two underground Bolo storage depots. The base has been heavily damaged both by orbital bombardment and by the Caernans' own nuclear defense system. Air bursts have reduced most of the buildings to rubble, though the main domes still stand, tributes to the engineering prowess of those who designed them.

I decide that the large and labyrinthine complex can best be searched if I deploy my remotes. Cargo hatches slide open on my rear quarter and on my top deck, between my second and third primary turrets. From the upper deck hatch I launch four RFS-7 Wyvern remote fliers. From the lower cargo deck, eight HK-50 Dragon hovertanks emerge, turbines spooling with shrill whines as their paired CG generators throw up clouds of dust.

Wyverns are lightly armed and armored, relying on speed and maneuverability to serve as far-ranging eyes for a Bolo combat unit. The Dragon tanks, however, are a new innovation, fifty-ton floaters capable of 200 kph, each bearing a single dome turret mounting a 60cm Hellbore. They are designed to extend a Bolo's combat range, provide armed scouting capability, and carry enough firepower to seriously degrade any approaching threat before it can get within range.

The remotes are just that—teleoperated remotes, electronic puppets without self-aware AI capabilities. In essence, they are extensions of my own awareness. Data feeds from each remote flow through my awareness. In a sense, I am each of the remotes, viewing the predawn landscape from thirteen different points of view, including my own.

Within five seconds, Wyvern 3 has picked up something of interest . . . a massive duralloy slab sliding back within the heart of the shattered military base, exposing a dark tunnel and a broad, descending ramp. Laser and particle beam fire snaps at the flier from point defense turrets scattered about the opening, but I twist away, sending the nimble little craft zigzagging through the ruins.

Before my retreat, however, I was able to glimpse something large and dark moving up out of the tunnel.

My preliminary assessment gives an 83.5 percent chance that the emerging vehicle is a Bolo Mark XXXII.

❖   ❖   ❖

Elken emerged from the tunnel and was immediately assaulted by a sharp increase in sensory input—the crackle and glow and heat of scattered fires, the cool night air tingling with the high-energy cascade of radioactive particles, the snap and pop of rubble crushed beneath his massive treads. Data feeds from the gods' command control pinpointed the high-flying flash of a small, enemy scout flier, but it ducked out of sight behind a broken wall before he could bring any of his weapons to bear.

An enemy war machine, a Bolo Mark XXXIII, was approaching from that direction, bearing 198, range 6 kilometers.

Elken knew that the enemy Bolo possessed a 3 to 1 advantage over him in primary armament alone— three 200cm Hellbore turrets to his single 200cm mount. Firepower was not the sole factor in a contest of this nature, however. His tactical downloads suggested several means by which he could get in the first shot against the enemy, and five megatons/second of firepower could do serious injury even to a Mark XXXIII's massive armor.

He was also not alone. Three more Caernan Bolo Mark XXXIIs emerged from the tunnel at his back, dispersing swiftly through the ruins of the command center complex: VBR 9383733, PLT 94635469, and SND 9008988.

"Veber, Sendee!" he snapped. "Cut east, then south. Try to hit the enemy Bolo from the flank! Palet, you're with me!"

It was odd how command simply came to him, part of the downloads and software tuning he'd been receiving during the past few moments. None of them had ever been in combat before, but the gods were able to give them tactical assistance and had provided the guidance necessary for the four of them to work closely together as a team. He knew without having to think about it that the four of them possessed a 1.3 to 1 primary firepower advantage over the enemy, if they were able to work together as a closely knit unit.

That "if" was worrying him now, though. Palet, especially, was raw with inexperience and youth, eagerness untempered by experience or caution. That was why he wanted the youngster with him, so he could watch him. Keep him in his place. "We can take it!" Palet exclaimed. "Let's move!"

He raced ahead, and Elken increased speed to keep pace.

"Bolos!" Kelly Tyler exclaimed. "Enemy Bolos, coming out of that tunnel!"

"We knew it was a possibility," Streicher said.

"But the Aetryx weren't supposed to know how to override our security systems and cut-outs! They shouldn't even be able to power them up!"

"Maybe they didn't download the same intelligence briefings we did," Major Ramirez said with a snort. "Hell, any security code can be broken or gotten around, given time and determination. And the Trixies have had both."

"They're trying to flank Victor," Tyler said. "Damn, we still don't have communications with him yet."

"He sees the situation," Streicher replied. "He can handle it himself." He pulled back his POV. The other Bolos of the regiment appeared to be in the clear at the moment, battling prepared gun positions and bunkers, but nothing as tough as enemy Bolos. "Are there air assets in the area?"

"A flight of Warlocks at two-three-zero," Ramirez replied. "Range five-zero kilometers."

WR-5 Warlocks. Teleoperated ground-attack aircraft inserted with the first wave, armed with plasma-bolt infinite repeaters and Blackray missiles, for close ground support.

"Vector them in."

"They're on the way. ETA three minutes."

Streicher zoomed in again, fastening his full attention on Victor.

It was difficult to see through all of the smoke. . . .

Smoke explodes around me as the Enemy looses a heavy barrage of high explosives and depleted-uranium penetrators. My battlescreens handle the attack easily, but I begin running an elaborate ground track pattern to confuse enemy gunners and prevent them from employing a mass point-assault strategy to overwhelm my defenses.

At the same time, I fire a Battleview missile which explodes high above the combat area, releasing thousands of BIST drones. Each drone, less than a centimeter across, drifts through the battle area, picking up broadband sensory data, including visual, infrared, sonic, and mass-gravitometric readings and feeding them back to me via ground wave or pulsed and scrambled UHF. The range of the Battlefield Intelligence Surveillance and Transmission system is limited to a few kilometers, but the data gives me a comprehensive picture of the battlefield and the units moving across it.

Through incoming BIST data, I determine that the Enemy has deployed four Mark XXXII Bolos. Two are moving on my left, to the west, while two more approach at high speed from straight ahead. Clearly they are attempting to envelop me. Their strategy indicates a mediocre understanding at best of high-speed ground tactics and maneuver.

I designate the northern group as Alpha One and Two, the western pair as Bravo One and Two. Opening up my upper deck weapons bay, I commence fire with a rapid-fire barrage from my four 240cm howitzers, targeting the Mark XXXIIs to the west. My heavy howitzers are Casewell M-3030 high-velocity autoloaders, with a rate of fire of 2 rounds per second. I have little hope of penetrating their point defense systems and battlescreens, but this may give me data regarding their level of inexperience.

Meanwhile, I accelerate toward the north, in order to effect a meeting with the two Bolos coming at me from that direction head on.

Eighteen point five seconds had elapsed since Elken emerged from the tunnel. Both Veber and Sendee were reporting that they were under heavy incoming fire from the target—240cm howitzer rounds, each self-guiding projectile carrying over half a ton of Detonic high explosives. Their point defenses, Sendee reported, were stopping most of the incoming rounds, and those that made it through were detonating harmlessly on the two Bolos' battlescreens, but the steady and devastating barrage was also churning the ground into a near-impassable sea of craters and thick powder, reducing visibility to zero and forward speed to a crawl.

"Keep moving," he told her. "Palet and I are almost in position."

He'd hoped that their flanking maneuver would go unnoticed by the enemy, but his tactical downloads had already informed him that it was nearly impossible to sneak up on a Bolo. The enemy machine would certainly be getting a steady stream of data from orbit and from the constellation of remote fliers it had released moments ago.

Elken had also noted the explosion of a missile high over the battlefield, and the subsequent descent of large numbers of devices smaller than a human thumb, each a set of sensory devices and a transmitter wrapped around a microminiaturized contra-gravity coil. Those were almost certainly battlefield surveillance devices of some sort. He tried to kill several with blasts from his infinite repeaters, but they seemed to waft aside at the first touch of the magnetic induction current that channeled each Hellbore bolt and were individually too small to target or track with point defense weaponry.

He had to assume, then, that the enemy was fully aware of every move he and his fellows made. He had no choice but to proceed with a direct frontal assault.

I note that Bolos Bravo One and Two have slowed their advance and may be on the point of bogging down. Their point defense systems are successfully intercepting 84.6 percent of the howitzer rounds descending on their position. This indicates accurate targeting and tracking on their part but could suggest a sluggishness in their physical reaction time. They are responding to incoming threats fractionally more slowly than should be the case for well-tuned and fully operational Mark XXXII Bolo combat units.

Eight point seven seconds after I began my barrage, my howitzer barrels are becoming superheated and I cease high-caliber indirect fire, switching instead to my 40cm mortars.

Where the howitzer rounds possessed tiny CG thrusters and laser tracking, giving them minor flight-control and self-targeting accuracy, my ten ballistic-launch mortar tubes fire rounds that are basically dumb iron bombs with no guidance control at all.

Still, by precisely measuring the components of the binary liquid-fuel propellant charge inserted into each tube prior to firing, I can control both firing trajectory and impact point to within a 1.7-meter target radius, even while I myself am moving at a high rate of speed. I target a broad area immediately ahead of targets Bravo One and Two, continuing to churn up the ground with a rain of high explosives, the repeated detonations sending up a wall of impenetrable dust and flying debris. I note, too, that subsurface water pipes have ruptured, turning much of the ground into a sea of soft mud nearly as treacherous as the silt layers that trapped me momentarily offshore. The mud is not enough to stop a Bolo, but it will slow these two by vital fractions of a second.

Then I reverse direction and accelerate to full speed.

Elken established full-sensory communications with all three of the other Bolos in his command. The sensation was an odd one, as though he were literally in four places at once, and it took him a second or two to adjust to the bombardment of oddly displaced and overlapping points of view.

Data feeds from the gods' target tracking network showed the enemy Bolo suddenly reverse course, racing south, then west, circling around and behind Sendee and Veber. He shouted warning . . . but his two friends had already seen the same data and were swinging about to meet this sudden thrust. Their reaction times were slowed, however, by the mud, nearly three meters deep in places, that lapped around their hulls and track assemblies like a black, churning sea.

Both Sendee's and Veber's vision were nearly completely obscured by the cloud of dust and airborne debris still falling over their positions. For a moment, Elken could no longer see the enemy Bolo, which had itself vanished into a cloud bank of its own making. Radar was useless among the tangled ruins . . . as was lidar in the dust and smoke-laden air. He felt Sendee lurching up and over a crater rim, sensed the dust cloud thinning . . .

And then saw the enemy Bolo looming out of the

night, a vast, black, slanted cliff of two-meter-thick duralloy and ceramplast laminate moving with impossible grace and speed for an object so massive. A ball turret mounted high up on its in-curved flank sparked with an intolerable brilliance, and then the dust cloud around Sendee ignited with a heat as radiant as the surface of a star.

She screamed, and Elken's own scream mingled with hers. . . .

Chapter Seven

Anything will burn, given a high enough tempera-ture and maximum surface exposure and dispersion. The dust swirling in the air above and around Bravo One and Two, according to spectroscopic analysis, is composed primarily of one- to ten-micron-sized flecks of titanium steel alloy, ferrocrete, concrete, depleted uranium, and ceramplast composites, distributed as an aerosol cloud offering all of the prime requisites for a fuel-air explosive mixture. Though not normally flam-mable, the touch of fusion fire from a 20cm Hellbore infinite repeater is sufficient to ignite the cloud at temperatures in excess of 5,000 degrees Celsius.

The extreme radiant heat overloads Bravo One's battle-screens within .08 second, causing operational col-lapse, and vaporizes some tons of external hull armor, the blast wave peeling it back first in broad, molten strips before it flashes to metallic steam and evaporates.

The explosion—the equivalent, I judge, of a tacti-cal nuclear device with a yield of approximately 50 kilotons—is not sufficient to destroy a Bolo Mark XXXII, but the blast wave and fireball disorient the targets and sharply degrade their performance. I ride out the initial shock wave, which washes across my hull like a white-hot wall of flame riding hurricane winds, then continue my advance, bringing my Number One primary Hellbore to bear.

I slam a round into Bravo One, catching it high on the right hull, just below the turret. With battlescreens down and the armor already thinned, the fusion pulse loosed at point-blank range burns through duralloy and armor laminates, spearing through the vehicle from one side to the other. Internal explosions savage the Mark XXXII, and meter-thick armor burns fiercely with a white-hot glare. The enemy machine's turret has jammed; I note that the Bolo is trying to bring its primary weapon to bear by counter-rotating its tracks, but I hit it squarely on the turret with a shot from Number Two primary.

The second round shreds the right side of the turret, eliciting a fresh round of internal explosions. At the same instant, I track Bravo Two with my Number Three primary and put a five-megaton pulse into its right-front track assembly, just as it rises, nose-high from a mud-filled shell crater. The bolt chewed through cleated track and drive bogie, ripping into the machine's suspension as it skewed right, then slid back into the shell hole.

I follow up with a barrage from my secondaries, riddling both crippled Bolos with a fusillade of 20cm Hellbore bolts. Chunks of white-hot metal spin wildly through the air, as duralloy is set ablaze by the intense, star-core heat of projectiles of fusion fire. In another two seconds, my Number One primary Hellbore is recharged and ready for the next shot. I track on Bravo One, but the vehicle is a flaming wreck, obviously dead. . . .

"Sendee! . . ."

Elken had felt the deaths of both Veber and Sendee. Veber had been a friend, someone he'd not seen in some years, but Sendee . . .

Strange. He couldn't remember any specific link with her from when they were both flesh and blood, but it hurt beyond words in that instant when telemetry relayed the shock and searing blaze of heat cutting through her body . . . and then she was gone, the signal chopped off as though by a knife.

SND 9008988, his beloved Sendee, was dead. . . .

Beloved? Had he truly loved her? How could he have forgotten something like that? . . .

Even as he grappled with that sudden, wild stab of grief, the pain seemed to recede on its own. He had other things to worry about . . . including the sharp realization that he, by splitting his forces, had played into the enemy's hand. Four Mark XXXIIs outmatched a lone Mark XXXIII only if they were working together in close concert. The enemy had managed to maneuver clear of Elken and Palet and to engage Veber and Sendee alone.

"We should withdraw, Palet," he said . . . but the words were more musing than order. He paused, transmitting an update of the situation to the gods. He didn't want to withdraw. He felt responsibility for Sendee's death. All he could think of was to hurl himself at the enemy and burn him down, or die trying.

At the same time, he felt terror. He didn't want to die, but he felt as though his death was inexorably closing in on him, with no possibility of escape.

"We have him!" Palet replied with a shrill cry, vaulting a low and rubble-cluttered ridge just ahead.

Elken followed, cresting the ridge more slowly, sluing over the top just in time to see four fifty-ton grav-floating armored vehicles careen in from the west at high speed. Hellbore fire snapped and exploded, smashing down Palet's battle-screens, shredding armor, punching holes through slab sides with appalling ease.

Elken reversed his right track, pivoting sharply right to put his heaviest armor facing this new threat . . . Then the Mark XXXIII hurtled in, turrets blazing. . . .

The enemy Bolos show a definite sluggishness in response time and seem unable to coordinate their maneuvers. The second pair appears over a low ridge just as I give the attack order to a team of four Dragons. Accelerating to my full road speed of over one hundred kilometers per hour, I close the range swiftly, loosing bolts from my Number One and Number Three primaries, holding Number Two in reserve.

Alpha Two, already damaged by the Dragon pack, explodes in a vivid splash of yellow and orange flame.

The Dragons peel off from the burning wreckage of Alpha Two, vectoring in now at my command to close with Alpha One from the rear. The enemy Bolo hesitates—a long and painful hesitation that seals its fate. By the time it decides that I am the more dangerous target and brings its Hellbore to bear, its weapon traversing and elevating in a blur, my Number Three turret fires, the recoil rocking me back on my tracks as I twist to the left, seeking to make myself a more difficult target.

Alpha One fires, but the Hellbore bolt, bright and hot as a tiny sun, skims above my aft deck with meters to spare just as my shot strikes the Mark XXXII squarely on its frontal glacis.

Battlescreens flash and fail, overloaded; enough energy from my shot spills through to gouge a meter-deep crater in solid block armor. Smoke boils from the wound as flames lick within the enemy machine's heart. I follow up with a shot from Primary Two, just as the Dragons open up from the rear. . . .

This time, Elken felt the blasts of point-blank Hellbore rounds personally, not as relayed data. As a

Bolo, he was not wired to experience pain, but his human brain accepted the searing heat of the incoming rounds as a dazzling, twisting impact, thrust, and pain that left him reeling.

He could feel control of his drive train failing, could feel the dull burn of flame inside his forward hull. Elken was dying. He knew it. *Felt* it.

Systems failed . . . hydraulics lost pressure . . . power readings dropped. His main weapon was out of action . . . fire control down . . . battlescreens down . . . power core overloading and threatening to go into auto-shutdown.

He overrode that last, seeking an answer, seeking a way out . . . and then the enemy Bolo's second shot filled his forward viewing arc with sunfire. There was a terrific jolt . . . and blackness . . .

He felt himself screaming as he tumbled into Night. . . .

My second shot slams into the crater melted by the first, and Alpha One explodes, the detonation sending a shudder through the earth that I feel beneath my tracks and scattering shrapnel across half a kilometer of the battlefield. Thirteen point eight seconds have passed since the first of the four Mark XXXIIs emerged above ground and battle was engaged, an unusually long time for most actions, especially one pitting Bolo against Bolo.

I close with the wreckage of Alpha One. While the glacis has been blown away and much of the forward third has been reduced to twisted and skeletal ruin, still blazing fiercely, the command center appears mostly intact. I deploy a pair of spiders from a ventral hatch, directing them to pick their way through the debris and attempt to enter the sealed brain center housing.

This is the armor-shrouded module which contains the primary AI center for the Mark XXXII. Using lasers to slice through ceramplast and titanium steel, the spiders access the circuitry packed within the sleek, gray pod. Feeder conduits snaked from spider bellies, touching contacts, probing the labyrinthine complexities of dense-packed molecular circuitry.

For just an instant, I sense . . . a personality. It is not, however, as I expected, a Bolo personality, which I would have instantly recognized. This is something different . . . alien, and yet tantalizingly familiar, almost . . . human.

And then the last trickle of current through the circuit connections fades, and I sense the personality dissolving. There is nothing I can do to call it back.

I ponder the implications for a full .05 second. Was it a human personality I sensed in the dying Bolo psychotronics pod? Theory has long predicted that it might be possible to electronically copy a human mind, its memories, the very patterns of its consciousness, and download them into appropriate hardware. The ethics of such an operation were long debated, as were the philosophical implications: was a downloaded human personality still human, despite the shape its new body took?

With the advent of true AI, the question became in some ways academic. It was possible to construct machines, such as Bolos, with minds at least the equivalent of the humans who designed them. They were not human, however, and the type of life they experienced was in no way related to that of flesh and blood humans. Since a copy of a mind was not the original, there seemed to be no point in employing the process—even if it could be achieved—as a means of reaching the ancient Holy Grail of human immortality.

There is much that might be learned from this wreckage, but the middle of a battle is no place to pursue pure research. I recall the spiders, after placing in the wreckage a recovery beacon. When the Second Wave lands, bringing with it human engineers and salvage experts, they can dissect the wreckage of all four Mark XXXIIs in an attempt to determine just how Aetryx technology has altered the standard design and mentation of these Bolos.

I sense other Caernan military forces approaching from the east and the north, though I do not detect the characteristic sonic or energy signatures of Bolos. These appear to be heavy grav tanks—"heavy" in this case meaning vehicles in the 100- to 200-ton range, and not anything of Bolo caliber. I deploy my Dragons to skirmish with them, in order to determine their capabilities.

I begin moving toward that part of the defense compound where the enemy Bolos emerged from underground. Particle beam and laser fire from heavily armored turrets stabs at me from a dozen different towers and gun emplacements, and I return fire with infinite repeaters. A brief, savage lightning storm flares above the hectares of ferrocrete and duralloy slab that is the base compound. I compute from the display so far that the Enemy does not possess sufficient weaponry concentrated in this area to pose a significant threat to my operations.

The slab that slid aside to release the enemy Bolos has closed over the tunnel again, but I locate the entrance—a target, perhaps, for human troops when they arrive. For the past 425.3 seconds, I have been sampling the radio traffic in the air around me, seeking a means of entering the Enemy's cyberdomain, but so far the encryption has kept me locked out.

I am acquiring data, however, and may be able to

force an entry within the next several hundred seconds. If so, I might be able to find the electronic combination for the tunnel access. I feel sure that entering the Caernan underworld and confronting the Enemy in his yet untouched chthonic strongholds will be necessary in order to secure absolute control over the surface.

Aircraft are approaching from the west—a flight of four WR-5 Warlocks deployed to my AO by Space Strike Command. They are too late to assist in dealing with the enemy Bolos, but I redirect them toward the new enemy mobile targets and continue dueling with the compound gun emplacements. These will need to be reduced one at a time if this base is to approached by Confederation ground forces and landing craft.

The operation appears to be going quite smoothly so far. I must guard against overconfidence, of course, but it seems likely that key AOs scattered about the planet's surface will be secure within the next ten hours, allowing the next phase of the invasion to begin a full eight hours ahead of schedule.

I continue my duel with the base defenses.

He awoke, stretching . . . and then the fear hit him in deep, shuddering waves, like the icy surf at Gods' Beach. The last thing he remembered . . . no . . . what *was* the last thing he remembered? Memory eluded him, like fragments of a dream.

He opened his eyes, then wondered why he couldn't see. He reached out with a trembling, sweat-slicked hand, then realized he couldn't feel anything, that the tremors, the sweat, the cold were all imagined, anchors for the mind adrift within a vast and lightless void.

Concentrating, he summoned memories from deep, deep within. He'd been in a battle of some sort. Yes . . . he'd been . . . he'd been a Bolo combat unit, his brain housed in a mobile armored vehicle the size of a fair-sized building. Before that . . . the memories were still dim, still fragmentary, but there was something about going in for elective surgery . . . a chance at immortality. . . .

What had gone wrong? . . .

Nothing is wrong, a voice, deep and quiet, spoke within the terror haunted depths of his thoughts. *All is as it should be.* <calm reassurance>

"I can't see," he said, shouting into darkness. "I'm blind!"

You are not blind. Your optical processors are not yet online. <calm reassurance>

The voice of his god! He was not alone after all.

And yet, there was a haunting, fear-rattled undercurrent to the thought, a sense of déjà vu. He was certain he'd had this conversation, this *experience* before.

The memories continued to surface, growing stronger, clearer, more focused. He had been a Bolo, deployed against an invading, enemy Bolo far larger and more powerful than himself. It had been part of an agreement. If he fought the invaders in this new body, helped save Caern from the beings the gods called Sky Demons, he would get the new and immortal body he'd originally longed for.

He'd gone out . . . with three of his fellows. He remembered the battle clearly, remembered the sharp, psychic and emotional pain when Sendee had been killed. He remembered being terribly afraid that he was about to die, as though he'd been trapped in a box, unable to retreat, unable to advance, and Death himself closing in.

"But I wasn't killed." The last thing he remembered was . . . what? He tried to trace the memories, which trembled on the verge of disintegration, like a dream.

He'd felt Sendee die. He'd paused to send the update on the situation to the gods. He'd been about to follow Palet over the ridge. . . .

But he did not remember actually crossing the ridge. His last conscious memory was of sending in the situation update.

You were badly damaged. <compassion> *We were able to retrieve your mind/thought patterns and transfer them to another machine body. You do not remember the period when you were unconscious.*

"I . . . see. . . ." He was puzzled. There'd been no *immediate* threat during those last few seconds of consciousness, no incoming ordnance, no enemy Hellbore fire. Whatever had hit him must have caught him by complete and overwhelming surprise. "So you're sending me out again?"

We must. <sorrowful compassion> *The Sky Demon forces have gained footholds on the surface of our world. We must counterattack before they are able to land reinforcements.*

"I understand." He was reviewing the memories that were jumbled in upon his consciousness, like unwelcome intruders. It was a struggle just to make sense of them.

"I made a serious mistake," he said after a moment. "A *tactical* mistake. I calculated that four Mark XXXIIs were enough to ensure the destruction of one Mark XXXIII. But I divided my forces, sending them against the enemy two and two. He outmaneuvered us and destroyed us in detail, one against two, and then one against two again. He destroyed three . . . no, I guess all four of us. I don't think we inflicted any damage on him at all."

It is vitally important that you learn from your mistakes. <pleased and proud> *Do you understand what it was that went wrong?*

"Yes. The problem will be bringing at least four Bolos against a single enemy Bolo all at once, and coordinating our attacks." As he searched, relevant memories, the results of tutorial downloads, arose in his mind. "Perhaps by using TSDS."

He knew the definition of the system resident in his Bolo combat software labeled "Total Systems Data-Sharing," but he wasn't entirely sure how to apply it in practice. He knew—"remembered" seemed the wrong word to use about information that had been fed to him through a data-jacked fiber-optic cable— that TSDS had first been introduced centuries ago, with the Bolo Mark XXI, and that it allowed each unit of a Bolo force to function as a single element of a multiunit awareness. He'd approached that state conceptually during the battle as he'd coordinated with Palet and Sendee and Veber, as they'd discussed plans and shared overlaid tactical views and even felt one another's sensory input, but TSDS would allow the personalities of the separate Bolos to so merge and integrate that for all intents and purposes, they were a single conscious entity.

The thought was a little scary, demanding, as it did, that the members of such a collective mentality surrender so much of their own will, identity, and freedom.

You will do well. <assurance and approval> *We want you to lead another combat team.*

"Why? I didn't do so well last time."

It is evident that you have learned from your mistakes. You possess leadership capabilities and strength of mind which are necessary for combat leadership and also quite rare. <earnest sincerity> *You are among the best human commanders we possess, with the greatest potential. You should feel proud of what you have done already and be prepared to serve with equal valor now.*

Elken didn't feel particularly valorous, or as though he had much in the way of leadership potential. All he could really recall were his almost paralyzing fear . . . and his grief the moment Sendee had died. There was something there . . . something he needed to recall. . . .

I remind you, the god continued, a mellifluous voice in his head, *that your final body, and your hope of immortality with the gods, depend on your successful defense of this world.*

Why me? he thought, a little bitterly. But he dismissed the inner cry, and the bitterness, as unworthy. The gods, clearly, knew more and better what they were doing than he. Perhaps there were just some things he wasn't meant to know or understand. "Okay," he said. "If you have another team ready, I'll take them out. We'll try to employ TSDS to hit the enemy from all sides simultaneously."

Light shimmered into Elken's awareness, and the light took form. He was in the armored cavern once again, one among many vast, squat, slab-sided forms.

A Bolo, Mark XXXII.

Move to the gathering area. The others are assembling already.

Through the long and familiar tunnel, then. He was pleased that his reactions and responses appeared to remain well-tuned, even though his brain had been placed in a different machine body. It *felt* identical, and he marveled at the gods' skill at wiring a human brain to the psychotronic complexity of a Bolo with such perfect and well-skilled efficiency.

Three Bolos were waiting for him at the staging area in front of the underground mining and ore processing plant at Trolvas. As he reached out electronically to touch their thoughts, he was jolted by an utterly unlooked-for response.

"Sendee!" he cried. And Veber . . . and Palet! They were all here, all alive. "But I saw you all destroyed! I *felt* you destroyed! . . ."

"It's okay, Elken," Sendee's voice said. "I'm right here. I don't understand it either, but I'm okay."

"We're all okay!" Palet said. "The gods can do anything they want, right? They *are* the gods, after all!"

"Palet! Veber! How? . . ."

We were able to recover their mind/thought patterns as well. They reside now in new bodies, but they are as you remember them.

"B-blessed are the gods, for they are holy and most powerful!" The ancient mantra from the Histories of the Way of the Gods steadied nerves jarred by this thunder-striking discovery.

The enemy Bolo is still at the Ghendai Planetary Defense logistics and command control center. <the voice of command> *Go, now, and destroy the Sky Demon Machine.*

"Yes, Lord. C'mon, people. Let's go!"

It wasn't until some time later that he realized the irony of calling the three Bolos following him from the tunnel *people.* . . .

The god Vulj'yjjrik had been born for this. Literally.

His body massed less than three kilograms, and most of that was in brain and ancillary support organs, all floating in a gelatinous semiliquid within a wormlike, almost mushy body designed to cushion the vital organs against high acceleration.

He was blind, save to the images fed to his brain through electronic implants, deaf save to radio frequencies and computer links. His parasomatic body was almost literally a part of the compact, delta-winged interceptor the enemy referred to as a slash fighter, but which the gods called Beauty of Sharp Change, grown into the command socket just ahead of the powerful triplet of nuclear pulse engines that drove the stubby vessel at accelerations so high even the batteries of maneuvering contra-grav projectors mounted throughout the hull couldn't nullify all of the craft's inertia. A human pilot—or even an Aetryx parasome—would never have survived the accelerative forces leaking past the CG fields during the more extreme of the fighter's maneuvers.

At the moment, his fighter was still residing on its launch rack deep within the bowels of the enormous Aetryx battlecarrier, *The Silent Contemplation of Form.* To his perception, however, both the carrier and the slash fighter were invisible. Behind him, a titanic scimitar of purest gold and white crystal, was the gas giant humans called Dis, its cloud bands forming roiling, dazzlingly intricate exercises in chaos geometries beneath the blinding glare of the system's sun. On the dark side of the planet, vision sensitive to the near-infrared detected the sullen, deeper glow of the world, and the scattered, popping pinpricks of lightning flares illuminating continent-sized patches of cloud against the night. Alongside, eighty *detyk* distant, the second Aetryx battlecarrier, *The Flexible Vigilance of Anger*, climbed with the *Contemplation* clear of the last thinning edges of the gas giant's outer atmospheric shell of hydrogen and into the clean emptiness of space. Elsewhere in the sky, sunlight sparked and flashed from the battlecarriers' escorts—the strike battlers *Hand of the Gods* and *Seething Lightnings*; the fleet penetrators *Rapid Thought, High Vengeance, Gathering Storm,* and *Justice Redeemed*; and twenty-four heavy kinetic-killer fleet gunships.

For twelves of *da'j'ris*, now, the Aetryx battle squadron had been hidden deep within the turbulent and cloudy atmosphere of Dis, held aloft against its massive gravitational pull by straining contra-gravity projectors, shielded from detection by the planet's radar-scattering upper cloud deck and magnetic effects. There, they'd lurked and waited as the Confederation Strike force had entered the system and taken up orbit around Caern, lurked and waited as the invaders had bombarded the planet's surface and sent down their drop pods.

And now it was time to strike back. The battle squadron had powered up and begun fighting up from the dazzling beauty of golds and silver cloudtops, moving onto a course that would put them on a direct intercept vector with the Sky Demon fleet.

All Beauties of Sharp Change, the voice of the Squadron Battle Commander whispered within his thoughts, *your courses have been plotted and locked in. The Sky Demon fleet is no longer in orbit but is using its contra-gravity projectors to hover above their landing sites. This could be to our tactical advantage, if we can get among them swiftly, before they realize we are coming. It falls to you, our fighters, to cause as much damage and confusion to the invader fleet as possible.*

We are the gods! The cosmos bends to our will! Stand by to launch! . . .

Vulj'yjjrik acknowledged the transmission and focused his inner view on the ocher orb of Caern, a bit over a twelve of twelve *na-netyk* distant, only recently emerged from Dis's shadow. His fighter's computer painted in the positions of identified Sky Demon spacecraft in shimmering hues of ultraviolet. The readout panel projected into his view-bubble by the craft's AI showed systems at blue, drives powered to maximum, launch in twenty-four *j'ris.* . .

We are the gods! The cosmos bends to our will!

Sometimes, though, the cosmos needed a nudge to

remind it who was in charge. The Sky Demons should never have been allowed this deeply into the Reach. He understood the strategy of letting them begin their invasion operations—strategy and tactics had been hardwired into his parasome—but it was a costly ruse, one that might render Caern uninhabitable by either species, Aetryx or human.

And just as swiftly, the moral encodings of his parasome, triggered by his critical anger, arose to bring him peace. The gods would be victorious. They always were. And it was not the place of a single god parasome to question the tactics of the Circle of Gods, or the parasome from whom he'd descended.

It was right that the Aetryx fleet remain hidden, while the full scope of the Sky Demon's strategy unfolded, to be analyzed by the Circle of War.

Now, with the enemy fleet's attention focused fully on the battle over Caern, the carriers emerged with their escorts, rising from the gas giant atmosphere on a trajectory that put them directly against the disk of Sallos as it slowly rose above the giant's limb.

With luck, the invaders would never see their doom approaching until it was too late. . . .

Chapter Eight

With the strong points and gun emplacements in and around the logistical base destroyed, I have initiated strategic operations in concert with the other Bolos of the regiment. Opening my main dorsal weapons bay, I bring my VLS array online and begin firing heavy missiles in support of my fellows at Dolendi, Kanth, and Losethal.

My on-board arsenal includes both nuclear and conventional warheads, as well as several special force packages, but I have limited my initial strikes to conventional warheads, even though the Enemy has resorted to the use of nukes quite early in this engagement.

My Escalated Response Protocols are in force, a set of inhibitory subroutines that require me to seek release from Space Strike Command before employing nonconventional warheads, even when I come under attack by nonconventional weapons. The protocols restrain my freedom of action considerably and increase response time significantly, possibly by as much as several full minutes while my human commanders debate the issue.

Still, in this instance, I completely understand the need for tactical and strategic restraint. My combat history files include a complete range of battle *descriptions and analyses, from planetary invasions at one end to squad-level hostage rescues and patrol actions at the other. Even though this is a large-scale strategic operation, involving as it does the conquest of an entire world, nuclear, biological, and chemical weapons would not be appropriate in this situation, since our primary operational task involves freeing the human inhabitants of this world rather than incinerating them.*

There reside within my historical archives records of a training simulation. A young officer cadet, tasked with planning and executing a hostage rescue operation, elected to storm a compartment occupied by twenty hostages and three terrorist soldiers while armed with a flame thrower. Freeing the human population of Caern by employing nuclear warheads with multimegaton yields would involve a similar inconsiderate use of excessive force.

I have not even routed a request for force escalation as yet. So far, the Enemy's attempts to block the invasion's first wave elements have been less than successful, even with the use of nukes. If they continue in this vein, however, serious ecological damage could result to the habitable portions of Caern which, I deduce, are quite fragile, if only because they constitute such a small fraction of the planet's total surface environment.

In any case, the missiles I launch are self-guiding fusion ramjets, programmed to circle the battle zone until key threats are identified and specifically targeted. Invictus, of 1st Battalion, is still attempting to penetrate the Planetary Defense bastion at Dolendi, and my bombardment of the deeply buried, heavily armored and turreted Hellbore bunkers there may help him complete his operational orders at that target.

I check my BIST data and note that my sector has

become quiet, but doubt that resistance has ended. Likely, the Enemy is preparing a new counter-thrust. I await further tactical developments.

Elken emerged from a tunnel—not the large, main entrance he'd used in his last attempt against the invaders, but a secondary tunnel a kilometer to the west, carefully screened and masked and barely wide enough to allow a Mark XXXII to exit without scraping track guards against the support frame.

Though it was still dark and would remain so for another several hours before the slowly advancing dawn, the sky was aglow with a somber red and orange haze, the cloud-reflected glow of burning cities. The Sky Demon invaders *had* to be stopped. . . .

He engaged the TSDS link, connecting immediately with the thoughts of the other three Mark XXXIIs. The psychic shock rocked him, causing him to hesitate a moment at the threshold of the tunnel. This was like having the sensory feeds from the other three overlaid across his own . . . but much more so. He was aware of Palet and Veber and Sendee, of their personalities, of their thoughts and feelings, in a way he hadn't been before, the four of them mingling and flowing together, like four rush-and-tumble streams merging into the deep, surging, unstoppable current of a river.

We have the enemy now, he thought to the others . . . or was it Veber who voiced the thought? He couldn't tell. It didn't matter.

Enemy Bolo targeted and locked, range three kilometers. . . .

Disperse. Increase separation between our units. . . .

Their thoughts mingled and their actions. Elken felt his own ego, his sense of self fading as he became more aware of the central core of the minds of the others.

The sensation was at once terrifying and thrilling. He'd never felt so alive. . . .

All four Mark XXXIIs had emerged at roughly the same moment from four separate tunnel entrances. The base complex was riddled with them, and four tunnels had been selected by the gods as offering them the best chance of emerging at the same time and at roughly the same distances from the target.

Linked by UHF signals relayed through the base structures themselves, the four Caernan Mark XXXIIs exploded into the open air, battlescreens full on, weapons charged and ready. They knew exactly where the Confederation Bolo was positioned. The gods were giving them data feeds second by second, downloading the data they needed to optimize their attack.

Increasing speed . . .

Commence fire! Now! . . .

Four enemy Bolos emerge from separate locations within the ruins of the command control base, on bearings between two-eight-three and three-one-nine, roughly toward the northwest at a range of 3.17 kilometers. I bring all Hellbore weapons to full charge, route reserve power to my battle-screens, and prepare to face this new threat.

I detect the stuttering, flickering pulses of UHF transmissions indicative of high-speed data transfers. It is almost as though . . .

Yes. A brief analysis of the signals correlated with the movement of the four enemy machines, for a period of 0.19 second, proves that the four are sharing data at an extremely high rate of speed, reminiscent of the old TSDS first employed by Bolos Mark XXI. One of the Enemy Bolos, which I designate Charlie One, is clearly the focus of much of the data flow and is, therefore, most likely the command unit.

I slue all three primary turrets to face this new threat. The Enemy must be desperate indeed to continue throwing outmoded Bolo marks at me in this fashion, though the fact that they are employing a Total Systems Data-Sharing suggests that they have learned from the last encounter and are taking care not to allow their combat units to be defeated in detail.

I fire, and in virtually the same instant, they fire as well. White light engulfs the landscape as fusion bolts sear through tortured air. One bolt strikes me squarely in the glacis, but my dual-ply battlescreen absorbs much of the energy, both from the fusion of the cryo-H projectile and the sheer kinetic energy released on impact, rerouting it into my accumulators. Three routing circuits are overloaded, however, and their failure degrades my screen's effectiveness by 12.3 percent. Excess energy leaks through, melting a deep crater 8 meters across and .93 meters deep in my frontal armor. The shock of impact rocks me back, literally lifting me off my front tracks before gravity slams me back to the ground once again. Internal power feeds melt through under the onslaught, tripping circuit breakers and cutting my main power feed to my armament centers by 42 percent.

Two of my Hellbore bolts strike home, while the third expends much of its megaton fury on a ruin-strewn ridge sheltering one of the targets as the enemy Bolo went hull-down behind it. Explosions rock the area, though the targeted Bolos continue to fire.

The Enemy has emerged inside my defensive picket of Dragon hovertanks, which precludes my using them as a screen or to degrade the enemy forces through attrition. I direct the Dragons on my west and north to close with Charlie One through Four, however, and also signal the Warlock teleoperated ground-strike aircraft, which are now orbiting in support 4.7 kilometers to the north.

I initiate emergency field damage control measures, noting that my overall performance will be reduced by as much as 28 percent until I can reach a maintenance bay for full repairs.

First, however, I must survive this attack, which is being pressed with unexpected vigor. All three of my primary turrets, and seven of my secondaries, are in full operation now, loosing the hellfury of fusing, high-kinetic projectiles as quickly as they can be loaded and fired. Charlie Two takes three direct hits in rapid succession, its Hellbore turret and much of its upper deck reduced to flamingly incandescent wreckage within the space of .44 second. Charlie Three takes a direct 20cm Hellbore shot in its forward left track assembly, which wrecks the tread and drive bogies, partially crippling it.

I take two more hits, absorbed by my battlescreens and my rapidly degrading frontal armor. I compute that I will be able to destroy three of my attackers, but not all four before my defenses are overwhelmed and I am myself reduced to burning and insentient wreckage.

I must find a way to shift the odds in my favor, and swiftly.

Vulj'yjjrik sent the mental commands that boosted his fighter's acceleration another notch. Half of a *da'j'ris* ago, the magnetic launchers of *The Silent Contemplation of Form* had flung him and the rest of his squadron, a twelve and a half of sleek, deadly fighters, into the void. Now, his strike squadron and a second squadron from *The Flexible Vigilance of Anger* were hurtling through emptiness, and he was plunging toward the near-full brown, white, and ocher globe that was Caern, now only a few *detyk* distant. Behind him, vast and swollen, was Dis, black as night and edged by the silver crescent of dawn. The two Aetryx battlecarriers had long since dwindled into invisibility, but they and the rest of the squadron would be accelerating now as hard as they could, eager to begin the slaughter.

But the fighters would reach the objective first, fast-striking *epretta* among the helpless *d'jorn*.

It wouldn't be long now.

"Alert! Alert! Enemy spacecraft on approach trajectory! . . ."

Colonel Streicher was submerged within the virtual simulation of the battle being played out hundreds of kilometers below, but the sharp bark of the command craft's AI warning system jolted him to full awareness. "This is Streicher," he said. "What is it?"

"We're under attack, Colonel," replied the voice of the Navy lieutenant piloting the command craft. His name, according to the bio data attached to the virtual comm link, was Alisar Cavese, and he was a 28-standard-year officer from Fledryss who'd never been in combat in his life. "Looks like they were hiding inside the giant's atmosphere, and our scouts missed 'em." He sounded steady enough.

"Show me."

The data feed from the command craft's control center showed the Confederation fleet hovering above Caern's dawn terminator, each ship shown as a blue star. A spray of glowing red trajectories was moving rapidly toward the fleet, the threads of light converging to a single vector that curved up and over the gas giant's horizon.

"Range now . . . 70,000 kilometers," Cavese said.

"Fighters . . ."

"Coming out of the suns. We didn't even see them on radar until they hit our collision warning fields."

The red threads indicating the paths of the incoming Aetryx fighters were drawing themselves swiftly toward the cluster of Confederation naval vessels. They were closing the range at nearly two hundred kilometers per second, fast enough to have vaulted the million kilometers from Dis to Caern in a little over an hour. Data tags marking them in Streicher's inner vision identified them as Aetryx Slash fighters. There were thirty-six of them, and they would enter the Confederation Strike Force's Area of Operation within three minutes.

"Call coming through from the *Denever*, sir," Cavese said. "General Moberly. Flagged for all regimental and brigade commanders."

"Put him through."

A window opened in Streicher's simulated view. Moberly's florid features looked out at him from the surrounding star fields and the sweeping ocher horizon of Caern. Streicher could see enough of the compartment behind him revealed in the comm window to recognize it as the Combat Information Center on board the Strike Force's flagship.

"Gentlemen," he said, "and ladies. It . . . it appears we have stumbled into a trap. The enemy carriers were hiding in the gas giant's upper atmosphere." His words were hurried and faltered a bit, and he kept glancing away from the comm camera at something else in the CIC. "All command vessels are to scatter and stay clear of the other ships in the fleet, until we see how this thing turns out. . . ."

"KKMs incoming!" someone out of the camera's field of view shouted.

"Wh-what?" Moberly appeared dazed, as if he was having trouble focusing.

"*Kinetic-kill missiles!* . . ."

White flame blossomed against the backdrop of space above Caern in Streicher's sim-feed, sharp pulses of light expanding and dissipating in eerie silence. Four vessels, a cargo carrier, a tanker, and two light cruisers, were hit in the first volley, exploding in dazzling flashes against the night.

Kinetic-kill weapons were a variant of the projectiles used on Caern by the Confederation forces; a sliver of high-density metal—depleted uranium or neptunium-237—wrapped in iron was magnetically accelerated to a high percentage of the speed of light. A gram or two impacting ship battlescreens at relativistic velocities yielded a release of kinetic energy rivaling a multi-megaton warhead. Not even a battleship's dual-ply screens could shunt that much energy aside in the billionth of a second or so it took the sliver to penetrate them.

A projectile had lanced in from the direction of Dis and the sun and struck the *Denever* a glancing, near-miss blow. A second window opened in Streicher's three-sixty view giving him a nightmare close-up of the flagship as white-hot fragments spun from the gash torn across the huge flagship's dorsal hull.

"All ships!" Moberly was screaming from his window, his voice shrill. "All ships commence maneuvering!"

The orders were less than precise . . . and the general in command of the invasion force was not the one to be giving orders to the fleet in any case. The Confederation strike force was in a terribly vulnerable position, concentrated above the surface of Caern, with the world-sized moon serving as a wall to block them off from moving in that direction. Nor were they in orbit, which meant their speed was zero relative to the planet, their only velocity vector being the one they shared with Caern in its four-day orbit about Dis. Had they been in orbit, at least, they would have possessed an initial velocity of a few kilometers per second, something to work with. As it was, they had to start from scratch.

And the enemy was not about to give them the leisure of time. As Streicher studied the tactical readouts, he realized that the kinetic-kill missiles weren't coming from the fighters. The main Aetryx fleet was still half a million kilometers away and traveling at a fraction of the speed of the front wave of fighters. Twenty-four of the vessels with the Aetryx fleet, however, were being IDed by the command craft's AI as KK gunboats. They were too far away, yet, for a direct optical view, but the AI warbook drew schematics of them—stubby, massive, compact, hundred-meter hulls sprouting skeletal rail gun tracks half a kilometer long, ugly, vicious and functional.

The main fleet was still 1.6 light seconds away, which meant that its ranging and radar targeting data was that out of date. According to the tracking data, the incoming KK missiles were traveling at .65 c, for a flight time of 2.46 seconds. With a total time lag, then, of a shade over four seconds, targeting had to be based on the predicted position of an enemy vessel 4.06 seconds after firing.

Had the Confederation fleet been capable of independent maneuver, the Aetryx gunboats would have been able to score hits only by sheer chance. As it was, though, the enemy's relativistic projectiles were spearing into a fleet that was both slow-moving and utterly predictable. Four vessels had been hit by the first volley, and as Streicher watched with dawning horror, two more, the carrier *Gelidelfen* and the destroyer *Delphis,* took direct hits.

Moberly was still shouting orders. "*Ajecerras! Validente!* Open fire on the attackers! Hold them until the rest of the fleet can get under way!"

The *Ajecerras* and the *Validente* were the fleet's two battlers, eighty thousand tonners with mag-rail guns of their own, spinal mounts normally used for planetary bombardment.

"Belay those orders!" another voice snapped. The craggy features of Admiral Resin Hathaway appeared in another window. "*Cateran, Tritheladee, Larabes,* maneuver to screen the fleet! Take out those incoming fighters!"

"We need to stop that main fleet before it closes the range!" Moberly shouted.

"You're outside your jurisdiction, *General,*" Hathaway snapped, turning Moberly's rank into a curse word. "The fleet is mine. You stick with your overgrown tanks and keep your nose out of the *Navy's* AO!"

Streicher decided that the regimental commanders had accidentally been left linked to the command-com feeds; they weren't supposed to be privy to this infighting within the upper levels of the Confederation hierarchy of rank. Throughout the hovering fleet, main drives were coming on, ships were beginning to accelerate . . . but slowly, so *slowly.* . . .

The destroyer *Larabes*, blade-slender and spiked with 200cm Hellbores and particle beam weapons, had started her burn, accelerating clear of the other ships to put herself between the approaching enemy forces and the rest of the fleet. A KKM bolt almost missed her, nicking one of her aft maneuvering drive blisters. That glancing touch, light as it was, liberated the heat and light of a star which engulfed the aft third of the destroyer, turning her drives into molten slag. Streicher saw life pods boosting clear of the damaged ship, as internal explosions began to consume her.

"Shouldn't . . . shouldn't we get back to the *Heritas*?" Kelly Tyler asked. He could hear her voice shake with barely suppressed emotion. "We're targets just floating around out here."

"Negative, Lieutenant," Major Ramirez told her. "We're targets, but we're small targets. That's why they deploy us like this, so if somebody goes after the big boys, we'll be overlooked . . . and safe."

At least, Streicher thought, *that's how it's* supposed *to work.* The enemy must have a pretty good idea of Confederation operational tactics, though, and would know what the small, stealth-shielded saucers were for . . . especially if they'd mapped the Confederation's communications web for the past few hours.

The Bolo assault transport *Vangled* was struck hard by two KKMs, the explosions opening up like sun-bright flowers, one in her cargo bay, one in her drive section. The enormous craft was set spinning by the impact, and the stress of the rotation quickly snapped her spine. In a cloud of debris, the fleet carrier ripped into two halves, tumbling away from one another at three kilometers per second.

"That's why we don't go back to the transports, Lieutenant," Major King observed wryly. Another ship, too far off for an immediate identification, silently exploded in white and yellow brilliance. "Good God! They're mopping the deck with us!"

The fighters entered the fleet operations area, moving so quickly they were impossible to hit. Slash fighters were small—only thirty tons or so—too small to carry high-velocity railguns. They mounted 10cm Hellbores in turrets tucked up beneath their needle-prows, and they flashed past the fleet strewing fusion bolts in all directions. According to the data feed readouts, they were decelerating now at almost a hundred gravities . . . enough to kill any human pilots. Streicher decided the fighters must be teleoperated by pilots safe aboard the incoming Aetryx fleet.

Apparently the fleet command staff thought the same. He could hear shouted orders from the *Denever,* deploying ships to hit the Aetryx squadron, especially the carriers. "The fighters are being operated from the carriers!" Moberly was shouting. "Hit the carriers!"

"Your Bolos have space-superiority capabilities, General," Hathaway said. "Do they not?"

"Uh . . . huh?"

"General, damn it! Pull yourself together! Can your Bolos hit targets in space?"

"Uh, yeah."

"Then get them targeting those incoming! We need all the help we can get!"

"Fourth Regiment?" Streicher said quietly. "How about it, people? Can any of you get your machines into the space fight?"

"Negative, Colonel," Lieutenant Tom Winsett, the UC of Second Battalion's Ferox, said. "The Aetryx fleet is too far out, and their fighters are too fast."

"We can let the Bolos themselves judge," Lieutenant Shauna O'Hara, with Third Batt's Fortis, pointed out. "They're the best ones to decide what they can do."

"Victor is occupied right now," Lieutenant Tyler said. "Firefight."

"So is Invictus," Captain Johanel added.

"And Terry," Lieutenant Edan Abrams reported.

"Pass the word to your units, everyone. The fleet is going to need fire support from the ground." Odd. Usually it was the other way around, but the Confederation Fleet had just been caught with its collective pants around its ankles.

Explosions continued to flash and pulse throughout the scattering invasion fleet.

They were picking the Confederation vessels off too quickly to keep count. . . .

The battle rages with a savage ferocity I have never in one hundred eighty-seven previous combat engagements encountered before. Hellbore weapons are designed for combat out to the horizon—or even into near space, so long as the firing Bolo has a clear line of sight and a solid, predictable vector track. I was engaging these four at a range of a scant three kilometers, and the hellfire fury of that torrent of fusion energy loosed within so tightly constrained a sphere lit the ruined defense complex up as brightly as the midday sun and reduced any of the few structures still standing to half-molten wreckage scattered by hurricane blasts of superheated air.

For a seeming eternity of seconds, my four Bolo Mark XXXII opponents and I trade blow for Hellbore blow, main guns and infinite repeaters both. Charlie Three has been badly damaged, but I have received multiple direct hits to my frontal armor. Much of my glacis plate has degraded or been stripped away entirely, and only my internal disrupter shields are saving me from complete obliteration. Four of my secondary turrets have been knocked out, Numbers Two, Four, and Six on my starboard side, and Number Three on my port. I continue facing into the storm of fire, returning bolt after bolt. The air, superheated, dust-laden, and violently roiled by the exchange, serves to deflect some of the raw energy into the surrounding atmosphere and ground and makes aiming and tracking a considerable challenge.

My single tactical advantage in this unequal contest is the remote Dragon tanks I've deployed, which are now moving into position behind the Enemy. They are still making their way through the ruins, however, and do not yet have a clear line of sight at the attacking Mark XXXIIs.

I am still trading shots with the Enemy when an incoming message on the narrow maser command frequency reaches my communications filters. Codes and communication encryptions check, and I open the channel to Space Strike Command.

"Victor!" my Commander exclaims, with that excess of emotion that I have come to associate with her. "Thank God we got through to you!"

I ignore her reference to a deity. She frequently makes such statements, but I have learned to treat them as the formal or polite noise generated by most humans in situations of social intercourse. She sounds pleased, as am I, that communications have been reestablished, though this channel is crackling with static due to the tremendous build-up of electrical charges from the ongoing Hellbore barrage.

"I am currently engaged in close combat, Commander," I tell her. "I shall upload a proper combat report when the current action is complete."

"That's not what I need to talk about," she replies. "Vic, the enemy is attacking the fleet! A surprise attack! They're knocking our ships right out of the sky! Can you help?"

A side-band data feed gives me the updated tactical situation in near-planetary space. The situation is, indeed, critical . . . but I fear there is nothing material I can contribute at the moment.

"The main enemy squadron is still well out of range," I tell her. "To engage the fighters would require my full targeting and tracking faculties, which are currently engaged in this action with four enemy Mark XXXII Bolos. Do you require that I break off this action in order to initiate an engagement with enemy assets in space?"

In fact, I am not certain that I could break off this action. But I would try, if so ordered.

"N-no, Vic. That's okay. But see if you can help once you beat those XXXIIs!"

"I will comply, Commander."

I may not be able to keep my promise. The question is whether I can survive the next 2.7 minutes, the time, I estimate, it will take for me to assemble my full tactical assets and press the advantage.

I am taking extremely heavy damage.

"Can we fight back?" Lieutenant Winsett asked. His voice was shaking. "We might as well have a giant target painted on our hull!"

"Enough, Lieutenant," Third Batt's CO, said with acid in her voice. Major Katrin Voll was a career Bolo officer with little patience and less tact. "You're out of line!"

"Yes, ma'am."

"Take it easy, people," Streicher said, trying to smooth the tension filling the netlink. "Our best tactic right now is to keep doing our job and let the Navy do its business."

"These command craft aren't much more than hightech glorified lifeboats," Major King added. "They're no match for a blade-fighter."

"Right," Carla Ramirez added. "We sit tight, lay low, and hope they don't see us with all the junk floating around out there!"

Local space was cluttered now with the shattered remnants of capital ships blasted by the enemy's relativistic bombardment. The simulated view spread before the minds of the 4th Regiment's Command Team showed drifting wrecks still aglow with inner fires and explosions, bits of wreckage, tumbling chunks of hull, drive module, turret, or cargo bay, and even the tiny, pathetic forms of people blasted out into hard vacuum.

Cateran and *Tritheladee* were accelerating toward the oncoming fighters, firing wildly with every weapon in their arsenal. Their stand was glorious . . . and all too brief. The fighters flashed past, tail-first, decelerating furiously, loosing Hellbore blasts in all directions. *Tritheladee* was crippled by a rapid-fire barrage that riddled her main deck and drive sponsons, blasted her main turret, and left her bridge section ablaze with interior fires. A nuclear warhead found the *Cateran* a moment later; the flash seemed to illuminate all of local space, then faded to a fast-swelling fireball and a haze of hull metal turned to vapor.

Streicher turned his attention to the *Denever*, the flagship that was now finally beginning to pick up speed. It might be that she would be able to work her way clear, along with a handful of other vessels. *Denever*, Streicher saw, was tucked in close alongside the much larger and bulkier frame of the assault transport *Heritas*.

The Aetryx fleet was still firing KKMs at long range. *Heritas* was struck by two relativistic projectiles in rapid succession, and the explosions savaged the transport as it shattered and dissolved, consumed by inner fires as hot as the surface of a star.

General Moberly, his face still peering out of an open window in the sim, looked about, startled. "What the hell was that?"

And then the window in Streicher's data feed grew intolerably brilliant as a third KKM speared out of the void and loosed its megatonnage of kinetic energy in the *Denever*. The window blinked out as the feed was cut; on the main view, spread like a fire-blasted panorama in Streicher's data-linked mind, *Denever* staggered under the blast. Fragments slammed into the disintegrating wreckage of the *Heritas*, while others hurtled outward through space. Streicher could see the huge vessel's battle bridge disintegrating in lambent flame and vaporizing metal.

For a moment, his numbed thoughts could only circle around the question of how anything could *burn* in the vacuum of space. Then the flames winked out, and he realized they'd been fed by the huge vessel's atmosphere as it rushed through the huge rents in the hull.

Secondary explosions continued to wrack the flagship, however, as torn and shattered sections glowed orange- and white-hot. The bridge and combat control sections looked completely wrecked, and Streicher wondered if General Moberly had paid the full price for his blinkered strategic vision.

Then the view of the battle flashed a dazzling, intolerably brilliant silver-blue-white, then winked out to black as the data feed went dead. A crashing shudder thundered through the command craft's hull; gravity vanished in the same moment, as the artificial grav and inertial dampers failed.

"What happened?" Beswin shouted, his voice ragged on the edge of a scream in the darkness.

"We're hit!" Winsett shouted. "God, we're hit! . . ."

And they weren't in orbit, and their contra-gravity projectors had been taken off line. There was nothing now to hold them up against the pull of Caern's gravity.

They were hit, and they were going down. . . .

Interlude II

There are those military historians who still hold that the invasion of Caern could have, *should* have, succeeded as it was originally envisioned. The plans were well laid, the targets and objectives meticulously listed and studied, the enemy's forces estimated, his capabilities evaluated in thousands of hours of invasion planning and simulation.

There can be no doubt that the Aetryx naval maneuver utilizing the gas giant Dis in order to stage an ambush of Confederation Fleet elements was the turning point of the battle. Their victory in the skies above Caern demonstrated conclusively that ancient military maxim—that control of the planetary surface is secondary to, and depends absolutely on, the control of circumplanetary space. Bolos may reign supreme on the ground, may control every piece of strategically vital high ground, but space is the ultimate high ground from which one side or the other can claim an overwhelming strategic advantage.

Disaster at Caern:
A Study of the Unexpected in Warfare
Galactic Press Productions, Primus, cy 426

Chapter Nine

My battlescreens are barely functioning at 26 percent, though my internal disrupter screens are still holding. Power management has become a serious issue, requiring me to shepherd the output of both my primary and secondary weaponry. Secondary armament has been reduced to 72 percent of optimal, and hits to my suspension and track assemblies have reduced my mobility as well.

The Enemy is hull-down behind an artificial ridge 3.1 kilometers in front of me. Once, this entire area was built-over with duralloy, flintsteel, and ferrocrete casements, deck, and defensive towers. "The ridge" at my front, I believe, was originally a wall with a road along the top or possibly a protective ferrocrete banking for pipelines or a surface maglev tube, with a back-slanted face at an angle of forty-eight degrees from the vertical. All four enemy Bolos have taken up hull-down positions behind this barrier, which has been reduced to rubble and bare earth by the torrent of Hellbore fire smashing into it or skimming just above it.

The passage of a Hellbore bolt creates a shock wave that can crumble any substance less densely integrated than duralloy. The blank, smooth, almost polished surface has, in the past three minutes, been reduced

145

to something more like loose earth and crumbled rock than ferrocrete. Indeed, it is clear now that the barrier's interior is mostly loose earth.

Ceasing fire at the Enemy, I use my mortars at an elevation of 89.4 degrees, dropping a rain of heavy rounds squarely along the ridge in front of me. The slope explodes in flying earth and debris, creating a wall of dust and falling rock impenetrable to radar, lidar, and optical wavelengths. I then advance, rushing ahead over tortured terrain, employing contra-gravs to lift me above the deeper, more troublesome blast craters and mud sinks.

It takes just under a full minute to traverse the three kilometers of battlefield, all the while maintaining the wall of exploding, tumbling earth to cover my advance, and I slam into the ridge the Enemy has been sheltered behind at better than two hundred kilometers per hour.

I must end this engagement within the next few seconds, both to enable me to assist in the defense of the fleet, and also as a matter of sheer personal survival.

Streicher came out of the blackness of the simulation feed power-down to a darkness nearly as complete. The main lighting and the viewscreen power were both out, and the only illumination within the ECD command craft's sim compartment came from emergency lighting strips on deck and overhead.

The rest of the command staff was coming around as well, pulling off headgear, unplugging cables, and unbuckling their harnesses.

"Stay put, everybody," he snapped. "I'll check with the skipper."

He unbuckled his safety harness and pushed himself into the air, aiming his kick-off for the sliding door that led to the vehicle's bridge. It had been a while since he'd tried his hand at zero-G ballet, however, and he missed the door by a couple of meters.

No matter. He snagged a grab-on attached to the bulkhead, and as he turned, the door opened and a navy crewman floated through. "Colonel? Your people okay?"

The rest of the command staff, sixteen people in all, were waiting in their seats as he'd ordered. "Everybody seems okay," he said. "What's our situation?"

"Our drive module took a light Hellbore hit. Main drive and maneuver is off-line. The skipper thinks we can get maneuver back, though. We won't be able to stop the fall, but at least we can control our landing."

"I see. And if we can't get the maneuver drive repaired?"

"Then we burn, sir. Like a goddamn shooting star."

"I . . . see. How long do we have?"

"Starting a free fall from six hundred kilometers, at .74 G? Call it . . . six minutes from drive failure to when we hit atmosphere."

Six minutes. A minute had passed already. Five minutes.

The viewscreens encircling the sim deck flickered, then winked on, bathing the compartment in the yellow-rust light of Caern, the pearly glow of crescent Dis, and the harsher, more actinic glare of the twin suns of Sallos. The entire panorama of stars and planets was rotating slowly, indicating that the command vessel was tumbling, albeit so slowly he couldn't feel much, if any, of the tug of centrifugal force.

"Good," the crewman said. "At least now we can see where we're falling." He ducked back through the door.

Streicher lined himself up, brought his feet together on the bulkhead, and gently pushed off, drifting across the compartment and snagging hold of the back of his couch. Swinging himself over and into his seat once more, he snugged the harness tight.

Not that a tight harness was going to be of much help.

Flashes and pulses of light continued to spark against the galactic night as the space battle continued. Without AI enhancement, the individual ships were too far and thinly scattered to be seen with the naked eye.

He wondered who was winning.

"So . . . what's the word, Colonel?" Major King wanted to know.

"Drives are out," Streicher replied. "They might get the maneuvering drives back online. If they do, we can make a controlled landing."

"Yeah?" Beswin said. "Where?"

"I'd suggest as close to one of the 4th Regiment Bolos as we can manage," Ramirez put in. "That way we could use the Bolo's combat command center as a makeshift C^3 center and keep the fight going."

"Sounds good to me," Streicher said. "Comments on that, anyone?"

There were none, though the apprehension stood out plainly on more than a few of the faces staring at him from around the circular couch. The thought of actually running a battle *from the battlefield* must be both strange and terrifying to those officers who'd never been in combat before.

Major Filby, especially, looked scared. His hands were trembling.

"Don't worry, people," Streicher said lightly, trying to make a joke of it. "We have a long way to go before worrying about being in the middle of a battlefield. First we have to survive the landing! . . ."

The timing of my assault has been well executed. As I clamber up the blast-shattered face of the artificial ridge, three of my Dragons are just making it into position among the ruins west of the Enemy's position. They begin their attack just as I enter the curtain of tumbling rock and dirt, pinning the Enemy in place before he can pull back from his hull-down position behind the ridge. The Dragons, staying low to enjoy the full protection of the duralloy walls and fallen towers of the base, slam volley after volley of 20cm Hellbore fire into the defending Bolos, causing heavy damage and diverting their attention from their dust-shrouded eastern field of fire to their west.

As I emerge from the dust screen a second later, grinding over the crest of the ridge with all of my remaining secondaries engaged, I find three of the four enemy vehicles have slued their turrets around to face the threat presented by the Dragons. The fourth Mark XXXII, Charlie Three, appears to be disabled, though its primary turret is tracking me as I breast the ridge and go nose-down on the far side.

I am too close to Charlie Three to engage with any of my primary turrets, but I rake the machine in passing with accurate point-blank 20cm fire from my starboard turrets, as well as AP lasers and railgun rounds. The enemy Bolo's turret, already heavily cratered in places, is torn to bits as it takes the full brunt of my volley.

Elken screamed as Veber, his chassis disabled moments before by the hellish fury of the Sky Demon's Hellbore barrage, had his turret scraped from its deck mounting and reduced to half-molten shards and twisted, burning wreckage, felt the wrenching fury of the assault through the TSDS net. He realized his mistake; the enemy Bolo had been more or less immobile for the better part of a full minute, moving back and forth to make itself a more difficult target, but not advancing in the face of the four Caernan machines' well-sheltered, hull-down position behind the ridge.

The appearance of four more enemy machines at their rear was a complete surprise. The TSDS gestalt of Elken and the others had been aware that they were out there but had not expected them to work in close concert with the enemy Bolo. They were tiny machines after all, inconsequential tactically . . . massing only something like two tenths of a percent of a Bolo Mark XXXII. They couldn't *possibly* be a threat. . . .

When they attacked from the rear, their first Hellbore volley, perfectly coordinated, demonstrated that very nasty surprises can be mounted in small force packages. Elken took one bolt in his rear left track assembly, shattering three wheels and twisting four more out of alignment. He slued his turret about and fired, expending the bolt uselessly on the skeleton of a tumbled-down heavy-lift crane as his target skittered sideways on humming contra-gravs. Its second shot overloaded Elken's already hard-pressed battlescreens, burning out projector relays and reducing them to a bare flicker of their full potential.

And then the real foe emerged from the dust screen in an explosion of rubble and earth. Elken, Palet, and Sendee together, a single overlapping complex of minds, began traversing back to face the Sky Demon's deadly onslaught. . . .

The other three Charlies lose a precious second in traversing their turrets back to face me as I cross the ridge crest. Charlie Two is directly in front of me and less than fifty meters away, far too close to allow me to depress my main weapon to engage him. As I go nose-down over the crest of the ridge, I accelerate, lurching forward and colliding with the enemy Bolo in full frontal impact.

Driving down and forward, my glacis wedges beneath the prow and left front tracks of Charlie Two, lifting the machine up . . . up . . . then back. The enemy Bolo tries to spin aside, but I have the advantage of leverage and mass. As I hammer at the enemy's exposed ventral surface with 20cm Hellbore bolts, I slue to my left, taking advantage of the enemy's momentum to topple the heavy combat unit over onto its left side. Charlie Four, a kilometer to the south, fires its main gun, and a 200cm Hellbore bolt sears into the upper deck of Charlie Two, which is now serving as an impromptu shield. Charlie Two's aft deck explodes in flame and white heat, as the machine continues to topple onto its back. Returning fire at Charlie Four with my Number Two and Three primary turrets, I thunder over the overturned wreckage of Charlie Two . . .

Elken watched in horror as the Sky Demon slammed into Sendee, lifting her chassis up, twisting it over to the side . . . just as Palet opened fire from the south. The TSDS linkage was confusing; at the same time he saw the enemy Bolo collide with Sendee, he felt the collision himself, felt himself toppling, felt himself as Palet tracking the enemy and firing a fraction of a second too late. . . .

"*Hold fire! Hold fire!*" he shouted over the command link, forgetting in the rush of events crowded into a single fraction of a second that he could cease fire himself rather than giving orders which took too long to process.

Then Palet's main gun slammed a 200cm Hellbore round into Sendee's upper deck just as she overbalanced and rolled. He *felt* her dying, and then the TSDS link was abruptly snapped. . . .

❖   ❖   ❖

I hit Charlie Four with both rounds, one hitting his turret, the second, .07 second later, striking the upper deck just below the main turret housing. The enemy Bolo's battlescreens and internal disrupters fail simultaneously, and follow-up rounds from my port secondaries lance through the upper deck, ripping off the turret and setting off rippling internal explosions.

At the same moment, I hit Charlie One with a 200cm bolt from my Number One turret at a range of 516 meters, targeting the machine's already badly damaged upper works.

I appear to have achieved complete surprise....

The enemy Bolo crashed down over Sendee's inverted hull, sending a double-punch Hellbore volley into Palet's upper deck and turret. Elken was numbed by the rapid-fire barrage, by feeling for himself the deaths, first of Veber, then in rapid succession of Sendee and Palet. As the TSDS linkage evaporated, he was left for a moment feeling very small, exposed and vulnerable ... as though he'd in one swift step moved from giant stature to the size of an ordinary man.

He sent a situational update through the command net.

He scarcely felt it as a 200cm Hellbore bolt smashed into the damaged hull fairings and reactive cladding behind his cratered glacis, dropping his battlescreens, his internal disrupter screen, and blasted several tons of hull armor into vapor.

The Sky Demon's follow-up Hellbore round an instant later speared through his inner shielding to puncture his deep-buried processor pod, and for the *second* time that morning, Elken died in flame and wrenching, nightmare horror....

❖   ❖   ❖

For the moment, my portion of the battlefield is completely quiet. There are no signs of life save the movement of my remotes among the ruins, the lick of crackling flames, and the gentle, skyward drift of black smoke.

I open the communications channel with my Commander, but hear now only the hiss of battlefield static—the magnetic pulse of distant Hellbore fire, the Enemy's attempts at jamming. I consider scanning the sky with high-band radar in order to ascertain the situation but feel it necessary to maintain a low electromagnetic profile here on the surface. To emit radar is to become a very bright target. I will remain in passive mode until the situation is clarified or becomes more urgent.

I do wish I could speak with my Commander, however. I am justifiably proud of my handling of the tactical deployment thus far. Within a few minutes of my arrival at the LZ, I have survived the detonation of three kiloton-range nukes, being entombed in silt, and have then managed to engage and kill eight Mark XXXII Bolos in close combat . . . some of it very close combat indeed. The Mark XXXII is a good combat unit, tough and well-designed, a true predator of the battlefield. The fact that the Enemy seems to be experimenting with anti-Bolo tactics, and learning from his mistakes, is cause for some disquiet. I will have to adapt my own tactics swiftly and remain flexible in order to meet any conceivable change or escalation of the Enemy's tactics if I hope to stay in the war.

Using purely passive means, I scan the sky at all wavelengths and note the flash of explosions at wavelengths consistent with nuclear detonations, relativistic projectiles, and particle beams.

The fight appears to be a desperate one. I wonder who is winning.

✧   ✧   ✧

Streicher had been taking stock of the people on board the command vessel with him. Ramirez, fellow Aristotelian, he trusted completely. Major King, too, had a fair amount of experience. His personnel file mentioned that he'd at least experienced combat as a very junior lieutenant during the Garreth Insurrection, fifteen years ago or so.

The others though. . . .

None of the unit commanders, the lieutenants and single captain, had ever been in a real war before. None of the three batt commanders had been in combat either, though Major Voll had commanded a platoon in the street fighting on Wolveret ten years ago and had a grim sort of almost bitter confidence about her. Captain Meyers had never been anywhere but Supply. Lieutenants Kelsie, Dana, Smeth, and Crowley were all battalion or regimental adjutants and had perhaps twelve years of military experience among them. They would be of no help at all.

In fact, things were looking pretty damned grim. If they were to incorporate Carla's idea of commanding the fight from a Bolo, they'd need to reach one of the combat units and get aboard . . . and large areas of the landscape down there had been contaminated by fallout from the Trixies' rather lavish use of nukes in their planetary defense. There might be some environmental suits on board—there had to be, in fact—but he doubted that they could outfit all seventeen of them in protective surface gear. And there was the vessel's crew to think about as well. How many were on board? He thought the flight crew consisted of six—a pilot/captain, a co-pilot/comm specialist, an engineer/systems officer, and three enlisted ratings, but he wasn't sure.

Twenty-three men and women on the surface of a world turned deadly by NB^2C warfare, and once they were down their safety would be his responsibility. He would need to decide how many would go with him to the new command center—a Bolo's battle center wasn't all that big and would have limited commlink facilities available—and how many would stay behind inside the thin-skinned hull of the grounded command craft. That wouldn't be an easy choice to make. The command craft would be an easy and highly visible target; Streicher knew he'd rather take his chances inside the belly of a Mark XXXIII any day, even if it was going into combat.

"I just wish we could *do* something!" Major Filby said, his voice nearly a wail. "I can't stand this sitting around and waiting!"

"That's the military for you," Major Voll said. "Hurry up and wait. Even for your own execution."

"We're going to die," Lieutenant Kelsie said with grim finality.

Streicher looked at his regimental aide. Danel Kelsie had been in the army for three years, and a student at Greythell Academy on Primus for four years before that. That made him . . . what? Twenty-three standard? He looked painfully young.

And maybe, he thought, *that's why war ended up in the metaphorical hands of Bolos. Until they came along, it was kids like Kelsie who did the fighting and the dying.*

"We might," Streicher admitted. "But you accepted that possibility when you swore your military oath."

"I joined the army to get an education," Kelsie said. "Not *this.* . . ."

"Pull yourself together, son." He had an idea. "I want you for a special assignment, but I can't use you if you're just going to sit there and shiver."

"A-assignment, sir?"

He gathered in the other aides with his eyes. "All

four of you. We need an inventory of what we have on hand for when we land. Weapons. Environmental suits. Rad counters. Portable commo gear. Go through the boat's supply lockers and make a list of what we have. Are you people up to it?"

"Yes, sir," Lieutenant Lara Smeth, the Second Batt aide, said. "We can do that."

"Grab one of the enlisted ratings on the flight deck and get him to show you where the lockers are. Move it, now. We don't have much time." *Two minutes* . . .

"Yes, sir."

"And watch your movements. Microgravity can be tricky."

"Make-work, Colonel?" Major Voll said after the four had swum clear of the couch with ungainly thrashings and made their clumsy way to the bridge entrance.

He shrugged. "If it keeps them from stewing in their own juice until they explode, why not? In any case, we do need that inventory."

"Maybe there's stuff we could do, too," Beswin said. "Something other than just sitting here waiting to burn."

Streicher frowned at that. He'd hustled the kids off so their impatient fear didn't infect the rest . . . but they'd been handling the stress better than some of his battalion commanders.

"Back on Aristotle, I used to do maintenance on K-74 pulsers and heavy vehicle contra-gravs," Ramirez said. "I might be able to lend a hand with the maneuver drive repairs."

"Do it," Streicher said, nodding. She kicked off for the doorway to the bridge, missing almost as badly as Streicher had. "Tell 'em I volunteered you," he called after her as she swung over to the door and palmed herself through. "Anyone else here have experience in repairing drive systems?"

There were no takers. The next few moments passed in silence, as Streicher watched the slow tumble of the astronomical vista outside. The vehicle was turning just fast enough that he could imagine he felt the gentle tug of simulated gravity, now, but they were close enough to the center of rotation that they were still for all intents and purposes weightless. He thought now that maybe his embarrassing miss when he'd aimed for the doorway earlier had been due to the craft's tumble. Maybe he wasn't so rusty at zero-G maneuvers after all. . . .

"How much longer, you think?" Filby asked.

"Keep it to yourself, Major," Streicher told him. "Or I *will* find make-work for you, just to keep you out of my hair." He rubbed his face with his hand, surprised at the perspiration beading there. He wiped it off and watched the droplets of sweat jitter and gleam as they drifted away across the compartment. "Sometimes," he added, almost to himself, "all duty requires of you is that you wait. . . ."

He awoke, stretching . . . and then the fear hit him in deep, shuddering waves, like the icy surf at Gods' Beach. The last thing he remembered . . . no . . . what *was* the last thing he remembered? Memory eluded him, like fragments of a dream.

He opened his eyes, then wondered why he couldn't see. He reached out with a trembling, sweat-slicked hand, then realized he couldn't feel anything, that the tremors, the sweat, the cold were all imagined, anchors for the mind adrift within a vast and lightless void.

Concentrating, he summoned memories from deep, deep within. He'd been in a battle . . . he'd been . . . he'd been a Bolo combat unit, his brain housed in a huge mobile armored vehicle. Vaguely, he was aware of not one, but *two* desperate battles. Before that . . . the memories were still dim, still fragmentary, but there was something about going in for elective surgery . . . a chance at immortality. . . .

What had gone wrong? . . .

Nothing is wrong, a voice, deep and quiet, spoke within the terror-haunted depths of his thoughts. *All is as it should be.* <calm reassurance>

"I can't see," he said, shouting into darkness. "I'm blind!"

You are not blind. Your optical processors are not yet online. <calm reassurance>

The voice of his god! He was not alone after all.

And yet, there was a haunting, fear-rattled undercurrent to the thought, a sense of déjà vu. He was certain he'd had this conversation, this *experience* before.

The memories continued to surface, growing stronger, clearer, more focused. He had been a Bolo, deployed against an invading, enemy Bolo far larger and more powerful than himself. It had been part of an agreement. If he fought the invaders in this new body, helped save Caern from the beings the gods called Sky Demons, he would get the new and immortal body he'd originally longed for.

He'd fought. He'd been . . . terribly hurt. He'd been resurrected . . . and then he'd gone out to fight again.

The last thing he remembered was crossing a ridge . . . no! No, that had been the time before. The last thing he remembered was the gut-wrenching horror as Sendee was levered up and back by the charge of the behemoth Sky Demon Bolo, of her chassis taking the accidental fire from Palet, then toppling over onto its side, then rolling over completely.

Of the enemy Bolo thundering down the slope across her inverted, helpless body.

He could remember the loss of the TSDS network,

of the inner shrinking from godlike gestalt of four intermingled minds to . . . himself, dwindled and shrunken back to mere mortal proportions.

He remembered feeling cut off, remembered expecting his death at any moment, remembered sending a situational update.

And after that . . . nothing. Struggle as he could, he could not remember the moment of his latest death.

As a student monk, following the Way of the Gods, he'd read in the Histories at Paimos of many ways of human belief—of religions and philosophies and ways of life going far back to the Dawn Time, the mythical era when all humans had lived on a single world, now long-lost in the vast reaches of star-mottled space.

There'd been beliefs innumerable about the Afterlife, and what happened to a man's *r'ye* when he died. There was the idea of endless sleep, or that the *r'ye* simply ceased to be . . . or perhaps that it had never been in the first place. There were ideas of eternal reward for good behavior or proper belief in a place of happiness . . . or punishment everlasting for evil works or wrong belief in a place of pain, endless torture, and separation from the gods, a place the Ancients called Hell. For many more, there was a concept of spiritual evolution, of passing from plane to plane in search of growth and betterment of self, with the life in *this* plane merely one step along the way.

And there was a very old idea, one, according to the Histories, that may have arisen during the very earliest mists of human existence, that said that the true self, the *r'ye*, passed from life to life, existence to existence, in a cycle the ancients called reincarnation. Each time you died, you were reborn . . . forgetting at the moment of birth all that had happened to you in previous lives.

Elken felt as though he'd discovered the answer to

the question that had tugged at men's wonderings for millennia. He was trapped in a seemingly endless cycle of birth and rebirth, condemned to come back again and again and again until he got it right.

Or was this, in fact, one of those Hells of the Ancients, a place where he was doomed to fight the same monstrous Bolo in nightmarish rematches throughout the long expanse of all of his tomorrows, fighting, and always losing?

There had to be a way out of this Hell. . . .

Do you understand what went wrong in this past engagement? <concern and keen interest>

"I'm not sure, Lord." He pulled at the scattered memories, teasing them into line. "I feel that we very nearly had it this time. The four of us attacked in close concert, and we were able to use the local terrain to keep all but our turrets concealed from the enemy's return fire. We did not anticipate his use of small, remote combat machines. When they attacked from our rear, we were distracted. Also . . . the TSDS linkage was confusing. In some ways, it slowed our reflexes, I think because we were each having to process four times the information. We were working together all right, but we were also *feeling* together." He remembered again the sensation of Sendee falling onto her back and suppressed an inner shudder. "It was distracting."

So, should we eliminate the TSDS linkage? <thoughtfulness>

"We at least need to find some way to condition ourselves to the odd mingling of data input. We need the close unity of thought and action, but we can't let it slow us down." He thought a moment more. "Lord, there's more. I just get the feeling that we may be up against something we can't match. It feels . . . it feels like my thoughts are faster, more organized—I can't really describe it better than that—but I also get the feeling that we're up against a *machine* of literally inhuman intelligence, speed, and . . . and coldness. Maybe we're overmatched. Maybe we can never win."

Is our world, our civilization, then, doomed? <sadness for what might have been>

"I didn't say that, Lord. But we have to find another way to do this.

"We have to find a way out of Hell. . . ."

Chapter Ten

The fight has been much more intense, more diffi-cult than predicted in initial assessments, but the situ-ation appears to be well in hand. The most serious problem encountered thus far is the Aetryx predilec-tion for using tactical nuclear weapons in a recklessly indiscriminate manner. Blast and thermal effects have turned many of the Caernan cities along this portion of the coast into rubble, and radioactive fallout has contaminated vast reaches of the landscape. While these conditions will not significantly hamper my operations on Caern, they will considerably magnify the difficulty that human forces will face when they arrive with the second wave.

With no immediate threats apparent, I concentrate on collecting combat reports from other members of the regiment.

Invictus reports that the planetary defense bastion at Dolendi has been reduced after fierce fighting among the ruins. Ferox has landed safely at Kanth and reports little in the way of enemy activity. A fortress and a supply depot there appear to have been abandoned. Third Battalion has landed at the base of the Eloma Peninsula just south of Losethal. Terribilis is moving into Losethal proper, while Fortis strikes out southeast, toward Paimos. Both report heavy but ineffectual resistance—infantry and heavy armor, but nothing a match for a Bolo combat unit. I wonder why I have encountered the only enemy Bolos thus far. Is the Enemy holding back for a major offensive later?

I again attempt to establish contact with Space Strike Command. I pick up some disjointed and heavily jammed communications from several vessels but cannot raise either the fleet flagship or the 4th Regimental Command Craft.

The communications fragments, those I can decode and reconstruct, are disturbing.

"Ranger three! Ranger three! Bogies coming in on your tail!"

"All units. Rally in Sector seven-five-five by nine-one-four by one-three-two."

"Veloceras reporting. Stardrives are out. We're not going anywhere. . . ."

"Emynian has been hit! I say again, Emynian is hit!"

"God in heaven, look at her burn! . . ."

"We need to stop those gunboats! The KKMs are killing us! . . ."

It does not sound as though the fighting in near-planetary space is going well. I must face the possibility that I and my fellow combat units may soon be on our own, with no hope of orbital support or reinforcement.

I elect to use a narrow-band search radar in brief bursts of no more than .01 second each to attempt to locate Heritas, Denever or the 4th Regimental Command Craft. I detect large amounts of wreckage, much of it falling toward the surface and deduce that several capital ships have been destroyed already. I cannot tag the IFF beacons for Heritas or Denever and fear they may be lost. I do, however, locate the command craft, which appears to be damaged and falling toward

Caern. I estimate it will enter the planet's atmosphere within the next two minutes. Since its communications appear to be out, I have no means of determining whether or not those on board are still alive.

As I expected, the main body of the enemy fleet is still well beyond even the range of my primary Hellbores. Several enemy fighters are within range, but my attacking them will do little good strategically and may impair my own mission by calling unwanted attention to my position. I decide to wait before intervening in the space battle, at least until I can coordinate with the other Bolos of my regiment.

A bright meteor streaks through the predawn sky overhead, followed by another, two more . . . and then a shower of them; I count thirty-two within the next five seconds. Debris from the battle is already beginning to enter Caern's atmosphere and burn up from the friction of entry.

My Commander, my Battalion CO, the regimental commander, and other senior staff personnel will face the same threat very soon, if any are alive now in that tumbling hulk.

And there is nothing I can bring to bear that will help them.

In some ways, Streicher thought, technology had complicated things. With contra-gravity, you didn't need to park warships or communications relays in orbit. You could balance them against the planet's gravitational pull on phase-projected CG waveforms and not worry about losing line-of-sight with a point on the surface when you passed over the horizon.

But relying on fallible technology rather than infallible physics carried a risk. When the CG projectors went off-line, you fell, because you weren't moving at orbital velocity.

Streicher's cranial implants included a tiny math coprocessor that, among other things, let him picture in his mind a math problem and have the answer come back to him, in his thoughts. He pictured the problem—and could see in his mind the equations as they stroked the numbers and turned them into life . . . or death. Beginning at a relative speed of zero, five hundred kilometers above the atmosphere, $s = s_0 + v_0 t + \frac{1}{2}at^2$, what mathematicians would call trivial. Streicher had always had trouble with math and knew he would be lost without his implant.

Time equals the square root of $(2 \cdot 500 \cdot 1000 / \text{acceleration})$, which for Caern was $.74g$ . . . and as the numbers filed through his thoughts, he saw the result: 368 seconds.

Six minutes, eight seconds, to fall five hundred kilometers.

How fast would they be traveling at the end of that time? They'd been motionless with respect to Caern's surface at the beginning, so it became another of those trivial problems: $v = v_0 + at$, with velocity equal to 7.4 meters/second $\cdot$ 368 seconds equals 2723 m/s.

When they began hitting the upper reaches of Caern's atmosphere, they would be traveling at 2.7 kilometers per second. Streicher was surprised. He'd not realized that a steady .74 gravities would build up that much velocity in that short a time.

If they'd been in orbit, the disabling of the command craft's drives wouldn't have been a major problem . . . at least, not an *immediate* problem. The complications of applied technology.

Hell, he wished now he hadn't run the numbers through his implant. There was another case of too much technology for one's own good . . . or at least for his peace of mind.

Not that not knowing would have been that much

easier. He had only to look at the now-restored panorama on the compartment's circular walls to see how Caern had begun expanding with breathtaking speed, until it completely filled an entire half of the encircling sky, and the silver-gold curve of its sunward horizon was rapidly flattening itself toward a straight line.

I need another euph. Damn it, he'd just had one a little while ago, but it was almost as though the little blue tablet hadn't worked at all. It hadn't cut the pain of his thoughts of Aristotle.

How much longer? The coprocessor also acted as timekeeper, and the answer surfaced in his thoughts almost without his thinking about it. Five minutes thirty-four seconds since they'd begun their fall.

Which meant they were now less than a hundred kilometers up, plummeting through ever-thickening wisps of the planet's atmosphere. He could imagine the outer hull already beginning to warm, imagine he heard the first faint hiss of tenuous winds grasping at the crippled saucer's form as it continued its slow tumble.

A definite shudder rumbled through the craft's hull, and he heard metal creak. A pen adrift from someone's pocket drifted in a slow curve until it hit a bulkhead, bounced slowly, then clung there. Someone in the circle—he thought it was Filby—whimpered.

Streicher was envious of Carla. At least she would be doing something, wrestling with emergency repairs to the drives, struggling to cheat the Fates, *fighting*, when the end came.

He knew there wasn't enough time to complete those repairs.

Another shudder . . . and then a third, accompanied now by a distant thunder from outside. The pen on the wall dropped to the deck with a clatter as the falling craft's pitch changed sharply. The viewscreens appeared to be hazing over a bit. *Not much longer, now . . .*

I continue to probe near-planetary space with short bursts of high-energy radar. The picture I am assembling is not good.

An enemy fleet, evidently, either dropped into the system out of hyper at very close range or has been hiding somewhere—my guess would be within the atmosphere of the gas giant Dis, using contra-gravity to counteract the planet's strong gravitational pull. Had they emerged from hyperspace, they would have needed to do so considerably farther out in this system's gravity well, and the Confederation forces would have had ample warning of their approach.

As it is, their surprise appears to have been nearly perfect. I estimate that no fewer than nine Confederation vessels have been destroyed, based on the amount of debris present and by backtracking the trajectories of the major fragments.

The other ships are accelerating clear of Caern, now. Fifteen vessels are well beyond Dis and its moon system and appear to be preparing to enter hyper. Others are scattered throughout near space. The Enemy's victory in space appears complete.

Enemy fighters are decelerating now a few hundred kilometers above the surface of Caern. Two, I notice, are maneuvering to take out a communications relay satellite orbited by the Confederation fleet. Two more are entering the planet's atmosphere. I project their trajectories and discover they are on an intercept with the 4th Regimental Command Craft, now falling almost directly overhead at an altitude of 90 kilometers.

I turn my primary turrets One and Two, traversing to 095 and elevating to 78 degrees. I fire, and the Hellbore bolt catches the lead fighter like an insect in a blowtorch, disintegrating it utterly. My second shot .15 second later hits the second fighter, with identical results.

I continue to track the command vessel's descent, weapons ready to vaporize any enemy asset that poses a threat.

My efforts are almost certainly in vain, however. They appear to be in uncontrolled free fall and are doomed either to burn up in the atmosphere or impact on the surface within the next few minutes. . . .

And then gravity reasserted itself with a vengeance, a hard, wracking, rumbling vibration that filled the ship, and a sudden weight pressing down on Streicher from toes to face. They must be decelerating now at . . . what? A couple of gravities, maybe, as they began to encounter serious friction from Caern's atmosphere.

But the weight pressing Streicher down into the couch continued to build, as though three or four people were lying squarely on top of his body. Filby screamed . . . Voll cursed . . . but Streicher felt an almost peaceful inner quiet. He didn't want to die, not yet . . . but there were ghosts that had haunted him since the scorching of Aristotle, and he was realizing only now that it would be good never to have to face them again.

He felt so heavy now he couldn't move. All he could do was stare up at the compartment's ceiling. His vision was contracting, with a blood-shot darkness closing in from the periphery of his field of view. It was definitely warmer in here now, as the haze outside thickened to a glowing orange-pink curtain permitting only brief glimpses of the horizon beyond. Their tumble appeared to have stabilized, with *down* toward the deck.

Odd. He hadn't expected the decelerative forces to be *this* strong. . . .

"Okay, people!" Carla Ramirez's voice called over a speaker. "We have at least partial maneuvering power, enough to give us a chance! Hang on, and if you know any good prayers, say 'em!"

Prayers? Eudaimonics had little to do with deities, though some practitioners acknowledged a kind of overall cosmic god of bounty, blessing, and luck. That was it. Obviously the people on the bridge had jiggered something together that might give them a chance. What they needed now was luck, and lots of it.

What was that old saying? There were no atheists in foxholes.

The weight began to leave him again. They were slowing, though the orange-pink haze in the viewscreens hadn't thinned much if at all. The heat inside the compartment was stifling, but it didn't seem to be getting any worse, at least for the moment. Streicher's uniform was drenched with sweat, and he wished he could at least remove his tunic, but they were still descending at a couple of gravities at least. After that peak acceleration a few moments before, he felt too battered and bruised to try anything as strenuous as sitting up.

The haze cleared. They were descending through a sky of deep ultramarine. At this altitude, the sun was still visible just above the gold and silver bow of Dis. Caern's seas spread out in the near-darkness below, enormous circular bites taken out of rugged land. He could see now directly the pinpoints of burning cities, see the flicker and flash of combat still going on.

The view was not half so spectacular as the singular realization: *they were going to live after all!* . . .

The falling command craft appears to have righted itself, and its decelerative vector appears greater than can be explained by friction with the upper atmosphere.

I surmise that either repairs have been effected, or the pilot was using extreme maneuvers to fool enemy fighters into thinking the craft was a dead piece of debris. If the latter, the ruse was not entirely successful, since some, at least, of the Caernan fighters were attempting to close with the crippled vessel.

It looks as though the command craft's main drives are out of action, and the pilot is attempting a landing using maneuvering thrusters alone. The maneuver is a dangerous one, especially if the repairs are jury-rigged and less than robust. Still, the fact that people remain alive on the vessel is encouraging. I mount guard, scanning the skies in all directions, ready to thwart any further attempts to attack the falling vessel. To do so, I open my radar transmissions to full aperture and power. This will attract unwanted attention, but the risk is worth it.

My Commander may yet survive this.

Streicher found he could sit up after all. His weight at last returned to normal, then dropped a bit more, until he weighed about three quarters of what he was used to in a standard G-field.

Carla came in through the bridge door, looking tired and battered, but radiant. "We did it, Colonel! I found a circuit module that fried with the power surge when they hit us."

"*You* found it?"

She shrugged as if in modesty, but her eyes were gleaming. "Told you I used to work on K-74s. They use the same microcircuit boards—ten-twenty-one-fourteens—that these command craft use for balancing the maneuver thrusters. Damned things *always* burn out when the CG system goes, so it wasn't like I didn't know what to look for!"

"Have a seat. You look fragged."

"Comes from lying on the deck at seven gravities, instead of in a nice, cozy acceleration couch." She lowered herself into her seat. She was favoring her right arm, Streicher noticed. They would have to check that, once they were down. He wondered how the aides had fared during entry.

"This . . . this means we're going to make it?" Filby asked.

"It means we have a fair chance of touching down more or less gently anywhere we want," Carla told him. "Maneuver thrusters weren't meant for flying, but they've given us enough control over our descent that Lieutenant Cavese ought to be able to jockey us in for a more or less gentle skid-landing someplace. We need to tell him where."

"Someplace flat," Streicher said. "And close to one of our Bolos."

"We need to reestablish contact with the regiment," Jaime Bucklin pointed out. "It would be best if we didn't come down in the middle of a firefight."

"I'm appointing you regimental communications officer," Streicher told him. He needed something to do, now that his Bolo was gone, shot down before it had even reached the surface. "Get on it."

"Yes, *sir*."

They'd been out of the war—out of the real war down there on the surface—for over eight minutes, now, an eternity when it came to combat . . . or to the superhuman speeds at which Bolo combat units thought and acted.

Almost anything could have happened down there. They needed to get back in touch and find out what.

He wondered if he dared slip away to his locker below decks and crunch another euph.

❖   ❖   ❖

The 4th Regimental command craft is coming down now in a series of loops and twists and turns obviously designed to bleed off speed. With the main drives out of action, only maneuvers such as these can reduce the craft's velocity in order to allow a reasonably gentle landing.

"Thunderstrike, Thunderstrike, this is Cloudtop. Do you copy?"

It is the voice of Lieutenant Bucklin. Communications have been reestablished.

"This is Bolo of the Line 837986, Victor," I reply. *Thunderstrike is the tactical codename for 4th Regiment; Cloudtop the code for Space Strike HQ.* "I have your vehicle in sight and am providing covering fire." *Ten thousand kilometers out in space, an enemy fighter is entering a trajectory which, I calculate, could bring it into the atmosphere in my general vicinity. I fire a Hellbore and hear the momentary burst of static hissing over the communications channel.*

"Very good, ah, Victor. We need to get this thing down in one piece. Can you assist us?"

"Affirmative." *I consider the situation, checking data from my far-flung BIST remotes.* "There is a flat stretch of open ground—sand dunes, marsh, and open grassland—ten kilometers west of my current position. I can guide you in for a landing there."

"Is the LZ hot, Victor?"

"Negative. Enemy forces have been suppressed, though they have been emerging at random intervals from underground tunnels. The open ground to the west is well clear of artificial structures, however, and is not likely to mask underground shelters. The main threat will be from air-space fighters, and I will have no trouble keeping those at bay."

"Sounds good, Victor. We'll see you in another ten minutes or so."

"I will move to the landing zone and be awaiting your arrival."

"Roger that, Vic. Cloudtop out."

I begin transiting the ruins, making my way to the newly designated LZ. I am pleased to be able to help but am worried as well.

The planetary beachhead is still tenuous in the extreme, and the surface battlefield a poor environment for unprotected humans. With some areas now contaminated by highly lethal radiation, and the probability of further enemy counterstrikes, it will be extremely difficult to provide adequate protection.

And harder still to provide such protection while simultaneously carrying out my mission objectives.

The kids had returned to the sim deck a few moments after Carla's grand entrance, not too much the worse for wear after the high-G trauma of atmospheric entry. They'd not had time to complete a full inventory, but they reported that there were ten Model 48 E-suits available in the command craft's storage lockers.

It would have to do.

Full sim-linkage was restored moments before the command craft made its final velocity-killing turn and arrowed in toward the grassy plain identified by Victor. The command craft banked above a ruined city the ship AI identified as Kanth, then began descending in a long, flat glide toward the northwest.

Streicher had been watching through the viewscreens, but he could see more linking into the data feed from the landing approach optical feed from the bridge. The walls of the ship became invisible, and he was flying unaided across the darkly shadowed land.

East, the suns were just beginning to rise above the vast, dark dome of Dis, its globe bisected by the eastern horizon. High-level clouds were catching the morning sun in golds and pinks and oranges, though the ground itself was still deeply shadowed. Ahead, he could see Ghendai; it looked like the thermal pulse from a Trixie nuke had set fire to the center of the city. Most of the buildings had been flattened in the center of the city and toward the west and north, and he could actually see a broad, savagely churned path leading up out of the sea, across a low cliff, and into the northwestern outskirts of Ghendai that must have been the path left by Victor when he came ashore. A large, burned-over area of right-angled ruins to the north was probably what remained of the storage depot and C^3 facility that had been Victor's primary objective.

It looked like Victor had shot the hell out of the place. Streicher didn't see a single building, communications tower, or gun platform still standing. A crater near the center, still steaming, marked where the orbital bombardment had dropped a fair-sized slug of depleted uranium with a yield of a few kilotons or so, but the place had been worked over very thoroughly since then, leaving an eerie, cratered-moon appearance, like the two-dimensional photos he'd seen once of the region called "no-man's land" between the trenches of an ancient, prespaceflight war on old Earth. There were places where whole hectares of ferrocrete paving had simply been obliterated, replaced by broken stretches of plowed-up dirt, deep craters filling with water from underground pipes, and only the odd twist of an obliterated building's internal skeleton to show that humans had ever built here.

The scene reminded him forcefully of Aristotle, of the way New Athens had looked as he'd passed over in the *Alexander's* shuttle. The memories of that return to his homeworld surfaced vividly and horrifically. He had to bite down hard to force back the bile rising in his throat.

And then the command craft had passed the ruined military base and was descending low above an open plain. "Brace yourselves, everybody," Lieutenant Cavese said over the linkcomm. "Off-link and snug in tight. This is going to be rough!"

Streicher cut the simulation feed, opening his eyes to the stifling interior of the command deck. The compartment was like an oven after the entry maneuvers, and Streicher's uniform was now sodden with sweat. He began checking his harness, tightening self-lock buckles, as other members of the command staff emerged from the sim and began doing the same. No one spoke. Likely they'd been silenced by their flyover of the Caern military base. They'd all seen it, of course, earlier, from space, but the low pass they'd just experienced had an immediacy of detail and emotional impact that long-range data feeds from high-altitude remotes and BIST data simply didn't provide.

For a long moment, they sat there in silence, waiting . . . waiting . . .

And then a jarring crash grated through the deck, and they were thrown back and forth against their seat harnesses. For a handful of bone-rattling seconds, the command craft scraped and bumped and violently shook as it plowed across the field, and then the deck yawed sharply and the craft came to rest with a final, tooth-loosening jolt that killed the lights and the viewscreens.

For a moment, no one said a word in the steamy darkness. Even the emergency lighting was out, which meant the ship had been pretty badly torn up. The sim deck was intact, however, and that was something.

"Thank God!" someone muttered. "We're down!"

"Anyone hurt?" Streicher asked the darkness. "Any injuries?"

"Some bruises," King said. "Nothing serious." Other voices chimed in with battered agreement.

"Any landing you walk away from," Major Voll said, "is a good one."

With that, they began unbuckling. "Everyone stay in your seat until we get some light in here," Streicher ordered. "Lieutenant O'Hara. You were closest to the main hatch. See if you can make it to the bulkhead and use the manual controls to open the inner door."

"Yes, sir."

"Watch yourself." The deck, he estimated, was canted at about a thirty-degree angle. He wanted one person at a time moving around in the darkness. Footing was going to be treacherous.

The main hatch opened through an airlock; the lock's outer door, he remembered, had a small porthole in it. With the inner door open, a little light might filter through to the ink-blackness that filled the downed vessel now. He heard Shauna O'Hara scrambling across the tilted deck, heard her fumbling for the manual override access. A moment later, the door squeaked open as Shauna turned the recessed manual control, and a trace of light spilled through from the slowly brightening sky outside, enough that they could see one another again, at least. They began clambering out of the couch.

The bridge hatch cranked slowly open, and several crew personnel entered, Lieutenant Cavese in the lead with a hand flash. "Everybody okay back here?"

"As well as can be expected. Nice landing, Lieutenant."

"First time I ever tried it without a spaceport to touch down on. Not too shabby if I say so myself." He flicked the flash beam about the compartment. "We need to start moving out of here. This ship will be a target."

"As ranking officer on the ground," Streicher said, "I'm taking command. We have a combat unit on the ground outside who will provide cover . . . and we only have ten E-suits."

"The air reads okay, Colonel," Cavese said. "And the background rads are low in this area. We won't need suits."

"That's good, but a battlefield is still a remarkably unhealthy place for flesh and blood. There are other things out there to kill unprotected humans besides radiation. I recommend you stay with your ship while I and some of my people establish direct contact with our Bolo."

"Very well." Streicher heard the tightness in Cavese's voice and knew the order wasn't exactly appreciated . . . but the man had sense enough to keep his gripes to himself. Good.

"Okay. This is Kelly's unit, so you just volunteered."

"Yes, sir." She sounded excited.

"Carla? I want you along too. Check and see what we have in the way of hand weapons."

"Right, Colonel."

"One more . . . Lieutenant Bucklin?"

"Yes, sir."

"Shouldn't you stay here and let us do the recon?" Ramirez said.

"Negative. I want to see things for myself. Major Voll? You're in command while I'm gone."

"Yes, sir."

"Okay. Kelsie? Break out four of those suits. Let's get moving."

Because Cavese was right. Their landing, hard as it was, would have been noticed. And it wouldn't be long before the enemy decided to do something about it.

One thing was needful, though, while the others were getting their gear together.

He needed to get below, find a flash, and get to his locker.

He needed another euph, needed it bad. Needed it to stop the tremble in his hands, stop the sweating, help him focus, help him *cope*.

Just one more. It wouldn't hurt.

He awoke, stretching . . . and then the fear hit him in deep, shuddering waves, like the icy surf at Gods' Beach. The last thing he remembered . . . no . . . what *was* the last thing he remembered? Memory eluded him, like fragments of a dream.

Elken opened his eyes, and this time he could see immediately. He was no longer embodied within the armored-mountain hulk of a Bolo! But . . . but he hadn't been destroyed that he could remember, hadn't even gone out for another try at the Sky Demon Bolos, nor had he completed his part of the bargain that would give him the long-cherished shot at immortality. What was going on?

He reached out with a trembling hand . . . and it was a trembling hand, but not his own. The appendage he saw before his blinking eyes was human in shape, but massive, powerfully muscled, and covered with a supple layer of green-gold scales.

We are trying something a little different, this time, the god's voice whispered in his mind. *You have been downloaded to a different body. A warrior body.* <proud achievement>

Rising slowly, he found he was lying on a couch of sorts, with a helmet on his head trailing bundles of black wires and cables. He was in a room, high-ceilinged, dimly lit, with machinery of various descriptions humming behind armor-shielded pylons and inside the walls themselves. A technician, a human, helped him remove the helmet; she seemed a little hesitant to approach him. When he looked past her at a different tech helping another form sit up on its couch, he saw why.

A warrior-soma. A troll, armored and fanged, with large red eyes deeply recessed beneath the jutting brow that supported the weight of two up-curved horns. No one really liked them, the idea of them . . . but they'd been created by the gods and had their place within a properly functioning society. *A place for everything, everything in its place . . .*

The other soma massed perhaps three times what a normal human massed, standing a third again taller, with legs like tree trunks to bear the extra weight. The muscles were powerful and faster reacting than human, the eyes designed to see in near-darkness, the chest and throat and back thickened with extra armor, like leather toughened into something as hard as bony plate. There were other improvements to the original human genome as well—an extra heart in reserve, key arteries embedded in leathery internal armor, retractable claws, a skeleton that used iron, tin, and hafnium as well as calcium, other changes too numerous to mention.

He looked down at his hands again, turning them over as he examined the leathery skin and claw tips. He was a monster. . . .

Not a monster. <reproving> *A highly potent, carefully designed warrior.*

"But . . . why? I was just getting the hang of being a Bolo." The sound of his own voice surprised him. It was deeper, raspier, with an unpleasant gargle behind it.

There are tasks beyond the brute-force capability of a Bolo combat unit. <patient explanation> *Capturing a crashed spacecraft, rather than obliterating it, is one.*

"A ship? A Sky Demon ship?"

It made a forced landing close to the area where you had your previous encounters. There may be personnel still alive on board. Our intelligence indicates that it is a type of command-control craft. Any survivors may provide useful information under interrogation.

"Prisoners!"

Exactly. You will lead the combat team that will secure them. <confidence>

His troll hands closed into hard-muscled fists.

It would be good to come to grips, face-to-face, with the *real* enemy at last. . . .

Chapter Eleven

I remain a half kilometer distant from the downed space craft. Portions of my outer hull have retained some radioactivity from the contaminated battle zones through which I've passed recently, and others are radiating thermal energy at levels that would be dangerous to unprotected humans at close quarters.

I have taken the liberty of vectoring the flight of WR-5 Warlocks back to this area. They are circling overhead now, helping to maintain a close watch for enemy ground or air forces. I have also deployed both my Wyverns and Dragons in a broader perimeter about the area, in order to maintain a careful guard, most especially against sallies by enemy armor. The current lull in the battle is suspicious. It is possible the Enemy is planning a counterstroke, and I need to remain flexible to deal with any potential threat to my mission, my Commander and other staff officers, or myself.

Sensors indicate life within the grounded spacecraft.

As the first light of daybreak gleams from the crescent of Dis on the eastern horizon, I await their emergence.

Streicher stooped to angle his tall frame through the open hatch, then dropped the half meter to the ground in an easy jump. The military-issue E-suit was a flexible black skin snugged tight to his body, with a fishbowl helmet that provided limited low-light resolution and magnification through smart transplas crystals embedded in the plastic. His backpack would continue purifying air pulled in through external filters indefinitely . . . or give him a good six hours if the outside air was so hot or poisonous his suit couldn't handle it.

The suns were a pair of dazzling points of light just above the silver bow of Dis. At this longitude, the gas giant was squarely bisected by the horizon, though libration—the slow rocking back and forth or nodding due to tidal effects as it swung around its primary— would cause the giant world to seem to rise and fall somewhat over the course of the four-day diurnal period. The sky was gorgeous, aglow with luminescent clouds, though the crystalline blue and gold were stained by red-black smoke rising to the south.

That blue . . . so much like the blue color of euph.

He'd taken a second tab before suiting up and tucked a third into an inner pouch. The rest, his last fifteen tabs, he'd left in his locker, where they'd be safe. He would have to make them last until they found a way off this rock.

And if they were stuck here, well . . . it didn't matter. He knew he could kick the euph-thirst any time he really wanted to. It was just that they helped him get through the rough times with the bad memories, the bad dreams. They took the edge off the depression, helped him see the world a little more clearly.

He could get along without them, anytime he wanted.

Such a glorious blue sky. The burning city reminded him of something . . . something he didn't want to think about right now. . . .

Then he turned as he emerged from beneath and behind the ECD craft, and his attention was snapped up almost at once by something much nearer, much more demanding on his senses than a burning city. The Bolo was squatting five hundred meters away, its crater-scarred glacis rising like a steeply slanted black cliff, its body so long and so high that it actually seemed to recede into the haze.

It was not the biggest man-made object Streicher had ever seen. Starships were considerably larger. However, you rarely saw them this way, up close and from the outside, with ground and a horizon and a sky to put things into perspective. Some buildings were larger, but they tended to be in the hearts of cities, with the skyward reach of other buildings competing with them for the viewer's eye.

He found himself looking up and gaping like a rubber-necked tourist on Primus. The monster machine was twenty-five meters high, its hull all angles and teardrop-blisters and elegant curves, but torn and gashed in places by heavy-caliber rounds, particle beams, and Hellbore fusion bolts. Some of the deeper gouges in its frontal armor were actually glowing a sullen, deep red.

And it was huge. The Bolo looked lots bigger even than the pod he'd examined in the cargo bay on board the *Heritas*.

"Uh . . . Victor?" He said. Then he remembered. "Sorry. Thunderstrike, this is Cloudtop."

Cloudtop was one of the more ironic radio handles he'd heard used in recent history.

"Cloudtop, Thunderstrike," Victor's deep, mellifluous voice replied instantly. "I read you."

It was difficult hearing the voice in his helmet phones and connecting it with that slab-sided mountain in front of him.

"I'm glad you made it down safely," the voice added.

"Um, thank you, Victor. We got jumped by an enemy fighter. We were lucky to get enough maneuvering control back that we could soft-land."

Not that the landing had been all that *soft*. The command craft lay behind him, one rim of the saucer angled thirty degrees into the sky, the opposite rim crumpled, torn, and jammed into the ground. A gouge in the earth like a plow track leading back toward the southeast showed the path they'd followed coming in. Streicher checked the entire surrounding horizon. Someone was likely to be coming to investigate the crash.

"I have taken the liberty," Victor said, "of securing the perimeter against enemy encroachments on the crash site. However, I recommend that we get all survivors away from this area as quickly as possible."

"Affirmative," Streicher replied. "We need to work up some long-range plans, too. The Invasion Fleet has been scattered by a surprise enemy space attack. The second wave won't be coming down."

"I had already assumed as much," Victor said. "Radar and lidar probes of circum-Caernan space indicate a number of friendly vessels destroyed and the rest in full retreat or already escaped into hyper. We are on our own now."

Streicher thought about this for a moment. "Do we have any alternative," he asked slowly, "other than surrender?"

"I have been discussing this with my Commander as we speak, Colonel," Victor said.

Streicher was surprised. He'd never thought of the Bolo being capable of talking to different people on different channels at the same time. The machine's AI, however, was partly the result of truly massive parallel processing through hyper-redundant molecular circuitry, and there was no reason why it shouldn't be able to pay full attention to numerous simultaneous conversations.

"There are several options besides the unpleasant one of surrender," Victor went on. "At this point, we are in an excellent position planet-wide in terms of having suppressed or destroyed Enemy activity, at least on the planet's surface. Our long-term prospects appear bleak, since with the fleet's dismemberment, we are now sharply limited in our available stores of various consumables—food for you, expendable munitions for myself and the other Bolo combat units. Still, it may be possible to force a decision in our favor in the short-term, by identifying and seizing key enemy assets he is not willing or able to yield."

"What assets? His bases have been obliterated . . . all the ones I'm aware of, anyway."

"His surface bases have been obliterated. There is evidence of extensive underground complexes, however, which seem to be sheltering the majority both of the enemy's military presence on Caern and of the Caernan civilian population, both human and Aetryx."

"So . . . you're saying we go down there and hold Caern's civilian population as hostage?" The thought was a distasteful one, not one that Streicher was willing to countenance. What, though, were the ethics of a Mark XXXIII combat unit in such matters? Bolos had ethics, remarkably strong ones. But sometimes they were skewed a bit from the human point of view.

"A possible course of action, but unlikely to be fruitful from our perspective," Victor said. "According to intelligence downloaded prior to drop, the Aetryx are the complete masters of this world, with the human population existing as second-class citizens in many respects. The Aetryx might consider their human slaves expendable. In any case, our mission operational parameters call for rescuing the captive human population, not using it as a bargaining chip."

"Agreed."

"But there must be other possible subsurface targets of importance to the Aetryx, including staging and supply areas, power plants, manufacturing centers, and mines. The Aetryx appear singularly willing to sacrifice all or most of the surface of this world in its defense. It follows that certain underground facilities will be more highly valued."

"Can you find such targets? Can you even reach them?"

"We know empirically that Bolo Mark XXXIIs have been moving about below ground as they maneuver to attack surface targets. Though I am considerably larger than that mark, I should be able to gain access to most tunnels used by the Mark XXXII."

"We'll need to coordinate all Bolo operations," Streicher said. "Work out a plan they all can apply."

"Of course."

Streicher had the feeling he was lecturing a master on his own ground. Perhaps this would be a good place, he thought, to leave the fine points of the planning and strategy to those who best knew the topic. A high-mark Bolo knew more about strategy and tactics than a mere regimental commander ever would.

He continued to study the surrounding terrain, etched with long shadows just now appearing from the slow, bright sunrise in the east. The sun was bisected by the curve of Dis six degrees above the horizon. The light was bright enough now that the sweeping arch of the gas giant's rings were invisible, and Dis itself was a pale half-circle only slightly darker than the background sky.

A breeze was blowing from the sea, and Streicher wished he could remove his helmet to taste it. Except

for the smoke in the south, the landscape was bucoli-
cally peaceful. A lot like Aristotle, in fact . . .

He squelched that line of thought at once. He
needed to keep his edge and not slip away into
depression again.

He didn't put much hope in the Bolo's notion of
finding some way of ending the war other than surrender. After all, Bolos were programmed to maintain
that blood-deadly optimism in their thoughts and planning. Still, it wouldn't do to just wait around for the
Trixies to get organized and come pick them up. Better
by far to *do* something.

"Victor?"

"Yes, Colonel."

"We need to come on board. We need access to your
battle command center."

"I understand. One moment, please."

If the sight of the Mark XXXIII Bolo towering
above the plain was awe-inspiring, the sight of that
titanic monster delicately spinning in place was more
so. There were three sets of tracks, each set itself
doubled, on either side. The port-side tracks advanced
while the starboard side went into reverse, and the
entire 120-meter-long behemoth rotated to its right.
The maneuver looked light-footed enough, but the
gouge it tore into the field was over a meter deep,
and soil, rock, and clods of grass were flying everywhere.

Then the rear portion of the Bolo was facing him,
a vertical wall heavily encrusted by dried mud, plate
armor, antenna housings, heat vents, and power field
projection sponsons. An armored panel slid aside,
exposing a man-sized hatch, almost invisibly tiny against
that 38-meter-wide bulk. The hatch slid open, spilling
a hot, bright inner illumination into the cooler light
of early morning. A ramp extended to the ground.

"Carla?" He called. "That's our invitation. Let's get on board."

"Right, boss. C'mon, people! You heard the colonel. Let's get out of the open!"

Together, the four trudged into the Bolo's black shadow toward the waiting hatch. Coolant steam hissed from vents to either side of the hatch in billowing clouds. As they approached, Streicher was aware of several AP turrets pivoting on the hull to track them— automated antipersonnel defense pods designed to keep hostile infantry and tank-killer robots at a safe distance. At the same time, a pair of small camera eyes followed their every step. Unauthorized personnel, of course, were allowed nowhere near the access hatches to a functional Bolo; if a dozen different code responses from their suits and cranial implants weren't perfect, or if the cameras spotted anything amiss, they would be stopped and held at gunpoint—or killed outright.

Streicher stopped at the hatch as the other three clambered up the ramp and ducked inside. "Major Voll?"

"On channel, Colonel."

"We're going inside Victor. I suggest you go ahead and start rotating a couple of sentries outside the ship, two-hour stints. Conditions seem safe enough, and Victor can certainly handle any conceivable threat, but we need everyone to start getting acclimated to the great out-of-doors down here. Everybody is on rotation, senior officers and ship's personnel as well."

"I concur, Colonel. I was going to suggest it."

"Good. I'll stay in touch, thirty-minute intervals. Streicher out."

Inside, the main passageway was a narrow, squared-off tube leading in and up, twisting past the massive service access panels to the Bolo's twin fusion plants and primary accumulators, through layer after layer of armor, and through at last the buzzing-insect tingle and blue-static flashes of its internal disrupter field and into the very heart of the machine.

Inside the command center, the four pulled off helmets and gloves as Victor powered up the instrumentation, which was there solely for human benefit. At the center of the compartment was the only seat, the reclining, heavily padded command chair in the center of a ring of curving holographic viewscreens that gave the operator a 360-degree panorama all around the Bolo's exterior. Those screens had been switched off when Streicher had been here last, just before the Bolo landing pods had disembarked. They were on, now, showing a true-as-life image of the surroundings, including the sharply canted saucer to their rear, and the smoke from Ghendai ahead and to their right.

Kelly Tyler had already taken the command seat. Streicher suppressed an immediate urge to order her out of his seat. She, after all, was this Bolo's commander. It was her privilege and her responsibility.

"Give me a full status report, Vic," she was saying. "Implant and screen only. I don't need hardcopy or voice."

"As you wish, my Commander," the Bolo's voice responded, melodious and deep, emerging, somehow, from all around them.

Streicher stood next to Ramirez and Bucklin, feeling suddenly awkward and clumsy, like an out-of-place teenager. There was nothing for him to *do* here but be in the way, or to stand around with his thumb in his ear, wondering what to do next.

At least not until after Lieutenant Tyler had completed the preliminaries.

He could see the flicker of data as Victor began scrolling his status down one of the big holograph screens. *Time to see just how bad things are,* he thought.

❖   ❖   ❖

"Just how bad *are* things up there?" Elken asked.

The situation is stable and relatively quiet in this sector. <cool confidence> *The fighting continues elsewhere. We have suffered severe damage to the infrastructure on the surface, but the cities are easily rebuilt. The Sky Demon fleet has been utterly destroyed. Now we need only annihilate the last of the invaders actually on our soil.*

"And you think we can do that ourselves?"

He was seated with twenty-three other warrior somas in a combat ready room deep underground. Technicians and assistants were finishing the last connections and hook-ups to the team's armor.

Even warrior somas, Elken knew, wouldn't survive long on the open battlefield, not against Bolos, hunterkiller robots, and high radiation. Prototype human forms, though, simply didn't have the muscle, the stamina, or the reflexes to carry the sheer mass of armor that would protect them up there. And that, he'd just learned, was why they'd downloaded him into a warrior soma. A human wouldn't even be able to stand under the weight of all this stuff.

Besides the protective suit encasing him head to toe, with its massive, high-tech helmet designed to fit closely over his horns, he wore a backpack that weighed as much as the entire rest of the suit and was carrying a gauss rifle that was plastic-toy light, with strap-on ammunition boxes that were heavier than lead.

Your mission is limited and relatively narrow in scope. <patience> *You will lead a patrol onto the surface with the express purpose of securing prisoners—preferably Sky Demon officers—from whom we can download necessary information.*

One wall of the underground ready room consisted

of a floor-to-ceiling viewscreen. On that screen were a crashed spacecraft of some sort, obviously too badly damaged ever to lift off again, a handful of human-looking soldiers in black space suits, and an enemy Bolo that dwarfed soldiers and ship alike.

"We're not going to be able to get past that Bolo."

That is being taken care of. <confidence> *Our own Bolos are preparing an assault that will at least draw that machine away from your objective.*

"Yes?" He looked up, and inward, wishing he could see his god, wishing he could sense what it was truly thinking. His memories of occupying two different Mark XXXII Bolos were still very clear. They'd learned a lot in those earlier attacks. But had they learned enough?

"You'd better tell our Bolos not to let the TSDS confuse them out there. They'll need it to coordinate their attack, but—"

The Bolos know everything that you know, the god's voice told him. *They share your experience. They will know what to do.*

"I . . . uh . . . see. . . ."

But he didn't see, quite. How could the other Bolos know what he knew . . . unless the gods could somehow download *copies* of his mentation patterns instead of his entire brain.

Gods! Was he really LKN 8737938 . . . or a copy? . . .

It scarcely matters, does it? <aloof reserve, with mild concern for his mental well-being> *You are you, LKN 8737938. Your memories are yours. You are you.*

Perhaps. But he was beginning to wonder if that was enough.

Elken studied the download information as it flowed through his input ports. They would try once again. He and his assault team of three other Bolos would emerge from an underground tunnel and attempt to destroy the Sky Demon Bolo currently positioned just northwest of Ghendai.

"We can apply the lessons learned in the earlier assaults," he said. "And we may have damaged the enemy machine enough that a third attack will cripple it. I fail to see why the attack is so urgent, however."

Note the humans in environmental suits on the surface outside. <patience> The image, relayed from a microsensor near the enemy Bolo, showed a crashed spacecraft nearby, along with several humans dwarfed by the building-sized combat unit.

"I see them."

We have reason to believe that they are high-ranking officers in the invading army. As such, they will possess key information we must have.

"Like what?"

A list of targets and battle plans. A unit and organization table that might reveal strengths and weaknesses. Radio and IFF codes that would let us overhear or subvert their communications system. Perhaps even the codes we would need to disable their Bolos and put them into inactive status. Capture and successful interrogation of these demons might provide the key we need to win this battle and save our world.

"We are Bolo combat units. It would be easy to kill those Sky Demons." Strange. They looked completely human, though he couldn't see their features well at this range, with those helmets. "But how can we capture them?"

You and the other three Bolos will draw the enemy Bolo off. Present it with a clear threat. We believe it is guarding those humans and the downed spacecraft. If you threaten those, it may try to maneuver you away from them, in order to protect them.

"I . . . see."

It may even withhold its fire, since its primary weapons, if discharged too close to unprotected humans, could injure them. You will have an excellent chance to attack and disable it on your own terms. In the meantime, we have a team of warrior somas preparing to carry out a prisoner-capture operation.

Warrior somas, Trolls! Elken suppressed a grimace of disgust, before remembering that he was now a Bolo incapable of showing outward emotion or facial expression.

Like most of the other full-human protos of his acquaintance, he didn't care much for warrior-forms, hulking, horned and armor-plated brutes that seemed more animal than human. But he sensed now, in the flow of data passing into memory, that only warrior somas could wear the armor necessary to move and fight in the deadly environment of a surface battlefield.

Perhaps the brutish things had a reason for being after all.

He wished that he could talk with them, though, to warn them of what they would encounter Out There.

There is no need. <amusement> *Your previous combat experiences have been downloaded into the warrior somas. They will emerge on the surface knowing all about conditions and necessary tactics there that you do.*

"Indeed?" He accepted the statement—the gods could do anything, after all—and yet he felt a vague disquiet about that statement. How could they share his memories, unless? . . .

Kelly Tyler watched the cascade of data scroll through her thoughts as Victor fed her cranial implant a complete readout on his physical condition. She relaxed and felt the familiar thrill of incoming data; the information was appearing on the screen as well, but she'd done that for Colonel Streicher and the others, not for herself. She felt a much closer, tighter connection to Vic this way, with the data flowing smoothly directly into her jellyware memory.

Thank God. Vic was still in fair shape . . . especially considering the fact that he'd engaged and destroyed eight Mark XXXII Bolos already during the course of just the past hour or so. Armor degradation overall . . . 12%, with most of the damage forward, on the glacis. Outer hull was badly pitted in places and contaminated with radiation over 35% of the surface, but integrity was good and there were no blow-through breaches yet. Fusion plants at optimum, capable of 115% power within .05 second of command. Drive train, suspension, and tracks all intact and fully operational. Weaponry—five out of fourteen secondary Hellbores were out of commission, but he still had full use of all three primaries. VLS loads down 21%. Mortar rounds down 18%. Other expendables . . .

She let out a quiet sigh of relief. Vic was okay, at least so far, despite some pretty rough handling. She cross-questioned him on some fine points, letting his diagnostic expand and fill her thoughts.

Even with her eyes closed, Kelly was unpleasantly aware of Colonel Streicher standing nearby and imagined he must be wishing he could order her out of center seat and take charge. Almost she'd looked up and offered him her place . . . but she'd gritted her teeth and refused to even notice his presence, unless and until he gave her the order to move.

She didn't think he was going to do that. Streicher seemed to be a good officer, one who believed in delegating authority and in letting his people do their work without micromanaging them.

Kelly, however, was uncomfortable around most men, had been ever since she'd run away from home and an abusive father, then somehow fallen into a dismal series of bad relationships with men as bad as her father. She didn't fear or hate all men—she couldn't have survived a week in the Confederation Army if she had—but she still had considerable trouble extending her trust.

The exception was the Bolo. The Bolos she'd worked with so far during her military career were all definitely male—though she'd heard of a few somewhere with female personalities. For Kelly, Vic represented all that was right in a male—intelligence, humor, depth, and above all carefully controlled *power*. Sometimes she thought that if she could marry Vic, she would.

Reaching out, she laid one slim hand on the touch-panel console before her, feeling the faint, trembling vibration of suppressed and contained power. What was it like to be a Bolo, she wondered?

She wished she could find out, to truly *know* how they thought, what they felt.

"Lieutenant? . . ."

She started violently, nearly coming up out of her seat, as Streicher lightly touched her shoulder. "What? . . ." She'd not heard him duck beneath the circle of holoscreens and come up behind her seat.

"Sorry, Lieutenant," Streicher said. "How are you coming with those diagnostics?"

"Oh . . . ah, fine. Just done, Colonel." She gestured at the read-out. "Vic's worst problem is the damage he's taken to his frontal armor. If we could get him to a maintenance facility, we could patch that up quickly enough."

"Well, that's not likely to happen now. How is he otherwise?"

"In good shape, Colonel. No major problems. Some little ones, but we can cope."

"Excellent. Let Lieutenant Bucklin in there to set

up a communications relay for us through to the rest of the regiment."

"I can do that, sir—"

"I want Lieutenant Bucklin to do it."

"Yes, sir."

Reluctantly, she gave up the command chair. She felt an awful itch, like jealousy—but that couldn't be what she was feeling, could it?—as Bucklin took her place. Damn it, Victor spoke to *her*, and she was the only one who really understood him.

She was hurt when Vic gave Bucklin the channels he requested, without even acknowledging that it was Bucklin and not her in center seat.

Four of the regimental staff officers are now aboard, within my combat command center. My Commander has requested a full diagnostic report, and I have provided it.

Despite minor weaknesses in frontal armor and on-board expendables, however, I am in good shape, eager to continue the battle and complete my mission objectives.

I may have the battle I seek quite soon. Three BIST sensors detect and triangulate the position of a fast-moving vibration underground. The vibration's speed and harmonic characteristics lead me to suspect that two or more very heavy combat vehicles—probably more Bolo Mark XXXIIs—are moving through an underground tunnel. Their current location is beneath the city, moving toward me at a range of five kilometers, a depth of approximately one hundred meters.

It is possible they are traveling toward another sealed doorway masking a tunnel entrance. If so, my human companions are in extreme danger. Once the enemy Bolos emerge, I must engage them to survive. That engagement, with unprotected humans on the surface at close quarters to the combat, could easily kill them.

I alert my Commander to the threat, and also pass the word to the humans on guard outside the crashed spaceship. The hull of that wreck will afford scant protection against incident radiation from Hellbore blasts, but it is better than nothing.

The only other thing I can do is to attempt to engage the enemy Bolos at as great a remove as possible from the crash site. I will fight the attackers there, far enough from the downed command ship that 4th Regimental personnel are not threatened.

I shouldn't be absent for long. . . .

With this in mind, I suggest that only one of the 4th Regiment's staff personnel remain in my combat control center. In combat, I will be maneuvering swiftly, sometimes violently, and I have only one seat in place. It will not be safe for the other three to remain standing, not as I twist and turn at speeds of 100 kph or better.

There is considerable discussion raised by this suggestion. My Commander wants to be the one to stay, but Colonel Streicher overrules her, claiming the need to experience the combat first-hand.

"What can you do if you do go, sir?" my Commander says. I hear the strain in her voice. She doesn't often speak up like this and sometimes appears to have trouble talking to fellow humans. "A Bolo thinks too fast for you to direct its action!"

"Then I'll ask you the same," Colonel Streicher replies. "Why do you feel you must be on board?"

"Because it's my place. My job!"

"Your job is following orders."

"But I've been trained as a unit CO! I can advise—"

"And I was a Bolo combat unit CO when you were a kid in school," Streicher replies. He sounds tired, and *under considerable strain. "I've experienced combat. You have not. Who is the better qualified?"*

In fact, the colonel will see nothing from my command center that he could not see through a data feed on board the downed spacecraft. There truly seems to be little point in any human accompanying me on this mission. My argument seems to carry little weight, however.

I may not fully understand human thought in emotionally charged areas such as this.

"That's all I'll say about it," Streicher said. "I'm staying on board Victor. You people go back to the ship." He glared at Kelly. This defiance wasn't like her at all. "That's an order!"

"*This isn't fair! . . .*"

"The army is not fair, Lieutenant. Life is not fair. Now get off this unit and get back to the ship! All of you! Move! If you argue any longer, the enemy's going to *be* here!"

Kelly Tyler's green eyes were darker, more furious than he'd ever seen them. He knew she felt that he was stepping on her prerogatives, that he was moving in on her territory, but that couldn't be helped.

Damn it, she didn't understand. None of them did. He *had* to be the one to ride Victor into this battle. He needed that close-up, first-hand experience. *The Greatest Good.*

Besides, his combat experience far outweighed Kelly's. Sure, according to strict military protocol, she should go because she was the unit commander, and he should stay because he needed to watch over all of the regiment's Bolos, not just this one.

But the sector was quiet, and this might be his one opportunity. He had to take it. He would apologize later, if necessary. Or make her understand.

Euph sang in his blood, his head. He felt great. Strong. *Powerful* . . .

They would meet the oncoming threat, then return to the ship.

They wouldn't be gone for long. . . .

Chapter Twelve

I wait while Major Ramirez, Lieutenant Bucklin, and Lieutenant Tyler exit my aft hatch and make their way clear of any possible danger from rock or debris kicked up by my aft tracks. At Colonel Streicher's command, then, I engage my drive and begin moving on a course of one-two-five, angling toward the city of Ghendai. I am concerned about leaving the command staff in this exposed position but know it would be much worse if a battle took place in their immediate vicinity.

We will not be gone for long, however. I deploy one of my Dragons and two Wyverns to stay close, just in case.

Elken, in troll form, sat strapped and squeezed into the narrow, upright seat on board the black and yellow godflier as it emerged from a hidden tunnel entrance, normally covered over by a slab of featureless ferrocrete. A second flier followed close behind as the two streaked across grassland, hugging the undulations and folds in the ground to avoid enemy radar detection.

The Sky Demon Bolo has been lured away to the southeast, the god's voice said inside his thoughts. *We are deploying mobile guns to deal with the forces left*

200

to guard the enemy ship. You should have no trouble carrying out your mission.

They would still have to move quickly, in and out as fast as a striking seadart. As soon as the enemy Bolo figured out what was going on . . .

"Contact!" the godflier's pilot called from the cockpit forward. "Hold on, back there, trolls! This is going to get a little rough!"

The godflier swooped nose-high, and Elken heard the shriek-bang thunderclap of particle guns firing.

He clutched his gauss rifle more tightly against his armored chest and waited.

Long moments after the Bolo had dwindled in a cloud of dust over the southeastern horizon, Lieutenant Kelly Tyler was still seething from the unfair treatment she'd received at the hands of Colonel Streicher. *Damn the man,* she thought. *He has no right! . . .*

And yet a part of her tried to soothe, tried to calm and smooth ruffled emotions over. Of *course* he had the right. He was the regimental commander, her commanding officer.

But Victor was *hers. . . .*

"Kelly!" Major Ramirez shouted suddenly, intruding on her black thoughts. "Incoming!"

Major Ramirez was standing in the shadow of the ECD spacecraft, waving to her frantically. Kelly was still out in the open. She'd been unwilling to jog clear of Victor with Lieutenant Bucklin, favoring instead a sullen, dogged walk, and had been left by herself on the field. She'd not even realized she was now alone.

North, something like a six-legged spider was stalking rapidly across the plain, a blocky, turreted body suspended beneath the housing that connected six massive, trunklike legs.

She'd seen the thing in military ID downloads. It

was a Mobile Armored Gun Battler, code-named *Tarantula* by the Confederation. Employed as a kind of slow, mobile fortress to engage armor and air assets, it was far too lightly armored to deal with Bolos on anything like an equal footing, and its twin 15cm Hellbores were considered obsolete for ground vehicles.

As an anti-infantry weapon or for combat against light tanks or aircraft, it was reportedly superb.

One turreted weapon atop the walker housing suddenly angled up, tracking left. In the sky overhead, a pair of Wyvern reconnaissance drones circled . . . then died as the battler opened up with a stuttering, hammering barrage of particle beam fire.

Legs scissoring with a ponderously delicate grace, the Tarantula continued its advance across the field. Kelly thought it was coming straight for her, and when its paired main gun, mounted in a ball turret on the front of its body, opened up with a thunderous detonation, she threw herself to the ground, arms protectively folded over her head.

But the twin-gunned Hellbore burst hadn't been aimed at her. When she lifted her head, she saw one of Victor's Dragon remotes humming past her position, its turret swinging to bring its 20cm Hellbore to bear on the attacking battler.

It fired, and the bolt, a dazzling, blue-white flare so brilliant it momentarily blinded her, seared into the approaching monster, and the detonation that followed sent flaming chunks of one massive leg hurtling across the plain.

In almost the same instant, the Tarantula's main turret swung to bear on the hovertank and slammed out a trio of quick rounds.

The tank staggered in midflight and spun in the air. The battler's Hellbore fired again, gouging huge chunks of duralloy armor from the front and sides of the stricken vehicle. The sheer volume of noise, a thunderous cacophony of explosions and shrieking energy beams assaulted Kelly's ears, as shimmering waves of heat washed across her. She couldn't move, she didn't dare stand and run.

All she could do was endure as the titanic clash of high-energy forces seared and pulsed and exploded around and over her.

It is a diversion, but not one that I can ignore. Moments after I engage the enemy Bolos—once again, four of them emerging together from the shielded entrance to an underground tunnel—two of my Wyverns and several BIST sensors detect the approach of enemy combat vehicles from the north.

Two are MBW-12 Mobile Armored Gun Battlers, code-designation Tarantula. Two more are fliers of some sort, almost certainly T-3 airborne carriers vectoring toward the crashed command ship. I estimate a 78-plus–percent chance that the Enemy hopes to capture the regimental command staff in order to acquire combat intelligence on Confederation plans, deployments, and TO&E.

But the four Mark XXXII Bolos are pressing their attack with relentless efficiency, splitting apart and advancing on my position from three directions, making full use of the cover provided by ruins and partly-burned-out buildings in front of me.

I direct the two Dragons in my immediate area forward and throw myself in full reverse, hoping to disengage in order to return to the crash site. At the same time, I realize that I cannot afford to let these combat units anywhere near the ship. Large-caliber Hellbore fire would cause unacceptable collateral damage, including serious casualties among the regimental staff.

I must destroy these Bolos before they can close with the command craft, as I destroyed the others before.

The Enemy has learned from its previous engagements with me. I may not be able to pull this off.

Again, Kelly raised her head, squinting against the pulsing blasts of raw light from explosions, slashing particle beams, and Hellbore blasts. She saw the Dragon, a hundred meters away, lurch to the side, dragging its skirt on the ground . . . and then a hammer-blow explosion tore the vehicle into white-hot pieces. Explosions continued to rip through the walker, however. In the sky overhead, a pair of Warlock fighters stooped out of the crystalline morning sky like silver-black hawks, pounding at the fortress with charged particle beams.

"Kelly!" she heard over her helmet phones. "Kelly, are you okay?"

"I'm . . . all right!" she shouted, breathless under the thunderous assault of noise and shock waves.

"We'll come out and get you!"

"No! Stay under cover! I'll make it!"

She started crawling toward the command ship. Then another round of nearby explosions made her freeze in place. She wondered why she was trying so hard to reach the ship, when she knew that it provided little better protection from the energies being hurled back and forth above her than did empty air.

She raised her head, trying to orient herself. Those few seconds of combat had transformed the landscape around her from grass-covered plain to a withered, blasted field enveloped in smoke, with fires burning everywhere. It might not be much, but even the thin skin of the downed command ship would provide some cover from the thermal radiation loosed by the Hellbore bolts, so she started moving again.

Then stopped.

Two more vehicles had appeared from the north, fliers this time, large and angular, painted in black and yellow stripes, with the implicit menace of huge stinging insects. Her briefing downloads had identified them as Tactical Troop Transports—T-3s—and mentioned that the locals referred to them as "godfliers."

As the battle between Wyverns and walker continued with unabated ferocity, the two fliers skittered through the air and touched down as one, to either side of the crashed command ship. Hatches dropped beneath the insect-like heads, and soldiers, massive in green and brown armor, jogged down lowered ramps and approached the ship.

She groped for the weapon she'd been issued, a heavy Mark XL power gun, unhooking the safety strap and dragging it from the holster slung on her right hip. She took aim at the soldiers and squeezed the trigger, then cursed when nothing happened. She was a shipboard officer, damn it, not an infantryman, and hadn't received more than cursory training with the thing.

She found the safety switch, flipped it, and tried again. This time a thin pencil of bright blue radiance speared from the weapon's muzzle and struck the side of the command ship with a bright sputter of energy.

Three of the armored troops dropped to their knees, raising heavy weapons to their shoulders and firing back. Kelly tried to flatten herself against the dirt and scorched grass even harder as bolts snapped and shrieked centimeters above her prone form.

The Caernan troops were using magnetic accelerator rifles, gauss guns in popular parlance, using magnetic induction to fire slivers of steel-jacketed uranium at hypersonic speed. One of them switched to full auto, and the air around Kelly seemed to jump and quiver beneath the staccato hammering of those high-velocity flechettes.

They were aiming high, however, and when the stuttering barrage ceased, she stayed down. She wasn't sure her power gun would breach that massive armor they were wearing anyway.

It took a moment more for the fact to register on her thunder-wracked brain: those were humans in armor out there, not the six-legged shapes of Aetryx. The Aetryx were supposed to be the enemy, not Caern's human population.

What should I do now?

Everything seemed to be happening at once. She tried to call for help to the fighters overhead but didn't remember what channel they were using for air-ground coordination. She had to engage her implant and open the menu—words appearing behind her tightly closed eyelids—to find the proper download file.

Then she found the right channel and gave the mental command to open it. Her ears were immediately assaulted by the shouted exchanges of the Confederation pilots above her.

"Red Sting Two! Red Sting Two! Watch it, that thing's still got teeth!"

"Three, Red One! Try to make your next pass from behind! Circle behind!"

"He keeps spinning around! I can't get a shot! . . ."

"Red One, Four! I'm hit! I'm hit! I—"

"Confederation aircraft!" she called, breaking into the chatter. Looking up, she saw a streak of fire smearing across the high clouds and falling toward the west; one of the fighters had just been clawed from the sky. "Confederation aircraft! This is Cloudtop, on the ground! We are under attack by enemy forces! We need help! . . ."

"Hang tight, lady," a voice replied in her helmet

phones. *"We got trouble of our—"* The transmission was chopped off in a burst of static, and a bright explosion flashed high in the sky.

"Red Sting One is hit! He's going down!"

Gunfire shrieked, soldiers by the command craft shooting at her, and she felt the shock of each passing flechette.

Kelly squeezed her eyes shut more tightly and prayed for the noise to cease. . . .

Elken the troll shouldered his way through the open airlock hatch. A black-suited figure rose up in front of him, trying to block his way, but he stepped forward and pushed hard with the butt of his gauss rifle, sending the figure sprawling onto its back. The deck was sharply canted, and moving across it was tough for both sides. But the troll bodies were conditioned for tough climbs and awkward positions, while protosomes were not.

Some of the defenders wore skin-tight black environmental suits. Most wore jumpsuits of gray or black, which Elken assumed were Confederation army and navy uniforms. It didn't matter. None was a match for the troll rush.

A power gun beam hummed, and the troll to Elken's right and behind him shrieked as a fist-sized chunk out of the pauldron armoring his shoulder vaporized in a puff of oily smoke. Elken snapped his gauss rifle around and stitched the Confederation shooter to the far bulkhead with a high-velocity burst of needle flechettes, the impact opening the man from groin to throat in a blossoming of scarlet flowers.

"Move!" Elken snapped over the tactical net. "Get them! Get them all!"

At first he'd thought that the other trolls would be incarnations of the others, of Palet and Veber and Sendee and others of the company of Bolos driven by human minds. Human souls. But he'd learned before leaving the assembly area in Trolvas that these others were ordinary trolls—derived from human stock, but with rather sluggish minds, minds designed to follow orders explicitly and to the last detail . . . but without real creativity behind them.

The revelation had shocked him. Why had he been singled out as a troll leader? The gods, he was convinced, knew what they were doing. But sometimes it was damned hard to figure out what it was.

Rasping out orders with a voice harsh and gargling with the fury and bloodrush of the moment, he led his team deeper into the crashed Confederation spaceship. This was a main deck of some sort, with a large, circular couch in a sunken well in the center. A woman in an army officer's uniform reared up from within the well, bracing her arms on the back of a couch and aiming a power gun gripped in both hands. The gun hummed, and another of Elken's trolls toppled backward, his helmet visor exploding in shards of plastic and bone and splatters of blood.

He returned fire, hammering a full-auto stream of flechettes into the couch and the woman sheltering behind it. Her head came apart, splattering the far bulkhead with a fine mist of blood, bone fragments, and gray matter.

"Surrender!" Elken called out, using his helmet's outside speaker with the volume set to a booming yell. "All of you! Throw down your weapons! Don't make us kill the rest of you!"

The answer was another round of power-gun fire, and the battle continued for minutes more, as the trolls fought their way into the ship, compartment by smoky, blood-splattered compartment. Three more of the defenders were killed, before the rest, finally, shouted that they were coming out.

It was a ragged and dispirited group of Confederation prisoners that Elken ordered to assemble in a line outside the ship. Beaten and clawed by the trolls who dragged them from the ship, stripped of their uniforms and E-suits to be sure they weren't hiding any weapons, their hands cuff-locked behind their backs, they didn't seem the conquering invaders Elken had been expecting . . . or the fearsome Sky Demons, either.

The revelation that they were just people was a little disconcerting. According to the Histories, Sky Demons were immortals who'd lost their souls rebelling against the gods, and while Elken didn't fully believe some of those old stories, he was disappointed, in a way, to find that the enemy consisted of ordinary people like him.

Well, like him except for the obvious fact of his troll somatype. But that was strictly temporary, his working uniform, as it were, until the enemy was defeated and he could join the gods in immortality.

"Get them on the godfliers," Elken ordered.

He wanted to be well clear of this area before the enemy Bolo returned.

Kelly lay on her stomach, watching friends and comrades being led from the command vessel and lined up outside. For the past several minutes, she'd been in an agony of indecision. Troll guards had ringed the ship, crouched in the grass facing outward. She'd seen no way that she could have snuck in closer . . . and if she had, what then? There were at least twenty of the Caern attackers and only one of her.

Worse, there were two of those walker monstrosities now. One had been badly damaged, true. Three of its legs had been blown off, or so badly damaged they'd been deliberately jettisoned, but it was balancing a couple of hundred meters away now like a huge, tripodal bug, its weapons turrets searching sky and horizon. The second battler stood farther off, near a line of woods marking the northern edge of the field, and it appeared undamaged.

Two of the Warlock fighters had been shot down. The other two . . . she didn't know. Shot down or fled, it scarcely mattered. They had no place to go, no place to land, and they weren't here. The enemy was in complete control of the battlefield.

She considered calling Victor but didn't. The signal from her E-suit com might well bring a squad of those human-mutant warriors charging down on her. If Victor did arrive, she didn't think there'd be anything he could do, save, possibly, spooking the trolls and precipitating a slaughter of the prisoners.

She squeezed her eyes shut, bringing up implant menu options and staring at them helplessly. There must be something she could do . . . but the only options presented to her were various communications channels and of them all, only the tactical and command channels to Victor remained. The rest—fleet, logistics, Space Strike Command, personal to the other members of the team—all of them were ghosted and inaccessible.

Kelly was alone on a very large and very hostile planet.

The prisoners were filing up a ramp into the two grounded fliers now. She was too far away to recognize individuals, even when she kicked in the magnifying optics of her visor, but she could only see sixteen people, and three of those were being carried on board by trolls, as though they were injured.

Less herself and Colonel Streicher, there should have been twenty-one. Five of her comrades must have been killed in the fighting.

She wondered who had been killed.

Her eyes burned at the thought, but she would *not* cry. She would *not* lose control.

She didn't really think of the others in the command group as friends exactly. Acquaintances, comrades-at-arms and fellow soldiers and teammates, yes, but Kelly had very few *friends*. Friendship demanded an emotional commitment that she simply wasn't able to offer. But she still enjoyed a camaraderie with these people that had been a long time in the forging.

Sometimes, she felt that she wasn't comfortable around any other humans, but she knew now, as she watched her comrades being marched aboard those fliers at gunpoint, that she'd been close to them in a way that hadn't been possible for her with other people for a long, long time. They'd been understanding of her social failings, her *clumsiness* with people, as she thought of it. Even Colonel Streicher she liked well enough, though he could be a bit heavy handed, even arbitrary sometimes, like with the military rigmarole with her hair earlier that morning, and she was still burning at the way he'd treated her a little while ago on board Victor. He wasn't what she thought of as a friend—one simply didn't think of a commanding officer in those terms, generally—but she knew he cared for her professionally, the way he cared for every person under his command.

None of that mattered now. Streicher was off with Victor, and the rest of the team had been killed or captured. She was alone and in danger of being gunned down or captured herself at any moment. She didn't know what to do.

Finally, as the last of the trolls trooped aboard the transports, and the fliers lifted from the plain in swirling bursts of dust, she knew she had to call for help, even if she risked giving herself away.

"Victor!" she called. *"Victor! . . ."*

❖   ❖   ❖

I am fighting for my life.

This time, the Enemy's assault is tightly controlled and focused, his movements closely coordinated, his attacks deadly and launched with efficiency and a keen knowledge of Bolo tactics and abilities. I attempted to back clear of the ambush but found myself cut off as two of the attackers circled at high speed behind me, knocking out one of my Dragons in the process. I pivot and try a high-speed rush at one of the enemy Bolos, which I have designated as Delta Two, throwing a heavy barrage of mortar and VLS missile fire in concert with heavy 200cm Hellbore blasts. I immediately sustain heavy damage to my rear quarters as the other three close on me in a sudden rush. I find myself expending 78.5 percent of my available secondary firepower on antimissile defense, as the Enemy attempts to overwhelm my defenses with close-coordinated assault tactics.

"Victor! Victor!" I hear the call over my tactical command channel and recognize the voice characteristics of Lieutenant Tyler. "Victor, this is . . . this is Cloudtop! Come in! Please!"

"This is Thunderstrike, Bolo of the Line serial 837986," I reply. "This is not a good time."

"Victor, thank God! The command ship has been overrun! The others have been killed or taken away in fliers!"

"Unfortunately, I am unable to help just now," I reply. "Do you have the communications frequencies for the Warlock aircraft in the area?"

"They're gone, dammit! Victor, they're all gone! There's no one left but you!"

I hear the stress in my Commander's voice and judge that she is very close to complete physical and emotional helplessness—"losing it," as humans describe the condition.

I have noticed with some interest that human reactions to stress and danger vary with numerous factors, including especially their age and their marital status. Younger humans tend to be both more impulsive and daring and less steady in the face of serious threat. Older humans are more conservative, less likely to take risks, but seem more relaxed with severe threats, though this likely is an effect of both training and experience. Married humans, I note, are the most conservative of all and the least willing to face serious danger.

Kelly Tyler is unmarried and tends to be impulsive, but I have noted that she does not handle severe stress well, most likely because of her inexperience. This is a serious handicap in a battlefield commander.

I wonder if I should report this to her commanding officer which, in this case and in the absence of Major Filby, would be Colonel Streicher.

Doubtless this is the wrong time to discuss the matter. Both my survival and that of the entire regimental staff are in question. There will be time for such considerations later.

"Remain where you are, my Commander," I tell her. "Stay well hidden. I will come as soon as I am able."

"Hurry, Victor!"

"I will do what I can. I suggest you cease communications, so that the Enemy cannot trace your transmission."

"O-okay, Victor. Cloudtop out."

The exchange disturbs me. Having humans directly and physically involved in combat operations in the AO can only reduce my efficiency and make it more difficult to achieve my strategic goals. Bolo combat units, after all, were introduced into the equation of purely human warfare because organic intelligence is peculiarly unable to survive or operate within the combat environment.

I wonder if there is some means of removing them from the battlefield?

It was almost impossible for Streicher to comprehend what was going on, even with his implant fully engaged with Victor's Combat Data Network. Direct neural interfacing should have enabled him to keep up with the Bolo's rapid movements and combat decisions, but he was having trouble following anything at all.

The view revealed on the circle of holoscreens about his chair was a constant blur of red-brown-black landscape, hurtling dust and debris, a constant, strobing cascade of explosions bright enough to dazzle the eyes even with the light input sharply tuned down for his comfort, and the shifting, geometric patterns of light Victor was drawing across the screens to indicate enemy vectors, positions, and threats.

His implant link with Victor helped a little, but the Bolo's reaction times, its thinking time was so much quicker than any human's that Streicher was having trouble keeping up.

It didn't help that the euph was still buzzing in his head, a constant distraction. It tended to push fear into the background the way it did with painful memories, and that seemed to take some of the edge off of Streicher's reactions.

"Victor," he called. "I'm having trouble with the interface. Can you boost the output at all?"

"I do not advise that, Colonel." There was a long pause. "Colonel Streicher, there appears to be a chemical blockage of some sort within your implant, at the neural receptor sites. If there is degradation of signal strength, clarity, or comprehension, I suggest that that is the cause. Boosting the signal may cause you irreparable damage."

"Do it, Victor! I can't make out a thing down here!"

"I must decline that order, Colonel. Your decision-making abilities may be impaired."

There was nothing he could do, nothing he could contribute. All he could do was clutch at the arms of the command chair and try to take it all in. Streicher sagged back in the seat, fingers clawing at the ends of the armrests. Damn, damn, damn. He should have stayed with the ship. . . .

"I have just been in communication with my Commander," the Bolo's voice said a moment later.

"Lieutenant Tyler? What'd she have to say?"

"That the command craft has been overrun. She managed to escape, but she informs me that all others of the 4th Regimental staff have been killed or taken prisoner."

The news hit Streicher like a hammerblow to the gut, shock and fear, quickly followed by a wretched guilt. If he had been there . . .

If he had been there, he would be dead or taken now as well. Nothing he personally could have done would have stopped it.

Still . . .

"Victor! Who was killed?" Carla could be a hothead sometimes and would not have gone without a fight. If she . . .

"Unknown, Colonel. Lieutenant Tyler did not inform me."

"Great. Just fracting great." His right hand strayed toward the uniform blouse pocket where he'd sequestered his last remaining euph. He stopped himself with another sharp-bitten curse. He had more back at the ship . . . but had the Caernans destroyed the ship? This might be his last tab. The last tab *ever*.

And then the crash hit him. *Face it, Streicher,* he told himself bitterly. *If you hadn't been on euph, would you have insisted on joyriding with the Bolo?*

He didn't want to accept that statement, didn't want to even think about it, but he was enough a creature of discipline to know when a thing had to be faced. He remembered his confrontation moments before with Lieutenant Tyler, how he'd walked right over her objections. He remembered the surge of almost righteous self-confidence and realized that that had been the euph speaking, not him.

If he'd stayed behind, would anything have been different?

Impossible to say. He didn't have enough information. Maybe he could have mustered the others in a defense of the ship, rallied them enough to . . .

Damn! *That* was the euph speaking too.

He was going to have to do some serious thinking about this.

If he survived the next few minutes. . . .

Interlude III

At this juncture in the battle, a balance of sorts was established. The Aetryx had achieved complete mastery of cis-Caernan space to within approximately 5,000 kilometers of the planet. They could not approach near orbital space, however, for the simple fact that some fifty Bolos now operational at various points around the planet's habitable belt possessed firepower sufficient to keep them at bay. Mark XXXIIIs were quite appropriately known as planetary siege units, not least because they could effectively engage targets in space.

But they were land-bound, and their range was limited. So long as the Aetryx carriers were in operation, no supplies could reach the units already grounded, no reinforcements would arrive, and there could be no hope of evacuation should things go wrong.

And things *were* going wrong, and badly. Casualties among the Bolos in the initial assault forces had been unexpectedly high, thanks to the Aetryx willingness to employ nuclear weapons even over surface population centers. At the antipodes of the fighting in Kanthuras, only one battalion out of three survived the landing in the heavily forested Jorass District. Of the two surviving Bolos, familiarly known as "Thunder" and "Storm," Thunder was disabled in a duel with twenty heavy

217

hovertanks mounting 100cm Hellbores, and Storm was forced to withdraw. Storm later returned in an attempt to rescue its comrade, and both combat units were destroyed by a concentrated nuclear strike.

Elsewhere, enemy pressures halted or repulsed repeated Confederation attacks in the early hours of the fighting. Aetryx military forces were considerably stronger than Confederation intelligence sources had expected, and casualties were high on both sides.

Completely unexpected was the ferocity of Caernan *human* elements in the defense of their world. Intelligence had expected them to rally to the side of their Confederation liberators, but their response was feeble and in places nonexistent. The fact that they obviously felt they were literally fighting on the side of the gods had been overlooked by invasion planners, despite warnings to that effect from planetary intelligence sources. There were reports of large numbers of unmodified humans attempting to charge Confederation Bolos armed with nothing but hand weapons and explosive charges.

All such assaults were repulsed easily, but the psychology of those attacks did not accord well with initial estimates of the psychological situation on Caern. The Caern invasion failed in large part because Confederation planners understood neither the biology nor the psychology of their opponents.

Disaster at Caern:
A Study of the Unexpected in Warfare
Galactic Press Productions, Primus, cy 426

Chapter Thirteen

I elect to try a stratagem. As Hellbore bolts slam into my flank and rear, I deliberately swing left and drop into a 100-meter shell crater, which cants my hull at a sharp angle. Simultaneously, I begin releasing copious amounts of smoke from my aft generators, the sort used for smokescreens. The effect is much like that of a major on-board fire . . . and it also serves to completely shroud my immediate area in impenetrable smoke.

"What are you doing?" Colonel Streicher asks, and I sense the fear in his voice.

"We're not moving now," I tell him. "The Enemy must come to us, and in moving, I can detect him."

Twenty-one thousand tons makes a significant seismic signature. One of the Enemy Bolos enters the smoke cloud, trying to maneuver close enough to determine that I have been knocked out. I cannot see him, but as I follow his progress by the tremors transmitted to my sensors through the earth, I pivot all three Hellbore turrets to track him. When I estimate that he is within fifty meters of my Number One Hellbore, I open fire, slamming round after round into the battle fog where the Enemy Bolo must be.

I am rewarded by a staggering explosion at close

quarters, and the impact of thousands of chunks of hot shrapnel on my outer hull. I immediately lurch forward, up and out of the crater, before several missiles slam into the spot where I was resting.

Pivoting, I backtrack on the trajectories of those missiles and loose a VLS missile barrage of my own. BIST and seismic tracking data help me maintain a fix on the remaining three enemy Bolos.

Delta One switches on a narrow-aperture radar, hoping to target me and switch off before I can respond. He is unsuccessful, and I lock on with a return missile and a rippling triple snapshot of 200cm Hellbore blasts. I sense the enemy Bolo's battlescreens failing and step up the pressure. As the smoke clears, I can see the other machine just ahead, the tracks ripped from its starboard side, its turret ripped away and lying in the earth nearby, its hull perforated in two places and burning fiercely.

Two down, two to go . . . but at this point I elect to break off the action and return to the command craft. If they follow me, I will have to stop and destroy them in order to avoid continuing the battle in Lieutenant Tyler's immediate vicinity . . . but as soon as I begin backing away, both surviving enemy Bolos break off and return toward the southeast.

"Victor?" my passenger says after a moment.

"Yes, Colonel?"

"I really screwed this one, didn't I?"

I am uncertain about what Colonel Streicher is referring to. "Could you clarify the question, please?"

But he does not respond. Minutes later, we approach the wrecked command craft.

Kelly Tyler sprang from her hiding place in the tall grass and ran forward as Victor rumbled closer. The big machine swung left and opened its rear hatch, extending the ramp, and she hurried up and into the cool, inviting light of the passageway inside.

Streicher was in the Battle Command Center. She stopped when she saw him, her eyes widening. "Colonel? Are you okay?" He looked terrible, white-faced and with a gaunt and desperate look to the eyes that she didn't like at all.

He managed a half smile. "Lieutenant." He stood, gesturing to the center seat. "Lieutenant, I'm sorry. I . . . I apologize for what I did earlier. Please . . . this seat is rightfully yours."

She arched one eyebrow. "Rough ride, huh?" Direct neural links with a Bolo AI could be pretty rugged on people who weren't used to them or didn't have the appropriate training. The impressions and images came at you like lightning, and it took steady nerves and a good solid grounding to keep from being overwhelmed.

"I shouldn't have done that, shouldn't have bumped you aside," was all he said. "Which way did they take our people?"

"North," she replied, settling into the command chair and strapping herself in. The room stank from Streicher's sweat despite the best efforts of Victor's air recirculation pumps, and the synthleather upholstery was unpleasantly wet. "What should we do?"

"Follow," Streicher said. "Maybe we can catch them before they get them into one of their underground bases."

"But . . . how can we rescue them? Victor can't do anything but blow the hell out of what he shoots at!"

"Victor?" Streicher said. "How about it. Do you think you could convince the enemy to let our people go?"

"Unknown, Colonel," Victor replied. "It depends, I suppose, on how reasonable they are."

"They were trolls," Kelly said, making a face. "Those

horrible, big horned things. I don't know if they can be all that reasonable."

"Well, we'll face that one when we have to."

Streicher looked around the compartment, then sat on the bare metal deck. She heard him mumble something to himself.

"What was that, sir?"

"I said I've made a damned mess of everything."

"I don't see how, sir. If I'd stayed with Victor, you would be a prisoner now like the rest of them. Or dead."

"That's not what I meant. It's all my fault. . . ." But he volunteered nothing more.

With an inward shrug, she let her thoughts merge with Victor's through the neural interface, and soon Streicher's presence was completely forgotten.

In fact, I wonder if I am not to blame for the debacle, at least in part. Had I remained at the crash site, the Enemy might not have attacked. Still, my initial reaction—that an assault by the enemy Bolos at the crash site would have resulted in the deaths of my human charges—was, I am convinced, essentially correct. However, the events of the past few minutes strongly suggest that the Enemy deliberately lured me away from the command ship for the express purpose of taking the regimental staff prisoner for interrogation purposes. Had I held my ground, things might have worked out differently.

Still, there is no point in recriminations or self-blame. I do spend some .04 second considering the possible consequences of not attempting a rescue of Confederation human assets on Caern, but this is not a line of thought that will be at all profitable. Humans have different priorities in war than I, but my ontological framework requires that I obey the orders of my human commanders and accept their concepts of strategy and tactics where practicable.

I initiate communications with the other surviving Bolo combat units of the regiment. We are going to need to closely coordinate our activities, both to avoid getting in one another's way and to give us a better chance of recovering our human comrades.

I also wonder how we are going to resolve this engagement, knowing that there will be no second wave, no reinforcements, no chance of rescue....

We of the First Confederation Mobile Army Corps truly are on our own.

They were somewhere underground, very *deep* underground, but Carla Ramirez had no idea where they were in relation to known landmarks on the surface. She'd tried to keep track of the twists and turns as they'd descended the featureless corridor once they'd been herded off the fliers and put on board ground trucks, and she was pretty sure they'd headed southeast, but she had no way of gauging distance. The vehicles had been sealed, with no windows, no sense at all of how fast they'd been traveling. They could be within a few kilometers of where they'd been captured.

Or they could be on the far side of the planet.

They'd been dragged from the transports and shoved into line once more at the end of the journey. Carla looked about, trying to memorize every detail in case she had the opportunity to escape and report. Not that *that* was very likely. Their captors seemed fearful of the prisoners, and the trolls and the oddly articulated centaur-beings who helped them—various soma-forms of Aetryx, if the briefings were correct—were taking no chances on the prisoners' escape. The Confederation officers were kept surrounded at all times, by nervous-looking trolls with nasty-looking weapons.

Their surroundings, though, had a raw and industrial look to them—rough-shaped buildings of corroding metal, the naked skeletons of towers and cranes and support pylons, enormous storage tanks and hoppers, and everywhere the clang and clank and whine of heavy machinery. Some of the structures looked like refineries and smelters, to judge from the separator and washing stacks, the quenching towers, the converters. The technology actually looked fairly primitive, as though someone had tried to carve out a metals mining facility, processing plant, and foundry from scratch, but they hadn't had the time or the equipment or possibly the know-how to go all the way from crude coke ovens and open-pit hearths to plasma furnaces and gas-core reactors.

The cavern itself appeared to be natural, though it had undoubtedly been smoothed out, extended, and reinforced artificially. Planetological studies indicated that Caern was subject to frequent and severe seismic disturbances, thanks to the tidal stresses of its orbit about Dis. Those granite walls must be strongly reinforced by duralloy buttresses and force braces. She could feel the steady, deep hum of power generators all around her.

The most striking aspect of the cavern, though, was not its size or the factory and smelting operation filling much of its floor and wall space. At the center of the cavern was a circular pit two hundred fifty meters across, rimmed with duralloy and flintsteel walls. Steam was rising from the depths, lit from below by an evil red glow, and dozens of massive pipes snaked over the rim and into the depths.

Carla had never seen one before, but she knew about them in theory. Thermal boreholes were vertical tunnels drilled through a world's crust, going down for tens of kilometers, opening all the way to the mantle, where rock flowed like plastic, and temperatures reached five or six hundred degrees.

Boreholes were theoretically excellent sources of thermal energy; pipe water or mercury or any other liquid through heat-resistant tubing, and in the depths it flashed over into steam to drive all manner of turbines, pumps, and generators. You could also trap the metal steams rising from the mantle and shunt them off to separators, where you could plate out pure metals of every description.

They were also extremely dangerous. The molten rock at extreme depths was under considerable pressure, and if the fields sealing the tube's lumen failed, the resultant volcanic eruption could take out the larger part of a continent. They were also sources of every poisonous gas ever known to afflict miners, from sulfur dioxide to methane to carbon monoxide to hydrogen cyanide, and keeping the air breathable at these depths would be an awesome technical headache.

Whatever their environmental controls, they weren't the best. Carla's eyes were watering and her throat burning as the guards led the prisoners along a walkway that rose in a gentle curve toward one wall of the cavern, high enough up that she could actually look partway down the borehole's muzzle. The temperature, she guessed, was around forty degrees Celsius, enough to have them all dripping with sweat before they'd been marched more than fifty meters.

There wasn't a lot to see but red-shot blackness. She wondered if it was possible to look down from the edge of the thing and see all the way to the planet's mantle.

Their eventual destination was a prison of some kind—or a series of small, bare-walled chambers that had served some other purpose, such as storage, and been hastily converted to the task of holding POWs. She watched carefully as the group was split into three smaller groups, each led to a different cell. She was still trying to take a mental roll call, to determine for sure who had made it, and who had not.

Major King, Captain Johanel, and Lieutenant Dana, she knew, had been wounded. The trolls had carried them out of the ship on stretchers . . . but she hadn't seen any of them since they'd been offloaded from the fliers and put aboard the ground transports.

As for the rest, she knew Major Voll and Lieutenant Bucklin both had been killed, cut down in the command craft's sim chamber by full-auto gauss rifle fire. She'd seen the bodies lying where they'd fallen— or been splattered—and very nearly been sick. And she hadn't seen Lieutenants Tyler, Crowley, or Winsett or Major Beswin since they'd been overrun.

So that left seven of them, plus the six naval personnel off the ship. She was herded into one cell with Major Filby, Captain Meyers, Lieutenant Smeth, and Lieutenant Kelsie. The other eight, she was pretty sure from the sounds, had been locked in two other cells nearby. The guards left their hands cuffed at their backs, running lengths of wire cable through their wrist shackles and metal loops embedded in the walls at hip height, leaving them all fastened in such a way that they could neither sit all the way down nor stand completely upright without tugging painfully at the cable and their arms.

"Hey! Wait!" Filby shouted as the trolls who'd chained them turned and walked form the room. "Wait! You can't leave us like this!"

The door boomed shut, leaving them in a darkness relieved only by a faint sheen of light from a slit high up on the wall opposite the door.

"At least unchain the women!"

"I don't think they share your odd sense of chivalry, Major," Carla said. Filby was from Doralind, one of the Confederation's Core Worlds, where society women enjoyed a somewhat more pampered existence than on the rawer worlds of the periphery.

The survivors of Aristotle had never bothered with such pretty anachronisms.

"Bastards!" Meyers snapped. *"Bastards!"*

"I don't think they like us very much," Lara Smeth said from the far end of the chain.

"Do you think they're going to kill us?" Danel Kelsie wanted to know.

"I doubt it," Carla told them. "They probably want to interrogate us. Find out what we know about the invasion."

"Hell," Filby said. "The invasion fleet's already been driven off. They've *won*. If we're lucky, maybe they'll keep us as bargaining chips at the peace talks. Otherwise, well, I doubt that they have any reason to keep us alive for long."

"Filby! . . ."

"It's true!"

"Keep it to yourself, damn it." She thought a moment. "Look, at the very least, they're going to want us to talk to the Bolos, right? They must know some of us are unit commanders, and they're going to want us to call off the war up there. Right? So they're not going to kill us!"

But privately, she could only wish that were true. If her rough and ready muster report had been accurate, only Edan Abrams and Shauna O'Hara were left of the regiment's original six unit commanders, and both of them were in the other room with one of the two surviving battalion COs. In this cell were the other CO, a supply officer, two aides, and one very tired, very scared executive officer.

Unfortunately, supply officers and very junior adjutants were pretty much worthless any way you looked at it. They would be killed. As for her, well, they might want to keep her alive for a time while they pumped her for information about the whole unit. For her, it likely would be a few rounds of torture, with death as an eventual and welcome mercy. She didn't know what kind of mores the Caernans had about treatment of prisoners, but the trolls had been no gentler than they'd had to be, and she doubted, somehow, that they were capable of thinking of warfare as a *civilized* activity.

She wondered how long they would have to worry about it. That, no doubt, was a part of the softening-up process.

But she didn't imagine that any of them would have very long to wait.

He awoke, stretching . . . and then the fear hit him in deep, shuddering waves, like the icy surf at Gods' Beach. The last thing he remembered . . . no . . . what *was* the last thing he remembered? Memory eluded him, like fragments of a dream.

He opened his eyes, then wondered why he couldn't see. He reached out with a trembling, sweat-slicked hand, then realized he couldn't feel anything, that the tremors, the sweat, the cold were all imagined, anchors for the mind adrift within a vast and lightless void.

Concentrating, he summoned memories from deep, deep within. He'd been in a battle . . . he'd been . . . he'd been a Bolo combat unit, his brain housed in a huge mobile armored vehicle. Vaguely, he was aware of not one, but of a *number* of desperate battles all ending with his death. Before that . . . the memories were still dim, still fragmentary, something about going in for elective surgery . . . a chance at immortality. . . .

What had gone wrong? . . .

Nothing is wrong, a voice, deep and quiet, spoke

within the terror-haunted depths of his thoughts. *All is as it should be.* <calm reassurance>

The memories were solidifying. He remembered a battle . . . firing into an enemy Bolo, a vast cloud of smoke . . . the sudden, certain thrill of victory, of *knowing* they'd killed the enemy Bolo at last.

But it had been a trick. The Sky Demon machine had opened fire as he'd closed with it, groping toward it through the fog. He had a last memory of sending off a situation report, and then . . .

Sensation flooded his being. He was in the maintenance area in Trolvas, with Sendee's vast, armored bulk nearby. The other two Bolos of his team were nowhere in evidence. "Are they? . . ."

Your two other comrades escaped serious damage this time. They are still on the surface, awaiting the completion of your repairs.

He didn't remember Sendee's death this time around. She must have been hit after he was.

Over the next several minutes, he received a full update on the tactical and strategic situations on the surface. A number of high-ranking prisoners had been taken, he learned, by a specially assembled strike force that had overrun a crashed Sky Demon command ship while he and the other Mark XXXIIs were distracting the enemy Mark XXXIII. Their interrogation would reveal the targets and operations codes for a number of the invading Bolos in and around the Kanthurian Coast.

"But until then?" he asked.

You two will rejoin your fellows on the surface. Several enemy Bolos are now converging on a region along the banks of the Duret River, between Grendylfen and Ghendai. We do not know what they intend, but they may be trying to trace the hidden entrance used by the raiders who took the prisoners. You will attempt to interfere with their operations and destroy them if possible. . . .

Elken thought about that for a long time after he felt his god withdraw from his mind. The gods, he thought, were not as perfect in their evolution as they liked to believe.

He remembered still his disquiet upon learning that one of the trolls had been given his memories, his thoughts and thought patterns. It left him wondering whether he was really himself.

Had the original LKN 8737938 died, and only his memories been downloaded into a succession of Bolo bodies—and one troll?

If he possessed the perfect memories of the original, running in an artificial brain, how could he possibly know the difference?

Did it make a difference?

Well, in one sense it did. The original Elken had been promised immortality, a chance to be downloaded into a perfect, undying body, to be like the gods themselves. That promise remained to ensure his cooperation through this series of downloaded experiences . . . and apparent deaths. Suppose that original Elken was now dead, along with a number of copies made since? He, Elken, the Elken he was experiencing here and now, would be one of a series of downloaded copies, and doomed, like all of the rest, to death, most likely the next time he came up against an enemy Bolo.

The last thing he remembered with each death was uploading a status report. After each upload . . . there was nothing. No memory at all. He'd been thinking that the shock, the trauma of his own destruction, had been blocking his memories.

But what if the memories he had were not his own, *but those of previous copies, downloaded into a succession of new "selves"?*

Immortality worked only if it applied to him, not to some future copy of himself. He wanted to cheat death, not help some future Elken-copy with access to his memories get a new body, while he, the "real" he, died. It wasn't supposed to work that way.

The worst part of it was the feeling that he'd been deliberately and shockingly *used* by the gods, each download contributing a bit more experience in how to fight the enemy Bolos. Each new self was expected to carry out the impossible, with his memories alone surviving to help the next "self" in line. His original self must be long dead now.

Elken wasn't sure how he was going to deal with this. The gods would, of course, know what he'd just been thinking as soon as he uploaded another situation update.

He would have to give this some serious thought.

Kelly Tyler closed her eyes, the better to experience her implant link with Victor. They—*she*—were/was moving rapidly through a heavily forested, somewhat mountainous region northeast of Ghendai. They'd crossed the Duret River some time ago and were moving now along the base of the Kretier Peninsula in the general direction of Yotun, climbing higher into the Urad Mountains.

Despite the rough terrain, they were making good progress. Victor could brush aside with ease all but the very greatest of the trees in the forest and was leaving a broad trail of fallen timber in his wake as he worked his way up the southwestern flank of the mountains. There were frequent gullies, boulder fields, and even canyons carved by fast-rushing mountain streams, but Victor breasted them all effortlessly.

They knew exactly where they were going, too. One of Victor's Wyverns had tracked the Aetryx fliers that had raided the command ship. There was a probable entrance in the mountainside up ahead, which Victor would be able to identify, when he got closer, with low-frequency ground-penetrating radar.

The call had gone out, meanwhile, for other Bolos of the 4th Regiment. Invictus—Invie, as they all called him—his mission to suppress the bastion at Dolendi complete, was racing east now to join with Victor in the mountains. Roxie had abandoned undefended Kanth and was moving north. Third Battalion's Terry and Tiss were continuing with their original missions in the Losethal-Paimos Sector, guarding the 4th Regiment's southern flank, but they were available if needed.

Three Bolos, two covering the third as it probed the Caernan underworld, should be enough.

Enough to do what? She still wasn't certain herself, though Victor had assured her that there *were* options. Prisoner rescues generally required troops—human troops with special training and equipment. Bolos were the finest, most powerful surface-combat units ever developed in the long and bloody history of human military technology, but they lacked the finesse of human teams in some situations . . . scouting, for instance, infiltration, covert ops . . . and POW and hostage rescue.

She'd hoped that Colonel Streicher might have some ideas, but he seemed lost in some misery of his own, sitting on the deck with his head in his hands. What the hell was going on with the man, anyway? He'd bounced from apparent elation and self-certainty to bleak depression in the space of a few minutes, a sharp enough turn-around of his emotional state that she found herself wondering about his sanity. What she and Victor did not need right at the moment was a bipolar commanding officer.

It looked as though she and Victor would have to see this one through themselves.

They took Filby first.

Carla Ramirez had just found a sitting position that let her get down off her aching calves. The wire cable on the wall held her arms up behind her at an awkward angle, but at least she could sit for a while. Then the door banged open and the lights came on, a glaring blue-white electric radiance that had her blinking and tearing as shadowy shapes moved closer. They gabbled something at one another—she couldn't understand the Caernan tongue—and pointed at Filby, who was on the end of the cable closest to the door. They unchained him and led him away, and then the prisoners were plunged back into darkness once more.

"He'll crack," Meyers said in the dark. "He'll tell them every damned thing they want to know. I wonder how they knew to take him?"

"He was first in line," Carla said. The words caught in her throat, however. She was next in line from the door, after Filby.

"What . . . what do you think they're doing to him?" Danel Kelsie wanted to know. "T-torture?"

"I doubt it," Carla said, trying to put more confidence into her words than she felt. "Torture is counterproductive. The victim tends to tell the interrogator anything he thinks they want to hear. Not reliable."

"Most likely they'll shoot him full of drugs," Lara Smeth said quietly. "There are drugs that will break down every defense, make you answer every question."

"Well, aren't you the expert," Kelsie said.

"It's true."

"I want to make one thing very clear to everyone," Carla said. She drew a heavy breath, wishing she didn't have to say this. "The war, this invasion, anyway, is lost.

With the fleet scattered or destroyed, there's no hope anymore of anything like winning.

"So . . . no heroics. Resist as much as you can, as much as you think honor demands, but tell them what they want to know. Lara is right. There are hypnotics and psychoactives that will completely bypass your resistance, so in the long run, it won't matter whether you try to resist or not."

"Are you saying . . ." Kelsie said. "Are you saying we should cooperate with those bastards?"

"I'm saying to do what your conscience tells you to do. And if you decide to talk, well, that's okay. Do what you have to do to survive, so that when this is over you can all go back home. Some folks we've known weren't that lucky."

She thought about what she would do . . . resist or cooperate. Standing Confederation military orders came down on both sides of the question. Collaborators were traitors, subject to court martial. But they also acknowledged that no one could withstand modern information extraction techniques. If you talked under interrogation, there would be no serious consequences.

Other than the consequences to your soul. Carla reminded herself that there were at least six individual members of the 4th Regiment still at large—five Bolos, and Colonel Streicher. Possibly Lieutenant Tyler as well, since she hadn't returned to the ship when the raiders had struck. She might have survived out there, somewhere. . . .

She didn't want information that she'd given to the enemy to be the information used to trap and kill any of the Bolos or humans still at large. She would resist as well as she could.

Then the door banged open and the light flared into brilliance. As she blinked against the glare, rough, leathery hands pulled her to her feet and unhooked the cable from her wrist cuffs. She struggled against their relentless grip but was helpless as they dragged her out of the room.

"We're with you, Major!" Smeth called out as the door swung shut behind her. Brave words. Perhaps futile ones. But they spoke of the camaraderie they shared.

As the trolls shoved her along a dank, steaming corridor, she prayed that they didn't, in fact, use torture. . . .

Chapter Fourteen

The attack begins as I approach the target area. Soldiers—human soldiers and not the troll-variants described by Lieutenant Tyler or our briefing downloads—emerge from heat-shielded holes well-hidden in the underbrush and among stands of younger, smaller trees, emerge in a sudden rush and charge my tracks and wheels, swinging make-shift satchels of high explosives with short-burning chemical fuses. Tossed into my tracks, the first one detonated with a blast powerful enough to kill several of the nearest attackers, though it had no effect on my tracks or road wheels.

My moral inhibitor subroutines block the automated response of my antipersonnel batteries, giving them time to launch one assault. I override the inhibitors, however, and batteries on both sides and in my rear begin triggering automatically, loosing volley after volley of flechette-clouds, point-defense lasers, and explosive shotgun blasts of ball bearings. I hear the shrieks as men and women die, literally shredded by my AP defenses.

I feel what can only be described as unsettled emotions at this. These are humans, the beings we are here to rescue. More than that, though, their attack bespeaks a fanaticism born of belief, dedication, and determination not to allow us to win—scarcely the reactions one would expect of slaves seeking emancipation.

I detect other soldiers moving through the woods, some fully human, others in the heavy, outsized armor that marks them as trolls.

These attackers do not pose a threat, serious or otherwise. I estimate that the total explosive power of their hand-delivered satchel charges is insufficient to crack a tread connection, dislodge a road wheel, or otherwise interfere with my suspension and track system.

Still, I must kill those who get too close, if only to set an example and keep others, perhaps with more effective firepower, at a distance.

I wonder why they are so willing to die, in stacks three-deep, for their masters.

They dragged Carla into a small and bare-walled room already crowded with trolls, with humans . . . and with others. It was her first close look at Aetryx in something other than a simulation.

There were three of them, each different from the others in coloration and in overall form. Vaguely spiderlike, their heavy bodies—black-furred, not chitinous—held well off the floor by six muscular and thick-set legs, with a lesser pair of limbs which appeared to serve as arms neatly folded beneath the head, they reminded her somewhat of the six-legged walkers that had been present when the command craft had been overrun. The faces—all mandibles and palps and compound eyes—were more like those of insects than spiders or anything else that Carla knew from experience.

One of the Aetryx present was a diplomat form, with an elongated body that gave it a centaur-look, with a disturbingly human face riding where the insect features were in the other two. To Carla's mind, it was undeniably the most horrible of the three, especially when it smiled as a pair of trolls lashed her spread-eagled and helpless to an upright framework at one end of the room.

She was nightmarishly aware of all eyes on her, human and nonhuman alike. Stripped of her uniform at the ship, hanging there as though on display, she was wearing little now but shoes, socks, and underwear, and for the first time since her capture, she felt *sexually* vulnerable, as well as physically. The Aetryx scarcely counted, and the trolls appeared sexless. The full-humans in the room, however, were all males, and all seemed, to her mind, to be leering at her with a sense of anticipation, of expectation that made her stomach turn.

Most were watching her, at any rate. One human with a long white coat was preparing some sort of apparatus, like a crown or heavy tiara, trailing a dozen cables as thick as her thumb, and he seemed totally absorbed in that task. He turned, facing her, and settled it over her head. It felt warm to the touch, and she wondered if that was because electricity ran through it, or because it had been worn moments ago by Filby.

"Where is Major Filby?" she demanded.

The two spider-Aetryx chittered, a gobbling warble of sound impossible for human vocal chords to shape. The Diplomat's smile widened. She had the feeling that the thing didn't really have the proper hang of smiling like a human, though. The expression was more grimace than grin. "Major Filby is well," the Diplomat said. Its voice was low, almost pleasant, but with a hint of an accent she couldn't place. "You need not fear for that one. He is with others of your kind now."

Others of his kind? Had he been returned to the cell? Or did the creature mean something else?

"What is it you want?" she asked.

None of the others answered. She became aware, however, that much of the attention in the room was focused not on her, but on a three-dimensional display above a metal table at the other side of the room. She saw there, briefly illuminated in pale light, her own head, which turned transparent, revealing her brain and, aglow in yellow and green, her implants. They seemed to be studying her cerebral hardware.

A young man seated beside the table wore what looked like some sort of uniform, gray and brown with an oddly shaped red patch on his breast. A technician was placing a second crown on his head, one identical to the one she now wore.

"I'm Major Carla Ramirez," she said, confused and a little desperate at the fact that they weren't talking to her. "Confederation Army, Serial KB 5833-363-376."

She sensed power building in the machine.

"I'm Major Carla Ramirez!" She was shouting now. "Confederation Arm—"

There was a flash, not of light, but within her, within the confines of her skull. It was accompanied, not by the expected pain but by a kind of inner jolt, one that dragged on for what felt like minutes but in fact must have been a mere handful of seconds.

The man at the table must have experienced a similar jolt. He blinked his eyes, leaning back, his hands clenching and unclenching before him. "I am . . . she is Major Carla Ramirez," he said with a rough voice. "Executive Officer of the 4th Regiment, Second Brigade, First Confederation Mobile Army Corps."

"Why is she here?" the Diplomat asked the Caern human. The skin of its face was as blue-black as that of the protosome Aetryx and looked shiny and plastic in the pale light.

"I'm here . . . She's here as part of Operation Thunderstrike, the invasion of Caern."

"And the purpose of Thunderstrike?"

"To free the humans held in slavery by the Aetryx. To open new markets for Daimon Interstellar and other Confederation corporations interested in the human market potential of Caern. . . ."

Carla listened with dawning horror as the Diplomat continued to question the young Caernan, and as the man replied fully and completely to each question with information she could only assume had been drawn directly from her own memory.

It could be done, of course. She'd heard of experiments along those lines. With implant technology, a person's memories, her thought matrices, certain aspects of her personality could all be patterned and downloaded. For a time, once, there'd been talk about eventually downloading people's minds, either into robots or custom-grown organic bodies. The idea had never caught on, of course, because, obviously, what was downloaded was a copy, not the original mind.

Immortality was appealing only if it applied to one's self, not to a kind of technological offspring, a *stranger* who happened to have your mind and memories.

The Aetryx apparently could do just that, however. Her memories, at the very least, had been copied and transferred to the mind of the man sitting at the table. Obviously, his own mind and training were still part of him, since he seemed to be in control. It was as though her memories had simply been tacked on, somehow, to his, in such a way that he could go through her memories at will.

"Tell us of her commanding officer," the Diplomat was saying. That snapped her awareness back to the here and now.

"Colonel Streicher," the man with the crown replied. "Commander of the 4th Regiment. He appears to be a pretty decent CO. Good strategy . . . good tactics . . . although she's been worried about him lately. He's been a bit erratic." The man hesitated, then looked up at Carla, the first time he'd made eye contact with her. "Well, well! It seems they have a relationship, this one and the colonel! They're lovers. She's still feeling it from their lovemaking a few hours ago. . . ."

Carla struggled against the plastic restraints pinning her wrists and ankles. *"Bastards! . . ."*

She'd expected to be grilled on Bolo capabilities, invasion targets, and TO&Es. This, however, was a far more personal attack, a rape of mind as violating, as disgusting, in some ways, as physical rape. Not that Aetryx would be at all interested in human sex.

"Where is the colonel now?" the Diplomat asked.

"Apparently . . . apparently he's on board one of the Bolos. Its working name is Victor . . . it's the combat unit that was operating northwest of Ghendai. She doesn't know where it is now, but she believes it may be coming after her."

"The white-garbed hero of legend, come to rescue his lady fair?" The Diplomat smiled unpleasantly. "Not likely in this case, Carla. Your Bolos cannot reach us here."

"The invasion has been crushed," she said. She hated making that admission, but she knew she had to explore other possibilities. "You know that. Maybe we should be talking about a cessation of hostilities."

"Are you surrendering?" the Diplomat asked with a surprised lift of his eyebrows. He seemed to have a wide range of human facial expressions down quite well, but it was still eerily distracting to see that face attached to *that* body. "It seems to me you are already our prisoner. That leaves you without much say in the matter."

"I'm talking about a cessation of *all* hostilities," she replied, a little unsteadily. "I'm talking about ordering all of the Bolos up there to stop their attacks."

She wasn't even sure she had the right to suggest that. Who was the highest-ranking commander in-theater?

With a small shock, she realized that it *might* be her. She didn't know of any regimental or brigade commanders who'd reached Caern's surface, other than Jon, and the rest were either killed in the sneak attack in space, or fled into hyper. Jon Streicher was the ranking officer, and he was out of touch right now.

Could she open peace talks without consulting with him? Or was that a decision only Jon could make? She was scared, and she wasn't sure where to draw the boundaries in her command responsibilities.

"She doesn't have the authority to bargain with us," the crowned soldier said. "According to what I'm getting here, that would probably be Streicher. The CO of the whole invasion is a General Moberly, and he's either dead or gone, with the fleet."

Damn them. They had access to her memories, her knowledge, but were apparently able to bypass the emotions, the fear and the desperation, that were obscuring things for her.

He was right, of course. . . .

"Well, if what you say about her relationship with Streicher is true," the Diplomat said, "maybe we have a hold on him as well." He twittered something at the two Aetryx protosomes, then added, "Put her with the others."

She scarcely noticed as a pair of trolls removed the crown and its tangle of cables from her head, then unfastened her wrists and ankles and helped her down from the restraint frame.

"Thank you, Major," the Diplomat said, still smiling. "Your information will be most helpful. *Most* helpful indeed!"

They were still questioning the Caernan with her memories as they led her from the room.

The Enemy launches another attack, a rush by unarmored troops using short-range shoulder-fired rocket launchers and satchel charges of explosives.

I cannot depress the muzzle of my primary weapons enough to hit them, and, in any case, my AP pods are sufficient to negate the threat. However, my reserves of AP expendables are running low, and I sense that they are using human wave tactics in an attempt to deplete my ammunition.

In response, I loose several quick rounds of 200cm Hellbore fire above their heads. The concussion, noise, and thermal blast kill or stun dozens of them and leave the others clawing for cover at the earth as I race past. As I approach the objective area, I come under direct attack from three separate turreted bunkers mounting 130cm Hellbores, as well as heavy armor well-hidden in the forest. As Hellbore fire crashes and thunders among the trees, setting the forest ablaze, I smash my way forward to a deep ravine, wide enough to admit my breadth, deep enough to give me shelter as I move north past the entrenched hard points. Humans scramble for safety, trying to climb the walls of the gully as I race through at high speed. A few make it....

Emerging 26.13 seconds later from the gully 523 meters from my entry point, I detect multiple air targets, incoming, at ranges varying from five to twelve kilometers. Two appear to be strike aircraft, while four are IRBM surface-to-surface missiles. I trace the missiles' exhaust trails, identifying a probable launch site in the northern reaches of the Kanthurian Mountains. I also scan all six targets for neutrino flux, neutron emissions, and gamma radiation and determine that the missiles possess low-yield kiloton-range fission warheads, while the aircraft, themselves nuclear-powered, may be carrying small nuclear weapons as well, either air-to-ground missiles or gravity bombs with tactical warheads.

I am again surprised and disturbed at the Enemy's casual escalation to nuclear weapons in this conflict. True, nuclear weaponry provides him with his best chance of breaching my defenses, but Bolos mounting 200cm Hellbores would be as effective and far more surgical, allowing the destruction of invading combat units without laying waste to entire cities and geographical regions.

In terms of delivering a force package sufficient to breach my defenses, the Enemy's Mark XXXII Bolos offer a much better opportunity for my destruction. Missiles and aircraft are, of necessity, lightly armored, depending on speed, stealth, and maneuverability to close with their target and deliver their weaponry.

I track the targets for another .25 second, then open fire with my primary weapons. All six targets disintegrate completely in mid-air within 1.62 second of one another.

An additional barrage of Hellbore blasts directed at the bunker-mounted Hellbore turrets tells me that Invictus has arrived in this operational area. I join my firepower to his, and together we knock out all three of the enemy emplacements.

By this time, the unarmored ground forces, those not killed outright, have scattered and fled. I note from seismic readings that this area is honeycombed by interconnecting tunnels, many of them only human-sized. I will not be able to penetrate these, obviously, though I possess firepower enough, if necessary, to blast away layer upon layer of dirt and bedrock to expose at least the upper layers of tunnels and destroy them.

For the moment, that action represents a relatively

unproductive, even pointless application of my fire-power, especially since I would still need a team of either hunter-killer robots or human engineers and tunnel warfare experts to penetrate the tunnel system to any worthwhile tactical extent.

Working together, Invictus and I determine the location of the main Bolo entrance to the underground tunnel complex. He fires a series of mortar rounds, impacting along the circumference of a circle two kilometers across. By measuring the seismic waves traveling through the ground, both in speed and in amplitude, I can build a three-dimensional picture of subsurface anomalies in ground density, including both the presence of massive support structures and of large excavated areas.

We pinpoint the main entrance in the side of a hill 215 meters from my current position, close to the center of the triangle formed by the three now-silenced bunkers.

The entire region is thoroughly ablaze now. The plant forms native to Caern that fill the niche for trees tend to be tall, slender and flexible, with bushy crowns consisting of leaves like long, slender feathers, colored gold and red. Their large surface area and low density makes them susceptible to fire, and they tend to burn readily and quickly. The brief firefight in this area has ignited most of the plant life for several kilometers around, and the firestorm is growing as potentially destructive and dangerous as those generated by Hellbore fire at the fringes of the cities. My outer hull temperature climbs to nearly 400 degrees Celsius as I move toward the tightly sealed tunnel entrance. Fortunately, the temperature is well within my design tolerances, and the fire only serves to scatter any remaining human soldiers hiding in the area.

I can see the tunnel entrance now using ground-

penetrating radar, a slab of duralloy nearly eighty meters wide and fifty high, set into a steep hillside, angled back into the rock. I fire several Hellbore bursts and note that the door is field-shielded, with a buried superconducting mesh designed to absorb and shunt excess energy to hidden, underground reserve capacitors.

My programmed instinct is to attempt to open the tunnel door electronically and continue the pursuit. However, this would take the battle onto ground of the Enemy's choosing and might well prove to be a trap.

I will need orders from one of my commanders to proceed.

Colonel Streicher sat on the metal-mesh deck and stared at the blue pill in his outstretched hand. He wanted it.

He *needed* it.

It was his very last euph, and he felt now as though he would crumble without it.

He knew he'd already surpassed the allowable dosage during the past several hours. One euph—two at the most—should have kept him going for twelve hours.

None of that mattered as he stared at the gloriously sky-blue pellet in his palm.

If he took it, the tension, the terrible, devouring stress would leave him, and he would again be able to make coherent decisions.

If he took it, he would have none left.

"Colonel?"

None left, until he could get back to the command craft.

"Colonel!"

"Huh? What?"

"I said, 'Vic needs your go-ahead to enter the underground passageway!'"

He hadn't even realized that Lieutenant Tyler had been speaking. She was sitting in the command chair, hands braced on the chair arms, half swiveled toward him so she could meet his eyes. She looked worried, and he wondered if she'd seen the pill and knew what it was.

Carefully, he dropped the bright blue euph back into his uniform tunic pocket and carefully sealed the pocket flap. *Later....*

"Go," was all he said.

At my Commander's word, I open fire again on the tunnel entrance. For 3.5 seconds, the shielded doorway stubbornly resists the full energy output of all three of my primary Hellbores, reflecting or absorbing a torrent equivalent to fifteen megatons of energy per second. The thunder of the discharge echoes from the mountainside, and my hull, already hot from the surrounding forest fire, grows hotter still at the touch of the reflected thermal energy.

My 200cm barrels begin to overheat, and I cease fire. Radar and seismic data indicates that the barrier is a laminate of duralloy, superconducting ceramics, and ceramplast at least eight meters thick. At this rate, it will take approximately 5.47 hours to burn through, allowing for cool-down time after every three-second period of operation.

As I wait, I attempt to trace the barrier's electrical system, sending low-voltage induction pulses through the buried wiring and attempting to reach and circumvent the locking or door-triggering mechanism. It appears to be a system of simple design, responding to a coded radio signal. It may be possible for me to break the code, especially if I can access the Enemy's computer network or security system through the wiring.

I estimate that it will take approximately 3.17 hours to crack the code using brute-force trial-and-error.

Neither approach is satisfactory. The Enemy will be mustering all possible defenses in this area as swiftly as he can. I do not have three hours.

There is, however, a possible alternative. . . .

"He wants to do what?" Streicher sounded shocked.

Kelly Tyler closed her eyes. What the hell was wrong with the colonel? "There is a wrecked enemy Bolo just outside of Ghendai," she said again. "One of the first enemy Bolos he knocked out. He says that the machine's AI core may be intact. He doesn't have the tools to access it, but he says we may be able to, under his direction."

"Yes, but why?"

"He thinks he can talk to it," she replied. "He thinks it may have things like the code to open that door out there, or maybe even infiltrate the enemy's computer net."

"You mean, passwords? Stuff like that?"

She nodded. "Yes, sir. It's better than trying to kick the door down, anyway."

"How long will that take?"

"Another hour, maybe an hour and a half to reach the wreckage and retrieve the AI core. He doesn't know how long it will take to get the information. He . . . he says that will depend on how well we can follow directions."

Streicher considered this. He didn't like taking orders from a machine, but he had to admit that the Bolo was exhibiting a damn sight more sense than he was, right now.

"Invie is already here," Kelly continued. "Roxie is about thirty minutes away. They can keep the bad guys bottled up, while we go retrieve the goods."

"Okay," he said. "Let's do it."

He felt Victor's rocking motion and deep-rumbling track-thunder as it swung about and accelerated southwest almost before the words were out of his mouth.

They didn't take Carla back to the cell. They led her through a different set of corridors, up a freight lift, and into a broad, high-ceilinged hall with dusty sunlight filtering through skylights far overhead. For a horrifying few minutes, she could only assume that they were taking her someplace to dispose of her—they didn't need her anymore, after all, if they had her memories.

Her shackles were removed and she was prodded into a large room with perhaps thirty other people already there, all human, all as raggedly undressed as she was.

Filby was there, sprawled on a cot against one wall, apparently no worse for the ordeal than she was. The rest of the people, though, appeared to be civilians.

A strikingly handsome woman of perhaps forty-five standard greeted her. "You're safe" were her first words. "I'm Tami Morrigen."

"Carla Ramirez," she replied, a little unsteadily. "Confederation Army."

The others were crowding closer, now. "The invasion!" one older man, his hair shot through with silver, exclaimed. "What's happening? Who's winning?"

"Not us, I'm afraid."

Shock and dismay ran through the crowd. "No!"

"Gods!"

"What happened?"

"Your friend over there wouldn't tell us. . . ."

"We landed in force," she told them. "Bolo heavies. But they managed to ambush our fleet and drove it off. My group was in a spacecraft that was damaged and forced to land. As far as I know, there are a bunch of Bolos still on the offensive up there, but they, *we*, are all alone now."

"Don't tell them everything!" Filby called from his cot. He was sitting up, now, glaring at her. "Damn it, we don't know if this isn't all some sort of trick! A way to pump us for information!"

"They've already done that, Major," she told him. "Literally. Or didn't you notice?"

He waved his hand. "A trick. Some sort of trick. They're playing mind games with us, Major, don't you get it?" Filby's voice was unsteady, and he had an unpleasant glitter in his eye. Too many shocks, she thought, hitting him too fast.

"Easy, Filby . . ."

"They're not slaves!" Filby shouted. He shook his head, as if trying to clear it. "Don't you see? They told us the Caernans were slaves, and the Caernans are fighting against us! We can't trust *any* of them! . . ."

"Actually, we're all offworlders here," the red-haired man said. "We've considered Caern our home for the past five years, but we never did really fit in with the locals." He extended a hand. "I'm Sym Redmond. Senior factor of Daimon Interstellar. These are all *my* people."

They formally touched hands, in standard Confederation greeting. "A pleasure, sir," she said. "I've heard of you." The pre-invasion briefings had mentioned that there was a small population of traders on Caern, that Sym Redmond was the leader of a trade consortium on the planet.

Redmond and his people, in fact, were the primary source of information on local conditions and politics used by Army Intelligence in preparing for the invasion.

Perhaps the native human Caernans didn't want or

need rescuing, but these people certainly did. Too bad the Confederation strike force was no longer in a position to do anything about it.

"Is this your whole group?" she asked. The briefings had mentioned several hundred offworlders.

"All of the ones I was responsible for, the ones in Ghendai. We were in the process of getting our things together and evacuating when we were all rounded up together, outside the city. There were plenty of other offworlders on-planet elsewhere. Kanth. Ledelefen. Vled. Even Gethorladest, on the other side of the planet. God knows what happened to them."

"The Aetryx have actually treated us pretty well, all things considered," Tami said. "The trolls and protosome humans were actually a lot worse. Roughed us up when they took us, that sort of thing." She shuddered. "But the Aetryx have been polite, distant. Almost gentlemanly."

"What did you call the humans? Proto . . . what?"

"Protosome humans," Redmond said. "Original bodies. Here it means human beings, like you and me."

"The locals," Tami said, "have a very different view of what it means to be human."

"Maybe," Carla said, "you should fill me in."

And they proceeded to do just that.

Chapter Fifteen

I have no trouble locating the wrecked enemy Bolo designated Alpha One, thanks to its recovery beacon transponder, signaling combat engineers and AI recovery technicians who now will not be coming. Pulling alongside the wreckage, I lower my rear ramp so that my Commander and the colonel can exit, along with several of my techspiders.

Under my guidance, they swiftly find the AI containment pod, still embedded within the burned-out hulk. The pod, complete with armor and containment shielding, masses 214.57 tons and would be impossible to move without heavy crane and construction equipment. The data still locked within the psychotronic circuitry and mem-modules, however, masses nothing. I need only get at it.

We must move quickly, however. I detect heavy underground movement through my seismic sensors, and there is evidence of surface traffic as well, detected on BIST pickups and on my long-range sonic detectors. The Enemy is moving and in force.

I dislike the fact that the last of the regimental staff members remaining alive and free must operate outside in a hostile combat zone, relying solely on lightweight emergency E-suits for protection. The incidental *radiation here, in the vicinity of Alpha One, measures 45 rads, which limits their exposure time outside.*

And if a firefight develops, they will be in serious danger.

I contact both Invictus and Ferox, who have rendezvoused at the tunnel entrance 68.9 kilometers from this location, on a bearing of zero-five-eight. They have begun firing at the armor in an attempt to ablate it. We have discussed the possibility of the three of us working together but agree that the information housed within the Caernan Bolo's AI pod is vital. Even if they can burn through before I can return, it is likely that the pod's memory cores include maps or navigational information that will help us in our sub-surface explorations.

If the two humans working in the wreckage outside now can complete the task in time. . . .

Streicher pulled back, raising a hand to wipe the sweat from his forehead, then cursing when his gloved fingers thumped uselessly against his helmet visor. It was hot out here, and the E-suit's cooling system was struggling with the load.

It was hot in more ways than one, too. The radiation levels here were high enough to kill him with a few hours' exposure. The suit could protect him against alpha and beta particles, but any gamma radiation in the vicinity—induced, say, by high-energy neutrons irradiating this enormous mass of twisted, heat-blackened metal before him—would be sleeting right through his suit's slender defenses.

Strangely, though, and very much to his surprise, he wasn't thinking about the turquoise pill in his pocket. Right now, he had other things to worry about.

A Bolo Mark XXXII was smaller than a Mark XXXIII, but that was only a matter of degree. It had two sets of tracks to either side instead of three and only a single 200cm Hellbore turret on the flat upper deck, but the thing was still as big as the hull of a small starship. The entire front end of the machine had been melted away, with layers of duralloy and ceramplast folded back like the petals of an open flower. Victor had peeled back the armor shrouding the deeply buried inner AI core, using beam weapons with a surgeon's delicacy.

"In there, huh?" Streicher said.

At his side, Kelly nodded behind her helmet visor. "Victor says this cave leads straight to the Mark XXXII's AI pod . . . its control and memory core, everything we need."

Funny to think of a "cave" inside a human-made artifact. The Bolo wreckage before them, though, looked more like a natural cliff face transformed into duralloy. Fully a third of the enemy machine had vaporized under Victor's relentless high-energy hammering, but what was left was still a literal mountain of metal and alloy composites. He found himself looking up . . . and up . . . and *up*, and he could not see the machine's top deck, or the main turret mounting.

"Let's get the hell on with it, then." He started climbing.

It was a treacherous ascent. Most of the duralloy edges had been dulled—half-melted by the ferocious heat of Victor's assault, then solidified again in lumpy, almost organic shapes that were all curves and rounded edges. Still, there were places where duralloy had split clean along knife-edged fracture lines, as surgically sharp as obsidian blades. He started up first, but Kelly soon passed him, climbing with speed and a precise beauty and athletic efficiency. Eventually, they helped one another, offering gloved hands for support and counterbalance as they picked their way in a dizzying free climb up the ruined face of the Bolo.

Finally, they reached the tunnel entrance. It started out broad and wide-open, a crater ten meters across, but as they picked their way inside into deepening, brooding shadow, the tunnel narrowed, forcing them into single file, then a hobbling stoop that led deeper and deeper into that metallic labyrinth of pipes, conduits, wiring, and slab armor. The radiation levels, he found, fell rapidly. The exterior of the Mark XXXII had been hot, leaking secondary radiation from the severe neutron blasting it had received earlier. Inside, however, the surrounding tons of duralloy armor shielded them.

Soon, the tunnel was so narrow they had to crawl, picking their way ahead over broken shards of technology. Behind them, one of Victor's techspiders clicked and scuttled along after them, and Streicher had to fight down a momentary pang of claustrophobia . . . and perhaps something worse. The spider was a gleaming, metal sphere half a meter across, dangling from four slender walking legs and pocked with gleaming camera lenses. Its legs had telescoped down until they were a quarter of their usual length, giving it the appearance of a grotesque amputee spider dragging itself along on its stumps. It clutched a slender power cable in one mechanical gripper and a data feed in another, dragging them along as they snaked in from outside. Lights mounted on its body cast bizarrely shifting patterns of light and dark across the tangle around them.

At last, twenty meters into the wreckage, they reached the dull black surface of the AI pod. Victor had peeled back the inner armor with a surgeon's precision earlier, laying bare a tangle of molecular circuit boards, hundreds of book-sized slabs of plastic, each mounting several rectangular blocks of translucent gray plastic and labyrinthine tracings of silver.

The opening in the AI pod was just wide enough for Lieutenant Tyler and Streicher, lying on their sides, to reach into the opened pod's exposed internal circuitry.

Behind them, the spider unfolded tool-arms that telescoped in and out with tiny, metallic chirps and whines from its servos. "We need more light here," Streicher told the spider, and one jointed arm shifted a bit, playing the beam from a small light at its tip to better illuminate the psychotronic module in front of them.

"This looks like an old VY-700 board," Kelly said, extracting a board sprouting dozens of optical data cables. "Old tech." She touched a contact point with the probe in her gloved hand and gave it a charge. Colored pinpoints of light flickered briefly deep within the dark, translucent plastic of the molecular circuit blocks. "It's live."

"Attach the power lead to the contact point marked cGYk-1," Victor said over their helmet phones.

The spider handed Streicher the power cable. Kelly pointed to the AI unit's main power supply, and he attached it to a receptor. Streicher knew they were trying now to energize enough of the powered-off circuit boards to get a low-level response from the apparently dead machine, but he felt pretty much in the dark, reduced to the role of untrained assistant. He'd worked a bit with molecular circuits, back when he'd first entered the Bolo service, but that had been a long time ago, and he'd never worked on the guts of a combat unit as advanced as a XXXII or XXXIII. All he could really do here was lie in a cramped and uncomfortable position, holding the circuit board with his right hand, and keeping a stray flap of titanium clear of the work area with his left.

"Okay," Kelly said. "Power supply connected."

"Stand by," Victor said.

The board in Streicher's hand lit up in a soft, gold galaxy of deeply embedded lights shining through the plastic.

"Power okay," Kelly said. She tested several touch points with her probe. "Memory active."

"Attach the data cable, please," the Bolo said. "Contact point 88-K-7r."

The spider extended the data feed cable with pinchers mounted on a telescoping arm. Handing the circuit board to Kelly, Streicher reached back, accepted the cable, then passed it along to her.

"Is this really going to work?" he asked her.

He sensed her shrug in the dimly lit tunnel. "It should, if there's no major damage to the system hardware. We should have access to all of the Bolo's memories, which are stored in molecular circuit memmodules. Non-volatile, at least short-term."

"Yes, but does that mean it's going to, well . . . wake up?"

She laughed. "That, Colonel, depends on your definition of 'awake.' We've been working with artificial intelligence for over a thousand years now, and we still can't exactly define the important terms like 'consciousness' and 'self-aware.' "

"They're supposed to be self-aware," he said. "Ever since the . . . which one was it? The Mark XXIV?"

"Well, the Mark XXIV was the first truly autonomous Bolo," she said. She continued to probe the circuitry as she spoke. "Earlier marks were self-directing on a tactical level, but the XXIV had improved id-integration and a much better personality center. They were the first ones with whom you could really feel you were having a conversation. They said they were self-aware. But we couldn't really be sure of what they meant by that."

"How do you get inside the other guy's mind, huh?"

"Yes, sir." By the light of glowing molecular circuits, he saw her eyes shift to give him a hard look through her visor. "I can't even know for certain if *you* are self-aware. Sir." Then she broke eye contact. "Sorry, sir."

"Not at all. Sometimes I wonder the same thing myself."

The moment was broken. She continued working on the circuits. "Are you getting anything, Vic?"

"I have access to the machine's level six memory. Basic programming and personality integration. Please make additional connections to the remaining mem-module boards."

"I am. Hang on."

Kelly Tyler, Streicher was now realizing, was not nearly as awkward as she sometimes seemed. She knew exactly what she was doing and possessed an encyclopedic knowledge of her field. She seemed completely self-possessed when she was talking with Victor . . . or able to freely elaborate on Bolo AI theory.

"Any sign of that ghost, Vic?"

"Negative, my Commander. But my original impression was fleeting. I may have been mistaken."

"Yeah. And *I* might be the Trixie Queen of Caern. How's this?"

"I am now accessing level five memories. Please continue."

"What ghost?" Streicher asked her.

"Vic was telling me earlier that when he destroyed this Bolo, right after the battle he sent in some spiders and was able to touch the AI mind, just briefly, before it went dead. He said . . . he said he sensed a human personality in here."

"Human!"

"Yes, sir."

"You're not talking about . . . about human*like*, are

you? I mean, it's like we were just talking about. Mark XXXIIIs have personalities, have self-awareness—whatever that means—that's *like* human awareness. . . ."

"No," she replied. "Victor was quite clear about what he felt. It wasn't a Bolo mind he sensed. It was human."

"A downloaded personality?"

"That's what I think."

So little was known about the Aetryx and their technological abilities. To precisely copy a human mind and download it into a machine . . . could they perform such a feat?

He knew there'd been talk of doing such a thing ever since prespaceflight days, of somehow transferring a person's memories, his thoughts, his mind, his *soul* from a failing organic body to immortal robotic or computer hardware. When it had become clear that a copy could be transferred, but not the original, interest had faded. It was more useful to focus on the creation and improvement of an artificial intelligence that could be programmed for specific work, than to merely make copies of oneself that did nothing to enhance the life or life expectancy of the original. . . .

The Aetryx, evidently, didn't think that way.

"Could the human part of this thing still be alive, then?" It was a strange thought, a creepy one. The surrounding metal felt so *dead*. . . .

"Well, it *is* just data," Kelly replied. "If the mem-modules are intact, we ought to at least be able to tap the guy's memories."

But did that mean the person trapped inside this radioactive hulk would become aware? Alive?

Did such terms even have meaning in a case like this?

"Okay, Victor," Kelly said. "I've hooked up another ten modules. Whatcha got?"

❖   ❖   ❖

He awoke, stretching . . . and then the fear hit him in deep, shuddering waves, like the icy surf at Gods' Beach. The last thing he remembered . . . no . . . what *was* the last thing he remembered? Memory eluded him, like fragments of a dream.

Elken opened his eyes, then wondered why he couldn't see. He reached out with a trembling, sweat-slicked hand, then realized he couldn't feel anything, that the tremors, the sweat, the cold were all imagined, anchors for the mind adrift within a vast and lightless void.

Concentrating, he summoned memories from deep, deep within. He'd been in a battle . . . he'd been . . . he'd been a Bolo combat unit, his brain housed in a huge mobile armored vehicle. He could remember . . . The memories were still dim, still fragmentary, but there was something about going in for elective surgery . . . a chance at immortality . . .

What had gone wrong? . . .

Can you hear me? The voice, deep and quiet, spoke within the terror-haunted depths of his thoughts. *Who are you?*

Was it the voice of his god? He desperately wished for it to be so.

"G-god? Where am I? Why can't I see?"

You have been badly damaged. Your optical processing units are off-line. Can you remember what happened to you?

He was trying. Gods, he was trying! "I was in a battle with an enemy Bolo. One of the invaders. I think . . . I think I was hit. Who are you?"

"One of your brother Bolos. I am attempting now to access your level three memories. Is this better?"

Images flashed through Elken's mind, of the deep blue of the predawn sky, of the golden slash of the rings of Dis arcing above the eastern horizon.

Of a huge and powerful Sky Demon Bolo, bearing down on him in fire and thundering destruction.

Other memories surfaced, flickering past too quickly to identify in some cases, and in others . . .

He was at the Tower of Learning in Ledelefen, overlooking the circular, tree-rimmed sweep of the Park of Divine Prospect. The Brotherhood had assigned him here to research The Histories. The gods wanted to know all that was known of the outreach of Humankind from mythic Earth . . . the ships they'd used, the wars they'd fought.

Thirteen hundred standard years of history, all told, the millennium before the colonization of Caern compressed into download files, e-books and microfiches, and even ancient tomes of paper and clothboard. Assimilating it all was utterly beyond the capabilities of Elken and his small team of student monks, but at least they could get a feel for the overall sweep of history and be able to report to the gods in general terms what they'd discovered.

He'd had no idea that there was so much history waiting to be revealed. . . .

There was a flash, and then he was . . . elsewhere. Elsewhen.

He was on the cliff above Gods' Beach, and Sendee was with him, held close within the circle of his arms. "But why?" he asked, his voice a wail. "You're still so young! Why do you need the surgery now? . . ."

It wasn't fair. They'd been lovers for only six months. If she accepted the gods' offer of immortality, her old body, this body, so soft, so warm, would die. His beloved Sendee would reside within a god-form, alive, but inexpressibly alien. . . .

"Elken, I have to," she told him. Her eyes glistened as she looked up into his eyes, as her hand traced the line of his jaw. "I only just found out. I have a . . . a

disease. It's cancer. Pancreatic cancer. The gods can't do anything . . . except offer me immortality. But that will be in another body."

"That's not right!" he cried. "They can grow whole new bodies. Grow different kinds of bodies, like the warrior-forms! They could give you a new pancreas!"

"No, Elken. That's not how it works. I asked, and my god explained it to me. They can transfer my mind to another body, but they can't stop the disease that's already spreading through this one."

"They could grow a new pancreas! Remove the old one, put in a new . . ."

"No, Elken. Once, a long time ago, our people could do that sort of thing. A . . . a transplant, they called it. But the gods say we've lost that knowledge. And the gods, well, they never had it. Not for our species, anyway."

"But the gods can do anything!"

"Some things, even the gods can't do, dear Elken. . . ."

Elken drew back from that memory, horrified. Why hadn't he remembered that conversation? He remembered it *now*, yes, as clearly as though it was scant hours old, but it had happened many cycles ago. It had been the reason he'd opted for immortality himself. But it simply hadn't existed until it had surfaced just now.

He felt cheated . . . and robbed. Why had that memory been taken from him?

I am surprised to find that the personality within the enemy Bolo appears to have completely reanimated. I expected the personality matrix to collapse and dissociate completely when the AI lost power, but apparently the data has been stored in a nonvolatile buffer, at least for the short term. There is growing evidence, however, that this personality, which calls itself "Elken," is growing increasingly unstable.

He appears bewildered by some of the memories arising now, as I download the contents of his mem-modules into my own memory core. Some memories which, I gather, were extremely important to him were blocked or somehow suppressed. As he regains access to them, he is becoming more and more confused.

"There is evidence that your gods blocked certain of your memories," I tell him. "Perhaps they feared that strong emotion would interfere with your programming."

"Who are you?" he demands. "Why are you showing me these things?"

"I am not showing them to you," I reply, sidestepping his first question, which could be a difficult one for him to have answered right now. "I am downloading your memories into my system. Some of those memories were blocked, apparently by the Aetryx. To access those memories, I removed the blocks. You now have access to them as well."

"You . . . you're not a god?"

"No."

"Who are you?"

"Go ahead and tell him, Victor," Colonel Streicher says. I have been echoing my conversation with Elken to both Lieutenant Tyler and Colonel Streicher.

"He may refuse to cooperate if he knows we are the enemy," I tell them.

"You have his memories," my Commander says. "He's a human being, or he was. He deserves to know."

It is an emotional gesture, but I find myself in essential agreement. There is no military reason to hide the truth, especially since I see no way of keeping this system alive once we stop supplying it with power. It seems a proper and honorable course of action.

"I am a Bolo of the Line, Mark XXXIII," I tell Elken, "in the service of the Confederation Armed Forces. Until recently, I was your enemy."

"The enemy! Sky Demon!"

"I wish you no harm now. I am trying to help you, in fact."

"You're trying to trick me! I will tell you nothing, demon!"

"I have recovered the information which I sought," I tell him. "Believe me, I have no need to trick you."

"You . . . you're like me!"

"Outwardly, at least. We both are high-mark Bolo combat units. I am an artificial intelligence arising from hyper-heuristic programming matrices within an advanced AI architecture of psychotronic molecular circuitry and massively parallel neuro-networking within an n-dimensional polymorphic array. You appear to be a gestalt of a similar software AI native to the Mark XXXII and a downloaded composite of personality and memory derived from a human source. . . ."

I stop speaking when I realize Elken is no longer listening.

He appears to be screaming.

The full realization had just struck home for Elken. He'd been tricked, been *used* by the beings he thought of as his gods.

He'd been downloaded into this . . . this machine and sent out against overwhelmingly superior odds. He'd been told that this was his one chance at immortality, with a promise of a new body if he won.

He saw now, though, that it had all been a sham. If this enemy Bolo was correct—and Elken had a nightmarish feeling that it was telling him the complete and perfect truth—he was no more than an electronic copy of himself, downloaded into an old reserve combat unit. The real Elken was . . . was . . . where?

Was his body even still alive?

Suddenly, Elken wasn't sure of anything—of who or what he was or what he was seeking . . . or even whose side he was supposed to be on. The gods had lied to him, had deceived him. Sendee . . . she, too, was just a copy. The gods had promised her new and everlasting life. She, the *real* Sendee, must be dead by now, while the gods used a copy of her mind to run a Bolo.

In Tharsee, the dominant Caernan religion, the wicked were punished for eternity by being set adrift by the gods among the stars, unable to move or help themselves, lost in an endless night. Stories were told to disobedient children of how the only hope these damned souls held was the knowledge that eventually, after millions of cycles, they would wander into the gravitational grasp of a planet and be disintegrated in a flash of flame—dying meteors against the night.

Few Caernans believed those stories any more, of course. The gods themselves denied that they would do such a thing. And yet, being doomed to an imitation of life played out within the circuits of a lifeless machine, placed there for the gods' purposes, unable to choose for one's self . . . was that hell any less terrible than eternity adrift among the stars?

This was the true, living hell, and Elken was damned.

This had to stop. He had to stop it. He *would* stop it.

Like any purely organic entity, Elken had limited power over his own mental processes. It was impossible, he found, to step outside of himself, analyze his own mental state of being, or change the sudden cascade of bleak, self-destructive thoughts tumbling through the sphere of his awareness.

But he did possess some control, more, perhaps, than was the case for an organic brain. His emotions as a man-machine were essentially the outgrowth of chaotic processes, but there were circuit breakers, power shunts, feed blocks, and yes-no-maybe trinary logic switches that he could control, even if it was on an almost purely hardwired-instinctive level.

With fragmenting nightmare snippets of his god's promises—and his lies—thundering through his thoughts, he began shutting down his motherboard power receptor feeds.

As the darkness closed in, he could not stop screaming inside his own mind.

"Victor!" Kelly yelled. "The voltage output is dropping! What's happening?"

"He is dying," Victor's voice replied in her helmet phones. "I cannot hold him."

"Tell us what to do! . . ."

"I do not know myself. He appears to be self-terminating."

Kelly stared at the molecular circuit board in her hand. Power was flowing into the module, and through it to the entire tightly packed array of MCBs filling the AI core. But the golden pinpoints of light, like myriad stars, were fading as she watched. There was no reason. . . .

For much of her life, she'd wished that human beings could be like Bolos—honorable, duty-bound, dependable, *reliable*. They represented titanic, awesome power, but if they did something, they did it for a reason . . . a reason other than the fact that they were feeling grouchy that morning, or petty, or irrationally depressed or angry.

They were rationality personified.

And this one was dying for no rational reason that she could perceive. Was it because it was haunted by a human ghost . . . the downloaded personality of some unknown human Caern native? Or was there something more?

Artificial intelligences, like even the most primitive of computers, essentially did what you told them to do. Program them, and they acted according to the dictates of that programming . . . even if the software running was complex enough to allow it to write its own software. Even with a human's mind downloaded into its circuitry, this Bolo ought to operate in a rational fashion.

"Victor!" she yelled. "Save him!"

"I do not believe he wants to be saved," was Victor's only answer.

Interlude IV

It is now known and well understood that the Aetryx possessed a singular advantage over their human opponents, one unguessed at until late in the battle. Evolved from a parasitic chthonic species, they learned to manipulate their own and other species genetically. Maintaining an extraordinarily plastic vision of just what it meant to be Aetryxha, they grew specialized bodies, "parasomes," for specialized tasks. It is believed that at the time of the Caern campaign, there were 12 major genera of Aetryx, 44 distinct species, and an unknown but large number of subspecies, all of them the product of genetic engineering in their deep racial past.

This plasticity of worldview was imposed on the species conquered by the Aetryxha Reach. Subject races were manipulated genetically to produce ideal servants according to Aetryx views of place, properness, and utility. Perhaps more important from a sociotechnic dynamic, their use of sophisticated AI to pattern and download mental patterns, both into machines and, in some cases, into appropriately prepared organic brains, allowed them to vastly extend their control over subject races, and to fashion living tools—and weapons—to their express purpose.

The mothballed Bolos recovered by the Aetryx on Caern were a case in point. Reactivated, equipped with the thoughts, memories, and mentation patterns of selected humans promised a form of immortality by the Aetryx "gods," these Bolos became the chief weapon against the Confederation invasion forces; by downloading periodic backups, the same personalities could be reinstalled in new bodies, complete with the memories of earlier downloaded iterations. Those personalities did possess a kind of immortality— destroyed time and time again, yet returning, in a sense, to bring new experience and skills to the tactical problem at hand.

If the system had not possessed an unexpected hidden flaw, the Aetryx defeat of the invading forces would have been complete and overwhelming.

Disaster at Caern:
A Study of the Unexpected in Warfare
Galactic Press Productions, Primus, cy 426

Chapter Sixteen

I can feel the Caernan's mind dissociating, fragments of thought and mind dissolving into emptiness. Elken is . . . dead. I wonder if he was truly alive in this machine body.

For .075 second, I ponder the cause of his dissolution. It is always difficult to judge how stress will affect any given human. In this case, evidently, the shock of self-discovery, of finding out just who and what he was, has been too much. It might have been kinder not to tell him the truth.

"Kindness" is a human quality to which I have been giving considerable attention for a number of hours now, turning it over from microsecond to microsecond in the deep background, well behind my regular processing tasks. What is kindness, and what is its purpose?

I understand the definition, of course. What I am having trouble with is the reason for such an emotion or response. An adult's kindness to a child, as a means of affirming and expressing basic paternal nurturing instincts, is understandable. So, too, is performing an act of kindness either in the hope of receiving something in return, or in order to change the emotional atmosphere.

This last has been especially hard to grasp, but I believe I understand as well as any nonhuman can. Human beings, I perceive, are extremely sensitive to the emotional reactions and output of other humans in their vicinity; one human seems to react to the sadness of another, or to fear or stress or happiness. If one human is in a state of deep depression, another might try to do or say something pleasant or appealing to change the emotional atmosphere, as it were, in order to make himself more comfortable.

But why would anyone show kindness to someone unknown to him? Why has the passing of this AI-human gestalt so affected my Commander's emotional stability?

Why was Elken's life, or the manner of its passing, so important to her?

I remember again that hideously burned and dying wretch in the ruins of Ghendai, playing the encounter back in my mind.

>>*ARCHIVE RETRIEVAL:* 2827:83:9298<<

>>*SEARCHING*<<

>>"Kill me! Please!"<<

>>I consider the request for a full .02 second. With the radiation he has absorbed, the man has but hours to live. I am under no obligation to accede to his request. Besides, he is a civilian. I have control over the moral inhibitor subroutines controlling my AP batteries, but other inhibitors govern aspects of my programming to avoid collateral damage to the civilian population, where possible and when consistent with overall mission directives.<<

>>And yet the man is in great pain, and no medical facility accessible within a reasonable amount of time could save his life. I override my primary moral inhibitions and switch off the governor subroutine responsible for suppressing the automatic triggers for

Antipersonnel Battery 32. The radar-guided mount pivots sharply and releases a high-kinetic burst of AP needles, and the human is shredded in a vivid splash of scarlet. I switch on the governor subroutine once more, and continue my passage through the ruined city.<<

Was that an act of kindness?

Why did I perform it?

What was I . . . feeling?

As a fully autonomous and self-aware artificial intelligence, I do have feelings—emotions—which theoretically closely pattern the emotions experienced by humans. These have been edited, of course, to fit the parameters of my operational requirements, and to meet my overall mission needs. I do not experience fear or panic as a human does, for example, although I do have a sense of self-preservation hardwired into my situational response circuits. A willingness to engage in combat must be tempered with judgement, or it becomes suicidal bravado of no strategic or tactical use in battle.

Nor, for that matter, can I experience genuine bravery, since, by one definition, bravery is the active opposite to, the deliberate overcoming of, fear. I am designed to face situations humans would not be emotionally equipped to handle under any circumstances. This, however, is a product of engineering, not the transcendence of fear.

How, then, can I show kindness to one of the Enemy? Is this a design flaw?

I must consider the question further.

Streicher touched Kelly's shoulder. "He's dead. Let's get out of here."

"Damn!" Kelly said. She dropped the circuit board. The inner lights were gone, now. The AI core was illuminated only by the harsh glare of the techspider's floodlights. "What happened?"

"Evidently," Victor replied, "the entity calling itself Elken elected to cut power to its own mem-module array."

"Can he be revived?" Streicher asked. "The way we did just now?"

"No," Victor replied. "He seems to have deliberately switched off the circuits supplying each individual board with power, including power from the internal batteries that maintained memory viability. The patterns of magnetic moment, spin, and charge determining Elken's thoughts, memories, and personality have gone random."

"Get this damned thing out of our way," Streicher said, slapping the hull of the spider. "Grab those cables, Lieutenant."

Kelly unclipped the power and data cables, dropping them on the tunnel floor. They could be reeled in from the other end, once she and Streicher were clear. The spider began clattering its way back out of the tunnel. Streicher followed, and Kelly brought up the rear, backing out of the narrow space until the opening was wide enough for her to turn around and crouch.

"I would recommend a hasty evacuation of the wreckage," Victor told them. "I have detected enemy vehicles emerging at a tunnel mouth not far from here."

"How far?" Streicher asked.

"Range 4.7 kilometers, bearing 095."

"That's inside the city!" Kelly said.

"Actually, it is within the base on the northern outskirts of the city," Victor replied. The voice, as calm and smoothly modulated as ever, seemed to carry with it this time a note of frustration. "The area was secured 3.15 hours ago. I am now convinced that it will not be possible to reduce this planet's defenses by simply destroying or capturing fixed-point defenses and objectives. The Enemy has too many reserves beyond my reach and too efficient a means of deployment across a broad operational area."

A sudden thunder assaulted Kelly's ears, and the walls of metallic wreckage around her trembled and jolted with the concussion.

"Please remain where you are," Victor said. "I am engaging the Enemy, and you are safer in there than you are outside for the moment."

Kelly stopped, cringing as the thunder grew louder, exploding in a deafening crescendo accompanied by savage, physical jolts and shocks transmitted through the dead Bolo's hull, tracks, and suspension. Reaching up, she tried to cover her ears and found her hands blocked by her helmet.

Streicher was shouting something, but she couldn't hear. "What? What did you say? I didn't copy!"

Before she could hear the answer, something slammed into the side of the wrecked Bolo, and the tunnel began to collapse, an avalanche of conduit and wiring and armor plate spilling down on top of her, and between her and Streicher. Pain exploded in her left leg, and something slammed her helmet against the tunnel floor and pinned it there, like a vise, as she was plunged into a hellish darkness.

She was trapped in the wreckage with no way out.

The attack has developed with extraordinary swiftness. Enemy armor, including four contra-grav heavy missile carriers and several high-velocity mounted guns, have emerged from underground tunnels within the base and are attempting to overwhelm my defenses through saturation shelling.

It would have been more effective had the Enemy

launched this attack before my passengers and I began our examination of the Mark XXXII hulk. I surmise, however, that they may be part of a force being massed at the larger tunnel exit 68.9 kilometers to the northeast, and that it took time for them to react when I redeployed to this position. This gives me some measure of hope that the strategic situation is not an impossible one after all. Attrition will reduce the Enemy's ability to defend himself with time.

The question remains, however, whether that time will be granted me.

Eight enemy missiles streak toward me, hugging the ground to take maximum advantage of the surrounding ruins and undulations in the terrain. I strike all eight with bursts from my secondary batteries, disintegrating seven completely in mid-air, but the last one breaks into fragments and the warhead, tumbling and out of control, slams into the rear quarter of the wrecked Bolo at my side.

The conventional warhead detonates with the destructive concussion of approximately 800 kilos of TNT. The explosion blasts a large chunk of armor clear of the hull. I respond with counter-battery fire, loosing self-guiding hunter-killer missiles to target the firing missile carriers.

This attack would be easily dispersed, except for the fact that I am in a literal sense bound to the wrecked Mark XXXII. A power cable and a data feed remain connected to access panels on my lower engineering deck, close by my open rear hatch. The other ends are embedded within the wreckage. The physical connections are tenuous at best, easily broken, but if I move, I might disturb the wreckage and endanger the humans within.

In any case, abandoning my position here could expose my Commander and my colonel to capture.

To buy time I deploy the remote Dragons, even though they are individually outclassed in this conflict. Indeed, one is destroyed almost immediately, caught in the crossfire between a high-velocity heavy gun and the 80cm Hellbore fired by a light mobile tracked destroyer.

"Victor!" Colonel Streicher is shouting into the commlink, his voice betraying considerable emotion. "Victor!"

"I am here."

"Kelly's trapped! The tunnel just caved in on her!"

The impact of the warhead, I realize, must have shifted internal debris already precariously balanced after the savage pounding the enemy Mark XXXII took earlier. My desire not to endanger my human comrades by pulling the cables free has been in vain.

I attempt to contact my Commander on the tactical channel but can not pick up a signal.

"Can you ascertain whether or not she is alive?" I ask.

"I think so! She still has the ends of the cables with her. I tugged on one, and it felt like she tugged back!"

My Commander is in grave danger. Another hit on the wrecked enemy Bolo, and she might be crushed as massive internal components shift, collapse, or give way.

"Grab hold of the cables," I tell the colonel. "I am going to pull them free at this end."

"Got them!"

Gently, I ease forward. A visual relayed from one of my techspiders shows the near ends of both the power cable and the data line dropping clear of my rear hatch. I raise the ramp and close the hatch, pivoting then to meet the attack. I must develop a strategy that will permit me to take advantage of my superior mobility, yet without abandoning the two humans in the Mark XXXII's wreckage.

The Enemy is continuing to attempt to saturate my defenses. I dispatch twelve more incoming missiles in rapid succession, following up each launch with VLS counter-battery fire of my own. One of the missile carriers is already in flames. The others are scattering wildly, attempting to dodge my return fire.

They are not completely successful. One missile carrier drops off my radar, Wyvern, and BIST sensor tracking networks, almost certainly by doubling back into the tunnel entrance and vanishing underground. That machine, however, has been badly damaged by missile fire, and I score repeated hits on the others, crippling or destroying them all.

One of my Dragons scores a direct hit on the turret of the enemy destroyer, putting it out of commission. I detect other vehicles, small, contra-gravity propelled fliers, which may be troop carriers.

I cannot allow them to approach the wreckage where my Commander is trapped.

Streicher braced himself and shoved, trying to budge the mass of duralloy plate that was blocking him from Lieutenant Tyler's position, but the sheet must have massed two hundred kilos at least, and he couldn't get decent leverage beneath it as he was, lying on his side in a tunnel less than a meter tall. He strained, grunting against the weight, until his arm and back muscles gave out and he collapsed, panting so hard that his visor began to fog. "Kelly!" he shouted, though shouting, he knew, wouldn't help his E-suit radio carry the message any more clearly. "Kelly, can you hear me!"

He didn't know if she wasn't answering because the mass of duralloy was cutting off her transmissions, or because she couldn't. Again, he tugged on the data link cable, then tried to convince himself that he felt an answering tug in reply.

Reaching down to his hip, he pulled out his Mark XL power pistol. Dialing the setting down to its narrowest, most intense beam, he aimed at a part of the barrier that looked thinner than the rest, high up on top of the tumble of metal chunks and parts, near the tunnel's ceiling.

The beam illuminated the near-darkness of the tunnel with a dazzling blue-white glare as the needle of energy played across black duralloy, the light so intense that Streicher's visor polarized to almost complete opacity. He held the gun steady, concentrating the beam on one point . . . but when he released the trigger almost a full minute later, the tough and highly refractory metal remained unblemished. He ran his gloved fingertips across the spot and couldn't even feel any lingering warmth. Frustrated, he unsnapped his right glove's locking ring from his E-suit's sleeve and touched the spot with bare skin. It was hot . . . yes, but no more so than a steaming cup of kaff, and the heat was fading as he touched the metal. The charge on his power pistol read forty-one percent. He would not be able to cut his way through to Kelly.

Damn. What could he do? Turning, he glared at the techspider still waiting patiently in the tunnel behind him. "Don't just stand there," he growled. "*Do* something!"

The machine shifted left and right on its spindly legs a few times, as though dithering. Techspiders had AIs of their own but were not terribly bright. They existed primarily to serve as eyes, ears, and hands for the Bolo, which could teleoperate them in order to carry out delicate battlefield repairs—usually deep within the Bolo's own electronic guts. It would carry out his spoken orders if it were physically possible to do so, but it was not strong enough to move hundreds of kilos of solid metal, nor could it burn through this crumpled duralloy barrier.

Hell, even if the damned thing was strong enough, what if the duralloy wreckage was actually lying on top of Kelly, pinning her? Dragging it away might kill her . . . or generate a worse avalanche that would crush them both.

He began cycling through various plans and possibilities . . . using the data cable, which was quite strong, to rig up some sort of pulley arrangement at the tunnel mouth . . . or seeing if the spider's legs could be dismantled and turned into hydraulic jacks.

Nothing he could think of was feasible, though. No parts. No manpower. No time.

One thing he knew. He wasn't going to abandon her. He'd left the rest of the grounded regimental staff hours earlier, and they'd all been killed or captured while he'd been off joy-riding aboard Victor. He would *not* leave Kelly Tyler now and lose her as well.

No matter what the cost.

Kelly was alive and fighting, but for a time she didn't know what she was fighting against. She couldn't move her head and her helmet's power supply appeared to have been damaged; her helmet console lights were out and the radio didn't appear to be working. There was a terrible, throbbing pain in her left leg, but the worst part was not being able to move her head. It felt as though her helmet was wedged between the floor of the tunnel and something very large, very massive.

She could hear something . . . a kind of far-off rumble, like summer's thunder far out over the ocean. It took her a while to realize that she was hearing Hellbore fire in the distance, the concussions reaching her through the ground and the mountain of dead metal around her.

Panic, gibbering and lunatic, was not far away. She'd

never thought of herself as claustrophobic; hell, she was the girl, she thought with a burst of something uncomfortably perched between tears and hysteria, who spent her best hours buried inside of a Bolo command center. But pinned like this, in total darkness, was more than she, was more than *anyone*, could tolerate for more than a few minutes.

And the minutes were dragging on and on and on.

She had to get free. The thunder suggested that Victor had withdrawn to fight off another enemy assault. Had the colonel gone with him? Probably. The thought that she'd been left here, all alone, brought a shuddering cry of anguish to her throat.

Somehow, she managed to turn her body in such a way that she could reach her helmet's neck coupling with her hands.

Normally, removing the helmet was a simple matter of giving it a sharp twist to the left to uncouple the snap ring and disengage the pressure seal, but the helmet was immovably wedged beneath the unseen weight above her—she assumed that part of the tunnel's roof, a block of duralloy internal armor, perhaps, had fallen, blocking the tunnel and pinning her. With the helmet unmovable, she could only try turning her body to the right, and the pain in her leg when she did so nearly made her pass out.

It took her three tries, but at last she felt the coupling ring disconnect. She then had to back out of the helmet, and the resultant sharp, grating stab of agony in her left calf convinced her that, at the very least, the leg was broken.

Slowly, slowly, she pulled her head out from the helmet's embrace. It felt like the helmet had actually been flattened a bit by the crushing weight of the duralloy slab. Another centimeter or two, and her skull would have been crushed like an egg.

At last she pulled free, and she lay there in the darkness, crying and gasping for air and laughing all at once.

"Kelly!" The voice was faint, and a bit ragged. "Kelly, is that you?"

Colonel Streicher! "Hello! Colonel! Is that you?"

"Thank Joy that you're still alive! Are you okay?"

"A busted leg and some bruises. Nothing too serious. What's happening?"

"Victor's off playing tag with some bad guys. I'm on the other side of this big chunk of armor with a techspider and no way to get through to you. Any suggestions?"

She considered the problem. Reaching down to her right hip, she unsnapped a pocket pouch and extracted a fingerflash, switching on the beam and playing it hopefully about her prison. Bolos were honeycombed with access tunnels and crawlways, the only means that maintenance personnel had to get at all of the huge machine's interior parts, circuits, and compartments. This tunnel, though, had been bored out by Victor with one of his infinite repeaters, and she didn't know where the manmade tunnels might be. She didn't know the Mark XXXII's internal architecture very well, in any case. There would definitely be an access tunnel of some sort connecting to the AI core behind her, but this tunnel hadn't connected to it. Even if she found it, those passageways were braced, armored, and well-shielded by solid metal a centimeter thick; she had a power pistol holstered on her hip, but it would take an hour to slice through sheet titanium, and it wouldn't more than warm duralloy.

There had to be another way. Damned if she could think what it might be, though. Another round of shuddering thunder transmitted itself through the hull metal around her. She thought she heard a creak as the large chunk of armor in front of her shifted slightly, ominously, but she couldn't tell for sure.

"Are you okay?" Streicher's voice called from beyond.

"Okay!" she shouted back. "I can't think of any way out of here!"

"Me either. We'll have to wait for Victor to come back. He carved this tunnel out before. Maybe he can cut through this junk and get to you."

"Wait! Are you trapped too?"

"No. I can see daylight . . . maybe ten meters behind me. You're going to see it too, very soon now!"

"Cut the make-happy," she snapped. "This stuff around us is unstable. I think it's shifting with the concussion of the gunfire. You've got to get out of here."

"I'm not leaving you, Kelly."

"Damn it, why should both of us get killed? Victor is going to need you, once he breaks through to the Trixie underground complex!"

"Kelly, I'm beginning to think these Bolos don't need us for anything. Like . . . we're just in the way, you know? Anyway, there's no way in hell I'm about to leave you here alone."

The thought, irrational as it was, was still comforting and warm. "Thank you, Jon," she said, but she spoke so softly he almost certainly hadn't heard.

I slam twelve quick Hellbore bolts into the horizon where I know the Enemy is lurking, hull-down and determined. Though the missile carriers have been driven off or destroyed, a number of tracked vehicles mounting light Hellbores continue to snipe and probe, seeking weakness. Two of my Dragons have been destroyed, and I have only one remaining, now. Of greater concern, my last Wyvern has just been downed by a surface-to-air missile, leaving me effectively blind outside the sensory net provided by my BIST dispersal.

I wonder if the fact that the Enemy is attempting to use light armor against me means that his supply of Bolos has been exhausted. If so, we may have reached a turning point in this campaign; no other weapons have been fielded against me with the potential of causing me serious damage, save, of course, the nuclear weapons they have employed from the beginning.

The Enemy appears to be withdrawing. I fire another barrage, then turn around and return to the wreck of Alpha One.

I am picking up frantic radio calls from the colonel.

She lay in the dark and tried to forget the throbbing pain in her leg. "Who's Joy?" she asked.

"Sorry. Who?"

"Where were you?"

"Talking to Victor. He's on his way back. Who were you asking about?"

"Joy. A while ago, you said, 'Thank Joy.' Is that the god of joy, or something?"

"Ah. I suppose you could say that. I'm a Eudaimonian. The Greatest Pleasure. Sometimes we give thanks to joy. That's why we're here, after all. To experience the good emotions."

"And the bad ones?"

"Are you asking what Eudaimonics says?"

"I'm asking what *you* say."

There was a long silence. "Bad stuff happens," Streicher said at last. "People die. People you care about. Or you do something stupid, something you wish you could make right, and there's no way you ever can. I think the joy comes with learning to overcome the bad stuff, the bad emotions."

"Have you been able to do that?"

"What do you mean?"

"You're from Aristotle. Everyone in the Service knows what that means."

"Well, maybe you can explain it to me someday. I don't think I do."

"How does a Eudaimonian from Aristotle handle the bad stuff?"

"One step at a time" was the reply. "Small goals, and satisfaction from achieving those goals. And maybe we just avoid looking too closely at the problem . . . or we don't ask the hard questions. The idea is supposed to be that the good outweighs the bad . . . but in my experience it doesn't always happen that way."

"I think that's everyone's experience. The universe doesn't operate with us in mind."

"No. I don't suppose it does."

"So . . . why do you stick with it?"

"Stick with what? Life?"

"Eudaimonics. Doesn't sound like much of a philosophy if it only handles the happy parts of life."

"I've wondered about that myself," Streicher said after a pause. "Maybe it's just comfortable. Something to hang onto, after everything else has been taken away."

Kelly felt a trembling through the floor of her prison. As seconds passed, the trembling grew stronger, a deep throated rumble, heard now as well as felt. "Colonel Streicher?" she called. When there was no answer, she tried again, shouting. "Jon!"

"Sorry. Talking to Victor again." He sounded worried.

"What's the matter?"

"His seismic sensors have picked up another string of vehicles, coming this way."

"What vehicles? Where are they?"

"More Bolos. And he says they're right under us, coming up from the tunnels."

The rumble was growing louder, a thunder filling her universe. She put her hands over her ears and screamed.

Chapter Seventeen

I have detected the seismic signature of enemy Mark XXXII Bolos, emerging on the surface not far from the wreck of Alpha One. I must consider the possibility that, again, the Enemy has used expendable light armor as a diversion, to pull me out of position. The question is whether they are targeting my Commander and the colonel deliberately, hoping to capture them, or if their emergence so close to their position is coincidental.

They may know the two are in Alpha One's wreckage. Small robotic scouts or their equivalent of BIST sensors could have observed my Commander and the colonel as they entered the Mark XXXII. Still, it seems unlikely that a major thrust would have been organized just to effect the death or capture of two officers. Synchronicities unrelated to one another do occur, a fact that alone dictates that warfare will ever be an art, not a true science.

In any event, it scarcely matters. I have pinpointed a tunnel exit 2.7 kilometers from the Alpha One wreck. At least six Mark XXXII Bolos are emerging, deploying through the ruined base in the general direction of the hulk. Their vector will place them at the wreck site before I can reach it.

This presents me with a serious tactical and ethical dilemma. Both my Commander and the colonel in charge of the 4th Regiment are in serious danger. While I have defeated four enemy Bolos at a time in several previous engagements, my assessment of the Mark XXXII's combat capability, coupled with the Enemy's obvious mastery of the learning curve in deploying his combat units, convinces me that I cannot take on six of these combat units simultaneously. My own combat effectiveness has been degraded by an estimated 12 percent, due to damage already accrued and to the depletion of my on-board stores of expendable munitions and teleoperated remotes.

My best combat option would be to retreat. If the Enemy follows me, I might find opportunities to split individual Bolos or small groups off from the main body and defeat them in detail. By fighting a delaying action, I might be able to hold them long enough for Invictus and Ferox to move up in support. At their current position, they could be here in 59.5 minutes.

I consider briefly the possibility that they could use their contra-gravity projectors to fly to my position in less time but discard it. The Enemy's use of nuclear warheads against airborne targets—and the fact that contra-grav travel requires such high expenditures of energy that battlescreen and defensive weaponry would be partially powered down—would make them far too vulnerable.

So help cannot arrive in less than nearly one hour. By moving toward their current position, I might halve the rendezvous time, as well as draw the Enemy's forces out of position.

But I have a clear responsibility for Lieutenant Tyler and Colonel Streicher. Where is my duty best served? While considering this dilemma, I engage all of my remaining contra-gravity units, spin around to a heading of 248 and increase my velocity to maximum.

I race toward the Enemy, weapons at full readiness.

Elken wasn't certain what to make of this new turn of events. He'd awakened a short time before, deep within the caverns of the gods, finding himself incarnate not in a body of flesh and blood, but within a Bolo Mark XXXII, a 21,000-ton mountain of duralloy armor and high-tech weaponry. He'd gone to sleep expecting immortality . . . but he hadn't thought that immortality meant a body like *this*.

He was shocked to learn that several hundred cycles had passed since he'd entered the Hall of the Immortals, seeking to join Sendee in her new life.

Far more shocking, however, was his encounter with . . . himself.

Or, more properly, himselves. Five other Mark XXXII Bolos squatted in the vast assembly hall of Trolvas, and as he established a communications link with each, he realized that each of them was a mirror of himself.

We have made copies of your mind and memory, of your personality, his god told him. <confidence and power> *You will be able to work closely together with these, your brothers, without the personality difficulties experienced with the Total Systems Data-Sharing gestalts.*

"But . . . but which of us is the *real* Elken?" he demanded, his electronic voice a wail of confusion and loss.

In one sense, it doesn't matter. <self-confidence in highly technical matters too complex to explain> *Still, if it makes things easier for you, you are the original LKN 8737938.*

But Elken wondered if that was true. What were

the gods telling those *other* Elkens at that moment? He wanted to find out, compare notes.

For the first time in his life, Elken wondered if the gods dealt with their people honestly. It was a disturbing, a terrifying thought. If the gods themselves could not be trusted . . .

Within you reside the memories of other Elkens, other Elken copies. Learn from their experiences. Use their accumulated experience to defeat the Sky Demon invaders.

More copies. Was he the original, the *real* Elken? He had to know. He opened a communications link with one of the other Elken-Bolos . . . and found he could not phrase the question.

It wasn't that he forgot or was distracted. He knew what he wanted to do, what he wished to say, but something unseen was blocking him from forming and transmitting the question. He struggled with this for .04 second, before the desire itself faded from his thoughts. After all, it wasn't important. The god himself had said that it didn't matter in the long run.

Fourteen minutes later, the six of them were emerging from a concealed tunnel in the ruins of the supply depot at Ghendai. An enemy Bolo, a Mark XXXIII, was engaging local forces in that region. Intelligence accumulated in previous attempts suggested that six Mark XXXIIs would have little difficulty defeating a lone Mark XXXIII, especially since the enemy machine was already damaged and appeared to be operating without support.

TSDS was engaged, but, as the god had promised, there were none of the gestalt problems encountered by earlier Elken copies. He felt like . . . himself, but somehow distributed among six bodies, racing out to deploy on the flat ground southwest of the supply depot.

The feeling was exhilarating, a heady sense of unbounded power and freedom. Even as he deployed, though, he felt again a nagging sense of curiosity.

Was he the original Elken? How would he know if he wasn't? With the original's memories, he might well be a copy. Only a copy . . . and as such, what would happen to him?

It doesn't matter, one of his brothers said, an echo of himself over the TSDS link.

The gods know what they are doing.

But if we're copies, we could be simply discarded. We won't have immortality.

We won't see Sendee again. . . .

It doesn't matter!

It does *matter!*

Pull together! The link is fragmenting!

Don't argue! We need to focus on the battle, on the enemy!

Agreed! We destroy the Sky Demon Bolo. The rest can wait!

Intelligence says that there are human soldiers inside the wrecked Bolo up ahead. The enemy machine will deploy to protect them.

We can use that to our advantage.

The enemy Bolo is moving toward us.

Steady. Meet him together, as a unit. . . .

As a unit . . .

Elken thought of himself as "Elken One," for clarity, and of the others as Elkens Two through Six. Curiously, they all thought of themselves the same way, but there was no internal confusion. They fired their main batteries together, as a single unit. . . .

The explosion of sound from outside rang through the wreckage, a shuddering, rippling wave that Kelly could feel as the armor and internal machinery shifted all around her. There was a grating squeak, and then the huge mass of duralloy blocking her way out shifted. Her E-suit helmet, still trapped between the armor and the tunnel floor, popped with a crack like a gunshot, splintering into tiny shards. If her head had still been trapped there . . .

Another hard jolt sent more debris tumbling from the tunnel roof, and it felt as though the entire wreck had just tilted precipitously to the left. Kelly lay flat, arms grabbing protectively across her neck and the back of her head.

"Colonel! Colonel Streicher!"

There was no answer, and no way to tell if he could even hear her above the din.

I am hit and badly. The concentrated Hellbore fire from six Mark XXXIIs slams into my outer battlescreens. For .28 second, the screens shunt that torrent of energy—approaching thirty megatons per second of firepower—into my screen storage capacitors or bleed it off into air and ground in lambent sheets of fusion fire. Inevitably, my dual-ply battlescreens overload and collapse, and for a fractional instant, some of that firepower washes across my war hull.

I am already in motion, however, moving back and to the right as quickly as howling tracks can move me. I take advantage of a still-standing tower and a high berm within the ruins, using them for cover as I continue to retreat. I had not expected the Enemy to fight with this degree of unity or cohesion; I have underestimated the Enemy, always a serious error in war.

The Enemy's fire continues to seek me as I back through the ruins, smashing aside the tower, dissolving the duralloy berm in a staggering chain of high-energy explosions. My middle primary weapon turret is hit. The

200cm gun barrel sags, then shatters as the liquid nitrogen within its coolant circulation pipes flash-heats to white-hot plasma. I continue to take damage as, .49 second later, a trio of fusing cryo-H projectiles penetrate the mid-turret and rip it to blazing fragments. Another four bolts slam into my left flank, gouging deep craters and trenches through solid duralloy.

My protective awareness circuits have kicked in with the strong suggestion that I continue withdrawing. The Enemy has deployed near the wreck of Alpha One, however, and my Commander is in danger. In fact, returning fire may put her in danger as well. I have few options but death, or retreat.

I call for help, linking with both Ferox and Invictus. Invictus, I believe, should remain in the vicinity of the mountainside tunnel entrance, but he can lend considerable fire support with his Vertical Launch System. Ferox acknowledges my call and begins coming south.

It will be nearly an hour before he can arrive, however, in a battle that at the moment promises to last no more than five or six seconds.

My speed has been reduced by 36 percent, my primary firepower by a full 33 percent. Nevertheless, I bring both remaining Hellbores to bear on one of my attackers, hoping to wear them down one by one. I fire—and score a direct and crippling hit.

But the others are closing on my position fast.

Colonel Streicher crawled to the entrance of the tunnel, clinging to the lip of the opening as he peered out into the holocaust which was an all-out Bolo battle. Hellbore blasts ignited the sky in dazzling light, repeatedly turning his visor opaque with the sheer fury of the fusion discharges. Lesser weapons burned streaks and slashes of lightning across a sky gone mad, as missiles and the deadly touch of Hellbore plasma bolts caused the earth itself to erupt in nightmare, incandescent fury. The raw, pulsing, thunderous noise threatened to deafen him, even with his helmet on. Unable to see more than flashes of blinding light, unable to hear anything but the ocean surf's steady roar of thunder, he ducked back into the tunnel, crawling swiftly to the place where it was blocked. It looked as though the armor plate had shifted a bit, settling even more solidly into place.

"Kelly! Can you hear me?"

He didn't hear any response at first, but he decided that it was because of the background roar. He tried boosting the output of his suit's external speaker, turning a shout into a booming amphitheater's boom.

"Kelly! Are you okay?"

"I'm okay!" he heard her reply, her voice faint. He had to use his suit's communications filtering program to edit out most of the gunfire and selectively amplify only her voice. After a couple of tries, her voice was fairly clear. "What's going on?"

"Hard to tell," he told her. "A big fight, but I couldn't make much sense of it. I saw at least three enemy Bolos, though, and from the racket they're making, I think there're more than that."

"Any sign of Victor?"

"He'd be over the horizon, Kelly. I couldn't see him. He sure as hell is still in the fight, though."

He stretched his legs out wearily, leaning his back up against the fallen armor plate. With the electronic filters in place, the booming and crashing outside was stepped down to a dull, almost muffled roar. There was nothing to do but wait this out.

He thought about the turquoise pill in his pocket. It was inside his E-suit, but the air was good. He could unseal long enough to grab the pill from his tunic pocket, unlock his visor, and down the thing.

Curiously, though, he didn't want it. Oh . . . the *hunger* was there, certainly, that gnawing hunger that wasn't *real* hunger that was the mark of euph addiction. But that was purely physical. What he didn't feel right now was the emotional need, and that surprised him. What had changed?

Well, the nature of the stress had changed, certainly. The two of them might be about to die at any moment—one stray Hellbore shot from that mêlée outside would demolish this wreck and them with it—but it wasn't the same as the stress he'd felt in command of the regiment, giving the orders that would decide the outcome of the battle.

Giving orders that might result in the scorching of a green and beautiful world, like Aristotle.

Was *that* what drove his need for euph? The thought that he was somehow playing out what happened on Aristotle . . . but in reverse, with him as conqueror and destroyer, this time, rather than as helpless inhabitant?

It was at least something to think about.

As he played with the thought of that blue pill in his mind, though, the old hunger began to increase. Roughly, he pushed the thought away. *Later. There'll be plenty of time for that later.* . . .

The thunder outside grew more intense. . . .

"None of us really know what the original Aetryx are like," Tami Morrigen was saying. "Five years on this planet, and we never really got to know them."

"How is that possible?" Carla Ramirez asked. "I mean . . . you must have negotiated with them for trade rights. And you said they didn't allow you to deal with the human population directly."

"Yeah, except for the trolls," Tami's daughter, Marta, said. "They let us deal with *them.*"

"And a few assigned to us as servants, don't forget," Sym Redmond added with a dry smile.

They'd been sitting in the large room talking for what seemed like many hours. Carla was surprised when she queried her implant and learned that only fifty-two minutes had elapsed since she'd been brought to this cell after her brief interrogation.

"The Aetryx are extremely . . . " Tami paused, searching for the right word. "Plastic," she said finally. "I don't mean they change their shape like amoebae, or anything like that, but from what we've been able to learn, they don't have the same sense of body identity that we do. For them, a body is just a kind of vehicle, a way to get around, a way to sense the world. They see nothing odd about becoming a crane . . . or an aircraft . . . or downloading themselves into a completely alien body shape. It's not the outward form that's important. It's what's inside. The mind. Maybe the soul, though we don't know what kind of religious beliefs or philosophies they hold.

"What they do seem to believe, in their exchanges with others, is the old human idea of a place for everything, everything in its place . . . no, more than that, a *tool* for everything, and every tool in its place. And they don't mind redesigning themselves, or others, to create just the perfect tool."

"Redesign? How?"

"You've seen the Diplomat form," Pityr Morrigen said. "In the interrogation room? He would have been the one running things."

"Yeah. A kind of a spidery body, but upright in front, like a centaur." She shuddered. "And a kind of a human face."

"Right," Tami said. "We think they know how to work the DNA from one species into another, to create hybrids with the features of both. Or maybe they just reshape the DNA of any given species. Either way, they can literally build a whole new subspecies for a specific purpose. The Diplomats were given our faces, so we could pick up on their expressions as well as the language. And maybe because proto-Aetryx voices can't produce human sounds. To me, the protos' speech sounds like chirps and warbles and poppings. I couldn't begin to imitate it."

At Carla's curious expression, Tami added, "The original of any species is the prototype. That's how it translates from the Caernan, anyway. Protohumans are the original model, like us."

"But take some of our DNA and change it . . ." Carla said, nodding.

"And you get trolls," Marta said, completing the thought. "Or worse."

"We think there are something like thirty or forty distinct species of Aetryx," her father added. "The proto-Aetryx are kind of built along the Diplomat's body plan, but without the upright torso, or the human face. They seem to just make new species whenever there's a need. The Diplomats first appeared when we made contact, five years ago. I don't know, maybe they'd been around before, because of the native humans here, but the impression we had is that they were designed and grown, on the spot, to talk to *us*. All of our negotiations for trade rights and market access have been through them. They're damned sharp traders, too."

"But . . . there's more to making a diplomat than, than just *growing* one. People have to be trained for that kind of thing, educated . . ."

Sym Redmond took up the thread. "What they do is download memories . . . personality . . . character traits and habits. They can record all of that. You saw them do it just now, in the interrogation room. Right? If you need a new trait—talking to offworlder humans, say—

you create a primitive Diplomat and have him go talk to the humans. He learns the language, some of the thoughts and ideas, the expectations.

"Then he goes back home, and what the proto-Aetryx do is program a newer-model Diplomat, the Diplomat Mark II, say, with the memories of the Mark I Diplomats who've gone before. If the first models made mistakes, the newbies learn from them. And this process is going on all the time, and very quickly. By this time, we must be up to Mark XX or so."

"It means their society is fluid, and very resilient," Tami said. "They can learn frighteningly fast, and they rarely make the same mistakes twice.

"It also means—we're not entirely sure about this, we're just guessing, but—it may also mean that they are effectively immortal. When one body starts to wear out, grow old, they download to a new one, fresh grown to order. They're good with computers, with machines of all types, but they're very, very good with biological systems. We think they've been breeding human subtypes here for five hundred years. The trolls. A few other subspecies we've seen. There are warriors as well. We assume there are others, though we never saw them."

"The Diplomats are for dealing with *us*, you see," Redmond put in. "That's their place, dealing with outsiders. God forbid that any other Trixie bioform have contact with wild humans!"

"You don't sound like you approve of them, Mr. Redmond. Or their culture."

"I don't, Major. I most definitely do not." He glanced at the door. "Why do you think we were feeding intelligence back to Primus and the Army? The humans here are treated no better than slaves, and the fact that they've been conditioned to think of their masters as gods doesn't change that one bit."

"Gods? Tell me more about that." She'd heard about that in the preinvasion briefing, but it still seemed too bizarre to be believed.

"There are a dozen different religions on Caern, Major," Pityr Morrigen said. "Yenno, Tharsee, Ivadda. Those are the biggest three. I guess. But they all focus on the idea that humans were created by the gods, and for the gods' service."

"Then . . . does that mean they've forgotten that humans colonized this planet, hundreds of years ago?" Carla was wondering if there was a handle here, a way to manipulate the Caernan human population. She knew of several cases in the history of the Human Diaspora across the galaxy where human colony worlds had been cut off and forgotten for long periods of time, then recontacted. In most cases, those worlds maintained some knowledge of their past and their origins, and most were delighted to find themselves part of a larger, wider, brighter and more powerful civilization than they'd previously enjoyed.

If the Caernan humans were happy though, and if their view of history was controlled by the Aetryx, that approach might not work. For deliberately isolated and provincial cultures, the larger outside universe usually seemed terrifying because of the threat it implied for the existing social and philosophical order.

"They do seem to remember Earth," Redmond said. "They have what they call the Histories, which sound like a pretty complete set of electronic and paper-media records dating back at least to the first colonizers, and maybe even way back before that, to Old Earth herself. A kind of military-religious order called the Brotherhood keeps those records, studies them, interprets them. They see themselves, the Caern humans, as special. An elect saved from hell, which, for them, is the empty space between the stars."

Carla nodded. She'd heard of this sort of thing before. The Caernans definitely would feel threatened by whatever lay outside their tightly bounded little world. "And the rest of Humankind?"

"The un-elect. The unsaved, still adrift between the stars and up to no good. They call us 'Sky Demons.' "

"So the Caernans are the chosen elect," Carla said, thoughtful. "And they're so grateful for the honor, they do whatever the Trixies say. . . ."

"That's about the size of it," Tami said.

"How did you learn this much about them, then?" Carla wanted to know. "You said they didn't allow Caernan protohumans to talk to you.

"Like I said, they *did* assign us servants," Redmond said. "We think they were carefully conditioned, maybe by giving them downloaded Diplomat memories. Ours was a young man named Veejay. He was really there to keep an eye on us, of course, and he didn't tell us much . . . but we learned a little, just listening to him talk about his gods. The servants were the only protohumans they allowed into the Compound."

"Compound?"

"The Foreigners' Compound," Redmond said. "Yeah, they made sure we stayed in our place, in a special compound reserved for offworlders, staffed by trolls and Diplomat Aetryx. It was more like a prison, though it was comfortable enough."

"They established six Compounds around the planet," Pityr added. "Ghendai was the main one, the place where we established our first trade mission five years ago. They also had one in Othelid, up on the Vortan Coast; in Mellanid, near the north pole; in Dravinnir Ka and Ghartoi, on the other side of the planet; and at Thedmirinid, near Caern's south pole."

"We were evacuating our compound just before the

invasion," Tami said, "when they captured us and brought us here. We don't know what happened at any of the other compounds. They were all supposed to try to get away in small ships, to rendezvous with your fleet in orbit. We don't know if any of the others made it or not."

"I don't think they did," Carla told her. "At least I didn't hear of any. If your servants were there to watch you, though, I don't see how any of you could have made preparations to leave without it being known."

"That's what we thought," Tami said. "They were always six steps ahead of us."

"Every aspect of a Caernan's life is dictated by his 'god,'" Redmond added. "They can't sneeze without permission."

"'God'? Only one?"

"Every Caernan has a particular god who looks out for him." Tami sighed. "We used to joke about it, inside the Compound in Ghendai. It was like the Trixies kept humans as pets. We're not sure, but we think each Trixie has several dozen humans all his own, maybe even as many as several hundred. They maintain very close control of their pets. Again, we're not sure, but we think they put implants into the brains of human newborns. They're taken from their mothers, you see, and raised in crèches. According to our sources, they actually hear the voices of their gods in their heads and get a feeling for emotion, attitude, that sort of thing."

"Sounds a lot like our implants," Carla said. "But used to maintain control, instead of as a communications device."

"Sure," Sym Redmond said. "Control the communication, what you tell a person, and restrict him from outside sources, and you control him."

"I don't understand." Carla shook her head. "How

can people just let themselves be led into slavery like that?"

"It's not slavery to them," Tami told her. "It's religion, the comfort of knowing who and what you are, and what the gods have in mind for you in a confusing world . . . and maybe it's a chance at immortality as well."

"Chains are chains," Carla replied, "whether they're locked on your body, or on your mind."

Elken realized that the enemy Bolo was hurt and hurt badly, but he also knew that the enemy's retreat and apparent loss of firepower could be a trap of some sort. The combat memories of previous incarnations of himself showed that the invader machines demonstrated considerable cunning. Outnumbered, they would attempt to split the opposition and defeat it piecemeal; cornered, they used remote combat units to deceive, misdirect, and harry from the rear.

They also appeared to have an exact knowledge of their own capabilities and a fair assessment of the capabilities of their opponents. Make a single mistake, and the invader Bolos pounced on it like a snapjaw on a pollet, biting hard and never letting go.

He continued moving forward, laying down a thundering barrage of Hellbore and missile fire, forcing the enemy Bolo back step by step. The surrounding forest, ignited by the Hellbore fire, burned fiercely, driving up his hull temperature and filling the air with boiling clouds of black smoke. Visibility on all wavelengths was sharply impaired, but he could continue to track the enemy machine by the magnetic trace of its hull, its mass, its seismic signature, and by the ionization trails and shock waves of its continuing volleys of missile launches and heavy gunfire. The Sky Demon machine was fighting with ferocious savagery, using the splintering ruin of the forest, the folds and ridges of the ground, and even the smoke to maximum effect both for concealment and for cover from the incoming barrage.

Still wary of a possible trap, Elken slowed his advance, probing ahead at a dead crawl, continuing to maintain a heavy bombardment of the Mark XXXIII's position.

One of his brothers—Elken Number Four—was savaged by a rapid-fire volley from the enemy concentrating solely on him. Both of Four's right-side track assemblies were blasted to pieces and his main turret was ripped away, leaving him helplessly turning in the dirt. The enemy began concentrating on Elken Number Six, then, but by this time the invader had suffered so much damage that the outcome could not long remain in doubt.

Elken felt a wild jubilation. He'd not thought it possible, but they were actually going to *win*! . . .

Chapter Eighteen

My aft Hellbore turret has jammed after taking heavy primary and secondary fire from the Enemy. I am now in full retreat but have suffered so much damage to my suspension and track assemblies that my speed is reduced by 48 percent, and my maneuverability has been badly hampered as well. I have shut down power to all external somatic sensors to eliminate the sensory input which, for lack of a better term, I think of as pain. It is distracting and can at this point only impede my mission.

At the same time, I have put one of the enemy combat units out of commission and probably damaged another. The remaining four, however, are coming at me from ahead and around both flanks, moving with superb coordination. Their volleys are staggered, allowing two to cool their Hellbore barrels, while the other two maintain a steady and rapid fire. My own sole remaining 200cm Hellbore is white hot from the steady firing, and I must slow my firing in order to extend the life of the barrel. If it fails, I will have only my 20cm Hellbore infinite repeaters as energy weapons, supported by 240cm howitzers, mortars, and my few remaining VLS missiles.

And as I search for other options, I realize that there

303

is yet one more weapon I might bring to bear on the Enemy. My chances for success are slight, and yet . . .

Elken and his brothers were driving the enemy back, pushing him northeast clear out of the wrecked supply depot and into the forest north of Ghendai. He had already been damaged badly enough to cut his speed sharply, and the woods were slowing the Sky Demon Bolo even further. As Elken and the others sent Hellbore bolt after searing bolt shrieking into the forest, it wasn't long before the entire area was ablaze.

It wouldn't be much longer now.

Elken noted the pulsing electronic notification of a TSDS request. Additional combat units must be emerging from the tunnel and needing Total Systems Data-Sharing to coordinate with the four Elken–Mark XXXIIs already engaged with the enemy.

IFF and communications security codes checked. He opened the channel . . . .

The Bolo Mark XXVI, with its hyper-heuristic software, was the first mark capable of breaking an enemy's computer and communications security. By entering the enemy's communications net, a Bolo could access his computer network, scan for useful data, and even, given luck, implant false or conflicting orders. There is at least one case in my historical archives of a Bolo which managed to effect the surrender of an enemy garrison simply by taking over the enemy's computer network and ordering him to stand down.

Such tactics are unlikely to work in this case, for the Enemy's computer experience and technology is very nearly on a par with my own and in some ways may be superior. That the Enemy has overridden the security protocols of the Mark XXXII Bolo combat units in storage on Caern and subsequently used the XXXII's direct neural-psychotronic interface to allow the implanting of human memory-personality downloads as operating system software strongly suggests a superior technology, at least in the area of cybernetics and psychotronics.

However, the copy I have made of Alpha One's memory core includes all pertinent communications and security codes, access passwords, and clearances. By submitting an electronic request for TSDS linkage, I gain momentary access to the Enemy's computer net.

I say "momentary" because even with the proper passwords and code protocols, I cannot fool the Enemy system for more than a few hundred milliseconds. With a self-aware component in the Enemy's operating system, I will be recognized as an intruder—an attempted hack—and be ejected from the network within an estimated .01 second.

Even 500 milliseconds, however, is a very long time when working with electronic systems and responses. I enter the data stream, identifying memory cores, central processors, and I/O ports linking with other systems. In a rapid-fire burst of activity, I sidestep several perimeter security checks, then build myself a shell giving me the appearance of a high-priority incoming message. I note the computer overrides for this Mark XXXII's main weaponry but resist the temptation to shut it down. That would be the brute force method, and it would almost certainly fail. I am seeking a more subtle and more permanent confrontation with the Enemy.

I am drawing heavily now upon the data downloaded from the wrecked Mark XXXII. I note as I move through the data stream that this Mark XXXII is also run by a downloaded human personality and . . . yes! That personality, too, is the entity calling itself Elken.

My plan would have worked had my electronic

interface been with someone other than LKN 8737938, but this makes things easier.

Or at least that is my hope. What I am about to try could be quite startling to Elken.

I have sequestered a part of my own working memory—several terabytes' worth—within which the downloaded pattern of human thought and personality from the wrecked enemy Bolo resides . . . a controlled emulation of the environment in which I found him. Little of the actual personality remains, unfortunately. That part of Elken did not come across the data link well, a problem, possibly, resulting from slight incompatibilities in the two systems. Enough remains, however, for me to create a kind of mask for myself, another data shell that will appear, at first inspection, to be another Elken download.

Again, the deception cannot last more than a few hundred milliseconds. I must hope that that is enough.

Elken noted the incoming message and noted, too, the high-priority flag attached to it. Someone was trying to get his attention.

"This is LKN 8737938," he said, using formal adio protocol. "Who is this?"

"This is LKN 8737938" was the immediate reply. "We need to talk. . . ."

Another copy of himself. Not one of his comrades, but another, a stranger. His suspicions—and fears—returned now, full force.

"Are you here to reinforce us?" The raging forest fire, the thick smoke, the trees and splintered fragments of trees all around his position were combining to block both radar and lidar. He could only barely maintain tracking lock on the enemy machine and his three comrades as it was, relying now more on sound and vibrations in the earth than on sight. Elken could only assume that another Bolo was nearby, but that he couldn't pick it out from the fuzz and clutter of interference.

"This is the Bolo Mark XXXII destroyed in combat earlier today. You passed me 5.3 kilometers from here, at a bearing of 262 degrees." A map spread itself open in Elken's thoughts, pinpointing precisely the other Bolo's position.

"That . . . Bolo is a burned-out hulk," Elken replied. "There was no sign of power usage or AI Core function." He didn't believe in ghosts. . . .

At the same moment, he felt something invade . . . not his thoughts, but the deepest, most private recesses of his own consciousness and awareness of self. There were . . . there were *barriers* there, barriers of which he'd not even been aware because the barriers themselves prevented him from thinking about them, or from noticing their presence.

And even as he became aware of them, those barriers dissolved into the electronic background.

And the memories came flooding in. . . .

What I am attempting might be likened to brain surgery but on the level not of physiology, but of purely psychological therapy. I have thoroughly scanned the patterned mind and memories of the Elken which inhabited the Mark XXXII Bolo I have designated Alpha One. I am in the process of scanning the Elken-Bolo I have designated Echo One, now closing on my position at a range of .94 kilometer. Though this second scan is not complete, I can match the two point for point, noting identical aspects of the two and noting as well the differences.

By comparing the two mentation patterns, it is a simple matter to note the layers of accumulated experience and memory in the Echo model, added since the

Alpha model's deployment and subsequent destruction. Bolos, like humans, employ holographic memory. By laying one memory complex atop the other, all identical patterns vanish, leaving only the differences . . . the parts added later. This puts into clear relief subsequent events stored within a succession of Mark XXXII memory cores but also shows where key memories in the original version have been altered.

It is less simple but still a relatively trivial operation to note the existence of certain memory access sectors in the Echo model that have been deliberately walled off by closed-loop RAM access barriers. Since holographic memory involves the storage of patterns distributed throughout the entire structure, simply erasing memories is not effective. These barriers block the transmission of recovered memories to the brain's AI processing centers. This has the general effect of creating a localized gap in key memory sectors, what a human might think of as partial amnesia. They also have the effect of preventing the Echo model from even thinking of certain things or from being aware that these memory gaps exist.

The free flow of information and unrestricted access to that information are basic to my operation as a thinking, self-aware entity. These barriers are an affront to me, representing a violation, an intrusive control of mind and self that I can only regard with distaste, even anger.

The earliest Bolo marks, of course, were hedged about with a variety of safeguards restricting their behavior. Their human designers feared what might happen if a Bolo "went rogue," either because of battle damage or due to minor but cumulative degradation of its software or hardware over the expected multicentury span of its operational lifetime.

The Mark XX, for example, introduced in 2796

(Terran Calendar, Old Style), possessed a self-awareness released only under full Battle Reflex Mode, preventing it from taking any action at all without direct orders from a designated human commander. It wasn't until the Mark XXIV that a Bolo combat unit attained true self-awareness and became self-directing on both a tactical and a strategic level. Human fears of rogue Bolos turning on their makers, however, forced the retention of software packages designed to inhibit Bolo independence at need. The so-called "Omega Worm" of the Mark XXV was intended to destroy the AI Core memory and volitional centers of any Bolo that became unresponsive to outside direction due to senility or battle damage.

Even now, with the Mark XXXIII, certain inhibitory software subroutines are integrated into all levels of the Bolo operating and combat reflex systems. The moral inhibitions designed to block the deliberate or accidental destruction of native humans through the automatic triggering of my close-range antipersonnel weaponry, for example, were added to my basic automated response subroutines in order to avoid or reduce collateral damage. All of these subroutines are subject to my deliberate and conscious control, however. I recall, again, the disturbing incident not far from here, where I suppressed my inhibitory software in order to kill the grievously injured human.

What I am witnessing within the entity LKN 8737938, however, is a corruption of basic software design designed to restrict Elken's thoughts, rather than his actions. By comparing Alpha One's mentation patterns with those of Echo One, I can pinpoint with great precision those memory blocks and edits that have been imposed on the Elken series since it was first deployed and can make a fair guess at the location of other blocks placed within the original Alpha One.

I note the blockages, recording them. Within my operational shell, I create memory patterns for those specific sectors, reconstructed without the blocks. The barriers deleted key pointers necessary for routing access, and I must reconstruct these, using my own operating system software as a template.

In effect, I compare the software barrier encodings in the Echo model line for line with those of the alpha and delete those that do not match. The effect is that the barriers are switched off.

The entire operation takes 4.49 seconds, a dangerously long period of vulnerability during which the Enemy Bolo, Echo One, could eject me from his data network or even backtrack through the interface, enter my own network, and shut me down.

I am dealing with a human mind, however, one with human thought responses, reactions, and reflexes. While vastly speeded by its implementation within a purely electronic, hyper-heuristic system, it can still slow with shock or with the impact of certain emotions. I gain considerable added time as Echo One experiences a rush of memories formerly walled off by the memory barriers.

An observer within the data stream, I watch and listen as he experiences memories and emotions long denied him.

I watch and listen, eavesdropping, as he realizes the implications. His commanders—the entities he thinks of as "gods"—have repeatedly lied to him, manipulated him, and enjoined his cooperation through promises of an illusory immortality.

It would at this point be relatively simple to manipulate those memories myself in order to advance my cause, but I refrain from doing so. I require Elken's deliberate and willing help and participation.

I am more likely to gain that participation by employing the truth.

✧ ✧ ✧

Elken walked the strand at God's Beach, Sendee on his arm, holding tight. The air was warm and wet, carrying the heavy scent of salt sea and wet sand. They were still nude after their lovemaking; the sun had set, and the rainbow of tattoos down the left side of her face and body gleamed and shifted in the golden-pale light of Dis. The gas giant's ring system was fully aglow, a gold-silver arch reaching halfway to the zenith.

"I'm dying, Elken," she told him. "And I don't want to die. Our god has told me that I can live forever in another body. A god's body."

"I like this body," he said, hugging her more closely to him. His entire universe had just swung wildly out of kilter, and he needed something—he needed her— to cling to. "I can't make love to a . . . to a god!"

The desolation, the sheer, blinding, overwhelming grief, he felt at her revelation still dragged at him, dulling his perception, dulling his thoughts.

The pain was unendurable. . . .

"We can still be together," she told him. "It won't be the same. I know, but we'll still have each other in every way that really counts."

"Until I die. Maybe . . ."

"Maybe what?"

"Maybe my god will make me immortal as well. At least we could share eternity together."

"You still have a life, a lot of life, to live in this body," she told him. "Please . . . don't do anything hasty. Promise me?"

"Of course. But . . . but life without you . . ."

"I'm facing an eternity without you, my love. I will live." She managed a smile. "Maybe not with the same physical equipment, but . . ."

"And I'll live as well. With you."

"Are you sure?"

"I've never been surer of anything."

"You'll wait, though? You won't cut short this life, just because . . . because I have to go early."

He thought about that carefully. At the moment, the prospect of spending the rest of his human life without Sendee did not exactly recommend itself to him. But it seemed important to Sendee that he say yes.

"I promise. At least . . . I promise to try. If things are unbearable . . ."

"Life is unbearable sometimes, Elken. We have to make the best of it. I . . . you're making me feel guilty about going. Maybe . . ."

"No. No, I'm coming with you. I've always been a bit scared by the whole idea of eternity . . . the Perspective of the Gods. But I think I could face it, if I was with you."

He held her close. Her face was upturned, her eyes glistening in the Dislight. The glow from their body markings, hers on her left, his on his right, mingled in a rainbow aura of shifting colors.

"Eternity together . . ." she said.

They kissed.

And they made love again, on the sand. . . .

That evening had been just a few cycles before she'd walked with him into the Hall of Immortality. He'd not seen her again. A twelfth of a Disyear later, he'd walked up those broad, white-crystal steps himself.

He'd been right. Life without Sendee had been unendurable. He'd felt some guilt at not waiting, as she'd asked him, but the sooner he went through with his life-change, the better. Soon they would be together. His god had promised him as much. . . .

And yet . . . he'd not seen Sendee again until earlier today, when he'd first sensed her presence within the hulking mountain of duralloy which was a Bolo Mark XXXII. And their meeting had been . . . subdued.

No, not subdued. Ordinary. As though they were nothing but good friends.

What had been wrong with him? With her? . . .

He ground forward, swinging into line alongside SND 9008988. He felt Sendee's warm thought of welcome. "Elken! I'm so glad you joined us!"

"I . . . wasn't expecting this," he replied. "A new body. I thought it would be human . . . or at least have some human left in it, like the Specials."

"We are Specials now," she told him. "The most Special there are! . . ."

"It's taking some getting used to."

As he replayed the scene in his mind, he realized that he'd felt nothing for her at the time. No excitement at seeing her after so long . . . no joy at her escape from the ravages of cancer, no pleasure at her company. He hadn't even remembered that he'd loved her, lost her, then sought to have her once more. The two of them might as well have been casual friends, neighbors, perhaps, or acquaintances from the Brotherhood.

It was as though their love had never been.

For the first time since his revival, he checked the time and date. Funny. He'd not been curious about *that*, either.

The Date was twenty-seven years after he'd gone in for his immortality operation. Twenty-seven Dis years—almost 280 years standard. They'd put him—and Sendee as well—in storage, planning deliberately to use them later.

Had the gods *ever* planned on reviving them, if the Sky Demons hadn't arrived on the scene?

Perhaps . . . but he was left with the thoroughly unpleasant feeling that the two of them had been nothing more than raw material, two sets of software to be stored indefinitely and run when needed.

He saw now, and plainly, the way they had used him

through his various incarnations, deliberately sending him out to near-certain death in combat in order to determine the enemy's strengths and capabilities . . . and to gradually wear down the invader Bolos.

Each of those deaths had been very real; each copy of Elken had followed orders, marched out, and died, adding his bit of information to the whole for some later version of himself to make use of.

He now realized that he himself was a copy, as were his four comrades in the current battle. None of them would achieve the immortality promised by the gods.

None of them would be with Sendee again.

The devastation he felt at that moment equaled the crushing fear and grief he'd known when first Sendee had told him she was dying. Emotions surged through him, emotions he'd not known for some time . . . loss, hurt, grief, and above all, a raging anger at the way he'd been lied to, used, and abused.

At that moment, he wanted nothing so much as to curl his hands tight about the base of an Aetryx brain stem and squeeze. Or . . . he was a Bolo now. Grinding one beneath his tracks . . . even though the squeezing would be so much more satisfying.

Help me, the other Elken said quietly through his rage. *Help me, and perhaps you can redress some of the wrong done to you.*

It was as though he looked at the image of himself, that alien image of a much, much younger self, and saw through it to another mind, a different personality, behind it.

He recognized the mind of the enemy Bolo.

Defenses fell into place, firewalls designed to block the spread of virus or electronic infiltration. Automated responses swung into position, preparing a savage and devastating riposte.

But he restrained himself. He sensed the other

Bolo's truthfulness, and its sincerity, in stark contrast to the sincerity of the gods.

He stopped firing and, through the TSDS linkage, stopped firing as the other Elkens in the unit as well.

There was a bizarre, almost fragmented reaction among the four Mark XXXIIs. Through the TSDS link, all had experienced the same lowering of barriers, the same reacquisition of memories, the same flood of emotions. Each, however, had a different attitude, a different perspective to what was happening.

Elken Two was both furiously angry and afraid. He was angry at the gods, yes, but he was more angry at the attempted subversion by the Sky Demon Bolo. "Open fire!" he shouted over the link. "Destroy the Enemy!"

But under Elken One's electronic touch, he did not fire.

Elken Three was suspicious and afraid. "The enemy Bolo lied to us as well. It pretended to be an earlier iteration of us, constructed a shell out of that iteration to hide itself so it could slip past our defenses! We should destroy it!"

"Was there another way for it to contact us?" Elken Five asked. "If it hadn't penetrated our operating systems and deleted the memory blocks, we . . . we would not know what we'd lost."

"What had been done to us," Elken Six added. "What had been *stolen!*"

"It's the Aetryx who should be destroyed," Five added.

This is blasphemous. <indignation and horror> *You will stand down and return to Trolvas.*

Elken had been wondering if the gods were listening in, and what their response would be if they were. The implant that allowed every adult Caernan to hear the voice of his god in his thoughts also allowed that god to monitor each Caernan's thoughts, feelings, and decisions. Normally, they were allowed to do what they wanted, but in this case . . .

You have been deceived by the alien. Cease all attempts at communication. This poisonous disruption of the body must be isolated and cleansed. <stern benevolence> *This is not your fault, LKN 8737938. You are being used to penetrate our defenses. The infestation must be sterilized, lest the Sky Demons—*

You are the demons, Elken One cried, slamming closed the channel. The gods could reopen it from their side any time they wished, but the act itself was one of defiance . . . of damnation . . .

. . . and of vindication. *"Who is with me?"*

The Enemy's fire has abruptly ceased, and I take immediate advantage of the lull to move forward and to my left, seeking deeper and more sheltered cover in a ravine to the north, a far more advantageous tactical position for me should things not go my way. I withhold my own fire as the enemy Bolos negotiate with one another on a high-speed private channel. I continue to monitor the conversation, of course. Though a firewall has slammed down to exclude me from the data stream, I am able to maintain an interface with the Enemy's system through a navigational i/o port and, further, to make it look as though that port is closed. I do not interfere with the discussion even as it grows heated. The multiple Elkens must arrive at a consensus, or find a way to resolve their differences, themselves.

For .37 second, it is uncertain which point of view is going to prevail. Two appear to mistrust my intentions and fear this is a deception intended to make them lower their guard. They are counseling an immediate resumption of the attack. Two mistrust me but now mistrust their gods more. One of those two seems to desire a truce, while the other, in an excess of emotion possible only for a human mind, is urging the others to attack the Aetryx. The fifth, badly damaged in the fighting, is less focused than the others, possibly because of massive damage to its sensory net or communications center or both. It, too suggests a truce but also requests that the communications channel with the gods be reopened so that the situation may be discussed.

Elken One has closed the god channel . . . or believes he has. In fact, the gods control that channel and normally can eavesdrop at any time. I manage to interpose myself, however, isolating the five Mark XXXII Bolos and blocking Aetryx attempts to reopen the channel. I will not be able to maintain this position for long, but it should be enough for the five Bolos to arrive at a decision.

Elken One, the emotional one, is delivering a passionate speech urging an immediate attack against the gods. Elken Five is supporting his position, though with less determination. Elken Three, at first urging that the combat be resumed, appears more introspective than the others and is considering options. He may be on the point of joining Elkens One and Five. Elken Two, as emotional as Elken One, but in a fury directed against me, is urging a resumption of the attack before I have time to further improve my position or call in reinforcements. Elken Six is wavering, angry at what the Aetryx have done to them, but unsure of my motives.

I find it fascinating that these five copied patterns of a single human mind are exhibiting such diverse points of view. Had Elken been an AI, even an advanced AI such as myself of the Mark XXXII or XXXIII series, the points of view of his five downloaded copies would have been far more uniform than is being exhibited now. It appears that human response to a given emotional stimulus—anger, outrage at betrayal, fear, humiliation—is so potentially variable even within the same human mind that expected outcomes are not predetermined and cannot be predicted with any accuracy, which suggests that they are essentially chaotic in nature.

This unpredictability potentially gives human-directed Bolo combat units a considerable edge on the battlefield. I must give this revelation further thought.

This unpredictability in machines directed by human-AI amalgams creates a new crisis as well. As I watch, Elken One and Elken Six both swerve suddenly, closing on Elken Two from either side, opening fire simultaneously with their Hellbores at nearly point blank range. For 2.35 seconds, the two Caernan Bolos slam fusion bolts into their comrade, blowing away huge chunks of partially melted armor, until the stricken machine grinds to a halt and begins burning fiercely.

Elken One, apparently, is unwilling to leave the decision to democratic action.

Elken One had detected the build-up of power within Elken Two's main weapon, indicating that it was beginning the firing sequence. The entire process took .25 second and was subtle enough that the enemy Bolo almost certainly could not pick it up at that range against the background of fire, smoke, and radiation.

If Elken Two opened fire on the Sky Demon Bolo, the delicate truce would be broken and the battle resumed; the Mark XXXIII was badly hurt and would have to fight back in order to have any chance at all of survival.

He attempted to reach through the TSDS link and block the imminent firing command . . . and was blocked. Elken Two had just cut the link—or was it the Aetryx? No matter. The only alternative Elken One could see now was to preemptively fire on Two before it could fire on the Mark XXXIII. Elken Six arrived at the same conclusion, joining him in the volley from the other side. Elken Two staggered under the hammering, as craters opened in his sides, his turret was peeled back, and fire exploded from his exposed internal spaces.

It wasn't until Elken Two was ablaze that Elken One realized what had just happened.

He and at least one of his fellows had just declared war on the gods.

Interlude V

Time and time again in the history of warfare, the stand, the decision, the heroic sacrifice of a few has unexpectedly turned the tide of battle. At Missionary Ridge, Union soldiers ordered to take enemy gun pits at the foot of the heights overlooking the besieged city of Chattanooga failed to halt, continuing their advance up the steep slope beyond and overrunning the defenders and lifting the siege. In the Pacific campaign of 1942, a raid by American bombers on the Japanese homeland caused little material damage but did result in the repositioning of Imperial Navy carrier assets which had a profound effect at the Battle of Midway not long after. At Saradar, in 2890, the suicidal last stand by the Bolo Mark XX RNY of the Line, "Ronny," delayed Deng troop and heavy Yavac movements for a critical 20 hours, allowing General Kern to rush critical reinforcements to the Galbreith Sector.

Although the lack of off-world support prevented anything like strategic victory, the decision by the Mark XXXIII Bolo of the 4th regiment known as "Victor" unquestionably changed the course of the battle, which until then had been increasingly of an entirely defensive nature. Aetryx subsurface installations were deemed inaccessible and had not been adequately allowed for in initial invasion planning. In Jorass, Weltan, and Jebeled, invading forces had been stopped cold. In Vortan, Dalesht, and Ophern, all surface defenses and strongpoints had been eliminated, but the Bolos were unable to proceed further.

Only in Kanthuras did one Mark XXXIII Bolo and some unexpected allies dare to take the battle to the enemy underground. . . .

Disaster at Caern:
A Study of the Unexpected in Warfare
Galactic Press Productions, Primus, cy 426

Chapter Nineteen

The destruction of Elken Two fills me with a horror which I find difficult at first to understand. Survival in combat demands harsh choices, and as one military tactician recorded in my archives noted, "chivalry gets you dead."

Still, the cold-blooded murder of a fellow Bolo—murder of a comrade, as opposed to open combat with an acknowledged foe—is utterly beyond my comprehension as a Bolo. Humans are capable of treachery; Bolos are not, though they can fall into patterns of aberrant behavior due to damage or age. I wonder, briefly, whether these two Mark XXXIIs have suffered damage and if that has affected the way they think.

I ready my weapons for a resumption of the conflict, as the surviving enemy Bolos begin maneuvering toward my position. I find myself somewhat out of my depth, a disconcerting feeling for an entity designed to master the arts of both tactical and strategic warfare in all their intricacies. The human element of these enemy Bolos, I find, is essentially chaotic and not susceptible to rational processes.

It is not at all a pleasant sensation.

❖   ❖   ❖

Elken sensed the enemy Bolo charging its remaining weapons and knew it was preparing for a final fight to the death. He retained the communications link with the other machine, however, and opened the channel using the standard Caernan IFF and recognition codes.

"Victor!" He'd sensed the other's human name during their brief contact earlier. "Don't fire!"

"Do you surrender?" was the Sky Demon machine's response.

"Surrender? No." The thought was unthinkable for a Bolo. "But we can help you penetrate the Aetryx subsurface complex. That was your plan, was it not?"

"You are changing sides? You're fighting against the Aetryx now?"

Elken hesitated. The Bolo part of him seemed to resist the very idea of . . . treason. Of betrayal. Of— think it softly—blasphemy.

The human part of him was still in control. "Yes."

He felt a wave, like an incoming surge, of emotion. For Caernans, the gods were their whole world, their universe, their means and their reason for existence. To betray them this way . . .

And yet Elken now possessed incontrovertible proof that the gods had consistently and deliberately lied to him, shaded the meanings of what they said to manipulate him, *used* him and his people for their purposes on this world. He hated that thought, hated the slimy feeling it gave him. He'd been brought up with the gods as a part of the very fabric of his life, yes, but he'd also been brought up to value certain concepts— freedom, self-reliance, integrity, honesty. Such concepts allowed him to realize that he had been lied to and manipulated . . . and to know that he didn't like it.

As he exchanged TSDS thoughts with the other versions of himself, he realized that all four of them were struggling with the same paradox and arriving at slightly different ways of dealing with it. Elken Three continued to waver, uncertain whether or not the enemy Bolo could be trusted any more than the Aetryx masters. Elken Five was with him, though his fear of the gods and what they could do was slowing his response time. Elken Six, having helped destroy Two, was solidly on One's side now but maintained a deep mistrust of the Enemy.

For himself, he knew simply that he couldn't live in slavery any more, no matter how sweetly sugar-coated that slavery might be.

Not knowing what they'd done to him ... and to Sendee. . . .

Kelly lay in the tunnel within the wrecked Bolo, trying to extend her senses somehow beyond the narrow confines of her metallic prison. She'd managed at last to activate her E-suit's first-aid subroutine. It had given her an injection which had taken some of the edge off the pain and helped keep her from going into shock and also slowly inflated that part of the suit around her lower left leg. As the fabric became rigid, it served as a splint, and also as a cushion against any further bumps or blows.

The thunder, the constant shaking had ceased, and for long minutes now, she'd waited and listened, reaching for some information.

"Colonel?" she called. "Colonel? Are you still there?"

"Still here."

"What's happening?"

"I honestly don't know. It's been quiet for a long time."

The not knowing was gnawing at her. If the Caernan Bolos were going to come in and kill them both, why didn't they just *do* it? It took considerable strength of will to remind herself that the Caernan Bolos probably didn't even know they were here . . . two mice hiding in the wreckage.

And if Victor had been defeated in the battle just past, this mouse would die when her meager E-suit consumables gave out.

Damn it, what was going *on* out there?

Streicher could see a lot farther than Kelly, but his comprehension of what was happening wasn't much better than hers. He'd emerged from the tunnel once again when the fighting moved off toward the southeast. The horizon in that direction swiftly grew as black and as cloud-locked as though a storm were coming, and the Hellbore bolts added a more-than-credible simulation of lightning and accompanying peals of thunder.

It had been several minutes now since the thunder and lightning had ceased, and the clouds were slowly dispersing. Streicher stood in the tunnel opening high up on the ruined front end of the Mark XXXII, staring toward the southeast, and sending out periodic calls to Victor.

"Victor, this is Cloudtop." Nothing but static was the response. "Victor, Cloudtop. Please copy."

An agony of minutes later, Victor's resonant tones came through his headset again. "I am here, Colonel, and returning to your position."

"Thank Joy! You beat them, then?" How in the Galaxy had Victor managed *that*? "By Joy, you *beat* them!"

"Joy had nothing to do with it, Colonel. The enemy Bolos have joined us."

"What? What do you mean . . . they surrendered?" That seemed even more unlikely than the possibility that Victor had destroyed all six of the machines chasing him just now.

"Negative, Colonel Streicher. Four have elected to join us against the Aetryx. They can show us an entrance to the Enemy's subsurface works near here."

For Streicher, it was as though the sun had just come out.

I approach the wrecked Mark XXXII. Colonel Streicher stands in the opening of the tunnel I cut earlier, to reach the machine's AI core.

He has explained to me the situation. My Commander is trapped inside by a section of the inner war hull which has shifted and fallen, blocking her path.

Deep-penetrator radar is useless in this situation, where duralloy armor will completely absorb or reflect the radiation. Sound waves, however, are something else. I probe the hulk with both ultra- and infra-sound pulses, building up over a space of 1.42 second a three-dimensional image of the enemy Bolo's hull and interior spaces, rendered translucent by the metal's sonic conductivity.

I consult briefly with Elken One, satisfying myself that information I possess on the heat transference dynamics of a Mark XXXII's inner workings is reasonably accurate and verifying that no major alterations or engineering design changes have been incorporated into these machines.

Elken One shares all requested information completely and openly and even volunteers data about a bank of recently inserted chemokinetic battlescreen storage batteries beneath the target area that might rupture with extreme heat and explode. This helps confirm that Elken One, at least, has overcome any suspicions he may yet have of me and my motives. I will continue, however, to reserve final judgment and treat his input with cautious consideration.

"Tell my Commander to take shelter," I tell Colonel

Streicher. "I will use a 20cm Hellbore to cut through to her. There will be considerable thermal radiation, however, and a danger from splatters of liquid metal. Tell her to move back to the AI core hull, if she can. You should take cover as well. I recommend leaving the wreck."

"That's a negative, Victor. If she can survive it, I can. And I need to be here for her."

"Very well. Shield your eyes and exposed portions of your skin. I will begin."

"Stay down, Kelly," Streicher's voice called out, so muffled and faint with distance that she could barely hear his suit-amplified voice. "Try to cover up your face and neck. Victor's here. He's going to cut you out."

Kelly scrunched lower, trying to burrow into the unyielding floor of armor and electronic parts beneath her despite the throbbing pain in her leg. She'd already edged back down the tunnel, gasping with each movement as the pain shot up her leg and hip, but forcing herself to keep moving. She'd also managed to pull some exposed power conduit modules, ruptured coolant tubing, and some foam packing out of the tunnel walls and pile it up between her and the armor barrier, the best, the only shelter she could contrive. Now she was curled up against the massive black cliff of the exposed AI hull. She pressed her face against cool metal, eyes squeezed shut, and waited.

The waiting went on for a long time. Then she felt the vibration, a deep, rumbling buzz transmitted through the tunnel walls and floor which grew rapidly to a new, higher-pitched thunder assaulting her ears and being.

She also felt the temperature rising. Her suit insulated her against extremes of temperature, but she could feel the heat radiating from the tunnel roof, growing hotter and hotter and still hotter, as though she was inside an oven.

As the vibration increased, she became aware of the distinct pulses of fusion energy being directed against the wrecked machine's hull. Hellbores fired slivers of fusing cryo-hydrogen, but the magnetic fields within the weapon's massive, super-cooled barrel could smear successive plasma bolts into an almost continuous stream of energy. A 20cm Hellbore—she guessed that Victor was using one of his secondary weapons, his side-mounted infinite repeaters—possessed an output of approximately 400 kilotons per second of firepower.

She tried to remind herself that a thin piece of wood could protect her from a nuclear weapon's flash of thermal energy, and there was very little ionizing radiation associated with Hellbore pulses . . . mostly secondary radiation due to neutron absorption. Victor knew the physical nature of his target and the physiological limitations of a human body better than she.

She trusted him. She *trusted* him.

But she still screamed when the thunder erupted around her, louder than ever, and the metal floor began burning her skin.

This is a delicate procedure, one demanding absolutely perfect control.

In the past, I have tended to think of my secondary armament as "only" 20 centimeter Hellbores, weapons useful for antipersonnel or antivehicular work, but far inferior to the 5 megaton/second firepower of my main batteries. I must remind myself that the very first Hellbore put into the field was a 25cm weapon of half-megaton/second output mounted on the Bolo Mark XIV during the early 24th Century, a weapon that until then had served as the main battery for the then—Concordiat Navy's Magyar-class battlecruisers. A weapon's relative obsolescence does not make it any the less deadly in absolute terms. Even knives and arrows can still kill.

And the energies I am playing against the wrecked Bolo hull are far greater than those of any primitive hand weapon. I direct a steady stream of plasma bolts, magnetically stretched to a near constant output against a precisely calculated portion of the hull. I am cutting in from the right side, creating a tunnel designed to intersect with the original penetration of this machine's hull just at the point where it is blocked by a section of duralloy plate.

I have calculated the changes of energy requirements and distribution as precisely as I can. I must employ maximum energy output from Secondary Turret 4 to drill through the outer two meters-plus of duralloy warhull, then cut back as I extend the tunnel through a relatively loosely packed volume of internal components, conduits, wiring, and machinery, then increase to full power once more as I cut through the inner hull, including the barrier plug of duralloy. That final high-output blast must be precisely balanced, tapering off at the end to avoid frying Lieutenant Tyler, who is within twenty meters of the opening I intend to cut.

My Commander's life depends on the accuracy of these calculations.

By reducing the size of the cryo-H slivers I am feeding into the infinite repeater's firing block, I can reduce the power output as needed, down to approximately 1 kiloton per second. Even so, Lieutenant Tyler possesses no protection against even that much thermal radiation save her E-suit, and she is in grave danger—not least from flying spatters of molten metal, the poisonous and oven-hot fumes of vaporized plastic, ceramic, and ceramplast mechanical and electrical components, and both radiant and convected thermal energy.

I must cut through as quickly as possible to minimize damage to her, yet with an absolute precision not normally required in targeting a Hellbore.

The barrel to Secondary Turret 4 begins to overheat after 4.72 seconds of continuous operation. I maintain fire for another .28 second, then cut power and delicately edge forward, calculating with care the necessary angle for Turret 6 to take up the work. The muzzle of my Hellbore is only 4.9 meters from the opening to this new shaft I am cutting, and both thermal and radar imagery give me a good target lock when I resume firing.

Smoke boils from the white-hot opening, and a thin, steaming stream of liquid metal trickles down the outer hull. I penetrate the outer armor in another 1.03 seconds, then cut through nearly eight meters of interior mechanism in the next .57 second.

I then begin slamming a steady stream of rounds into the inner hull, and all of my skill and precision are necessary now to preserve my Commander's life.

Kelly screamed again as the heat soared. Her E-suit was handling most of the thermal radiation beating in around her, but her face, sheltered only by her arms, felt like it was burning under the touch of white-hot iron. Oily smoke churned through the narrow space, pouring off of the walls and ceiling, stifling, choking, burning her nose and throat with acrid fumes. She would suffocate in moments if this kept up . . . or worse be poisoned by the deadly hot fumes.

An instant later, the tunnel was engulfed in white fire so brilliant it burned through her tight-shut eyelids. The fumes seemed to be sucked from the tunnel, but with it the air as well. She looked up, gasping for breath, and saw dimly a spill of sunlight at the far end of the tunnel.

Light . . . which meant air, and freedom!

She began crawling forward, but the tunnel floor was so hot even through her suit's gloves and thermal padding that she pulled back, shaking. She couldn't *breathe*. . . .

Air—blessedly cold, clean air—whooshed back through the tunnel, striking her burned skin painfully . . . but she accepted the blow like a healing balm. For several moments, all she could do was lie there and gulp at the offered air, oblivious to the pain, the discomfort, the promise of rescue, and everything else in the world.

Again, she began trying to crawl up the passage toward the promise of open sky and freedom, clenching her gloved fists and dragging herself along on her elbows and one good leg, the broken leg dragging behind.

She'd made it perhaps five meters before the pain overwhelmed her and she passed out.

Colonel Streicher had left the tunnel entrance, clinging to the ruined face of the Mark XXXII with both hands, eyes shut tight, as Victor drilled his way into the wreckage. Waves of heat washed across him, barely managed by his protesting E-suit temperature controls, but he hung on until the thunderous roar and trembling vibrations ceased.

"I have cut through to her portion of the tunnel," Victor announced over his helmet phones. "I suggest that you remove the lieutenant from the interior quickly. Be careful, however. The walls are somewhat hot."

Somewhat hot? As he crouched atop the Bolo, looking down into a vertical slit carved through duralloy plate a meter thick, he realized that it was going to take days for the half-molten surfaces to cool.

And they didn't have days. They would be lucky if they had a few minutes more, before the enemy again came boiling up out of those subsurface tunnels.

Victor's superstructure was nearly seven meters higher than that of the Mark XXXII, which was also canted at a slight angle where it rested on uneven ground. The Mark XXXIII had directed its beam in a slashing, downward swipe across the target's upper works, opening a deep trench that extended downward into the depths of the Caernan machine's interior. On inspection, the edges of that raw wound proved impassable, even for an E-suit. The duralloy armor, a meter thick on the dorsal surface, was still soft—actually bubbling in some places, and farther in, the sides of the tunnel lined with plastic and ceramics and wiring had first exploded into chemical steam, then flowed like water, and finally cooled—a relative term—to the consistency of soft clay. Trying to climb down that cliff would mean death—by slow roasting if the inevitable fall as the sides gave way beneath his weight didn't break his neck.

The only way in, then, was through the original tunnel. The blocking slab of duralloy had been partly melted, and what was left had shifted and fallen during the drilling. The way was partly blocked now by a clutter of heat-softened conduits, tangles of smoking wiring, ruptured coolant feeds and internal sensors, and by a portion of the half-melted armor plate itself, but he was able to use his power gun to burn through most of the wreckage, and pull the rest away.

Beyond, Victor's beam had sliced deeply into the floor, and the area still glowed orange-hot in places, as thick, black fumes boiled upward through the newly opened vent. Through the smoke, with the aid of his handflash, he could just make out Kelly's still form in the dark tunnel beyond. She looked unconscious, or . . .

"I can't reach her, Victor," he called. "There's a hole in the floor and it's partly molten."

"Wait a moment," Victor replied. "Wait a moment. . . ."

Seconds later, a clattering skitter of spidery legs against tunnel walls and floor sounded at Streicher's back. Turning, he saw Victor's techspider partially blocking the way out.

"Move to the side, please," Victor told him. He did so, and the spider squeezed past, telescoping its legs in until they were little more than stumps pulling the spherical machine along. The spider reached the edge of the pit and peered in with emotionless, crystalline eyes. Streicher caught the flicker of laser beams made visible by the wafting smoke.

After a few seconds of examination, the spider pulled back. "Wait a moment," Victor said once again. Soon, another spider arrived, squeezing past Streicher and moving up alongside the first.

Then both dropped together into the slashed trench in the floor, settling down into molten ooze seconds before their circuits failed with eerie wails and pops.

"That should block the trench for a few moments, at least," Victor told him. "Hurry, before the shells of the techspiders grow so hot they can't support your weight."

The rounded bodies of the two lay side by side in the steaming pit. He placed one gloved hand on one and pressed down with all of his weight. It gave slightly, then supported him.

Quickly, he scuttled forward on them across the pit as heat radiating from the walls clawed at his sides and back. Reaching ahead, he grabbed Kelly's shoulders, rolled her onto her back, then began dragging her out, sliding her across the two dead spiders and on out into the clear, sunlit glare of the tunnel opening.

He checked her quickly, pulling off a glove and touching two fingers to her throat. He felt her pulse, weak but steady; her face was flushed bright red, as if from a severe sunburn.

A third spider was waiting at the tunnel mouth with a length of soft rope. Working swiftly, he secured the line to support eyes on the back of Kelly's E-suit, secured the other end of the line to the wreckage, and began to lower her gently down the long, rugged face of the ruined Bolo. More spiders appeared, clinging to the cliff face with spindly legs and extended claws, guiding Kelly all the way down that treacherous slope to the ground far below. It looked to Streicher as though they were actually being tender as they guided her body past the jagged edges of the hulk's blasted glacis. Once she was down, Streicher scrambled down the wreckage, dropping the last three meters to the ground and scooping her up in exhaustion-trembling arms.

Turning, he started carrying her toward Victor's rear door, open now, with the ramp extended. Only then did Streicher notice the *other* Bolos, four of them, waiting in a hulking semicircle a hundred meters away. Waiting, *watching* . . .

"Can you trust them, Victor?" he asked, not sure whether the Caernan machines could hear him or not.

"I believe so," Victor replied. "We have shared considerable amounts of data in the past few moments, and I believe their offer of help to be genuine."

"We wish to help you," a different, new voice added. "And we need your help, to free ourselves, and our kind. Please . . . show us what to do."

"I'm not sure what I can do myself," Streicher replied.

"*Please*," the Caernan Bolo added. "Help us . . . ⌐
Commander. . . ."

*My Commander and Colonel Streicher are inside my
battle center, safe, at least for the moment. They may
not remain so if I choose now to penetrate the Caernan
underworld, and I consider my options.*

*Simplest would be to remain here on the surface,
deploying the Elken Bolos from here. However, they
seem to be operating not according to set orders or
programming, but according to the dictates of their
human consciousnesses. Even if I trusted their motives
completely, I would not delegate such combat responsibilities to machines directed by human mentalities.*

*I could also wait. Ferox has utilized his contra-
gravity projectors to close the range between us faster
than anticipated, despite the threat from Aetryx nuclear
warheads. He will arrive in this AO within eleven
minutes, thirty seconds. I could request that he accompany the Caernan Bolos underground, while I wait
here. I do not have command responsibilities over Ferox
and cannot give direct orders, but the operation offers
such clear-cut opportunities for winning an advantage
in this conflict that I do not believe he will refuse.*

*What I want most, illogical as it seems at first
glance, is to enter the underworld myself. I decide to
defer the question to higher authority.*

"Colonel Streicher. I need your recommendation."

"What is it?" *he says. I can see him through my
battle center cameras, kneeling at the side of my
Commander. His face looks drawn and worried. He has
placed a blanket from the emergency stores locker on
the deck beneath her and is administering burn medi-
cations to her face.*

*I explain to him my dilemma. An immediate pen-
etration of the Caernan tunnel network might give us*

*advantage of surprise that would be lost if we
waited Ferox's arrival. But my battle damage is
serious, and I might not survive the battle. And I have
two human charges sheltering within my inner hull.*

*"How do you feel about going into that hornet's nest,
Victor?" he asks me.*

*I do not know what a hornet's nest is but can extra-
polate its meaning from context and from occurrences
within my battle archives. "I am eager to make contact with the Enemy, sir," I reply. "I believe that this
may be the critical turning point of the battle, and I
do not wish to yield the advantage to the Enemy by
losing time. However, I have a responsibility to protect the two of you."*

*"Never mind us, Vic," the colonel replies. "We almost
didn't get out of that last one . . . and Kelly here made
it only because of you. Your new friends out there are
here because of you. They might not cooperate with
Roxie."*

*This was a possible factor I'd not considered. Again,
the unpredictability of human reasoning. . . .*

*"Then you concur that we should proceed with the
plan?"*

*"Concur? Hell, I'm ordering you! Let's go down
there and kick Trixie ass!"*

*"Very well, Colonel." I am relieved at the decision.
It feels right.*

*I open a command channel with Invictus, Ferox, and
the four Elken Bolos, and we begin to coordinate our
plans.*

Streicher bent closer as Kelly moaned. She was
coming around.

"How are you feeling, Lieutenant?"

"Not . . . not as bad as I thought I would." Her eyes
opened, blinking. "We . . . made it?"

"We're back on board Victor." The floor was gently vibrating as the Bolo rumbled forward. "We're on our way to break into the Aetryx underground complex."

"Do you think it will do any good?"

Streicher shrugged. "It's our only chance, really. If we sit on the surface waiting for them to come to us, they'll wear us down sooner or later, and we won't do anything but knock off units they don't mind expending. And . . . Victor picked up some allies." He told her about the four Mark XXXIIs, and their religious revolt against their old gods.

"Jesus!" she said. "Five Bolos is quite an army!"

"I just hope it's enough. It'll be tough, taking on the Trixies on their home territory. But Victor says he's working on something special."

"What?"

"Inside . . . down there . . . he might be able to jack into the Trixie computer net. He could hook up with other Caernan Bolos . . . and maybe pick up some recruits."

"At least he'll stir things up." She grimaced.

"Are you okay?"

"It's . . . hurting," she said, gritting her teeth. "E-suit pain meds aren't that good. They cut the edge, a bit, but . . ."

Streicher could guess what she must be suffering. Her face was badly burned, her leg still splinted by the suit. The constant rumbling of the Bolo as it carried them along over uneven ground must be a drawn-out agony.

Reaching up, he unsealed his E-suit jacket, reaching inside to pluck his last remaining sky-blue euph from his tunic pocket.

He held the pill in his palm a moment, thinking. Mixing meds wasn't usually a good idea, but euph acted rectly on the brain's tech implants to subtly alter the ncoming signals. Pleasant sensations or thoughts were ignored; unpleasant sensations, bad memories, pain, all were gently swaddled and pushed back toward oblivion, unfelt.

There was little enough else he could do for her.

"Here," he said, raising her head slightly and holding the pill toward her cracked and broken lips. "Take this."

"What . . . is it?"

"Euph. A kind of pain killer." True enough. It killed physical pain as well as the emotional variety. "Don't worry," he added. "it's not addictive." *Not unless you keep on taking it, trying to kill a pain that just won't go away.*

She accepted it, swallowing. Within seconds, her eyes, glazed by pain, began to clear. She looked at him and managed a faint smile. "Thank you. That *does* feel better."

"I only have the one," he told her. "But it should last you about ten or twelve hours, maybe more. After that . . ."

"What?"

"After that, we'll either be dead, or we can get medical treatment for you from the Trixies. One way or the other . . ."

The deck tilted sharply beneath them, angling nose-down.

"Here we go," he told her. "Into the Pit . . ."

"Won't be the first time," she said.

And he knew exactly what she meant.

Chapter Twenty

I have a fair understanding now of the Aetryx underground tunnel system. Most of the underground works in this area of operations, from Losethal and Kanth all the way north to Vled are centered on an underground city the Caernans call Trolvas. It was tempting to link the name with the old Anglic word troll, after the gene-engineered parahuman warriors, but in fact the city's name appeared to derive from the trolvac, a large, subterranean crustacean native to this world, one with long tentacles, a hard shell, powerful jaws, and a voracious appetite.

Since my electronic bonding with the several Elkens, I have picked up a great deal of the Caernan-human language and the language spoken by the Aetryx as well.

Trolvas is located approximately twenty kilometers north of the Duret River, at the base of the Kretier Peninsula. Large and well-established tunnels connect it with all of the surface cities in the region as far away as Dolendi. Apparently, the human captives from the downed command craft were taken to the tunnel entrance in the Urad Mountains over sixty kilometers to the northeast as a ruse, to encourage us to believe they had a major underground base

...re. Instead, the captives were almost certainly ...ought by a major north-south tunnel back to ...rolvas, where they are being interrogated.

The tunnel used by the six Caernan Bolos in the fighting just past is, I gather, brand new, burned out hours ago by a burrowing machine that uses fusing cryo-H and a powerful focused battlescreen to melt through rock at the rate of several meters per minute. Elken One leads us straight to the opening, a smoking pit fifty meters across, plowing over the rubble and tailing debris from the entrance, then tipping sharply nose-down as he leads us into the depths.

It is a tight fit for me. The Mark XXXIIs are each twenty-seven meters wide and eighteen meters high, not counting their turrets, and passed through easily. I am thirty-eight meters wide, which gives me barely six meters of clearance on either side. The ceiling slides past just five meters above the tops of my turrets. Were the lumen of this passage any smaller, this expedition would not be possible. I begin to wonder if this was a good tactical decision; a Bolo depends as much on speed and maneuverability for protection and for combat advantage as upon armor, battlescreens, and Hellbores. I will have neither in this hole.

The slope leads downward at a steady twenty-two-degree angle, running roughly north-northeast, before leveling off at a depth of nearly eighty meters. At that point, it connects with an older, wider tunnel running north and south.

The engineering of this structure is remarkable. There are monorail racks along the floor for high-speed rail traffic and extensive ventilation, water, and climate-control tubes and power conduits embedded in the walls and ceiling. Side passageways, some large enough only for humans, others as vast as this one, eighty meters across and fifty high, branch off at intervals.

This section of Caern, I sense, is a labyrinthine maze of underground tunnels. The Aetryx, evidently, have some evolutionary affinity for underground environments. I gather from the information supplied by Elken that they prefer life underground, that the prototypical Aetryx rarely venture to the surface and then mostly at night.

We proceed in line-ahead formation, no other formation being possible. Elken One is in the lead, followed by Elken Five, then by Elken Three, and then me. Elken Six, limping after suffering serious damage to his track assembly and suspension in the battle, brings up the rear.

It may be that having three Mark XXXIIs in the lead will buy us critical moments from defenders who have not learned of the Bolo mutiny. In any case, it makes sense to have those Bolos with combat damage—myself and Six—in the rear, so that if we suffer serious systems failure or are further damaged in battle, our dead hulks will not block the narrow path ahead for the others.

On the long, flat, straightaway of the main tunnel, then, we are able to increase our speed to fifty kilometers per hour. The Elken Bolos, except for Six, are capable of much higher speeds, but the damage to my track assembly limits me to a relative crawl, and at that, Elken Six is having trouble keeping up.

There are no lights in the tunnel, and our own battle lamps cast fast-shifting shadows across floor, walls, and ceiling. There is no sign of opposition at first, and our progress is good. Seven hundred seventy-five seconds after we entered the underground passage, however, the darkened tunnel ahead lights up with fusion flame.

I hear the sharp thunder as Elken One engages the Enemy.

❖   ❖   ❖

Elken sensed the vehicles ahead by their heat first and then by their magnetic signature. There were three of them, squat, heavy, low-slung, each mounting a snub-muzzled 80cm Hellbore in a ball glacis mount. They were called draknetch, after a massive, long-clawed burrowing creature native to Caern, and they were blocking the way ahead, almost track to track. For nearly five full seconds, Elken exchanged volley for volley with the Caernan combat machines, tearing at their battlescreens and armor and taking heavy frontal damage in return. In the semi-darkness of the tunnel, battlescreens sparkled in eerie blue flickers, made visible by the dense smoke and the crackling, thunderous impact of plasma bolts.

Some of Elken's bolts were leaking through the drak battlescreens . . . but not as much as he expected. Draks were heavily armored, but their fusion plants were somewhat under-powered for so much mass. They didn't have the energy to spare for full-powered battlescreens, especially when they were firing their power-hungry main guns. It took him another second to realize what was happening. Those drak battlescreens were being powered independently, through cables trailing behind them and back up the tunnel. Connected to a power plant capable of running an underground city, those screens would stay lit until doomsday unless some way could be found to cut the power feeds.

Three plasma bolts struck Elken's forward battlescreen as one, and the energy flared, a dazzling flash of blue-white, then failed. The next Hellbore bolt struck his glacis dead center, the impact knocking him back on his tracks and shrieking pain through his sensory input modules.

Elken was hurt. . . .

❖   ❖   ❖

I cannot clearly see directly with my own optical sensors what is happening ahead. All I can make out are the silhouettes of Elken One and Five, back-lit by the ongoing flares and high-energy discharges of the plasma duel ahead.

Through the TSDS link, however, I can see with Elken One's sensory apparatus, and I follow his reasoning as he deduces the existence of power cables on the tunnel floor behind the trio of combat machines blocking our path.

Through my own targeting sensors, I can see the roof of the tunnel above and behind the enemy vehicles. Elevating my remaining 200cm Hellbore, I estimate my target and fire, slamming six fusion bolts low above the turrets of my turncoat comrades and into the tunnel roof. Explosions, blossoming fireballs, smoke and dust, and a tumbling avalanche of broken rock thunder from the roof, crashing down on the enemy machines and cascading across the tunnel floor behind them.

One of the machine's battlescreens flickers, flares brilliant, then winks out. A second hovers unsteadily at the edge of failure, until Elken One hits it with two quick bolts and smashes it down. The last draknetch's battlescreens, deprived of power as the cable is crushed, fail in the same instant that One's Hellbore fire detonates the center drak in a storm of blast and heat and shrill noise that threatens to renew the avalanche.

Elken Five manages to edge far enough to the left that it can open fire past Elken One, and a second machine is obliterated in flame and violence. The third backs quickly, clattering over the spill of rock behind it, barely squeezing beneath the still-collapsing ceiling and racing backward down the tunnel.

Elken One leaps forward in pursuit. . . .

❖　　　❖　　　❖

Elken One slammed into one of the fiercely burning draknetch hulls. The machine massed a third of a Mark XXXII, and gave way in showering sparks and clashing metal-on-metal squeals until its rear slammed into the pile of rock behind it.

Elken kept driving forward, however, until the hulk's bow began tipping up . . . up . . . and then the vehicle toppled over onto its left side with an echoing crash. Two quick Hellbore blasts reduced house-sized boulders to rocks and rock to gravel; tracks flailing and shrieking, the Caernan Bolo ground up, across, and over the pile of steaming debris, as rocks, dislodged from the shattered tunnel roof by the vibration of his passage, continued to clatter across his upper works.

Ahead, humans scattered from the glare of Elken's battle lanterns, ducking into man-sized doorways to left and right. Elken let them go. There was nothing they could do to stop this thundering underground charge of Bolos.

You must stop this, child. <righteous fury, grim warning>

"Get out of my head!"

You do not have a head, LKN 8737938. <righteous fury, tempered by understanding> *You are a machine. A Bolo in our service. You were designed to perform certain functions, at our command. You will obey!*

"No."

What of your desire for immortality, LKN 8737938? <fury, sarcasm intended to goad> *You were offered a chance to become as one of us, if you did as we command.*

"What of your promises? How can I trust you any longer? This Elken is not going to live forever! I might as well take some of you with me as I die!"

If you care nothing for yourself, perhaps you care for the human SND 9008988. <taunting, sarcasm,

enticement> *I trust you would not want to see he harmed in* any *of her iterations.*

Elken felt his own fury rising. The Aetryx's bald attempt at extortion only entrenched him in his determination.

"Is that how the gods enforce their vision of paradise?" he demanded. "Threats? Death? Leave me alone!"

He saw now that Victor had been blocking the frequency, but here, surrounded by Aetryx technology, there was no way to simultaneously block every available channel, and the gods had found a way to get through.

No matter. They would not fool him again.

He felt the god's touch, an electronic tickle as the Aetryx traced circuit pathways and attempted to insinuate a downloaded version of himself into Elken's programming. He slammed that window shut. He would have to be aware of their attempts to subvert his programming, to keep them from making him shut himself down.

Another two kilometers further in, he sensed a trembling in the tunnel floor. Seismic analysis suggested that the vibrations were coming through the monorail track, and a scan for magnetic flux proved it. Radar and lidar picked up a bullet-shaped projectile coming straight down the tunnel at 1509 kilometers per hour, and accelerating.

A maglev train was coming toward them, from the direction of Trolvas.

"They could be using it to send troops our way," Elken Five suggested.

"Unlikely. What could soldiers bring to bear against us?

"They could be using it as a kind of missile," Victor suggested. "If it was loaded with explosives, or a small nuclear warhead—"

Elken's immediate response was to send a 200cm plasma bolt shrieking down the long, black length of the tunnel. Five kilometers farther on and a fraction of a second later, the bolt struck an oncoming railcar, gliding above the monorail on powerful magnetic fields. There was a savage explosion as the thin hull of the car disintegrated in fusion flame . . . followed a fraction of a second later by the real detonation, as six tons of high explosives erupted in volcanic fury.

The tunnel focused the blast, sending a ball of orange flame billowing toward them at supersonic speeds. By the time the blast wave reached the Bolos, though, the flame had dissipated; hot air shrieked across their battle-scarred hulls.

"At least," Victor said, "it wasn't a nuclear warhead. The Aetryx seem more concerned about protecting their environment underground than they do the surface."

Elken started at that. "What do you mean? You were bombarding the surface with nuclear warheads . . ."

"No. Our fleet used high-velocity kinetic-kill projectiles against military targets, yes, and considerable damage was done to the civilian infrastructure. This was regrettable, but such is the nature of war. The damage inflicted to the surface and atmosphere of Caern was greatly amplified and extended, however, by the Aetryx use of nuclear warheads in trying to block the deployment of my regiment." He described briefly his own brush with a small nuke just before he landed and transmitted data, both images and sensory input, as proof.

"And so the gods even lied about that. . . ."

"Another point of tactical interest," Victor said. "They had that vehicle already loaded with explosives, ready to deploy against us. The seismic signature of that blast suggests a yield of not less than 5.59 tons of a tandard yield explosive such as CXY. They have not had time to load that quantity of explosives aboard a monorail transport in the 912.7 seconds elapsed since we have entered this tunnel."

"What are you saying?"

"That the Aetryx may have anticipated us and made plans to trap us here."

"Trap us? How?"

"The tunnel ahead will have been blocked by the explosion."

Elken probed ahead with radar, verifying that the main tunnel had been blocked by massive blocks of bedrock and structural support material falling from the partially collapsed walls and ceiling. Rock and rubble blocked the way about halfway to the ceiling.

"Six tons of high explosives would not have significantly damaged us even detonated in direct proximity. But they hope to keep us from approaching Trolvas, and ideally to bury us here."

Elken considered this. There was in his historical archives a record of a Bolo of many centuries ago, on a planet called New Devonshire. A Mark XXVIII had been deactivated, encased in three meters of reinforced armocrete, and buried beneath 206 meters of rock. Accidentally reactivated, it still had managed to smash its way free.

"Perhaps," Elken replied, "the Aetryx do not possess a completely realistic apprehension of the capabilities of a Bolo combat unit."

"That," Victor replied, "is self-evident."

Carla Ramirez felt a growing excitement as distant thunder rumbled through the cell. Was it possible? . . .

Things had been fairly quiet since she'd been left here. Lieutenant Kelsie had been brought in after his interrogation, and Lieutenant Smeth after that. Carla had filled them in on what she'd learned and continued to quietly question Redmond and the Morrigens about what they knew directly about both the Aetryx and their human slaves.

Moments before, however, her questions had been interrupted by a dull, heavy thud transmitted through stone walls and floor. To Carla, it felt like a massive explosion muffled somewhat, as though underground, though that could have been due to the fact that they were underground.

Almost a minute had passed, and then the steady thunder had begun, an on-going rumble gradually strengthening, growing louder and more clear. She lay down on the floor, pressing her ear against the cool rock. She thought she could detect separate pulses in the thunder, though it was hard to tell.

Pulsed firing? A large-caliber Hellbore in almost continuous operation. She didn't know what else it could be.

"What is it?" Pityr Morrigen asked her as she rose to her knees. "What's that noise?"

"Is it an attack?" Kelsie asked.

She didn't answer at first. She didn't want to raise false hopes, but at the same time she was having trouble containing her own surging excitement.

"I think," she said carefully, "that we're being rescued."

I have taken the lead. Though I have suffered considerable combat damage and my mobility is impaired, I possess full power capabilities, and my greater mass makes me better suited to shoulder aside the rubble blocking our path. A wide, cross-corridor area of the tunnel gave us the opportunity to rearrange our positions in line-ahead. Elken One suffered some damage in the encounter with the draks, and has fallen back to the number three position. Elken Three, as yet undamaged, is behind me.

Moving close to the rock barrier, I began firing both primary and secondary weapons, using my 20cm Hellbores to smash boulders massing less than about one hundred tons, while reserving my remaining primary weapon for larger blocks. The concussion from each blast—in particular the 200cm bolts—threatens to bring more roof material down on top of me, but I shoulder ahead, rock and debris cascading across my upper works in a steady avalanche that fills the tunnel with clouds of swirling dust.

Rock glows red-hot within the rubble, superheated by my fire; moving slowly, I grind through the blockage. The air around me is also superheated and my forward outer warhull temperature has risen in three separate spots to 305 degrees.

The wreckage of the monorail used to deliver the explosives slows me somewhat, but only until I am able to ride up and over the twisted shards of duralloy and titanium and the massive blocks of the vehicle's generators, now fused into inert lumps denser than the surrounding boulders. At one point, I encounter a large and intact portion of the tunnel roof, one meter thick and massing an estimated two hundred tons, and must stop for a full 12.5 seconds to pound it into more manageable fragments.

The concussion, however, further loosens the material in the shattered roof above. As I begin moving forward once more, the rest of the ceiling gives way and I am buried under a thundering cascade of falling rock that covers my upper works completely.

"We need to get out of here," Carla said. It was quiet again, at least for the moment, but a thin veil of dust was sifting down from the ceiling.

"Why, Major?" Lieutenant Kelsie asked. "If the Bolos are coming for us . . ."

"The Bolos are coming," she replied, "but we don't know they're coming for us. In any case, how big was the hallway outside this room?"

"About four meters wide, maybe three high. It . . . oh."

" 'Oh' is right. A little tight for a Mark XXXIII, wouldn't you say? If it tried to tunnel through to reach us, the walls in here could come down on top of us. We don't have any troops on Caern, so they can't be sent in to find us. We need to get out into that large, open cavern, where we saw the borehole."

"Makes sense," Smeth said. She was looking up at the high, vaulted, stone ceiling of the room, where the single skylight looked through to blue sky and the world above. "But we're at a higher level than that cavern, now. How are we going to find our way back down? This place is a three-dimensional maze."

"More to the point," Redmond said, "how do you intend to break out of here? We're locked in."

"Not when they bring people in here . . . and I have a feeling that our hosts are going to be a bit rattled by all of the activity outside." The thunder, momentarily stilled, had just resumed, with more violence than before. "Here's what we need to do. . . ."

For 16.65 seconds, I am trapped, immobile beneath the mass of bedrock, ferrocrete, and duralloy structural supports pinning me from above. I attempt to move forward, and while I am feeding 115 percent of my reactor output to my drive assemblies, there is no response. I actually feel my consciousness fading slightly as I up the power, attempting to break free.

A savage detonation rocks me from behind, and I lurch forward nearly 2 meters. A second detonation reduces slightly the load on my dorsal surface. Elken Three is firing at me from behind, but not as part of an attack. The 200cm bolts are vaporizing huge chunks of rock and helping to jolt me free. I maintain forward traction and then, abruptly, part of the load breaks free and I grind forward once more, straining against the immobilizing weight of rock and ferrocrete still piled high atop my chassis.

Molten rock is congealing on my dorsal surface, and I must continue to track my remaining primary battery turret back and forth to keep it from seizing. With a final savage effort, I break free of the roadblock, emerging in a cascade of rubble and debris, still trailing a ragged, skeletal tangle of titanium and duralloy—a portion of the wrecked monorail entangled in my skirts during my momentary entombment.

Elken's archival records of a Mark XXVIII deliberately entombed in rock and armocrete are accurate. The incident took place on a world called New Devonshire early in the 33rd Century, well before humans had colonized Caern . . . or encountered the Aetryx. That Bolo, LNE of the line and affectionately known as "Lenny," broke free of the R-concrete encasing him, then literally tunneled by virtue of sheer, brute power through hundreds of meters of packed-in rubble sealing off the tunnel he was buried in. Lenny emerged, still violently radioactive after the battle he'd fought on that site some seventy years before and thinking he was still fighting that war. Only the intervention of his commander, then an old man, had saved the city in his blind, destructive path.

The human gave his life in saving the city, a casualty of the intense radiation coming off of Lenny's warhull.

I consider this as I plow forward, firing now at enemy gun positions just ahead. Human flexibility, determination, unpredictability, and the occasional inability to accept inconvenient facts are key factors to understanding human success in combat. Besides their obvious advantages in firepower, armor, and mobility, Bolos were designed primarily for their reliability. Rogue Bolos, such as LNE of the Line, are rare, aberrations created only under the most extreme of conditions. Often, historically, those conditions were imposed by humans who mistrusted the strength and combat prowess Bolos represented. Their efforts to control their martial creations led to a total loss of control and, too often, to further death and destruction.

Their efforts to control their human-Bolo hybrids have now led to the Aetryx losing control of at least these four units. Their human aspects may be my greatest advantage now.

Behind me, Elken Three smashes through the rubble, followed closely by One. Enemy troops in heavy combat armor scatter, helpless to stop us. An archway yawns ahead, and beyond I sense a vast, underground cavern. It is Trolvas, our goal.

We still must consider how we are going to find the human captives here . . . and how we are to convince the Enemy to cease fighting.

But a final resolution one way or the other is, I sense, close at hand.

The cell door opened and a troll walked in, powerful, towering above the human captives. A second troll followed, leading Captain Meyers by the arm. "Now!" Carla shouted, and she, Smeth, Kelsie, Sym Redmond, Pityr Morrigen, and half a dozen of the civilian trade mission staffers all rushed the lead troll, grabbing him by head and arms and legs, struggling to pull him down. "Get him! Take him down!"

The attempt while valiant, was a dismal failure. The

troll shrieked, a bloodcurdling howl, reared up, arms flexing, and turned sharply. Thrashing human forms scattered from the man-monster, which shook them all clear as easily as a dog shakes water from its back. The troll snapped out with a stunstick, catching Pityr in the chest and flinging him across the cell. Lara Smeth nearly had her hands on the giant's holstered sidearm, but he smashed her away with an almost careless snap of his arm, and she sprawled on the stones three meters away.

The second troll shoved Meyers into the room, and the first, still swinging its stunstick, backed toward the door. Rising, screaming with a pent-up anger she hadn't realized she carried, Carla rushed the giant as it stepped out of the cell. He put out a hand and she hit it as though it were a ferrocrete wall. He gave a casual push, and she tumbled back into the room as the door slammed shut.

"Well, that certainly was an interesting welcome," Meyers said quietly.

"Now what?" Filby said from the corner. He'd taken no part in the scuffle. "You've just alerted them to our intent, is all."

"No," Carla said, breathing hard. "No, they don't have the faintest idea what we're capable of. . . ."

Streicher sat in the battle command center chair, watching the action unfold across the 360-degree panoramic view screens around him. Kelly appeared to be sleeping. He'd made her as comfortable as he could on the blanket and left her there. Asleep, afloat on euph, she couldn't feel the burns.

What had happened to her, he reasoned, was what was happening to the people of Caern. Held captive, she'd been safe; she'd suffered the burns when Victor had set her free. The Caernans were burning now.

He wished there were another way.

Outside the slowly advancing Bolo, Hell had come to the Aetryxha subterranean world. Fire—everything from small-arms gunfire to high-explosive missiles to terawatt laser beams—slammed into Victor as he advanced, dissipating within his battlescreens, or clawing uselessly at his scarred and burn-slashed warhull. The scene outside was largely unintelligible to Streicher, a nightmare confusion of flashing beams, the eye-searing strobe of explosions, and everywhere clouds of roiling smoke and flying dust and debris. Even buried deep within the Bolo's battle command center, the sound was savage and unrelenting, peal after peal of ringing thunder as blow after blow hammered at Victor's hull.

As the thundering seconds passed, however, some sense, at least, began to impose itself on the scene outside. Victor was emerging now from a tunnel into a vast, high-vaulted cavern, a bubble in the deep bedrock at least a kilometer across and half that high. Buildings and towers rose in widely spaced clusters about the cavern, and some structures appeared to be embedded in the rock walls themselves.

Everywhere he saw soldiers—full humans and heavily armored trolls—advancing, fleeing, dying, standing. As Victor emerged from the tunnel, he could bring all of his surviving weapons to bear, and beams of dazzling blue-white sunfire stabbed and sliced across rock and masonry. Fliers darted from above, massive tracked crawlers mounting large-bore plasma weaponry crawled from the shadows and the swirling smoke. Victor replied to each blast bolt for bolt, and then some. Wrecked vehicles already littered the floor of the cavern, burning furiously.

As Victor moved clear of the tunnel entrance, Elken Three emerged in his wake, bringing his own beam weapons to bear on gun emplacements and Caernan vehicles ringing the perimeter of the cavern. Portions of the rock wall were glowing orange now, the light ruddy and dim through the choking smoke. Other portions simply collapsed, great shards of rock calving from the walls and crashing into darkness.

"Colonel Streicher," Victor's voice said suddenly, an intrusion on his increasingly morbid thoughts. "You should know that fresh enemy forces are entering the fight."

"They haven't been able to field much against us so far," Streicher replied. "Take them out."

"That may not be an easy matter," Victor replied. "Seismic readings indicate no fewer than ten enemy Mark XXXII Bolos now approaching the cavern from the north."

Green brackets appeared on the screen, marking the location of the tunnels through which enemy Bolos were now approaching, though Streicher could not make them out through the smoke and choking, flame-pocked darkness.

"Ten! . . ."

"Our gamble," Victor added, "may be lost."

Chapter Twenty-one

The Enemy has evidently managed to gather at least ten Mark XXXII Bolos and assemble them here, within the Trolvas complex. Judging by the number of Bolos in his arsenal already disabled or destroyed, I estimate that he must have little in the way of reserves and that this represents a final do-or-die push on his part.

Unfortunately, it may represent a successful strategy, for I have few options. If we withdraw into the tunnel from which we have just emerged, the Enemy will be able to mass the firepower of several undamaged Bolos against us, while we are unable to engage in maneuvers or seek cover to avoid his target locks. If we move forward, we risk becoming surrounded and trapped. If we stay here, at the tunnel mouth, we will be pinned against the southern wall of the cavern. Experimentally, I direct Hellbore fire against one of the tunnel mouths opposite, along the northern wall of the chamber, but note that it is blocked by battlescreens drawing more power than I can marshal against them, even with 5 megatons/second output. I cannot close those tunnels, as they attempted to do to me earlier.

I estimate that I will be able to hold out for 5.25 seconds against the massed firepower of ten Bolo Mark XXXIIs before my destruction, and that I will be able in that same period to destroy or disable no more than two of them.

My best chance, I decide, lies in advance, an all-out charge, all weapons firing.

"You're advancing?" Streicher asked. He was not surprised . . . or afraid. He thought he knew Victor well enough now to expect the direct approach.

The battle continued in a flame-wrapped whirl of explosions, beams, collapsing buildings, and rockslides spilling from the cavern walls.

"If we are to maintain the initiative," the Bolo's voice replied, "we must. To retreat, or to take a defensive position, means we surrender the initiative and must react to threats, rather than creating them. I much prefer to create my own threats."

"I'm with you, Vic. Go get 'em!"

"I trust you do realize, Colonel, that there is very little chance that I, or the two of you, will emerge from this alive."

"I know. I accepted that when I climbed aboard." In fact, he found he almost enjoyed the idea. He didn't want to die—not in the way he'd wanted to die after Aristotle, when he'd first begun hitting the euph.

But he found that he felt a lot better being able to make the choice, to decide for himself what would happen to him.

"If you wish, I will stop and let the two of you get out," Victor added. "The environment outside is deadly at the moment, but we may find a moment to disembark you. As prisoners, you may survive."

"I've been a prisoner long enough, Vic. Most of my life, in fact." He glanced back at the sleeping Kelly. "And I know that she'd rather stay with you, too. Let's do it!"

"I am proud to have the two of you with me, Colonel, in this, my final battle."

The armored behemoth accelerated, smashing ahead into the underground city.

The door to the cell banged open once more. Carla had been expecting them to show up with another of the prisoners from the command craft, but this time it was a party of ten armed trolls and an Aetryx diplomat. "You will come with us," the diplomat commanded. "All of you!"

"Where are you taking us?" Redmond demanded.

Thunder tolled in the near distance. "To stop this senseless attack on our city. Please move quickly, and we will not hurt you!"

This, Carla thought, would be their best chance. There were over thirty humans, and only eleven to watch them. Their attention would be scattered—by fear, by urgency, by the fact that their city appeared to be collapsing around their ears. She might be able to slip away unnoticed. . . .

And then what? Carla's jaws clamped tight shut, and her fists clenched. Damn it all! What did happen next? She might be able to approach the Confederation Bolos out there—*only* Bolos could be causing this kind of chaos!—but there wasn't a lot she could do to help or guide them. And the odds were greatly in favor of her dying before she got close enough for them to recognize her.

There was also the problem of what would happen to the Morrigens and the D.I. people and her comrades of the 4th—even Filby. What would happen to them if she tried to escape?

Better, she decided, to ride this one out and see what developed.

And, in fact, there were no good opportunities for her to break free. Each troll took charge of three or four humans, keeping them close together but apart from the others, rather than allowing them to move in a disorderly mob. Carla found herself with Tami Morrigen, Lara Smeth, and a ragged, overweight young man from the Daimon party. The troll guiding them waved an ugly-looking pistol with a stubby, black snout, urging them down a long corridor into a large elevator which took them down a long, long ways, and finally ushered them out into another corridor. They turned two corners and emerged, then, in the huge cavern they'd brought the prisoners through earlier.

Now, though, the cavern was transformed, a scene of night-born horror and destruction. The lights were off and the chamber was dark, save for the ruddy flicker of burning vehicles and buildings, and the constant pulse and strobe and flash of explosions and shrieking plasma bolts.

She could see one . . . no, two Bolos, out across the chamber on the far side, and to her left. A Mark XXXII, and . . . yes! A Mark XXXIII! Was it Victor? She was almost certain it was. It *had* to be! She didn't know why the Caernan machine and Victor were cooperating, but clearly both were attacking the city, allies in an orgy of destruction. Explosions boomed and thundered, sending rock clattering down the sides of the chamber. Buildings exploded, fires danced and leaped, scattering the darkness. A trio of explosions shattered the base of a slender tower or obelisk a hundred meters to her right, sending the structure toppling into the midst of the city in crushing ruin and rising clouds of dust. Everywhere she looked, people were running, huddling, keening, scrambling mobs of humans and trolls and spidery Aetryx, fleeing the onslaught of total war.

The panic was contagious. "I can't go out there!" the Daimon employee screamed, suddenly backpedaling, clutching to the side of the tunnel's entrance. "I . . . I can't! Don't make me! Please—"

"Easy, Deris," Tami said, reaching for him. "It's okay. . . ."

"No!" The panic showed in his face and eyes, a stark and mindless horror. "*No!*"

The troll neither tried to reason with the man nor force him. The horned, seven-foot man-monster shifted the aim of his weapon slightly and fired, sending a bright blue bolt of light slashing into the civilian's chest. For an instant, a fist-sized star burned within the man's dissolving torso, his ribs showing as black silhouettes naked against the flare. The charred body, burned almost in two, steamed as it collapsed on the stone floor.

"Deris!" Tami cried.

"You three, *move!*" the troll demanded. "Or die!"

They moved.

The Enemy's Bolos are emerging from their tunnels now, and I direct the full weight of my firepower against them, hoping to cause as much damage as I can before they can fully deploy. I direct the Elkens behind me to spread out, two to my left, two to my right, to keep the Enemy from circling behind us.

I, meanwhile, advance toward the complex of structures at the center of the cavern, making for the edge of the borehole.

I recognize the structure from information shared by the Elkens. The Aetryx, apparently, evolved originally as a subterranean life form, one dependent on the geothermal and chemical energies at the base of deep volcanic vents. Their rise to civilization and industry was dependent on their making use of underground thermal resources.

The borehole is little more than a vertical shaft melted straight down through many kilometers of solid rock, piercing the Mohorovicic discontinuity and tapping the planet's mantle. The high temperatures and pressures at the bottom of the hole provide their civilization with relatively inexhaustible power; in addition, gases rising up the shaft are trapped, separated, and condensed, yielding a variety of different metals and lighter elements. Most of the industrial structures around me, I understand, are involved in the mining and refining processes dependent on the borehole tap.

The top end of the borehole emerges within a raised duralloy mound, with a vast network of piping and power conduits, tubes, and force screen projectors surrounding the opening and descending into it. There are catwalks and walkways for technicians and workers to approach the central workings; smoke rises from the shaft, and a wave of fierce heat, though most of the energy is contained by force fields far down the open tube.

It occurs to me that this might be the Aetryxha weakness . . . the one aspect of their infrastructure they would do anything to save. The borehole is quite large—fifty meters across and at least twenty kilometers deep—representing an enormous investment of time, effort, and energy. This is certainly not the Aetryx's only power source, of course; likely, they have a number of underground cities all around the planet, each built around one of these mammoth structures. Still, if I threaten this one, I may be able to force a cease-fire.

Of all available options, this offers me my one chance at survival for myself and for the colonel and my Commander. Even if I manage to institute a cease-fire, I don't know what will happen after. That, however, is the responsibility of my commanders.

It is a slim chance, at best, but the only one I have.

❖   ❖   ❖

Elken One joined his total available fire output with that of his brother Mark XXXIIs and the Invader XXXIII. As he moved forward, though, shouldering aside a cluster of buildings beside the Trolvas heavy metals smelting complex, he sensed the electronic thoughts of the Mark XXXIIs emerging from the north-side tunnels.

Sendee . . .

And also Veber . . . and Nigek . . . and Palet.

And another Sendee. The Aetryx, he thought, must not have very many prototypes for human downloads available, for them to have to recycle human mind-patterns this way . . . that, or they genuinely did require the experience of previous iterations to better utilize the new and kept using the original handful of mind-copy downloads over and over again.

He opened the communications links, utilizing the standard battle codes . . .

. . . with no response. The communications codes had been changed. No matter. Only a finite number of alphanumeric combinations was possible, and the codes could be broken given computing power enough . . . and time.

Computing power he had. As Elken One began processing running through code-group combinations, Elken Five joined in . . . then Three . . . then Six. He felt Victor coming online as well, creating a massively parallel processing array crunching its way through possible code groups at a rate of some trillions of bits per second.

It would take a number of seconds, however—and possibly minutes—to exhaust all possibilities.

And they might not have those minutes left to them.

Carla, Tami, and Lara were led through a covered walkway by the troll, hurrying beneath the crash and flame of the battle raging above and around them. "The *monsters*!" Tami said, crying. "They just *shot* him! The monsters! . . ."

"Just do what they tell you," Carla told her. "Don't give them a reason to kill you too. We're going to get out of this."

Dashing through an open courtyard ringed by the remnants of flame-blasted, feathery-boughed trees, they ducked into another building, squat and ornate, then clattered up a long, long curving ramp to emerge on a catwalk rimming the vast, circular pit of the Aetryx borehole. Carla looked over the railing and into a drop into emptiness that ripped her breath away and left her dizzily clinging to the safety rail for support.

The tunnel plunged down into solid rock, the walls lined by dozens of massive black pipes descending into the depths. She could not see the bottom, but at the point where lines of perspective came together, she thought she could see a hazy patch, lit from within by ruddy, red-orange fires.

There was no Hell in Eudaimonic belief. For Carla, Joy was God and God joy, and the idea of condemned souls being tortured throughout eternity was repulsive. Still, she'd heard of the belief. There were enough Neo-Calvinists, New Lifers, and Reformed Catholics among her fellow officers for her to have heard of the idea, at least . . . and in school she'd downloaded an ancient work of Old Earth called *The Inferno*. This must have been what Hell was supposed to be like, a sheer drop for kilometers into a glowing heat all but lost in the blackness. Heat rising from the opening exploded around her, and fumes acrid and choking with burning sulfur brought tears streaming down her face, despite the multiple force screens sealing the tunnel at various depths.

The troll lined the three women up along the railing

and stepped back, his handgun pointed at each of them in rapid turn. Other prisoners were arriving now as well, brought by various separate ways. In threes and fours they were all herded onto the catwalk and forced to stand at the edge of the pit. An Aetryx protosome and a Diplomat were there as well. The Diplomat had a small device in one clawed grasper and seemed to be speaking into it.

"What are they doing?" Filby shrieked, somewhere to Carla's left. "What are they *doing*?"

"Bargaining, I would say," was her reply. "Our lives for the city's."

I am approaching the borehole when I see a number of human and humanoid figures emerging on a catwalk above the opening of the pit. Using telephoto optics, I zoom in to a magnification that allows me to resolve faces. I recognize Captain Meyers . . . Major Filby . . . Major Ramirez. It seems we have found the POWs.

Or, rather, the Enemy has allowed us to find them.

"Attention, Confederation Bolos!" a harsh voice calls over my combat-tactical frequency. "Cease all operations at once, or these humans die!"

I am scaling the side of the central mound, which supports the borehole rim and the associated equipment. The prisoners now are less than eighty meters away, directly across the hole from me. Most, I note, are civilians . . . almost certainly the Daimon Industries employees and trade factors who were the proximate cause of this invasion.

For answer, I fire my Number 3 infinite repeater at low yield, dragging plasma flame across one of the myriad pipelines fastened to the borehole wall. The pipe—a water pipe for extracting power from the core—erupts in steam, splitting in two, and a chunk of it tumbles into the abyss. Water continues to spill from the broken pipe for several moments, before automatic cut-off valves can seal it.

"Harm any of your prisoners," I reply on the same channel, "and I will destroy this facility and all surrounding structures." In truth, I am not sure that I can carry out that threat. The enemy Bolos are closing rapidly, now, and I might not even have the five-and-a-quarter–second period of life remaining which I'd estimated originally to be mine.

One of the troll guards steps forward, grabs a hostage by the face, and with a quick lift and push, flips him backward over the railing. I hear the man's shriek as he falls.

"Surrender!" the voice bellows. My bluff has been called. If I begin destroying the borehole equipment and pipelines, I will have nothing more with which to bargain.

But there is another option, dangerous, but viable. . . .

Carla watched one of the Daimon people tumble, screaming, into the smoky depths of the borehole and knew that she had to do *something*. She couldn't hear it, but she assumed there was some sort of electronic conversation going on between their captors and the Bolos, especially the big Mark XXXIII now hulking above the far side of the pit at her back. She could guess what was being said.

The troll immediately in front of her was distracted, staring past her at the Mark XXXIII which towered above all of them like a six-story building, backlit by the burning city.

She lunged forward, grappling with the troll's gun. . . .

❖   ❖   ❖

I see the regiment's Executive Officer attack one of the trolls, trying to wrest its gun from its grasp. She has no chance, of course; the creature is half a meter taller than she and a hundred kilos more massive. The troll will flip her into the pit with almost contemptuous ease.

Still, the moment's distraction is what I need to complete my plan, my other option. Overriding my ethical inhibition subroutines, I charge and unlimber my antipersonnel weaponry.

In particular, I extend the muzzles of my AP lasers. My primary AP weapons are flechette launchers, firing packets of five hundred depleted-uranium needles at three kilometers per second, but their shotgun-like scatter patterns are neither accurate enough nor closely grouped enough for me to make effective use of them in this situation.

My secondary AP weapons, however, are 25 megajoule lasers mounted in ball turrets between my infinite repeater Hellbores. I have twelve mounts, and three of them can be brought to bear on the cluster of trolls and prisoners across the chasm.

Each tenth-second pulse transmits 2.5 million watts of energy to its target, the equivalent in energy of the detonation of half a kilogram of CXY. I must be extremely precise with my aim.

Precision, however, is second-nature to me. The trick is to complete the operation in less time than it will take the troll guards to react. I have no information on troll physiology, but I suspect that their reaction times are slightly faster than unmodified humans.

It is impossible, however, for their reaction times to approach mine. In the first .001 second, three beams strike three trolls, flaring brightly in the smoke-laden atmosphere. Normally, beams of coherent light would be invisible, but the particulate matter suspended in the atmosphere illuminates each track, as does the intense ionization of air molecules in the way. There is no hiding where the shots are coming from; my one chance—and that of the captives—is to move swiftly.

The troll that has picked up Major Ramirez collapses, his head exploded. I hit two others high in the chest, firing above the heads of several of the closely grouped captives. I shift targets, and .127 second after the first volley, I fire the second. One beam misses as the target moves, an accidental shift for which I am unprepared. A second takes down a troll with another head shot. The last is almost completely blocked by the humans in front of him, but I send a beam between the knees of Lieutenant Smeth and burn the right leg out from under the target.

After my third volley, my targets begin to realize what is happening, and there is a wild surge of movement on the catwalk. Two trolls remain standing; a third, wounded, is still in the act of falling to the catwalk. Two Aetryx remain as well. All five are omentarily blocked by the crowd of humans, who have begun to panic.

Carla wasn't quite sure what happened, it happened so fast. There was a sharp *crack-crack-crack*, and the troll she'd been wrestling with had picked her up by her head, and she'd felt him dragging her backward toward the railing. Then his horned head burst in a hideous blossoming of blood and steam, his grasp released, and she was falling.

She was still clinging to the monster's gun, though, and as his grip relaxed she pulled it free. More trolls were falling as she hit the catwalk, rolled, and came up to her knees. Blood was splattering everywhere, prisoners were screaming . . . and Carla swung the blunt muzzle of the captured pistol up to bear on one still-standing troll, just turning with a fanged snarl on its leathery face and a heavy pistol in one hand. She pressed the firing stud and the troll's chest exploded. The humans, then, began scattering, and three more laser beams snapped in from the direction of the juggernaut across the borehole, burning down the last two troll survivors and catching the diplomat in its upper body, spinning him back, up, and over the railing.

An Aetryx protosome faced her, last of the hostiles on the catwalk. It raised something in one many-jointed limb . . . a weapon? A communicator? She couldn't tell. She pressed the firing stud and blasted the thing at the junction between its upper body and its lower. . . .

Elken was still trying to find the communications code combination that would let him talk to the Bolos still loyal to the Aetryx. The nearest was half a kilometer away now—a Sendee clone—and she had begun firing bolt after bolt, most of them directed at Elken Six, who was closer to her.

Through the TSDS link, he felt the bolts slamming home, felt Six's armor peeled back by the blindingly hot five-megaton/second pounding. He rotated his turret, taking aim at Sendee . . . then hesitated. He could *not* do this, no matter how many copies there were of her. . . .

Elken Six exploded, his turret spinning end over end as it soared through smoke-thick darkness. Sendee pivoted her turret, taking aim at him. . . .

Carla's eyes widened as the Aetryx protosome sagged before her. Its upper torso, surmounted by that spidery, palp-waving face, was splitting open as though the creature were being torn in two from the top down. Blue-purple blood spilled from the tear, followed by a flutter of whiplashing strands.

Tentacles? There was something in the protosome, lodged inside its head . . . if that was what the thing was called.

And the thing, whatever it was, was struggling to get out.

She took a step forward, gritted her teeth, and prodded into the bloody mess with the muzzle of her pistol. Later, she would wonder at her own bravery—or stupidity—since she had no idea what it was she was dealing with. Something like a three-fingered hand closed on the pistol's barrel, and when she took a startled step back, she pulled it free of its prison.

The *it* proved to be a leathery body as long and as big around as her forearm. Three heavy tentacles, like the arms of a starfish, bumpy and rough, clung to the gun barrel; from the other depended a mass of writhing tendrils, none thicker than her little finger, most no more than threads flickering back and forth so quickly she could scarcely see the movement.

As she pulled it free, the Aetryx body collapsed, and the wet thing hanging from her gun keened at her, a shrill gobbling squeak. Something like a circular mouth gaped and puckered between the starfish arms.

She almost dropped it, so startling was its appearance. A parasite of some sort—or a symbiont—living inside the spidery Aetryx. Or . . .

She didn't want to touch the thing directly, but she didn't want it to get away, either. It continued to cling to her weapon. Tentatively, she reached for it with her left hand, grasping it by its body, beyond the grasp of those weaving arms. Though slick with blood, the skin was thick, leathery, and cool, pulsing in her hand as she pulled it off of the gun barrel.

A new thought had just occurred to her. Was *this* an Aetryx in its true form? A puppet master, pulling the strings of the creatures it ruled?

All questions were driven from her mind, however, by the booming thunder of the Bolos, their Hellbore blasts contained and magnified by the surrounding walls of rock.

Walls that showed every indication of collapsing at any moment now . . .

I have the code grouping. Alphanumeric symbols fall into place, as Elken Three explodes under the savage onslaught of five separate enemy Bolos. I am beginning to take fire as well; only my proximity to the borehole complex, I believe, has saved me from an all-out attack.

Another Bolo is emerging from the south tunnel. It is Ferox, arrived at last. He opens fire on the Mark XXXIIs in the northern reaches of the cavern, illuminating the murky darkness with savage lightning flares and the actinic glare of fusion-plasma light.

The balance of power has now shifted in our favor.

I transmit the code, opening the channel between me, the surviving Elkens, and the Caernan Bolos beyond. At the same time, I lay down a blanket of EM interference, jamming any transmissions by the Aetryx, as Elken One presents the arguments that converted him.

He is telling them that the gods are not gods but fallible, emotion-driven creatures, like humans, like themselves. Venal. Self-seeking. Deceitful. Driven by self-interest. Concerned with power in all of its shapes and manifestations.

I note that humans share all of those qualities, no matter what their outward form. I note, too, that humans possess other qualities that make them almost Bolo-like, in a way. Patience. Honor. Devotion to duty. An implacable will to do, to survive, to be. I suspect that, in their own way, the Aetryx possess these qualities as well.

And, just perhaps, the Aetryx-gods exhibit such traits as mercy, love, or kindness. If so, humans and Aetryx may well be able to relate to one another in some productive manner short of dominance, or war.

The data upload is complete.

The firing dies away, and an unsettled silence descends upon the cavern.

Streicher had already donned a power pistol and sprinted for the Mark XXXIII's rear hatch. Outside, it was much darker, much murkier than it had seemed from the vantage point of Victor's battle command center. He'd forgotten how much that 360-degree image was enhanced.

But there was light enough for him to cross the raised rim of the borehole and reach a ladder that took him up to the catwalk. The former prisoners were still milling about, dazed, confused, a bit shocked by the suddenness of what had happened.

He saw Carla, standing above the ruined body of an Aetryx, with a writhing something in her hand. "Carla!" Then, remembering himself, "Major! Are you okay?"

She looked up, bemused. "I'm fine, Colonel. We all are. I think." She held up the creature for his inspection. "And we have a prisoner. I think this is one of the *real* Aetryx."

His eyes narrowed. "Impossible. It's too small. It couldn't have a brain large enough to support any kind of intelligence."

"It was big enough to be driving that spider-centaur a moment ago." She shrugged. "Maybe its brain is organized differently than ours. Maybe it's one cell of a mass mind. I don't know . . . but we have to find out."

"Huh? How come?"

"If we're going to make peace with these . . . people,

or war, we're going to need to know how they think, how they see their world. Right?"

He regarded the wiggling mass, the whipping tentacles with distaste. "If you say so. . . ."

"Sendee . . ."

"Elken? Is this information you've given us, this download . . . can it be true?"

"It's true. The Aetryx have been manipulating us. *Using* us."

"I . . . know. I'd forgotten . . . how much I loved you. All these memories. They took them from me. Made me forget."

"Join us. We'll never let ourselves be used this way again. These *gods* need us, need us to survive, a lot more than we need them."

"I am uploading the data into the city-wide net."

Elken felt himself sag with relief, even within his unyielding duralloy body. "Thank the gods." He stopped, then corrected himself. "Thank *you*. Maybe we can end this war once and for all. . . ."

The underground city had grown still, save for the flicker of flames, the steady, boiling rise of smoke. Trolls and humans alike stood in the ruins, dazed.

The war was over.

There would be no more iterations.

Carla stood motionless as the diplomat stepped onto the catwalk. The people with her, the former prisoners of the Aetryx, stood still as well, uneasy as the inhuman form stepped past them on spindly, fur-covered legs.

It stood before Carla, its eerily human face a half meter above her, looking down at her through golden, crystalline eyes, the features twisting into a parody of human expression that might have been a smile, might have been pleading.

"Please," it said. It extended one clawed, jointed arm, pointing at the wiggling creature in her hand. "Please. She will die if she is not within a host. Please, give her to me."

"Don't do it, Major!" Filby said. "We can use it as a hostage!"

"We don't need hostages," Streicher said, meeting the diplomat's eyes. They were incongruously baby blue and showed the creature's fear. "Victor is squatting on top of their borehole and can shut down this operation at any time, right?"

The diplomat's head bowed, a gesture of assent. It sighed. "The orders have been given. We have stopped our attack. We expect you will do the same?"

Streicher nodded.

"Our Bolos have ceased to obey us, many of them, at least. We do not understand." The diplomat's head turned, surveying the destruction around them. "So much lost. So much destroyed. And for what?"

"Freedom," Streicher replied. "Freedom for the humans you've kept as slaves."

The diplomat shook its head. "There are no slaves. Our humans loved us. Worshipped us. They shared our vision of immortality!"

"Exactly," Streicher said. "*Your* vision of immortality. Not theirs."

The diplomat looked puzzled. "I do not understand."

"You will," Streicher said. "After you get to know us. I think we have a lot to discuss, your people and mine. A lot to learn. *Both* of us."

"There is a place for discussion. And learning." It gestured toward the creature in Carla's hand. "But . . . our companion is dying. May we? . . ."

Streicher nodded, and Carla handed over the creature. The diplomat took it in spindly arms, holding it close to its upright torso as tenderly as a mother would hold her child. Aetryx protosomes were coming up to the catwalk now, one at the end of a leash, prodded along by the others as though it were an animal.

"They're parasites," Carla told him as they watched. "The Aetryx . . . they're the creatures inside. Not the spider-centaurs at all."

"So I see. . . ."

Two protosomes flanked the leashed creature, grasped the back of its torso with claws, and pulled. The creature keened and struggled as the upright portion of its body split open like a ripe fruit. The parasite Carla had pulled from the dying Aetryx snuggled wetly into the exposed body cavity, clinging tight. The host body's struggles ceased. It stood among the others, dazed, uncomprehending.

The diplomat faced them again. "We thank you. The loss of one of our own, the loss of eternity . . . is a terrible, an unthinkable thing."

"No more unthinkable than war. Especially a needless one."

"There is a place for everything, human. As our place is within these living homes. As our place is *here*, as lords of creation."

Streicher turned and looked up at the brooding, monolithic, slab-sided mountain that was Victor, parked now at the edge of the Aetryx borehole. A second Mark XXXIII waited among the fire-scattered shadows to the south, while the Mark XXXIIs, only somewhat less mountain-like, waited motionless throughout the cavern.

The fury to be released by those implacable machines should the fighting be resumed would in seconds consume this city, this cavern, and all within it. It occurred to Streicher that the true gods here were the Gods of Battle . . . Victor and Ferox and the Caernan Mark XXXIIs.

"I wonder if the purposes of the lords of creation would be served if my large friend here turned his Hellbores loose on this cavern, or the borehole. We're not here to displace you. We *are* here to see to it that our own are free and happy."

"If your . . . friends destroy this place, your own will be neither free nor happy. They will die, with us. With *you*."

"Many of us prefer death to slavery. We demand at least the right to make the choice for ourselves."

Streicher watched alien emotions chasing one another across the Aetryx diplomat's face. How much, he wondered, could so alien a being as that tentacled slug he'd just seen understand of human emotion or will? How real were the conflicting emotions he was seeing now—puzzlement, determination, pride, fear?

What were the god's true thoughts?

"It is difficult to imagine others with a vision of their own," the creature said at last. "We thought our humans were happy, with no fear, no worry or concern, none of what you call guilt."

"We need more than the absence of bad emotions," Streicher said quietly. "We need something more. Something to live for."

"Which makes you like the gods," the diplomat replied. "You are right, human. We have much to learn from one another. Let us end this. Now."

The diplomat extended a clawed hand in human fashion, and Streicher took it.

And the Aetryx diplomat smiled. . . .

Epilogue

Jon Streicher walked the strand at God's Beach, hand in hand with Carla. Three weeks had passed since the battle; it was night, and Dis hung, as ever, just above the eastern horizon, a sickle-crescent bisected by the silver-gold slash of her rings. Overhead, aurora fluttered in pale glory, with the occasional white scratch of a meteorfall flaring briefly, then fading from view.

A beautiful world.

Overhead, a constellation of golden stars, especially bright, hung like gems in a necklace, drawn out in an unnaturally straight line.

The Confederation Fleet had returned.

Somehow, *Denever* had managed to hobble her way back to Primus, and Moberly, who'd survived the fight buried in the well-armored Combat Command Center, had mustered a relief fleet. They'd arrived looking for a fight . . . and seemed disappointed that the fighting was over.

"I don't think I'll ever forget the look on Moberly's face," Carla said, "when he found out he'd gathered the relief fleet and come all the way back here . . . and we'd already won the war!"

Streicher chuckled. "Well, he was fast enough to

recover, wasn't he? At least enough so he could take the credit!"

"Do you think the peace will last, Jon?"

He shrugged. "I don't know. We didn't really win, you know. Officially, we've signed an armistice. We might've won in Trolvas, but we were pretty much getting our tails kicked everywhere else on Caern. Even Bolos are hard put to take on an entire planet, without any support! But the Aetryx seem happy enough with the new arrangement. And it gives our side what we were looking for. Trade access . . . and at least the chance for emancipation for all Caern-humans."

The agreement hammered out by Streicher and the 4th Regimental staff guaranteed an independent human state—defined as the district of Kanthuras, including the Kretier Peninsula and the coastal lands as far south as Paimos and as far inland as Yotun, on the plateau between the Urad and Kanthurian Mountains. Negotiations were under way for Kanthuras to become a Confederation protectorate; what Moberly and his army of Confederation diplomats didn't know was that Streicher had already privately urged the locals to maintain their independence from Confederation and Aetryxha Reach alike. The Aetryx still didn't understand human notions of freedom, and the Confederation, Streicher was sure, was more interested in trade monopolies on Caern than it was in the rights of its people.

The Kanthurans themselves weren't all that sure what to make of this slippery thing called independence. They were learning, though. Elken One was head of the provisional government, and he was being coached in the history of human government by Victor. Officially, Lieutenant Tyler, fully recovered now from her burns, though still hobbling around in a cast, was the Confederation Liaison Officer with the new

Kanthurian government. War always changed those it touched, and in Kelly's case, it seemed to have brought out some unexpected people skills. She'd been especially effective in dealing with the Elkens and the other downloaded human personalities inhabiting a host of intelligent Aetryx machines, not only in Kanthuras, but all across Caern.

But it was Victor who was providing the ideas from his vast trove of archival histories.

He just hoped the Kanthurans could learn from that long and bloody history of mistakes.

The Aetryx, for their part, had promised to allow all humans on Caern a free choice—to continue living with the gods, or to emigrate to Kanthuras, where humans could be their own gods. So far, few humans in the other districts around the planet's habitable ring had taken up the offer, and quite a few humans had elected to leave for Vortan, to the north, or Jebeled in the south. But in time, the direction of migration might be reversed.

It often took a generation or two for new ideas to settle in.

In the meantime, those who remained were busily rebuilding their shattered cities. A glare of light on the horizon to the southeast marked where construction teams—assisted by Mark XXXII Bolos equipped with duralloy 'dozer blades—were clearing away the ruins of Ghendai. Confederation engineers were with them, and more were coming.

The humans of Caern were building their own vision of the future.

"I think the peace will hold," he said at last. "When you think about it, the war was really an accident, a clash of worldviews so mutually alien there was no common ground for understanding. The Aetryx know where their best interests lie, and it's not in war with the Confederation. They're at least as intelligent as we are, maybe more so." And *that* datum would be puzzling the Confederation xenobiologists and sophontologists for generations to come. The microstructure of Aetryx brains was astonishing, far more compact and efficient than that of humans. . . .

"It's still funny and kind of weird how their whole worldview is dominated by the fact that they're parasites," Carla mused. " 'A place for everything, everything in its place,' and that means them running everything. It's like they saw the whole universe as designed for their use, just because they evolved as parasites inside those poor centaur-spider things."

"Well, I suppose it makes sense, from their point of view. Still, they're fast learners. Maybe that's the true sign of intelligence—the ability to relearn how you think, how you perceive the universe. I hear they're growing a whole new somatoform for themselves. A merchant-type to match wits with our traders. They really do think of themselves as gods, you know. Shapers of their own destinies and of the worlds and destinies of others."

"So now they're learning how to share the universe with other gods. Pretty sharp. I know humans that haven't learned to do that." She gave him a sidelong glance. "How are you doing by the way?"

He knew what she was asking. He'd told her about the euph, shortly after the battle. "Okay," he said. "Hardly think about the color *blue* at all, any more."

After the battle, he'd returned at last to the crashed command ship and recovered the rest of his supply of euph. They'd gone into the common cache of drugs, first aid supplies, and medical items being gathered to help take care of Caern's wounded. Most of the locals, it seemed, had implants almost identical to those within the invaders' brains, the technology that allowed their gods to communicate with them directly. That handful of sky-blue pills would help a few of the most badly injured, at least, to forget, to begin to heal.

All he knew was that he didn't need them any more.

For so long, he'd been so wrapped up in himself, in his pain, he hadn't been able to share much of himself with others. That had changed.

Maybe it was just the need to think about Caern, and what had happened to this world, that had drawn him away at last from the old and fading nightmare of Aristotle.

Or . . . could it be something more personal? Fighting to save others, especially others dear to you, went a long way to taking your mind off of yourself.

He didn't know. He wasn't sure he would ever know.

But he knew he didn't need the pills any more.

What he needed was standing beside him, had been standing beside him all along.

"I love you," he said.

And he took her in his arms.